THE ELIZABETH TUDOR CONSPIRACY

The Marquess House Saga
Book Two

Alexandra Walsh

SAPERE
BOOKS

THE ELIZABETH TUDOR CONSPIRACY

Published by Sapere Books.

20 Windermere Drive, Leeds, England, LS17 7UZ,
United Kingdom

saperebooks.com

ISBN: 978-1-913028-49-7

To Deborah: who kept me sane
To Gemma: who always made things better with laughter
To Dawn: with her wisdom and patience
And to Jo: who was there from the beginning and never doubted me,
even when I doubted myself
Thank you ladies, you're awesome

DRAMATIS PERSONAE

Marquess House

The Woodville Rivers Family:
Dr Perdita Elizabeth Woodville Rivers — Unexpected heiress to a vast fortune
Piper Eleanor Davidson *née* **Woodville Rivers** — Perdita's twin sister, who inherits equally with Perdita
Mary Fitzroy — Grandmother of Perdita and Piper. (Deceased)
Jeremy Davidson — Piper's estranged husband
Hector Woodville — Mary's husband. Father of Louisa. (Deceased)
Louisa Woodville — Daughter of Mary Fitzroy. Mother of Perdita and Piper. (Deceased)
James Rivers — Father of Perdita and Piper. Husband of Louisa. (Deceased)
Cecily Fitzroy — Mary's sister, mother of Randolph Connors
Lettice Hawkland — Ancestor of Perdita and Piper
Bethan Bridges — Childhood friend of Mary Fitzroy. Mother of Sarah Eve. Grandmother of Larry and Billy Eve and Briony and Mark Llewellyn. (Deceased)

The Mackensie Family:
Dr Christopher 'Kit' Mackensie — Works for his family's company, Jerusalem. Lives at Marquess House
Alistair Mackensie — Father of Kit, Stuart and Megan. Husband of Susan. Owner of Jerusalem and integral to the

7

running of Marquess House

Susan Mackensie — Mother of Kit, Stuart and Megan. Wife of Alistair. Integral to the running of Marquess House

Stuart Mackensie — Middle Mackensie child. Works for Jerusalem. Lives in New York

Megan Mackensie — Eldest Mackensie child. Runs Jerusalem from the family home in Andorra

Pablo De León — Megan's fiancé. Works for the Andorran government

Lydia Brooks — Kit's ex-girlfriend

Suki Merriweather — Daughter of family friends of the Mackensies. Had a drunken New Year kiss with Kit when they were younger

Linda Merriweather — Family friends of the Mackensies

Toby Merriweather — Family friends of the Mackensies

Lara Cunningham — A friend of Megan's

Dr Olaf Dade — Colleague of Perdita's

The Marquess House Team:

Jenny Procter — Chief Librarian and Archivist at Marquess House. Distant cousin of Alistair

Izabel Barnes — Jenny's granddaughter and her assistant. Best friend of Meg Mackensie. Engaged to Mark Llewellyn

Sarah Eve — Head of Catering and Events at Marquess House. Godmother of Perdita and Piper

Alan Eve — Sarah's husband. Former Head of Security, now semi-retired

Billy Eve — Eldest son of Sarah and Alan. In charge of building maintenance and architecture at Marquess House. Cousin of Mark and Briony Llewellyn

Larry Eve — Younger son of Sarah and Alan. Head of Security, referring to his father while he learns the job. Cousin of Mark and Briony Llewellyn

Mark Llewellyn — Works at The Dairy. Engaged to Izabel Barnes. Elder brother of Briony. Cousin to Billy and Larry Eve

Briony Llewellyn — Runs the Louisa Woodville Trust, the animal sanctuary based at Home Farm, the childhood home of Perdita and Piper. Cousin to Billy and Larry Eve

The Black Family:

Dr Deborah Black — Mother of Elliot and Callum. Chief Librarian and Archivist at Castle Jerusalem in Andorra

Callum Black — Best friend of Kit. Younger son of Deborah Black

Elliot Black — Eldest son of Deborah Black. Pilot of the Jerusalem planes

Samantha Carver (Sam) — Wife of Elliot Black. Pilot of the Jerusalem planes

The Connors Family:

Randolph Connors — Son of Mary Fitzroy's sister, Cecily Connors. Father of Xavier Connors

Lady Marianne Connors *née* **O'Rourke** — Estranged wife of Randolph Connors and mother of Xavier Connors

Xavier Connors — Son of Randolph and Marianne Connors. Second cousin to Perdita and Piper. Father of Ruby and Pearl Connors

Amber Connors *née* **Prust** — Xavier's wife. Mother of Ruby and Pearl Connors

Ruby Connors — Elder twin. Daughter of Xavier and Amber Connors

Pearl Connors — Younger twin by half an hour. Daughter of Xavier and Amber Connors

Other Characters:
Stephen Haberfield — Head of MI1 Elite
Gary Ashley — Haberfield's assistant
Warren Dexter — Perdita's ex-fiancé. Works for MI1 Elite
Hannah White — Owner of one of the two ruby rings
Kirstin Chaplin — Girlfriend of Jeremy Davidson

The Tudor Court

Elizabeth I — Queen of England. Daughter of Anne Boleyn and Henry VIII's second wife, mother of Elizabeth I

Anne of Cleves — Fourth wife of Henry VIII, stepmother of Elizabeth I

Lady Isabel Baynton — Half-sister of Catherine Howard, who was the fifth wife of Henry VIII. Wife of Sir Edward Baynton

Henry Baynton — Son of Sir Edward and Lady Isabel Baynton

Lady Arbella Stuart — Orphan. Granddaughter of Lady Margaret Douglas. Granddaughter of Bess of Hardwick

Francis, Duke of Anjou and Alençon — One of Elizabeth I's suitors

Robert Dudley, Earl of Leicester — Elizabeth's favourite. Husband of Lettice Knollys

Amy Robsart — Robert Dudley's first wife. (Deceased)

Robert Devereux, Earl of Essex — Son of Lettice and Walter Devereux

Sir Thomas Perrot — Husband of Dorothy (Devereux) Perrot

Lord Robert Rich — Husband of Penelope (Devereux) Perrot

Henry Baynton — Son of Lady Isabel Baynton and Sir Edward Baynton

Sir Francis Knollys — Husband of Kathryn Carey. (Deceased)

Mary, Queen of Scots — Scottish queen. A guest of Elizabeth's

King James VI of Scotland — Son of Mary, Queen of Scots and her second husband, Henry, Lord Darnley, who was the eldest son of Lady Margaret Douglas and her husband, Matthew Stewart, Earl of Lennox

Mary of Guise — Mother of Mary, Queen of Scots

Mary Tudor — Former queen. Elizabeth's half-sister. Daughter of Katherine of Aragon and Henry VIII. (Deceased)

Edward VI — Former king. Elizabeth's half-brother. Son of Jane Seymour. (Deceased)

Lady Jane Grey — Former queen. Daughter of Lady Frances Brandon, daughter of Princess Mary Tudor (younger sister of Henry VIII) and Charles Brandon, Duke of Suffolk and Henry Grey, Duke of Suffolk. (Deceased)

Philip II of Spain — Widower of Queen Mary Tudor. Determined to invade England and reclaim what he believes is his throne

Infanta Isabella Clara Eugenia — Daughter of Philip II of Spain

The Ladies of Melusine:

Lady Katherine Newton — Great-niece of Catherine Howard, through Agnes Leigh, daughter of John Leigh, Catherine's half-brother. Catherine was a cousin of Anne Boleyn, Elizabeth I's mother

Elizabeth Talbot, Countess of Shrewsbury aka Bess of Hardwick — Married to George Talbot, Earl of Shrewsbury

Elizabeth Pierrepont 'Mignonne' — Bess of Hardwick's granddaughter

Mary Talbot — Bess's daughter

Lettice (Knollys) (Devereux) Dudley, Countess of Leicester — Daughter of Kathryn (Carey) Knollys and Sir Francis Knollys

Dorothy (Devereux) Perrot — Daughter of Lettice Knollys and Walter Devereux

Penelope (Devereux) Rich — Daughter of Lettice Knollys and Walter Devereux

Kate Howard, Lady Effingham — Daughter of Henry Carey, Baron Hunsdon and Anne Morgan. Wife of Charles, Baron Howard of Effingham. Later Earl of Nottingham. Also Lord High Admiral

Courtiers:

Ralph Fitzalan, Duke of Hereford — Elizabeth's confidant

Mary Fitzalan, Duchess of Hereford — Ralph's wife. Daughter of Katheryn Parr and Thomas Seymour, Baron Sudeley

William Fitzalan, Viscount Rutland — Son of Ralph and Mary, Duke and Duchess of Hereford

Sir Francis Walsingham — Elizabeth's spymaster

William Cecil, Lord Burghley — Friend and confidant of Elizabeth I. A high-ranking courtier who wields great power

William Paulet, 3rd Marquess of Winchester — Trusted courtier

Sir Edward Stafford — Member of Parliament, courtier and diplomat

Douglas (Howard) Stafford — Wife of Sir Edward Stafford. Mother of Robert Dudley's illegitimate son

George Talbot, Earl of Shrewsbury — Husband of Bess of Hardwick and Earl Marshal of England; his son,

Henry Talbot — Son of George Talbot, Earl of Shrewsbury

Sir James Croft — Politician and Lord Deputy of Ireland

Sir Christopher Hatton — Lord Chancellor and a favourite of Elizabeth I

Mr Edward Barker — Robert Dudley's lawyer

Sir Edward Montagu — Politician. A dependable Protestant and staunch supporter of Elizabeth I

Lady Elizabeth Monatgu — Wife of Sir Edward Montagu, daughter of James Harington of Exton in Rutland, also a dependable Protestant and staunch supporter of Elizabeth I

Sir Peregrine Bertie, Baron Willoughby de Eresby — Son of Katherine Willoughby, Dowager Duchess of Suffolk by her second husband, Richard Bertie

Sir Philip Sidney — Poet and best friend of Robert Devereux

Edward la Zouche, Baron Zouche — Diplomat

Richard Bagot — Deputy lieutenant of Staffordshire

Thomas Phelippes — One of Walsingham's most trusted codebreakers

Nicholas Berden — One of Walsingham's men

George Devereux at Lamphey Hall — High-ranking Welsh nobleman

Morgan Philipps of Picton Castle — High-ranking Welsh nobleman

Erasmus Saunders — A former mayor of Tenby

Charles Paget — High-ranking Welsh nobleman

The Barlow Family — High-ranking Welsh noblemen

Thomas Morgan — High-ranking Welsh nobleman and Catholic sympathiser

Thomas Revell of Forest — High-ranking Welsh nobleman

The Wogan brothers: Morris and William of Wiston and Alban Stepney of Prendergast — High-ranking Welsh noblemen

John Howell, Mayor of Tenby — High-ranking Welsh nobleman

Claude Nau — Secretary to Mary, Queen of Scots

Gilbert Curle — Secretary to Mary, Queen of Scots

Francis Mylles — Burghley's man

Jolyon Gillions — Bargeman. A trusted member of Robert Dudley's staff

Joan Gillions — Wife of Jolyon Gillions. The chief laundress at Robert Dudley's home, Leicester House

Thomas Dampard — Loyal member of the Dudley household, particularly to Lettice Dudley

Captain Hynde — One of Ralph Fitzalan's men

Sergeant Abel — One of Ralph Fitzalan's men

Golding — One of Ralph Fitzalan's men

Merrick — One of Ralph Fitzalan's men

Dominique Bourgoing — Physician to Mary, Queen of Scots

The Bowls Match:

Sir Henry Newton — Husband of Lady Katherine Newton

Lettice Fitzgerald — Half-sister of Lady Katherine Newton

Sir Ambrose Coppinger — Husband of Lettice Fitzgerald

Douglas Aungier — Sister of Lady Katherine Newton

Francis Aungier — Husband of Douglas Aungier

Anne Knollys — Cousin of Elizabeth I and sister of Lettice Dudley

Thomas West, 2nd Baron De La Warr — Husband of Anne Knollys

Elizabeth Knollys — Cousin of Elizabeth I and sister of Lettice Dudley

Sir Thomas Leighton — Husband of Elizabeth Knollys

Philadelphia Carey — Cousin of Elizabeth I and sister of Kate Howard, Lady Effingham

Thomas Scrope, 10th Baron Scrope of Bolton — Husband of Philadelphia Carey

Plotters:

Anthony Babington — Former member of Bess of Hardwick's household, plotting to overthrow Elizabeth I

Chidiock Tichbourne — One of Babington's loyal men

John Ballard aka Black Fortescue — A Jesuit priest who has been trying to recruit young scholars, through his links with Caius College, Cambridge. He has already recruited Chidiock Tichbourne and approached Charles Paget

Owen Lewis — Welsh Roman Catholic priest

James Beaton — Catholic sympathiser

Earls of Westmorland and Northumberland — Suspected Catholics

Baron Ughtred — Catholic sympathiser

Baron Vaux and his family — Catholic sympathisers

Richard White — Welsh cleric, known Catholic sympathiser and co-ordinator for the plotters.

William Vaux, 3rd Baron Vaux of Harrowden — Catholic sympathiser

Sir Thomas Tresham — Brother-in-law of William Vaux, charged with harbouring a known Jesuit named Edward Campion

Phillip II's men:

Gaspar de Quiroga y Vela — One of the most senior officials of the Spanish Inquisition

Alvaro de Bazan, 1st Marquis of Santa Cruz de Mudela — A Spanish admiral, organiser of the Spanish Armada

Bernadino de Mendoza — The Spanish ambassador in Paris, providing a safe house for anyone of noble birth fleeing from England

Joshua Page of Lyndesey — Maud's father

Prologue: London, 12 July 1557

"Where is she?"

The young woman threw back the cowl hood of her heavy cloak and ran through the candlelit house, her boots ringing on the wooden floors. "We have only a few moments; there are guards on the road this night," she called.

"This way, my lady," replied a woman holding a lantern, lighting the way through the midnight shadows.

The young woman entered the room on a wave of fear and adrenalin. Was this a trap? Another plot? Then she saw the prone figure in the bed and breathed in the scent of impending death. It took every ounce of her self-control not to gag. This was no subterfuge — this was yet another farewell.

Controlling her emotions, she threw herself on to her knees beside the bed and clasped the woman's hand. It felt cold and brittle but there was still the warmth of life. She was in time.

"My lady, can you hear me?" the young woman whispered, her voice low, insistent, urgent. "It is I…"

"I would know your voice anywhere, my dear," the figure croaked. Once she had spoken in clear, lilting tones — now her words were hoarse, rusted with illness and loss. "My request has put you in danger but my time on this earth is almost done and there is something you must be told…" She pointed to an exquisitely carved wooden box on the table beside the bed. "This is my gift to you. Your legacy. Inside this casket is the truth about your half-sister. No, not the one who holds your life in the balance," the woman continued, halting the girl as she made to interrupt. "There is another. She is a true princess, born in wedlock but hidden at birth."

16

"No," said the girl, her voice low with shock and disbelief.

"I tell you this to keep you safe," said the woman, her voice a rattling whisper. "You are the rightful heir but there are always men who would see you removed, who would use this girl as a replacement."

"No, this is treason…" The young woman recoiled from the box as though it were poisoned.

"You must listen, you must know. I promised her — my friend — that I would pass her secret on," the woman implored. "Open the box, I beg you…"

The younger woman hesitated, then unable to resist the request of the dying woman, she unlocked the casket. Inside a small velvet pouch sat on top of a stack of parchment. The girl opened the small bag and a ruby ring fell on to her palm.

"On the side," explained the woman, "is a catch. It opens the ring. We used them to pass messages."

"Who…?" began the girl but a sharp knock on the door interrupted them.

"My lady, we must leave now or risk capture," came another woman's tense voice.

"Go," entreated the woman in the bed. "I have put you in enough danger. The diary, the confession, it is all there, it will explain everything. Keep it safe, sweet princess, it may save your life one day."

The young woman nodded, then bent to kiss the parchment-like skin, sadness muting her fear. Here was another woman whom she had loved, who had cared for her, being taken from her too young.

"Goodbye, my lady," she replied, wiping the tears away as she hurried out of the room and ran with all her might through the house and out into the stable yard where her escort waited. Within moments she was mounted.

17

"Give me the box," whispered the woman who had accompanied her.

"But, Isabel, if we are stopped…"

"Better my head on the block than yours," she replied, strapping it to her saddlebag.

Biting her lip nervously the young woman was about to protest but one of the men gave the signal that all was clear and she knew there was no time to argue.

One day, she thought, *I will protect them all and they won't be able to argue with me.*

And with a smile on her lips at this thought, she urged her horse forward into the black night.

PART ONE: September, 2018

Chapter One

"No!" screamed Perdita Rivers.

She was falling, her body twisting out of control, her breathing ragged as she fought to regain her balance, but she knew it was impossible. She threw out her hands, the wind tearing the screams from her mouth as she fell headfirst, tumbling over and over, until she no longer knew where was up. A large, soft snowdrift finally stopped her fall and she lay face-down in the icy coldness, catching her breath. It was then she heard the shouts of concern, punctuated by stifled giggles.

Two strong hands grabbed her around the waist and hauled her into a standing position. With great reluctance, she looked up into the dancing blue eyes of her friend, Kit Mackensie. He was doing his best to look concerned as he dusted away her covering of snow but was making a very bad job of it. Perdita, too, felt the corner of her mouth twitch.

"Stupid snowboard," she muttered and Kit burst out laughing.

Behind them, she heard the whoosh of skis as the rest of their party arrived at her side. First to reach them was her twin sister, Piper Davidson, who skidded to a neat halt, followed by Kit's elder sister, Megan and her fiancé, Pablo. Piper was giggling.

"Oh Perds, that was hilarious! Shame you weren't able to work in a somersault!"

For the past few months, archaeologist Perdita Rivers and her artist sister, Piper, had been staying with the Mackensie family in their vast and impressive home, Castle Jerusalem. It was situated in the tiny principality of Andorra, which was perched on the Pyrenees mountains between France and Spain. The house, as the name suggested, was at its heart a 12th century castle that had belonged to the family for several generations. Over the years it had been extended and was now the headquarters of the Mackensies' vast historical research business, as well as a comfortable family home. Around the castle were the impressive ski runs and luxurious resorts that added to the glamour of the small but perfectly formed tax haven.

Together the group made their way, laughing and talking, back the short distance to the winding path that led to the side entrance of Castle Jerusalem. The sun was sinking over the mountains, streaking the sky with a magnificent show of red, orange and pink swirls. It was breath-taking but the sudden drop in temperature was stark. Perdita was looking forward to a hot bath and a change of clothes before an evening in front of the roaring fires.

"Hello!" shouted Megan as they arrived in the large ante room where the ski equipment was stored. "We're home!"

It was a Mackensie family tradition to shout this greeting, even if there was no one around to answer. But, as they all began stripping off their outdoor clothes, basking in the heat of the flaming log-burning stove, a voice none of them expected to hear shouted a response.

"Hey everyone!"

They all exchanged a surprised look as a slender, blonde figure hurried into the room.

"Izi!" exclaimed Megan, running over to her friend. The two women hugged, then Izabel Barnes grinned around at everyone.

"When did you arrive?" asked Perdita, also greeting Izi with a hug once Megan had released her. "How is everyone at Marquess House?"

"About an hour ago," she replied, "and everyone is fine — they all send their love and say hello."

Perdita smiled her thanks. Marquess House was the stately home in Pembrokeshire that Perdita and Piper had inherited earlier that year from their grandmother, the eminent historian, Mary Fitzroy. Izabel worked there with her own grandmother, Jenny Procter, who was the chief librarian and archivist.

"We didn't expect you until next week," Perdita heard Kit exclaiming as she pulled her head clear of a thick fleece.

"As chief bridesmaid I thought Megs could do with my help," Izi replied, grinning, and Megan beamed. "Nan, I mean Jenny, suggested I come over early, then I can help you with the wedding and, if you'd like —" she turned to Perdita — "I can assist with your research, too."

"Izi, that would be wonderful. I haven't begun yet, but I can't put it off forever."

The conversation had taken the group to the hall at the centre of Castle Jerusalem which was the conduit to all areas of the ancient building, from the original 12th century heart through to the modern business extensions.

"And," said Izi, turning to Perdita as everyone began to disperse to their bedrooms, "message from Alistair. He has some news and would like to have a chat with you and Piper before dinner."

It was early evening and everyone was gathered in one of the smaller sitting rooms in the castle. A huge fire burned in the carved stone fireplace, throwing out a cosy glow. Perdita sat on a two-seater sofa beside Kit, while Piper was curled in a wing armchair. Alistair and Susan Mackensie, Kit's parents, were on another sofa by the fire. Perdita was trying to keep her tone reasonable but she could feel her frustration growing.

"So, why can't we go home?" she asked. "Apart from Megan and Pablo's wedding, obviously; but once that's over, do you still intend for us to remain at Castle Jerusalem?"

"For the time being, yes, my dear — I think you're safer here than returning to Marquess House," replied Alistair Mackensie.

Perdita shook her head in irritation. She still found it hard to believe this was her life. Six months ago, she had been working on an archaeological dig when her then fiancé, Warren Dexter, had arrived with the news that her estranged grandmother, Mary Fitzroy, had died. The following day she had received a letter from Alistair, who had been Mary's solicitor, inviting her to her grandmother's stately home, Marquess House in St Ishmaels in Pembrokeshire, only a few miles from the dig site.

During the interview, Alistair had explained that she and Piper were the main beneficiaries of Mary's will and, apart from a few personal bequests, they had inherited everything — her manor house, an extensive research centre and a vast fortune. They were now worth in excess of £300 million between them.

It had taken the twins a while to come to terms with their inheritance. They could not understand why their grandmother had shunned them in life — abandoning them after their mother's death when they were seven years old — yet had embraced them in death. Determined to unravel this mystery and, with Piper in America accompanying her husband, Jeremy Davidson, Perdita had resigned from her university job, and moved into Marquess House.

Once ensconced, she had searched her grandmother's published and unpublished books for clues and, to her astonishment, had discovered a trail of information left by Mary for her to find. It seemed the key to Mary's behaviour lay in her unfinished manuscript *The Catherine Howard Anomaly*, which she had been working on at the time her daughter, Louisa, the twins' mother, had died in a road accident.

With the help of Alistair's son, Kit Mackensie, Perdita had uncovered more than she had imagined. Not only had she discovered the truth about her mother's death and the real reason Mary had stepped away from them, she also revealed an incredible but provable alternate version of Tudor history concerning Henry VIII and his fifth bride, Catherine Howard. Struggling to understand why such an incredible historical revelation had been covered up, Perdita was told of the real danger she now faced was from a shadowy section of the British Secret Service called MI1 Elite.

This organisation was tasked with retaining the accepted version of history, removing and destroying any evidence that emerged which might offer an alternative view to the one recorded in the history textbooks. What made matters worse was that her former fiancé, Warren Dexter, had been part of this highly secretive and dangerous section of the British government. It transpired he had been married throughout their relationship and had seduced her in order to discover what she knew about her grandmother's work. While Perdita had dealt with her own emotional upheaval, Piper's marriage to Jeremy had collapsed when he had an affair with a co-worker called Kirstin.

The twins were told they were protected by an ancient document called The Milford Haven Treaty that created a sovereign state within Marquess House, making them immune from arrest by the secret service while they were living there. However, in order to get around this, the new and ruthless head of MI1, Inigo Westbury, had reintroduced The White List, an assassination register of academics who tried to reveal more than the government was willing to allow. Although Alistair had been able to have the arrest warrants for treason quashed, it nevertheless meant Perdita, Piper and Kit had been in incredible danger and had been forced to flee for their lives. This was the reason they were currently in the Mackensies' stronghold in Andorra.

"But Dad," interjected Kit, his tone as constricted as Perdita's, "won't The Milford Haven Treaty protect us? You said the Home Secretary was investigating Inigo Westbury and we were no longer on The White List, which according to him, doesn't exist anyway."

"Quite correct," said Alistair. "My desire to keep us all here is nothing to do with the Treaty or even MI1." He paused, taking a sip of wine, then turned to Piper, who was gazing into the dancing fames. "Piper, I apologise now for what we have to discuss, as you may find it distressing. When Perdita first told me about the woman your husband has been having an affair with, Kirstin Chaplin, I sent one of my teams to investigate…"

"Why though, Alistair?" asked Piper, her voice low. "We know they're having an affair. Jeremy's plastering their pictures all over social media."

"It's not to discover what they are doing now," he explained. "It's to find out who she really is because she isn't an IT Consultant on a contract with Jeremy's company. I suspected she might be a professional mistress sent by a company who would subsequently try to persuade Jeremy to fight for at least half of your inheritance and access to Marquess House. However, at present, she seems to have no connections to any of the usual organisations who instigate this kind of high-level sting."

Perdita, Piper and Kit exchanged horrified looks.

"You think Jeremy and I have been set up?" asked Piper.

"We can't dismiss the idea."

"Rather like Warren and me," said Perdita in a quiet but bitter tone.

"Unfortunately, yes," Alistair said. "However, while Kirstin Chaplin is not affiliated to any of the usual companies that organise such stings, I have discovered she has links to someone else."

"Who?" asked Perdita.

"Randolph Connors," said Alistair. "The son of Cecily Connors née Fitzroy, Mary's younger sister."

"Which would make him Mum's cousin," said Perdita.

"Yes," confirmed Alistair, "and when you two inherited Marquess House, he was furious."

"Why?" asked Piper.

"It seems your father and grandmother had played their parts well over the years because Randolph believed the charade they set up after your mother's death. He was confident that when Mary died, Marquess House would come to him. However, under the terms of the will and the many covenants put in place over the years, even if he had been the only claimant, the house would never have been his; you see, Marquess House can only be passed to a female heir."

"I wondered," said Perdita. "Don't you remember, Pipes, we discussed it the first day we were told about our inheritance?"

"We joked about it," agreed Piper, "but we didn't know for sure. Isn't primogeniture usually all about keeping property and money in the male line?"

"It is, but your female ancestors were the ones with the money and they were very forward-thinking women. In order to scare away ruthless, fortune-hunting men, a clause was created that stated Marquess House and the money it generated could only be passed through the female line. When Mary inherited, then gave birth to Louisa and she gave birth to female twins, there was no question about where the trust would go with each generation."

"Way to go, Granny," murmured Piper, and Perdita smothered a grin, not wishing to seem disrespectful as Alistair explained his concerns.

"However, Mary had a younger sister, Cecily, who died young," he continued. "Her widower, Albert Connors and their son, Randolph, were told that they had a claim on Cecily's extremely large trust fund but would never be able to gain access or ownership to Marquess House. Albert had no interest in the house but his son, Randolph, in recent years has become obsessed with Marquess House and the aristocratic roots it represents."

"Does it?" said Perdita, surprised. "The house is old but not all period houses come with a title. We don't have any, do we?"

"Mary didn't use them," Alastair admitted, "neither did her mother, Eleanor Fitzroy. I think Lettice Lakeby was the last of your female relations to use the title officially."

"And what is it?" asked Piper.

"Haven't you guessed?" he said, with a searching look at Perdita.

"The title is connected to the house?" she clarified.

"Yes," confirmed Alistair.

"And is this a rather unusual female title?"

Alistair nodded.

"Marquess of Pembroke — the title bestowed upon Anne Boleyn so she was of a high enough social rank to marry King Henry VIII," Perdita said, slowly. "A male title given to a woman. I presume this is the reason Randolph Connors thinks he has a right to it? It should really belong to a man."

"It's possible," said Alistair, "and you're correct, Perdita, your official title, should you ever choose to use it is the Marquess of Pembroke and, as your heir, Piper is Viscountess Cleddau."

"This is insane," said Perdita.

"Connors is one of the richest men in the world," continued Alistair, "so money has never been his motivation. He is only interested in things he cannot buy, like the history and kudos of having an aristocratic title. When Randolph married Lady Marianne O'Rourke, they had one son, Xavier. Three years ago, Xavier married the heiress, Amber MacDonald and in May this year, Amber gave birth to identical twin girls, Ruby and Pearl. When Mary died in June, Randolph tried to claim Marquess House on behalf of his granddaughters."

"What?" Perdita was astonished but then something she had read in one of Mary's letters finally made sense. Her grandmother had written that things had changed and they must protect themselves. Was she referring to the birth of Randolph's twin granddaughters? Had Mary suspected Connors would try to claim Marquess House on their behalf?

"Randolph Connors is not the most stable of men," said Alistair. "He believes Marquess House should have been passed to his granddaughters, allowing him to administer and control it on their behalf, while also using the titles until they come of age."

"But he has no claim while we're alive..." began Piper, then realisation dawned and her voice faded away.

"Connors is wealthy and influential," said Alistair. "He has nefarious connections with dubious and powerful groups around the world. He might try to have you removed to clear the way for Ruby and Pearl."

"Do you mean murdered?" asked Kit, horrified.

With great reluctance, Alistair nodded. Perdita watched the blood drain from Piper's face and knew she was probably just as pale.

"And Kirstin Chaplin, the woman who is having an affair with my husband, has links to Randolph Connors?" confirmed Piper.

"I'm afraid so," replied Alistair. "While the Home Secretary has given me his assurance about MI1 being bound by the Milford Haven Treaty he refuses to issue any commands for further protection for you while you're in the UK, unless I can show proof that Connors is a threat."

"But why?" gasped Perdita.

"Because Connors donates heavily to many organisations, including leading political parties," said Susan, who had been silent until that moment. "The Home Secretary doesn't want to upset one of the government's best financial backers."

"Marquess House has proved that it is easily breached," said Alistair, "whereas Castle Jerusalem is an old fortress with better defences. I have also been able to secure a number of agreements with the French, Spanish, Italian and Swiss authorities to guarantee your protection. I refuse to take risks with any of your lives."

Perdita put the two mugs of hot chocolate on the long low table in front of the fire before sitting on the sofa in their private apartment and glancing over at Piper. After Alistair's revelations, neither of them had contributed much to the conversation over dinner, both relieved that Megan and Pablo's upcoming nuptials had dominated the discussions.

"Perds, there's something I don't understand," Piper said, picking up her mug, "does this mean we're related to Anne Boleyn?"

"We could be, but unless someone has researched our family tree going back to Tudor times, we won't know. If there are only certain people who can inherit, it makes the bloodline rather twisted."

"I bet MI1 Elite know," muttered Piper.

"I'll call them, shall I, and ask?"

"They might at least give us a straight answer."

"Shortly before they assassinate us."

"Perds, don't," said Piper, her voice harsh. "I keep having nightmares about being murdered — saying things like that seems like bad luck."

"I'm sorry," replied Perdita. "I didn't mean to upset you. It's this whole situation which is making me spiky. The endless drip-feed of information is so frustrating. I've decided to ask Alistair to sit down with us and tell us everything he knows, even if Granny told him not to. We're still here, she isn't, and at the moment I feel as though I'm operating blindfolded. If we're going to solve this mystery and stay alive, we have to know everything about our inheritance."

Piper sipped her hot chocolate, nodding in agreement, then asked, "If we're going to be here for a few more months, I've decided to accept Alistair's offer of setting up a studio on the top floor of the business centre. If I'm busy, time will pass more quickly. It'll also stop me brooding over Jeremy. Will you begin your research again now you know we're going to be here until at least Christmas?"

Perdita drained her mug and placed it on the table in front of her.

"Yes," she said, although her tone was flat. "I've been putting it off because it felt wrong to be working here. All the historical anomalies we discovered about Catherine Howard were connected with Marquess House, so it felt right to be revealing them within its walls."

"And now?"

"I have no choice; like you, I can't bear to sit around doing nothing any longer," Perdita replied. "I'll talk to Kit and ask him if the office opposite his is still free for me to use, then I'll ask Deborah Black in the library to bring the next lot of Marquess House account books out of storage."

"The story will continue then?" asked Piper.

"Yes — we've found the first ruby ring, which we think belonged to Catherine Howard, and I hope the account books will offer some clues to the whereabouts of the second ruby ring and the silver locket. Catherine Howard may have told us her story through her codex but now we need to discover what happened to her children."

Chapter Two

Each book was a sentinel of the past, laid out on its own separate, cotton-covered, foam wedge. The books stretched the length of the boardroom table, waiting to reveal their secrets. The ancient bindings were brown with age but they had been carefully dusted and now glimmered in the crystalline mountain light that was flooding through the floor-to-ceiling windows. Perdita approached the first book with great caution as though the inanimate object were a wild animal that could be scared away. "You realise what these are?" she said, her voice low and respectful as she turned to Piper, who was watching her from the doorway.

"Old books?" suggested Piper.

"These are the key to the past," said Perdita. "They hold the answers." She pulled a pair of white gloves from a pile that lay at one end of the table and slid them on. "Inside these pages is the truth about who lived and who died. The words collected here could change history forever."

"You're worrying me now, Perds," said Piper, joining her by the table. "These are old account books. They might be able to tell us a certain amount but please don't get your hopes up that they could solve the mystery."

Perdita turned her startling grey-green eyes on her sister, the gold glints within flashing; their depth as raw as a winter storm.

"It's too late for that, Pipes," she said, "my hopes have been up ever since I knew these books existed. It's taken me a while to find my enthusiasm again, but now they're here and I'm breathing in their scent, I know they're going to help me discover the truth. Even if they can only tell me the kind of feed they bought for the horses back then I'll feel as though I've discovered something."

"Perds, you're crazy," Piper said, laughing.

"No, I'm feeling better about things and exploring unexamined books always excites me. If they're anything like the other accounts book I've studied over the years, they'll be jammed full of small trinkets of information, minutiae that have been overlooked, missed or ignored but which could reveal a whole world of deceptions. Remember, Pipes, history is in the details."

"Exactly," Piper said, "and it's the details you could discover that scare me."

The twins stared at each other, then both moved at the same time and embraced.

"We no longer have a choice," said Perdita, breaking away first and holding her sister at arms' length, trying to impart some of her own strength to her nervous twin. "Either we find the truth first and use it as leverage or we spend the rest of our lives knowing we could be murdered at any moment, especially now we know Randolph Connors is chasing us as well as MI1 Elite."

"I'm going upstairs to the studio," Piper said, turning away.

"Pipes, I'm sorry, it was a stupid thing to say — I didn't mean to upset you," said Perdita.

"You don't need to apologise," said Piper. "We are in danger — why else would we be hiding here in a castle carved out of a mountainside? Good luck with the books, Perds, I'll see you later."

Piper gave her a watery smile and waved as she let the heavy door swing shut. Perdita cursed herself — she was not usually so insensitive. It must be anxiety, she reasoned with herself as she walked back to the books. Or eagerness, she admitted, not to be rid of Piper but to be able to disappear into another world for a while and forget the horror of this one. Scraping her long, thick dark hair into a ponytail, Perdita rummaged in her computer bag, set up her laptop, extracted a notebook and a series of pencils, then turned to the first account book entitled: *Marquess House, February 1543* and stared down at the heavy leather cover.

It was thanks to the ancient account books dated from 1542 that Perdita, Kit and the Marquess House research team had been able to unravel the final truth about Catherine Howard. The set Perdita was studying now had been held in deep storage in the Jerusalem archive in Andorra but had been requested by her grandmother, Mary, a few days before she had died. Rather than ship them to Pembrokeshire, Dr Deborah Black, the head of the library team at Castle Jerusalem, had kept them in one of their storage units, awaiting further instructions. To Perdita's frustration, they were not a complete collection, only six remained for 1543 — March through to September — and for 1544 and 1545, there were only a few — June, July and October for 1544, and January, April and August for 1545.

"Knock, knock," a tentative male voice announced.

"Oh, hello Kit," Perdita said, her eyes coming back into focus as she turned to look towards the door.

"Are you all right? You were miles away," he said, walking across the room to join her. He had his battered Fred Perry sports bag slung across his chest and was carrying a tray of coffee and pastries. Perdita pulled off her cotton gloves, then cleared a space on a small round table away from the priceless ancient books and relieved Kit of his burden.

"I was thinking about all this," she replied, sweeping her hand in an all-encompassing gesture, "our moonlight flit,

Granny Mary, Marquess House, Catherine Howard, the Llyn Cel mermaid, the ruby ring, everything that's brought us to this moment. It's been quite a bumpy ride so far."

"Yep, and it isn't over yet," said Kit with a frown.

Perdita stared up into Kit's piercing blue eyes, unnerved by this chink in Kit's usual armour of optimistic sunniness. At 5ft 7in, she was tall, but Kit towered over her at 6ft 4in, and with his mop of dark curly hair and toned surfer's physique he was an imposing figure, but today he seemed strangely fragile.

"What's happened?"

"Nothing." He paused, then turning away from her as though he were embarrassed, continued, "I had another nightmare last night and I can't seem to shake that feeling of dread."

Perdita's eyes were sympathetic. Since their escape, she had suffered bad dreams of being chased by faceless, terrifying strangers dressed in black. Piper, too, had confessed to experiencing similar unease.

"You don't have to pretend to be brave to me," she said, taking his hand and giving it a reassuring squeeze. "We went through a horrible ordeal. You wouldn't be human if it didn't trip you up every now and then. In fact, I'd be more concerned if it hadn't affected you in some way."

"You're right," he murmured, then to her surprise he drew her into a tight, almost suffocating embrace, burying his face in her hair. It was over in seconds and he released her, leaving her tingling all over, her heart pounding. "Sorry, needed some human contact."

"Any time," she replied, in a choked voice. They stared at each other, then Perdita reached for her coffee and walked over to the vast windows, sipping it, as her heart rate returned to normal. She watched Kit as he wandered over to the waiting books, enjoying the change in his expression as his professional expertise rose to the surface.

When he was not working with Perdita, Kit had two major roles within his family business, Jerusalem. The first was using his legal qualifications to act as an assistant to his father in the administration of Marquess House — a job he would take over from Alistair when he retired. The second, he shared with his siblings, Megan and Stuart, which was to rescue and restore important antiquities and documents. If they were of national interest the organisation would donate the items to the government of their country of origin. Megan ran the organisation from Andorra, covering Africa and Asia. Stuart looked after the Americas, while Kit concerned himself with Europe and Australasia.

"These are in exquisite condition," Kit said, after examining them. "How far have you got?"

"I haven't even opened them yet," Perdita admitted and he grinned, looking more like his usual self.

"Together?"

A thrill of anticipation and excitement ran through Perdita and she returned Kit's grin.

"Ready?" asked Kit, his hand positioned over the account book for *Marquess House, March 1543.*

Perdita mirrored his pose. "Set?" she said, then together they both shouted: "Go!" and in unison they opened the covers and began to read.

The familiar writing of the housekeeper, Mrs Helen Page, filled the page, once more beckoning Perdita into the past. It had been Mrs Page's accounts that had helped Perdita solve the final mystery of her grandmother's work. Although in conventional history books, Catherine Howard, the fifth bride of Henry VIII, was said to have been executed at the Tower of

London on 13 February 1542, Perdita had proved that not only had this been incorrect but that Catherine had been spirited away to Marquess House in Pembrokeshire.

The account books had shown that she had been preparing to give birth and Perdita had realised Catherine had delivered twins: a girl and a boy, a legitimate Tudor prince and princess, who for reasons she had yet to discover, had at some point been written out of history. Perdita was determined to discover the identity of Catherine's children so she could understand why there had been a systematic rewriting of historical events to wipe these children and their lives from all official records.

Perdita and Kit had also found a Tudor ring — an ancient ruby surrounded by a golden filigree case that opened to reveal a hidden cavity for passing messages and the Latin inscription *Iuncta Sanguine*, which translated to *Joined in blood*. As an expert in jewellery and its symbolism Perdita knew this ring was more than an ornament. It had significance and if she had guessed correctly, the matching pair to this ring was going to provide the evidence they needed to locate one of the children, while a silver locket would point the way to the other.

The only question was, how were they going to find them? This was where she hoped the account books would help. There might be unwitting clues in the daily lists of household activity, snippets of information that to the uninformed eye would mean nothing but which could give Perdita a clue. She had other sources to check that she hoped would provide corroborating evidence, but the search had to begin somewhere. Mrs Helen Page had helped them once, Perdita hoped she would offer the hand of service across the centuries once again.

As before, it took only moments for her eyes to become accustomed to the extravagant writing and she was soon making copious notes on her laptop. Beside her Kit was doing the same. After an hour, he stretched and looked up.

"How are you getting on?" he asked.

Perdita finished the sentence she was writing and pulled a face.

"Not bad. There are a few references to a wet nurse for 'the boy-childe' and orders of linen and swaddling clothes but there's no mention of the little girl. Do you think she died?"

"No," said Kit, looking enigmatic.

Perdita narrowed her eyes at him. "Come on Smug-Mackensie-Kid, what have you found?" The name had been a derogatory term Perdita's ex-fiancé, Warren, had once used about Kit but it had made Kit laugh so much, Perdita had been using it ever since.

"You know when we were compiling the list of anomalies in Catherine Howard's life and one of the odd things we came across was a baby who was supposedly lodged at the house of Anne of Cleves — a baby rumoured to have been hers and Henry VIII's child?"

"Yes, 15 November 1541, if my memory serves me correctly. Two of Anne's ladies-in-waiting — Jane Rattsay and Lady Wingfield — were questioned and denied any truth in the rumours. After an inquiry, Anne and her household were exonerated."

"Well, I've found a record of a gift of linen for 'the Lady Anne, sister to the king' — which was Anne of Cleves's legal status after Henry VIII divorced her — sent by 'Lady Tudor' who we know is Catherine 'for her kyndness in sheltering my daughter, late November last on her northwards journee…'."

"What? Let me see!" Perdita sprang from her seat and leaned over Kit, examining the ancient text. "The dates are incorrect for Anne's supposed baby but a tweaked date here or there is the least of our worries. I also remember that the child who was found was a boy but it's possible Anne said that in order to hide the true identity," she said, thinking out loud. "This proves that the little girl, Elizabeth, if the Tudor graffiti in Marquess House is correct, survived but that she was sent away almost immediately. I wonder why? And where was she sent?"

"Somewhere north," supplied Kit.

"Helpful, thanks," said Perdita. "I wonder why the daughter was sent away and not the son? Surely as a male heir, the longed-for second son, the duke of York, he would have been in more danger. There were already two Tudor princesses — Mary and Elizabeth. This little girl would have been way down the list of succession." Perdita wandered back to the table and picked up one of the pastries Kit had brought with him earlier. "It doesn't make much sense yet, does it?" she sighed.

A few hours later, Piper stuck her head around the door, bringing with her a smell of turpentine.

"Food, anyone?"

"Definitely," said Perdita and they headed for the enormous kitchen where lunch was served every day. Perdita explained their discoveries to Piper and then asked how Piper's portrait of Megan and Pablo was coming along.

"I'm really pleased with it; I hope Megan and Pablo will like it."

"If it's anywhere near as good as the sketch you did of them, they'll love it," said Kit. "Although, if I'm honest, the sooner this wedding is over the better. Megan is crazy. If I try to talk to her about work, I can't get a sensible word out of her."

"Only another few weeks," said Piper, patting his arm consolingly. "Poor Megan, she must be tearing her hair out. I was crazy in the weeks running up to my wedding."

Kit was tapping away on his phone, scowling. "See you later," he said, his tone gruff, before wandering away.

"What was that about?" asked Piper, watching his retreating back.

"No idea," said Perdita. "He's been fine all morning."

"Ah, there you both are," said a cheerful voice. Perdita and Piper had finished eating and were sprawled on the squashy armchairs in front of the enormous roaring fire, discussing what to wear to Megan and Pablo's upcoming wedding. Dr Deborah Black, the chief librarian at Jerusalem was beaming at them. In her early 60s, Deborah was a slim, energetic woman with deep auburn hair cut in a short pixie cut. "I have the results from the tests on the boxes."

Perdita sat bolt upright. "And?"

Before fleeing Marquess House, Perdita and Kit had found a ruby ring they believed to have once belonged to Catherine Howard. It had been protected for the intervening centuries by a wooden box, inside which was a leather jewellery case. Deborah had offered to run a series of dating tests on the boxes.

"Both boxes can be dated to the seventeenth century…"

"Which fits with all the information we've discovered about Penelope Fitzalan, who I think might have been the person who hid the ring," interrupted Perdita in excitement. "After all, she was the one who made us realise the significance of the pieces of jewellery. She claimed in one of her letters she would die to protect the secret of the ring."

"Yes, it does, but there's more. This is the report which you'll want to read in its entirety later," said Deborah, handing them both a bound copy. "In summary, though, the most interesting piece is the outer wooden box. The X-ray showed it had once been painted. There's a picture of it in the appendixes." She paused while Perdita and Piper flicked through until they found the relevant page. "In the top left-hand corner of the box's lid were written the words *Iuncta Sanguine, Iuncta* is at the top and underneath it is a red star, the letter 'A' and what we think may have been a green dot but it's very faded so we can't be certain of the original colour, with the word *Sanguine* at the bottom of this arrangement. On the right-hand side the pattern repeats but with a few differences: the top word is *Semper,* while the word at the bottom is *Sorores, Sisters Always.* The red star is there again, but the letter 'A' is changed to a 'C' and there is what looks like a faded blue dot underneath it."

"Those phrases are on the frontispiece of *The Catherine Howard Codex,*" said Perdita, "and the words *Iuncta Sanguine* were engraved on the inside of the ruby ring we found…"

"Exactly," said Deborah. "There's more though. If you look closely at the image, you'll see there is a curved line beside each of these patterns. I do wonder if they were jewelled or made from some form of gold leaf because they're very faint but they seem to have points at the ends as though they are directional arrows."

"Oh yes," said Piper, tracing her finger over first one line, then the other on the image, "one points to the left, the other the right."

"What's this at the bottom?" Perdita asked. "Oh my goodness, it says *Spe et Nereidum* — Hope and Mermaids — that's what was written on Catherine Howard's gravestone."

"Look at what else is there," added Deborah. "A curved line and in the dome of that is the letter P with a white star underneath. There's also a tiny mermaid engraved under the words *Spe et Nereidum.*"

Perdita considered the image for a moment, then flicked over the page where there was a picture of the leather jewellery box that had been interred within the wooden box. The interior of this had been padded with what had once been white velvet, which had long since crumbled and discoloured, and had three specific areas within it — two slots for holding the rings and an indentation that would have held an oval locket.

"The markings in the lid correspond with the positions of the pieces of jewellery as they would have been stored in the leather case," said Perdita. "The ring we found was in the left-hand corner and it had *Iuncta Sanguine* engraved inside. I think I've realised something." Perdita looked up and scanned the cavernous interior of the room. Kit was sitting at the large round wooden table in one corner deep in conversation with Megan's fiancé, Pablo. "Kit!" she called. "Do you have a minute?"

"What's up?" he asked, hurrying over.

Perdita explained what Deborah's team had discovered. "This pattern corresponds with the position in the box where we found our ruby ring," she said. "What if the red star represents the ruby, the green dot represents the emerald on the clip…"

"And the letter 'A'?" asked Kit.

"Anne," said Perdita.

"You mean, Anne of Cleves, who had the rings made for her and Catherine so they could pass messages to each other?" clarified Piper.

"Yes. We've found Anne's ring, not Catherine's."

"But, Perdita, if that's the case," said Deborah, "why would Lady Anne's ring be at Marquess House?"

"I don't know but this does corroborate something that was written in the story of the Llyn Cel mermaid. The noble woman in the story, who don't forget was named Catherine, gave her children tokens so they would be able to recognise each other. What if the story is referring to these pieces of jewellery: she gave one child her ruby ring and the other her locket? So, her ring wouldn't be at Marquess House, it would be with whichever child it was given to at the time."

"It's possible," agreed Kit.

"It'll also give us something to look out for in the account books," Perdita continued. "We know Catherine's daughter was sent away on a journey after her birth but there are records for a wet-nurse for the little boy, so he must have stayed at Marquess House. You never know, we might get lucky and find a reference to the item of jewellery that was left behind for him, then we'll know definitively which child was given which piece."

"If we're suggesting the 'A' inscribed in the lid refers to Anne, then it follows the 'C' will probably indicate Catherine, so who is 'P'?" Deborah asked.

"I would guess it's probably Penelope Fitzalan," said Perdita. "It was Penelope who wrote a series of letters referring to a secret hidden within Marquess House that she would be prepared to die rather than reveal. Catherine was the inspiration for the Llyn Cel mermaid, which is a story included in the anthology of legends written by Penelope, so somehow Penelope must have been given a ruby ring."

"Do you think she knew it was Anne's and not Catherine's?" asked Piper.

"She must have done, if she was the one who hid the ring in these two boxes with all this symbolism attached."

"But who was Penelope Fitzalan and how is she connected to everything?" asked Kit.

Perdita gave him a rueful smile. "I have no idea but she does seem to have a link to the story."

"The letters you mentioned, Perdita — when were they dated from?" asked Deborah.

"Mid-seventeenth century," she replied, "which is too late for her to be Catherine's daughter but she might be a granddaughter or even a great-granddaughter. I would guess she was a descendant but until we do some more research, we won't know."

Chapter Three

Perdita hurried down the stairs, her computer bag bumping on her hip as she headed towards the suite of offices in the west wing. She and Piper were meeting Alistair to discuss all aspects of their inheritance and what it meant to their lives, including an update on the situation with Randolph Connors. Alistair had promised to tell them everything, assuring her there would be no more secrets but as she headed towards his office, she realised she was experiencing some trepidation. The last time she had felt anything similar was when she and Kit had sat beside Llyn Cel while he told the truth about her mother's death.

Piper, who had been struck by inspiration for the wedding portrait, had promised she would be 20 minutes behind her sister and not to wait.

"Good morning, my dear," said Alistair as Perdita entered. "I hope you'll indulge us for a few moments. Kit bid for this document shortly after you moved into Marquess House. It arrived yesterday. Would you care to see?"

"Yes, please," she said, hurrying over to join them at the table.

The document was held down with soft padded weights and Kit was examining the extravagant swirling letters across the top of the page.

"Morning Perds," he grinned.

"It was a document allegedly showing ownership of the islands of New Zealand going back to the 1500s, therefore, predating Captain Cook who didn't discover them until April 1769, wasn't it?" she said, putting her bags on the floor before pulling a band from off her wrist and twisting her hair into a ponytail. "You were sure it was a fake. What do you think now you've seen it?"

"There are loads of tests to be done but I'm pretty certain this is an eighteenth-century forgery," he said. "The parchment is wrong and, look at that…"

She laughed. "In January 1558, the English monarch was Mary I, not Elizabeth as this claims! Elizabeth ascended the throne on 17 November 1558. And is that a Roman number four? Both of them were simply Queen Mary and Queen Elizabeth — there would have been no regnal number. Mary only became Mary I when the Stuarts put William and Mary on the throne as joint monarchs and Elizabeth only needed a regnal number, when Elizabeth II became queen in 1952."

Kit picked up a magnifying glass and examined the mark.

"It does look like a Roman numeral," he agreed. "How many monarchs have reached four in the regnal number?"

"There were six," Perdita replied.

"Really?" said Alistair.

"Yes, the English kings Henry IV and Edward IV, then George IV in 1820 but he was king of Great Britain, rather than only England."

"What's the difference?" asked Kit.

"In 1707, the last Stuart monarch, Queen Anne united the country under the Act of Union," explained Perdita. "It was when the Scottish and English parliaments agreed to form one political union, making her the first monarch of Great Britain. George IV was on the throne for ten years, then he was followed by William IV who died 1837. Apart from that there was a Malcolm IV in Scotland and the final one was James IV. He married Margaret Tudor, the sister of Henry VIII and mother of both James V of Scotland and with Archibald

Douglas, her second husband, Lady Margaret Douglas, later the countess of Lennox."

"You're like our own walking search engine," said Kit, grinning, when Perdita finished.

"Always happy to be of service," she laughed. "What happens to the document next?"

"I'll hand it over to Dr Black and her team. We can do a lot of tests in the labs here but if need be, we'll send it back to The Dairy at Marquess House to ascertain authenticity."

The smile faltered on Perdita's face. "You're right," she said, moving away from the table. "We can't take any supposed fakes at face value anymore."

There was a knock on the door and Dr Deborah Black arrived.

"Morning," she said.

"Good morning, Deborah," said Alistair.

"Is this it?" she asked, appraising the document with her expert eye.

"Yes," replied Kit. "What are your first impressions?"

Deborah was silent as she examined the ancient parchment, then taking off her glasses, she tapped them against her teeth before speaking.

"The parchment is suspect. It feels too thick to be Tudor. It'll be interesting to see what the carbon dating gives us but I can guarantee it won't be sixteenth century."

"Thank you, Deborah," said Alistair. "Is there any news on Callum?"

"Much better — he's flying back with Stuart in time for the wedding. I'll be relieved when he's home though."

"It's good news to hear he's recovering at last."

"Who's Callum?" asked Perdita.

"My youngest son," explained Deborah. "He's been working

in the US but caught glandular fever, then pneumonia. We've been very worried about him. He's much improved, although he's still battling bouts of intense fatigue."

"What about his job?" asked Kit.

"He was on a short contract and it ended a week before his illness — they've tendered it out to someone else now."

"We have a vacancy," said Alistair. "Only when he's well enough, though. We could use his IT expertise with all our upgrades and increased levels of security."

"Oh, Alistair, thank you," smiled Deborah. "I'm sure he'll be delighted; he's been saying for a while he misses it here. Now, Kit, will you help me with this, please?"

Between them, they rolled the parchment, stowing it in a protective tube. Tucking it under her arm, Deborah bustled off with a cheery goodbye.

Voices in the corridor announced Piper's arrival as she chatted to Deborah.

"Hi all, sorry I'm late," she called, hurrying in, her wild red hair tamed in a long plait and her glasses, rather than her usual contact lenses, perched on her nose. "The portrait is ready to be framed."

"You're not late," said Alistair, heading for the round table in the corner of the room.

"Are you staying, Kit?" asked Perdita, following Alistair.

"If you have no objections."

Before Alistair could speak, Perdita took command of the meeting.

"Alistair — Piper and I would like to begin with an apology to you, Jerusalem and the Mackensie family," she stated. "With all that's been going on, we've neglected our obligations concerning the running of Marquess House. We've realised

48

that apart from living in the property, we've made no offer to you and your team to help to run the estate in the way our grandmother did. From now on, we want to be as involved with Marquess House and its running as Granny Mary was when it was her home."

"Perdita, there is no need for either of you to apologise," said Alistair. "You've had rather a lot to deal with in the past few months. If it helps, when Mary inherited the house on her 21st birthday, my father, Kenneth Mackensie, fulfilled my role and he told me it was at least a year before Mary began to involve herself in the minutiae of Marquess House."

"What was she doing in the meantime?" asked Piper.

"Enjoying herself," replied Alistair. "She had inherited a huge house, full of history, which always was her *raison d'être*, as well as vast wealth at a time when rationing was ending and there was lots available to buy. I believe she spent quite some time in Paris and was a fan of the Christian Dior 'New Look'. I think some of her outfits are currently on loan to the Victoria and Albert museum."

"Something else we didn't know…" said Perdita and even to her own ears her voice sounded petulant.

"Enough, Perdita," said Alistair, his tone clipped. "You and Piper have been in possession of your inheritance for barely four months — you cannot possibly be expected to know everything that is going on or has taken place there. It took Mary years to be as conversant with the property and land as she became and, remember, as Kit is learning from me, I learned from my father how to administer your estate and it's taken most of my adult life. While I appreciate your need to understand what is going on, you're putting unrealistic expectations on yourselves. At the moment, your research skills and your expertise in the history of jewellery are far more precious and important than knowing what your grandmother spent her money on in the 1950s."

Kit was watching her with a guarded expression. Alistair, meanwhile was staring at her, awaiting her response.

"As ever, Alistair," she said, forcing her voice to sound calm and reasonable, "you are eminently practical. While I concur about the day-to-day running of Marquess House, the issue we have is that there still seem to be secrets you're keeping on Mary's behalf, like our titles. We understand she was acting with our best interests at heart but we are now adults and it is up to us to make such decisions. From today, as the eldest, I give you permission to disregard all Mary's instructions concerning secrecy. Whatever you know, we need to know. In trying to keep us safe, she may inadvertently be keeping key information from us that could be the difference between life and death."

Perdita fixed Alistair with what she hoped was a determined but approachable gaze. She had no wish to fall out with him but he did need to stop treating them as though they were the seven-year-old twins who had disappeared from Marquess House all those years ago.

"Of course," said Alistair with his usual smile.

Kit quickly interjected: "In the new climate of transparency, let's talk about the dig at Dale."

"The one Perdita was on in the summer?" asked Piper.

"Yes," he said. "You may not have realised but it was funded jointly by Jerusalem *and* Marquess House. Your grandmother hoped to visit but she was nervous about approaching you in case there was anyone from MI1 observing. Instead she had planned a large party to celebrate the end of the dig in order to meet you. Obviously, things didn't go to plan."

Perdita felt a lump in her throat. She had been so close to meeting her grandmother.

"Something that you won't have known is that the land on which the dig took place is part of the Marquess House estate," added Alistair.

"Really?" said Perdita.

"The reason we're discussing this now is because I've had emails from both Dr Olaf Dade, who headed up the underwater team, and Professor Maggie Cartwright, who was overall dig director. We informed them immediately of the change of ownership of the land and while probate and various other legal requirements were observed, all work on the dig and its findings had to be halted. Now, though, all the paperwork is complete and restoration of the artefacts can begin. As the landowners, you have certain rights over the antiquities and what happens to them. There is also the question of the golden mermaid cup and Olaf's request about returning to the site next year to continue the digs on both land and sea. He also has ambitious plans to raise the wreck."

"Would that be possible?" asked Piper. "Raising the wreck? It would cost millions."

"Between the two organisations I don't see why we couldn't put the funds in place," said Alistair.

"Wow," murmured Piper. "Would we fund it or is that you?"

"The companies would contribute equal amounts," said Alistair. "I would suggest that after the wedding, when we can all think straight again, I contact Olaf and propose a meeting to discuss his plans. In the meantime though, he has made a suggestion: Piper, how would you feel about working on the golden cup? Perdita has told me your expertise is sculpture and you use clockwork a great deal. This cup has a strange mechanism within its stem which we think is an early form of

51

clockwork — it was probably what drove the mermaid in the rim. There were also three keys in the box with the cup."

Perdita glanced at her sister, who seemed surprised but delighted.

"Well, I could certainly look at it and see if it's viable," said Piper. "Will Olaf be co-ordinating it?"

"Yes, although, Maggie Cartwright will be taking charge of the artefacts found on land. If you wish to accept the commission, I'll contact Olaf on your behalf and we'll draw up some contracts."

For the next half an hour, as requested, Alistair talked Perdita and Piper through the most recent events at Marquess House, including the requests for the artist's flats and studios, the plans for repairing the roof in the Victorian section of the property and the annual cleaning of the attics. Although Perdita knew she had asked for this information, she was soon quite bored and found her attention wandering back to the account books that were waiting for her and Kit in her office. In fact, Alistair was being so dull, she wondered if it was deliberate.

"And, finally, before you all scurry back to your research," he said, "Izabel has brought with her the first of the transcripts of the letters your grandmother had been using for her unpublished manuscript, *The Ladies of Melusine.*"

Perdita gave her full attention to Alistair.

"She will also be helping you and Kit," continued Alistair, "and now that Deborah and her team have finished the project they were completing for Megan, she has offered extra help too."

"Thank you," said Perdita. "It'll help to speed things up."

"Once I've sorted out framing the painting, I can help," offered Piper. "I have the algorithm I use when curating exhibitions. I could adjust it to search the Marquess House and Jerusalem databases to see if there's any mention of either the ruby ring or the silver locket."

"Good idea, Pipes," grinned Perdita.

"And, once again, Perdita, I'm sorry you and Piper have had such a difficult transition into your new life at Marquess House. There are no more secrets to be told, I promise."

Even though he was smiling and she had no reason to doubt him, Perdita felt that Alistair was lying.

Perdita, Piper and Kit made their way up the stairs from Alistair's office to the floor above. Once again, Deborah's librarians had laid out the account books but there was also the welcome addition of Izabel Barnes. She was seated at one end of the long table, reading the report Perdita had begun to write concerning the relevant information they had gleaned so far.

"Hi guys," she said, as they entered. "These books are fascinating."

Perdita put her computer bag down on the desk and pulled out her laptop, but then she noticed a pile of box files and a small leather case. It was identical to one Jenny had given her months before that had contained USB sticks holding her grandmother's published and unpublished works.

"Izi, what's this?" she asked.

"A present from Nan," Izabel replied. "Rather than email it, she thought it would be more secure to give you a USB stick."

"What's on it?" asked Piper.

"The transcripts of the first section of the Lady Pamela letters, as well as the research from Mary's other unpublished work and the first draft of the manuscript that was in the box. She had begun writing it, then she abandoned the project."

Perdita knew the reason why her grandmother had put all this information into storage: her mother's tragic death, orchestrated by The Watchers, the name Mary had used for MI1. Yet she could not quash the rush of anticipation she felt at delving into this hidden treasure trove. In Mary's other unpublished work, *The Catherine Howard Anomaly*, she had helped them to uncover a huge historical secret. Was it possible her grandmother had discovered even more, perhaps what had happened next? Maybe the inflammatory nature of what she had discovered was the real reason she had hidden this research.

"If you like," said Izabel, considering the vast amount of work spread out around the office, "I can cross-reference the report Nan made of the early Lady Pamela letters with the dates you're researching here?"

"Wouldn't that be a massive task?" asked Perdita.

"Not really. If you remember, the Lady Pamela letters cover quite a broad time period from 1541 to 1662. There aren't many from the earlier time period, so I could probably do it this morning. It certainly won't take longer than today."

"It might help us to clarify a few points," agreed Perdita.

"How many letters were there from 1543 until 1545?" asked Kit.

Izabel went back to her laptop and, after checking the details, said, "The first year we have an actual dated piece of correspondence is 1541 and there are three letters for that year, then in 1542 there are only two, however, for 1543 there are 15, the next year has 12 letters, then in 1545 there are nine. These numbers are fairly similar until we reach 1586, when there's an absolute explosion of correspondence which continues until 1589, after that there are only a few per year again until 1648, and then there are loads every year until 1662."

"There must be thousands of letters," said Piper.

"It's an incredible resource," said Izabel. "Nan thinks it could be as important as the Paston letters."

Piper threw Perdita a quizzical look.

"It was a collection of letters discovered by Major Thomas Weldon, the son-in-law of William Paston, the second earl of Yarmouth," Perdita explained. "Before his death, the earl had been struggling against bankruptcy and after he died, it was down to Weldon to sort through the detritus. Anything of value was sold, but the letters, which were sorted into several sacks, were set aside for burning with the other rubbish until their historical importance was noticed by antiquarian and local historian, the Reverend Francis Blomefield, in late spring 1735.

"They were mostly personal correspondence and covered the period from 1422 to 1509 — many of which were written during the Wars of the Roses. When they were published they caused a sensation, as they gave a whole new interpretation of the period as seen through the eyes of a family who had lived through the conflict. They were and remain one of the most important sources of Medieval history. If the Lady Pamela letters are anywhere near as informative, then Jenny's right, they could provide a new interpretation of events, one that MI1 would probably prefer to bury."

"Who would have collated them, though?" asked Kit, who was scanning the list Jenny had compiled of the names they had collected from the letters. "These letters are from a wide selection of women who were more likely to be friends than relations."

"Yes, but at least one of them was a Paston," said Izabel. "I wonder if she collected them and created an archive. She may have understood the importance of their letters or it could even have been by chance and she collected them because that's what the Paston family had always done."

"The letters cover 121 years, so she couldn't have overseen all of them," pointed out Piper.

"Who was the woman you were referring to, Izi?" asked Kit.

"Her name was Katherine Paston and she married Sir Henry Newton, MP for East Harptree in Somerset. What's fascinating is her connection to the work you've been doing."

"What do you mean?" said Perdita, a stillness coming over her.

"Katherine Paston was the daughter of Agnes Leigh," said Izabel, her eyes not leaving Perdita's face. "Agnes Leigh was the daughter of Sir John Leigh…"

"And Sir John Leigh was the half-brother of Catherine Howard," interrupted Perdita. "This is our link."

"How though?" asked Kit.

"Lady Pamela is descended from the Baynton family," continued Perdita. "Sir Edward Baynton was married to Lady Isabel Leigh, who was the sister of Sir John Leigh and the half-sister of Catherine Howard, making her and Catherine Howard great-aunts of Katherine Paston. Isabel had three children with Edward: Henry, Francis and Anne." Perdita glanced at one of the lists of correspondences Jenny had provided and pointed to one name. "I thought so — Elizabeth Talbot, Countess of Shrewsbury, better known as Bess of Hardwick is one of our letter-writers. There's a crossover here, because Edward's daughter, Jane, from his first marriage, married William St Loe of Chew Magna in Somerset, who subsequently married as his third wife, Bess of Hardwick. Not only that, the Anne Cavendish who married Edward and Isabel's son, Henry, was the daughter from Sir William St Loe's first marriage."

"They're all entangled," said Piper.

"It's quite incredible," said Perdita. "All these connections and all leading to Lady Pamela. Katherine Paston must have understood the importance of what they were doing and collated all the letters from this particular group of women. Is Penelope Fitzalan on the list of corresponders?"

"Yes," said Izabel, after consulting the list. "Her letters appear in the later sections, but we haven't transcribed those yet."

Perdita looked triumphant. "'A secret she was prepared to die to protect'," she quoted. "I bet the Lady Pamela letters contain a secret, too, and I suspect the packet of letters Penelope hid behind the portrait will fit perfectly into the timeframe and dates with this collection."

"But if these letters hold such a contentious secret, wouldn't it have been discovered before now?" asked Kit.

Perdita looked into his blue eyes. "Spoken like a man," she said, although her tone was not unkind. "You forget, Kit, women's chatter was deemed unimportant. Letters written by women were unlikely to have been taken seriously — after all, what could they write about that would be of interest to men? Yet these women were at the heart of the courts of England. They were often married to high-ranking members of the privy council. Many of them were ladies-in-waiting to the different queens. These women can give a unique perspective on what was happening and, if they were involved in keeping a secret, don't you think it might include what happened after Catherine Howard gave birth? The very fact they were written by women is what has protected that secret for so long."

Perdita turned away to stare at the long boardroom table. It was covered in ancient books, piles of notes, reports and the box files Izabel had brought with her. For a moment, Perdita felt overwhelmed by the sheer volume of information they had to assimilate into some kind of coherent whole. Looking for references for a ruby ring and a silver locket could take them years.

"Where do we even begin to unravel all this?" she sighed. "There's so much to search through."

Walking the length of the table she took several deep breaths and forced herself to calm down. Prioritise, she told herself, what's the most important task? Finding references to the jewellery to see if that can give us any clues to the identities of Catherine Howard's children, she thought. However, even that splits our attention — we need to focus on one thing at a time. But, which one: the ring or the locket?

"Perds?" asked Kit, tentatively.

"I've got a plan," she said, turning to face them. "We're nearly through the books for 1543, perhaps between us —" she pointed to herself, Kit and Piper — "we can go through the rest and see if there are any references to either the ring or the locket and which piece of jewellery was given to which child. While we're doing that, Izi, perhaps you could do the same with the letters we have for this time period, cross-referencing with the information we've already found?"

There were general nods of agreement and movement towards the table as they began to organise themselves.

"These books are our best clue as to what happened in the immediate aftermath of the birth of the twins," said Perdita. "Hopefully the letters will pick up the continuing story."

Perdita returned to the book she had been working on the previous week and consulted her notes. Opening it to the correct date, she once more began the painstaking work of searching for clues.

An hour later, as Perdita turned one of the pages and a cloud of dust puffed into the air, she sneezed. It was the first noise any of them had made since they had begun. There was a flurry of murmured "Bless yous" but nobody stirred, such was their intent on finding something relevant. Perdita closed the account book for June and after placing it to one side, moved to July. As she once again worked her way through the orders for grain, milk, barley and linen, she began to wonder if this was a waste of time and whether she would be better off reading the letters Jenny and her team had begun to transcribe, when something caught her eye.

"Kit, may I borrow your magnifying glass?" she asked.

"Here," he said, passing over a large, plastic-handled glass. "Have you found something?"

"Not sure, give me a moment."

She lined up the glass and squinted through it. Reading the words, her heart began to race.

"Perds, use this," said Kit, appearing by her side. He flicked a few switches and the huge computer monitor in the middle of the table buzzed into life. He was holding a camera-pen. "Hold it over the words and it'll come up on screen."

"Perfect," she said, and with great care she pointed the sleek silver tube at the words written over 400 years earlier. Kit, Piper and Izabel crowded around to share her discovery.

"The tiny writing at the bottom," said Perdita. "I think it says: 'Paid the same day by her ladyship's commandment to the engraver, Jacob Bryers, for the repair and decoration of Master Nicholas's locket...'"

"It does," breathed Kit, leaning close to the screen to study the magnified image. "It isn't conclusive proof, but I think we can assume with some confidence that this is a reference to the missing silver locket. Unless we find something to contradict this, we can presume the locket went to the son and the ruby ring went to the daughter."

"Which means, if we can find references to either piece of jewellery in other letters or documents elsewhere, we know approximately where each child was situated," said Perdita, her voice bubbling with excitement. "The question is, which one do we search for first?"

"Can't we do them both together?" asked Piper.

"I think it would spread our resources too thin," replied Perdita. "We have one reference to the locket — do we have any to the ring in the letters, Izi?"

"Twelve," replied Izabel.

"What?" asked Perdita, astounded.

"They're mentioned in the letters from this time period," she said. "The letters don't say much, only that the child went on a journey and this one —" she pointed to a short note — "confirms the ring was with the child when she left 'Lady A for the North'."

"Which corroborates what we found in the account books," said Kit.

Perdita considered the information for a moment, then made a decision.

"I think we should search for the ruby ring and Catherine's missing daughter first," she said. "It makes more sense to focus on one at a time, and if there are already that many comments about the ring in the letters, I suspect there will be more. We need to discover who Catherine's daughter went on to become. The biggest explosion of letters is between 1586 to 1589, which would be in the reign of Elizabeth I. By then the baby would have been 45. I think this is where we might discover her true identity."

"Assuming she was still alive," said Kit.

Perdita shot him a confused look, wondering why he was being so negative. Instinct told her this was the correct path to follow in order to find the missing Tudor princess in the same way it had guided her to the chapel at Marquess House in their search for Catherine's grave.

The research into the ruby ring had been put on hold as the start of the wedding celebrations took over Castle Jerusalem.

Tonight was the first drinks party to welcome the new guests. Perdita had arranged to meet Kit at the bottom of the staircase which divided the family wing from the towers she and Piper were staying in, once they had changed into their formal gear.

"Wow! Perds, you look beautiful," exclaimed Kit, as she appeared in a whirl of purple and black.

"You don't look too bad either," she replied.

Privately, Perdita thought Kit looked great. In the few months she had known him, Kit had usually worn casual clothes. During the summer in Pembrokeshire this had been surf shorts, t-shirts and jeans. Here in Andorra, with the cold weather intensifying every day, his work uniform had become jeans, boots and jumpers. Dressed in an impeccably cut black suit with pristine white shirt and swirling patterned purple tie, he looked more handsome than she had ever seen him. Even his unruly curls had been tamed and were swept back from his forehead.

"Shall we?" He offered her his arm.

Sliding her hand through his and walking closely beside him, Perdita could smell the faint lemon tang of his expensive aftershave.

"Who's going to be at this soirée?" she asked.

"Mostly local friends: the Merriweathers, who own the hotel and ski centre down the road. Other friends of Mum and Dad's, Pablo's family who live in the capital Andorra La Vella and some of Megan's contacts from the government, not to mention everyone from here. Where's Piper?"

"She went down earlier. Megan wanted her to check the decorations."

"Quick, come in here," Kit said suddenly, pulling her into a small sitting room off the large stone entrance hall. "I want to tell you something."

Before Perdita could protest, he had propelled her into the cosy, fire-lit room.

"Come and sit down." He ushered her towards the sofa but rather than sit beside her, he stood by the fire, gazing into the flames as though struggling with what to say, something which was unlike him.

"Has something happened?" Perdita asked.

"What? No." He came out of his reverie. "Sorry Perds, no. It's only me being indecisive about whether or not I'm about to make a colossal prat of myself."

"Whatever you say, you won't make a colossal prat of yourself," she reassured him.

He ran his hand nervously through his curly hair. "Maybe, maybe not," he murmured, then he took a deep breath as though steeling himself to get the worst over. "There's a strong possibility Suki Merriweather will be here this evening."

"Who's Suki Merriweather?" asked Perdita, thinking she sounded like a character from a children's book.

"She's the youngest of the Merriweather family. They're the closest thing we have to neighbours here and her parents, Toby and Linda Merriweather, are friends of Mum and Dad.

You haven't met them yet because they've been in Australia for the past few months."

Perdita had no idea where this was going but she had never seen Kit so agitated. Remaining silent, she waited for him to continue.

"Anyway, Suki arrived in Andorra this afternoon and she texted me. And —" he began to pace up and down, rubbing his palms together in a nervous gesture Perdita had never seen him use before — "well, some years ago, she and I had a bit of a drunken kiss one New Year's Eve and I wanted to warn you that she's a troublemaker, especially when she's had a few drinks, and that there's nothing between us, no matter what she might imply. I've always made it clear I wasn't interested in her, at all; and, well, I wanted you to know. I wouldn't want her to cause any problems between us."

He ground to a halt and Perdita sat in stunned silence. This was the last thing she had expected him to divulge. She would have been lying if she denied there was a spark of attraction between them but neither of them had ever referred to it, until now.

Kit looked at her imploringly.

"Thanks for telling me, Kit," she said, before joining him by the fire and giving him a hug. "I appreciate your honesty. I'll bear in mind all you've said if I meet Suki Merriweather this evening."

"There's something else, too, and this is the bit I need you to hear from me first," he said. "Suki's very pretty and she knows it," continued Kit. "She's also extremely dull."

"That's a bit harsh."

"In all the years I've known her, we've never had a conversation which hasn't involved her name-dropping several minor celebrities 'who are, like, my really good friends'," said

Kit, going into an exaggerated posh London accent. Perdita grinned. "She wants a rich husband, several homes around the world and the chance to suck up to anyone even faintly famous."

"And she's set her sights on you?"

"Oh no, I'm merely a conquest. She told me that years ago." Kit took her hand and stared into her unusual storm-coloured eyes, before continuing. "The thing is, Perds, even if she hadn't said that, I would never have been interested in her." Perdita stared back at Kit, unsure what to say. When she did not speak, he prompted her, "And we're OK?"

"Of course we're OK," she said.

He planted the lightest of kisses on her lips before taking her hand and dragging her to the party in the vast Grande Hall.

"Ah, there you are!" called Alistair as they entered the room, and before Perdita could protest, Alistair swung her away from Kit's protective arm, whisking her off on a round of introductions.

After an hour of small talk and sipping champagne, she caught sight of Piper talking to Stuart and hurried across the room to join them, hooking up a glass of red wine from a tray on her way over.

"Hi Stuart," she said, reaching up to accept the kiss on the cheek he proffered.

Stuart was a similar height to Kit but, along with Megan, he had inherited their mother, Susan's, colouring. His light brown hair and soft brown eyes were quite different from Kit and Alistair's more startling Celtic looks with their dark hair and piercing blue eyes.

"How's Megan?" Perdita asked Piper, as Stuart was accosted by one of Pablo's brothers.

"Glowing — look at her," replied Piper with a smile. "She and Pablo are so happy. I think she wanted one of us down here as moral support rather than for any decorating adjustments. She hadn't wanted to ask you because she knows how busy you've been."

"Oh, Pipes, I'm sorry," said Perdita, a wave of guilt washing through her. "I should have been here too. As of now, I'm officially at the beck and call of the bride, in any way she needs me."

"Brilliant, it'll be good to have some fun together," said Piper as they chinked glasses.

A waitress approached with a tray of canapés and, as they took one each, the doors opened to admit more guests, one of whom was a petite blonde, wearing a short, tight black dress. Her large brown eyes swept the room and fixed on first Stuart, then Kit, who was talking to Pablo's father. However, before she could walk towards him, Susan and Megan hurried over to greet the newcomers. Perdita watched the blonde woman for a few moments.

"Who's she?" asked Piper.

"I suspect she's Suki Merriweather who once told Kit she planned to have an affair with him."

Piper choked on her mouthful of wine, "What?" she croaked through streaming eyes.

"Kit told me before we came to the party," said Perdita, watching as Stuart and Kit went to greet the Merriweather family. "He also warned me they had once had a drunken New Year's Eve kiss and that she's a troublemaker."

"And what did you say in response?"

"Nothing, because it's none of my business."

"Don't kid yourself, Perds," snorted Piper but before she could say any more, Megan called them over to be introduced.

65

Suki was fascinated by the fact Perdita and Piper were twins and despite herself, Perdita found herself liking her. Suki was very funny, if slightly bitchy about any female who was not part of Megan's group of friends.

As the party progressed, Perdita was becoming increasingly aware of the height of her new heels. When she could bear it no longer, she grabbed Piper and whispered, "I'm going back to our room to change my shoes — these might be beautiful but they're eating my feet." As she left, she waved to Kit, who struggled towards her through the throng but she did not wait. Another part of the reason she needed to escape for a few minutes was the constant feeling of Kit's intense blue gaze on her.

After changing into more comfortable footwear Perdita wandered back towards the party. She had paused to admire the white beauty of the full moon against the dense blackness of the mountain sky when she heard her name. Two women were sitting on a padded seat in the curve of the corridor, the window beside them open while they smoked. One of the women was Suki Merriweather, the other was a friend of Megan's, Lara Cunningham. Perdita slipped into a shadowy alcove, wondering what they could be saying about her.

"And it's definitely her? Perdita Woodville-Rivers?"

"Dr Rivers," corrected Suki. "Don't forget her PhD. Lydia's always going on about it."

"Suki, I know Lydia's your friend but don't you think it's time you and everyone else impressed upon her the fact that Kit isn't going back to her, ever."

"Believe me, I've tried but she's convinced he'll, as she puts it, 'see the error of his ways and run back into her waiting arms'."

Lara took a deep drag on her cigarette, then exhaled out of the window before replying. "Has Kit given her any indication that he's going to change his mind? He's usually very honest — I can't imagine he'd be stringing her along. It isn't in his nature."

"None at all," admitted Suki. "He was very kind to begin with, because I think he felt so guilty about ending it, but he's losing his patience with her now. She's been texting and ringing him endlessly asking why she hasn't been invited to Megan's wedding. I think Kit feels too guilty to ignore her completely. He said he feels terrible because he knew Lydia had been expecting him to propose, but he had known for a long time that the relationship wasn't working. Plus, there was · another big reason why he couldn't ask her."

"Which was...?"

"He'd fallen in love with someone else."

"What?!"

"Dr Perdita Woodville-Rivers. Kit took one look at her and fell absolutely head-over-heels in love. The worst thing was, at that point, Perdita was engaged to someone else."

With that, they turned the corner and Perdita could no longer hear their conversation. She leant against the wall, shaking. This was not what Kit had told her when he had confessed that his relationship with his long-term girlfriend, Lydia Brooks, was over. He had made it seem a very casual, matter-of-fact event, claiming it had been a mutual decision between him and Lydia. He had not told her of the devastation his actions had caused. Nor, once he had returned to Marquess House after that fateful weekend at his friends' wedding, had he shown any signs of misery at his newly-single status. In fact, he had seemed positively gleeful.

Another sentence floated to the surface of her teeming mind, "Kit took one look at her and fell head-over-heels in love."

Surely, that was a mistake?

Perdita closed her eyes, wondering whether to flee back to the tower and lock herself in while she tried to make sense of this unexpected revelation, but she was astute enough to realise her disappearance would be noticed. This is gossip, she told herself. It's two women talking at a party — it might not even be true.

Shaking her dark hair back, she forced a smile on to her face and walked back to the party, determined to treat Kit in exactly the same way as always. As she re-entered the room, glancing around for Piper, Kit appeared and led her back towards the lively crowd in the corner. He had taken her hand on many other occasions but this time when he did it she felt a strange, and not unpleasant, tingling.

The next morning, Perdita and Piper were having breakfast with Kit and Megan when there was a flurry of noise at the door and Deborah's sons, Elliot and Callum, walked in. Kit gave a cry of joy and rushed over, pulling the dark-haired man into a huge hug, while Elliot laughed. Perdita grinned and turned to her sister, ready for the two of them to be introduced, but when she looked at Piper, she was horrified.

"Piper, what is it...?"

All, the colour had drained from Piper's face and fury filled her eyes.

"Callum Black!" she snarled, barely able to speak such was her rage. "What the hell is he doing here?"

"You knew he was coming," said Perdita, confused by her sister's reaction.

"But I never made the connection!"

"How do you even know him?"

"He worked for one of the subsidiary companies that employed Jeremy and he came to a tedious black-tie event we had to attend."

"And...?"

"He was Kirstin's date! We have to tell Alistair."

Piper stormed out of the kitchen before Kit could call them over for the introductions. Perdita hesitated, then went over to Kit and said a brief "hello" to Callum, before hurrying after her sister.

She found Alistair and Susan trying to calm Piper down.

"Piper has told us about Callum and Kirstin," said Alistair. "I wasn't aware of their connection, so I'll take it from here."

"Of course. Come on Pipes, let's get you sorted out."

Perdita led her sister up to their apartment and sat her down by the roaring stove. Piper's face was stricken. All the happiness of the past weeks had vanished and she was shaking.

"Pipes, tell me," whispered Perdita, "this isn't only about Callum, is it? What else is wrong?"

Piper gulped, wiping her eyes, then she took Perdita's hands and her words delivered a blow to Perdita's confidence.

"Do you think we can trust the Mackensies?" she asked, in a low, urgent whisper.

"What?"

It was the last thing Perdita had expected to hear.

"I've been wondering for a while; do you think we would be safer going it alone and heading back to Marquess House where the Milford Haven Treaty would protect us?"

"Piper, what's brought this on? The Mackensies have saved our lives more than once. Why do you doubt them? They couldn't have done more for us. And, anyway, with Connors on the loose, you know it would be unsafe for us to return at the moment."

"But what if it's a ruse to keep us here?" said Piper, her voice panicked. "They keep us here while you work out the truth before turning us over to the highest bidder: be that the authorities or Connors."

"Piper, this is madness…"

"What if the Mackensies are part of the conspiracy?" she interrupted. "What if they're playing both sides? What if they hadn't expected me to recognise Callum? Even the best criminals make mistakes."

Perdita knew a moment of pure fear as Piper's words tapped into every dark thought she had harboured since their escape from MI1 and the frightening news that Randolph Connors was circling them like a hawk. The three-o'clock in the morning doubts that she had always pushed to one side, the terror that no matter how far they ran and how well they hid they would never be safe…

Then reason came to her rescue.

"No," she said, her voice harsh but firm.

"But Perds…"

"If we begin thinking this way, we're lost. Alistair and Susan, all the Mackensies, have risked their lives to save us. Alistair has never given us any reason to doubt him…"

"But Callum Black and Kirstin? How do you explain that?"

"I can't — yet. We at least need to hear Callum out. His mum has worked here for years, he and Kit are best friends and before you ask, yes, I would trust Kit with both our lives. He's a good judge of character and, if for any reason, MI1 has got to Callum, you've alerted Alistair soon enough for us to be able to deal with it."

"But…"

"No Piper," said Perdita, her voice gentler now but determined. "We have to deal with this logically. I'll insist on being in the interview with Alistair and Callum. We will sort this out but I think some of this is your anger with Jeremy and Kirstin."

Piper sagged at her sister's words. For the first time, Perdita saw the fragility behind her sister's smile. The past months had been hard on them both but Perdita had thought Piper was coping. Now she understood her sister was struggling with their new lives more than she had shown and more than Perdita had realised, particularly the collapse of her marriage.

"You're right," Piper admitted. "I'm sorry, Perds. It's been so strange and confusing. Even though Jeremy has behaved appallingly, I miss him. Apart from you, he's been my closest companion all my life. But another part of me hates him and knows his betrayal has destroyed my trust in anyone."

"It's understandable, Pipes."

Piper wiped her hand across her eyes. "I'm OK," she said. "You go and talk to Alistair. Find out what's going on."

Kit and his father were exchanging heated whispers outside his office door.

"Callum is my best friend, he's practically one of the family!" Kit exclaimed. "There is no way he's involved with Kirstin or Randolph Connors."

"I'm sure there's a rational explanation," agreed Alistair, "but you understand we have to do this and it's better if you aren't involved."

Kit rounded on Perdita as she approached. "What's Piper thinking of accusing Callum of spying?"

"She didn't," snapped Perdita. "She doesn't know Callum but she did meet him at a black-tie event held by Jeremy's firm.

Callum attended as Kirstin's date. If he was anyone other than your best friend, you'd be the first one to mistrust and question him."

Kit looked as though he was about to argue the point but then he backed down, as ever, scrupulously honest. He gave a curt nod. "Fine," he said and turning on his heel, stormed off.

Alistair opened his office door and beckoned her inside.

A few moments later, Callum arrived, bemused at being so formally summoned. Alistair introduced Perdita, who nodded a greeting but did not speak. Instead she tried to put aside all her preconceived ideas in order to listen to the facts and assess them rationally.

"My apologies for this Cal," said Alistair, pointing to the chair opposite his desk, "but we have to ask a few delicate questions."

"Why? What's going on?" Callum asked.

"Perdita's sister, Piper, recognised you from an event you both attended while you were in the US," Alistair continued. "It's the woman you took as your date whom interests us and your connections to her."

Callum looked even more confused.

"Your sister?" he asked, looking at Perdita. "Who's your sister?"

"Mrs Piper Davidson, wife of Jeremy Davidson and you accompanied a woman called Kirstin Chaplin," supplied Alistair.

Callum's face cleared with understanding. "The tedious do in New York," he said. "Jeremy is on secondment from the London branch and is usually based in Austin, Texas, isn't he?" confirmed Callum, and on a nod from Perdita, continued: "A number of staff were flown to New York for the annual internal awards ceremony."

"And your date, Kirstin Chaplin?" prompted Perdita.

"She wasn't a date. As we were the only two who weren't coming with partners it was suggested we paired up and made up the final numbers of the table where Jeremy and his wife sat."

"So, you and Kirstin weren't or aren't romantically involved?" Alastair asked.

"No!" exclaimed Callum, laughing. "The first time I met her was in the lobby of the hotel where the awards ceremony was being held. We talked at dinner — she was very good at small talk and networking — and she told me about her two daughters and how one loves horse-riding, the other is a brilliant tap dancer. I told her a bit about Mum and Elliot but then it went back to work talk. I thought Jeremy's wife looked quite unhappy all evening. She didn't seem too keen on Kirstin."

"Was Kirstin interested in your mother's job?" asked Alistair.

"Only in passing," said Callum.

"Did you mention the name Jerusalem, at all?"

Callum considered this for a moment, then shook his head. "No, I said Mum was a librarian and Elliot was a commercial pilot. You've always told us to be circumspect when we discuss our jobs with strangers, so I followed your usual line. When the dancing started, Kirstin went off with Jeremy until, in the end, his wife cut in between them. I don't think Kirstin and I spoke again."

"And have you heard from or spoken to Kirstin Chaplin since?" asked Perdita.

"No, nothing," replied Callum. "As I said, I met her for the first time that evening and I haven't seen her since. What's this about Alistair? Why is everyone so upset?"

"Kirstin Chaplin is having an affair with Jeremy Davidson and was instrumental in the break-up of Piper and Jeremy's marriage. She has been the cause of a great deal of pain for Perdita's sister," said Alistair. "Piper was shocked and upset to see you. She thought you and Kirstin were involved and asked if we would check your connections."

"Poor thing!" Callum said, horrified. "It would explain a few things, though."

"What things?" asked Perdita.

"Why your sister was so edgy at the New York party. I remember thinking how beautiful she looked but how incredibly sad and I thought Jeremy behaved appallingly. He ignored your sister and was all over Kirstin like a rash. It was embarrassing."

"Thank you, Cal, your information has been very useful," Alastair said, standing up to indicate the interview was over. "However, if you could be thoughtful around Piper, we'd all be very grateful. Her marriage has broken down irreparably since her husband's affair with Kirstin Chaplin and she's in a great deal of emotional pain, something which probably isn't helped by the wedding fever gripping the castle at the moment."

"Of course," said Callum, walking to the door with Alistair. "I'll do whatever is best. I wouldn't want to upset anyone, but really, I have no connections with Kirstin Chaplin. I spent that one evening chaperoning her and she was more interested in..." He checked himself. "Well, she wasn't interested in me." They had reached the door and he turned to Perdita. "Please tell your sister I'm sorry to have upset her."

Callum hurried through the door. Alistair shut it behind him and re-joined Perdita at the desk.

"Do you believe him?" she asked.

"Yes," replied Alistair. "For now, we will have to put this down to unfortunate circumstances and coincidence, however, when the wedding is over, I will ask the team watching Kirstin Chaplin to dig deeper and see what else they can uncover. We know she has links to Randolph Connors. My guess is, Randolph employed Kirstin to spy on Jeremy and the fact she ended up being chaperoned by Cal was a pure chance."

Perdita considered all she had heard and looked into Alistair's clear blue eyes. Piper's question echoed in her ears: "Can we trust the Mackensies?" and Perdita swallowed as once more a fear that Alistair was lying rose in her. *Could they trust them? Granny had trusted them, so had Mum,* she thought, *and they are both dead.*

"Perdita, are you feeling all right?" She heard Alistair's voice through her unexpected panic.

And both your mother and your grandmother were murdered by MI1 Elite, her rational self answered. *An organisation Alistair has spent his life defeating. Do not let fear and paranoia destroy everything.*

"Sorry, Alistair," Perdita said, "I'm a bit tired after last night. If you think Callum is trustworthy, then I believe you." Smiling at Alistair, she walked towards the door. "Piper and I have a list of errands to run for Megan. I'm going to insist she comes with me — it will be good to get out of the castle for a while."

Hurrying back to their tower, Perdita's heart beat fast in her chest as she wondered whether she had made the right decision.

Chapter Four

Megan and Pablo's wedding day dawned with a crystal-clear blue sky and passed in a whirl of laughter and happiness, with the newlyweds leaving for a sunshine-filled honeymoon. As the last glass of champagne was drunk and the last song was played at the reception, Perdita could not help but think, "And now, I can get back to work."

Olaf had called her the day before to tell her his team had identified the name of the ship in Dale. Around the figurehead of a mermaid was the name 'Arbella Stuart'.

Somehow Perdita had expected it to have a connection with either Catherine Howard or Penelope Fitzalan, or even the Llyn Cel mermaid, which would account for the figurehead. Arbella Stuart was the last name she had expected to hear.

Perdita was still thinking it over the following Monday when she met Kit in his office to continue with their research.

"Remember the initials on the fourth bust in the chapel at Marquess House? A.S.?" she asked him. "I think they stand for Arbella Stuart."

"Great," said Kit, then he leaned back and folded his arms. "Who's Arbella Stuart?"

"She is the name of the wreck that Olaf and I were investigating last summer and, in Tudor times, she was the granddaughter of Lady Margaret Douglas," replied Perdita. "There was also a time when she was considered the most likely candidate to be named heir to Elizabeth I."

"Really? So why have I never heard of her?"

"Once James I was named as heir, Arbella rather faded into the background. She supposedly suffered from an illness called porphyria, which has also been prescribed to both Mary, Queen of Scots and George III by varying historians, which was said to cause the occasional bout of madness. What with this and being a woman, she was more or less forgotten for centuries."

"Yet she had a ship named after her?"

"Yes, and a ship with a mermaid figurehead," replied Perdita. "I've done a bit more research into mermaid imagery and iconography — after all, they're all over Marquess House, Catherine Howard was the inspiration for the legend of the Llyn Cel mermaid and then there's the Ladies of Melusine, the name Granny had been considering as the title of her second unpublished manuscript. Melusine being a water goddess who was half woman, half fish…"

"A mermaid," interrupted Kit, grinning.

"Indeed, a mermaid."

"Did you find any others?"

"Yes, quite a few. What's interesting for us, because it fits with the timeframe we're studying, is the array of mermaid symbolism during Tudor times, particularly in the Elizabethan era."

"Wasn't the mermaid a derogatory term suggesting a woman of low-morals?"

"Correct. Because of her tail, a mermaid was seen as impenetrable, therefore making her a tease," Perdita replied. "The women of the era viewed them in a different way, though. There's a very famous portrait of Elizabeth I called the Armada painting and there's a mermaid carved on to her chair of state. It's supposed to represent her feminine wiles in luring the Spanish sailors to their deaths."

Kit laughed. "Isn't that stretching the interpretation a bit thin?"

"Very," agreed Perdita. "Although, even more strangely, another more recent interpretation of this is the suggestion that the mermaid is supposed to represent Mary, Queen of Scots. It's claimed that the reason Elizabeth is facing away from the carving is because Mary and all the plots she aroused are behind Elizabeth. Mary, Queen of Scots was executed in February 1587 and the Armada followed a year later. You can't dismiss the possibility that the carving does represent Mary because there is surprising amount of mermaid imagery relating to her."

"Really?"

"The most famous images are those of a mermaid and a hare which were distributed after her third and much derided marriage to James Hepburn, 4th Earl of Bothwell. It was to defame Mary, suggesting she was little better than a prostitute for marrying him. There is also a passage in Shakespeare's *A Midsummer Night's Dream* which refers to a mermaid riding a dolphin. It's supposed to be a play on words of Mary and the dauphin, her first husband, the French prince, who became King Francis II of France. And, there's a house called Harvington Hall that has mermaid imagery from the Elizabethan era on the walls, as well as numerous carvings in churches, cathedrals and castles, including Stirling Castle."

"Which is fascinating," agreed Kit, "but doesn't help me understand who Arbella Stuart was in connection to the throne."

"Mary, Queen of Scots, who became monarch at five days old, grew up to marry three times like her paternal grandmother, Margaret Tudor. First she married Francis II, the king of France and was briefly Queen of France, then after he died and she had returned to Scotland, she married Henry Stuart, Duke of Albany, also styled Lord Darnley, then finally

James Hepburn, 4th Earl of Bothwell. Her second marriage to Darnley was the only marriage to produce a living child, a son, who was the future James VI of Scotland and I of England, the heir to Elizabeth I.

"Margaret Tudor — Mary's grandmother — had a daughter from her second marriage called Lady Margaret Douglas. Lady Margaret was part of Catherine Howard's court and was engaged to Charles Howard. But when Charles vanished from the pages of history, Margaret became engaged to Matthew Stewart, 4th Earl of Lennox and from this marriage she gave birth to two living sons, Henry Stuart, Lord Darnley and Charles Stuart, 1st Earl of Lennox."

"So, Mary, Queen of Scots married her cousin?"

"Yes."

"And Henry Stuart was murdered?"

"Mary was accused of being involved in his murder and that's when things went awry for her. Margaret Douglas's other son, Charles, was never blessed with the most robust health but she was very conscious of the fact he possessed a claim to the throne through her Tudor blood, so she was eager for him to marry and reproduce. Lady Margaret was already grandmother to one heir to the English throne and with Elizabeth I unmarried, she wanted to have more than one potential monarch in her arsenal. Particularly, as under the terms of Henry VIII's will, English monarchs had to be born in England to qualify and James VI had been born in Scotland, so he might not have been eligible."

"Margaret Douglas was quite an amazing woman," said Kit. "Imagine if she'd been alive today."

"She'd be running multi-national companies," agreed Perdita. "Even back then she was formidable and she was friends with another powerhouse of a matriarch, Elizabeth Talbot, countess of Shrewsbury, better known these days as Bess of Hardwick."

Understanding was dawning on Kit's face.

"Bess of Hardwick had a daughter, Elizabeth Cavendish, from her second marriage," Perdita continued, "who married Charles Stuart and they had Arbella Stuart, who was born in England and had royal blood, descending from Margaret Tudor. It always strikes me as odd that historians are so fascinated with Henry VIII, when it was actually Margaret Tudor who had the biggest impact on the monarchy and it's through her that the descendants of the Tudors still sit on the throne today. Although, Charles and Elizabeth's marriage did cause a bit of a scandal."

"Why?"

"Charles had royal blood; therefore, he was supposed to seek permission from the reigning monarch if he wanted to marry," explained Perdita. "Both Margaret and Bess were convinced Queen Elizabeth would say no to the match so they encouraged their offspring to elope and presented the queen with a fait accompli. She was very angry."

"Following the law of succession as laid down by Henry VIII, Arbella should have been Elizabeth's heir, then?" said Kit.

"Yes, because she was the English offspring of Henry's elder sister, Margaret. There were the Grey girls but they were descended from Henry's younger sister, Mary, so Margaret's offspring took precedent."

"And you think this somehow all links in with the ship that Olaf and his team have discovered, which is named the Arbella Stuart?"

"And don't forget the ceiling design in the chapel at Marquess House."

"But why?"

Perdita shrugged. "No idea, but I'm hoping Granny's next set of notes, *The Ladies of Melusine*, as I've decided to call it, might offer some answers. I'm going back to my office to read it and the transcripts of the Lady Pamela letters that Jenny and Izabel have sent."

"And I'm going to answer a few emails and do a bit of work for Jerusalem, then I'll do the same thing."

Perdita marched into her own office and shut the door. Throwing one last glance through the window at Kit, she made herself comfortable and began to read.

PART TWO: May, 1586

Chapter One

Elizabeth's face screwed up in fury as the ceremony unfolded. The nobleman glanced in her direction, then turned his back — the highest insult to pay a monarch. Urging the crowd to cheer, the man raised the crown he was holding aloft and, with great deference, he placed it on the head of the new incumbent: the one chosen by the people.

The young and beautiful girl who stood, staring out over her kneeling populace, smiled. As her lord chamberlain stepped away, he called for cheers for the new monarch and the crowd responded, their cries ringing through the sweet spring air. Atop the white horse, garlanded with flowers, the girl was led towards her and Elizabeth knew, that despite the fact she was a Tudor and a royal monarch, she had no choice but to pay fealty to the new queen.

There was a tense silence as the girl drew level with Elizabeth and, for a moment, she remained in her vast carved throne, staring at the child who shared her colouring and her blood. As the atmosphere grew uncomfortable, Elizabeth rose. In the hush, where the gathered hundreds held their collective breaths, she handed the girl a branch of rosemary, festooned with ribbons, then to the delight of the watching audience, Elizabeth curtseyed. Her smile broke across her face like the rising sun, washing away the faux fury she always displayed — an expression that was part of the lore of the ceremony.

"To you, Arbella Stuart, Queen of the May," called Elizabeth, her clear bell-like voice floating on the breeze. "You wear a crown for a day, my dear — use it well."

A ripple of wonder followed this statement as the eager nobles once more searched for clues as to Queen Elizabeth's successor. Fully aware of her words and intending them to have this impact, Elizabeth resumed her seat under her silken canopy and raised her hand, indicating the official beginning of the lavish May Day celebrations.

"Elizabeth, you are a terrible tease," murmured the woman sitting behind her.

"I know, Kate," she replied. "It's such fun. As if I would announce my successor at an event such as this."

Kate Howard, Lady Effingham, laughed and indicated for the pages to bring refreshments. The women were cousins through their shared Boleyn blood and Kate had served at Elizabeth's side throughout her reign. Elizabeth shaded her eyes, squinting to see the parade that had now reached the other end of the tournament ground where the excitement was shining on the face of the queen of the May.

Arbella was being garlanded in flowers as her May Day subjects danced and applauded their 11-year-old queen. Around her the minstrels played their jaunty tunes, mummers capered and Morris Men danced, their costumes glittering and twinkling in the bright spring sunshine as the bells on their legs jangled a merry accompaniment. There was joy in the air and Elizabeth watched her courtiers smiling in delight, rejoicing in the freedom of the warm weather after a long, hard winter.

"Your Majesty, my apologies for disturbing you, but I have the note," said a quiet voice, bringing Elizabeth back from her reverie.

"And who is it from?" Elizabeth's voice was low, carried on an edge of anxiety.

"From Calypso. I have translated it."

"Thank you, Katherine."

Katherine Newton bobbed a curtsey, then brushed past Elizabeth and with sleight of hand, slid a small square of parchment, unnoticed by those around them, on to Elizabeth's palm. Katherine took her seat with the other favoured ladies of the bedchamber in the shaded and cushioned chairs behind Elizabeth. The queen pulled a silken handkerchief from her sleeve and under the guise of dabbing her forehead, glanced down to read the short missive.

Our friend the nun has once again been approached by those who favour the old. She has heard whispers that there is an intention to breach the coast of the dragon. Ships are sailing.

Elizabeth bit her lip. These were not the words she had expected to read. The note had arrived as they were leaving for the May Day ceremony but Katherine, as their chief cryptographer, had remained behind in the chamber to translate the message that was written in one of their detailed codes. Although Katherine had converted this into English, she had left behind certain words known only to the chosen few who were part of Queen Elizabeth's inner circle. By leaving in this layer of subterfuge, the note would not be fully understood if it was read by someone unfriendly to their cause. The ladies in Elizabeth's close circle all had codenames, and Calypso was Lady Dorothy Perrot, daughter of Elizabeth's favourite cousin, Lettice Dudley, Countess of Leicester. Lettice herself was codenamed the 'She-wolf'.

"Katherine, pour me some sweet spiced wine," called Elizabeth. As Katherine fussed around, Elizabeth passed the note to Kate, whose eyes widened as she read the contents.

Katherine bent close, passing her the golden goblet of wine. "Calypso is currently with her husband at their family home of

Carew Castle. They hear news from her father-in-law and from the sailors, not to mention the pirates, who roam the coastline. Calypso must be certain or she would not write such a dangerous letter. Perhaps we could ask the countess of Shrewsbury to send word to Mignonne to see if she can corroborate the rumours."

The third codename, 'Mignonne', referred to Bess of Hardwick's granddaughter, Elizabeth Pierrepont, who was serving as Lady of the Bedchamber to Elizabeth's hidden half-sister. Elizabeth gripped Katherine's hand and gave the smallest of nods. "Would you?"

"Yes, Your Majesty," Katherine replied with a curtsey. "I will attend to it at once."

"Very well, Lady Newton, seeing as your head pains you again, you are dismissed," said Elizabeth, her voice raised so those around glanced over to see who had incurred her displeasure. She gave Katherine a complicit wink at the cover story they often used. In reality, Katherine's health was robust. "Your many ailments keep you often from my side — it is most disagreeable."

Katherine adopted a downcast expression before leaving the pavilion.

"Do you think this could be true?" asked Kate Howard, who had screwed the note into a tiny ball and placed it in the hollow at the back of the necklace she wore, intending to dispose of it later.

Elizabeth allowed her eyes to wander to the spectacle taking place around her while she thought. Having completed several circuits of the tournament ground, Arbella was reclaiming her May Day throne, which was positioned at the opposite end of the enclosure and matched Elizabeth's pavilion in every detail, complete with an array of courtiers. Arbella's court was made up of her contemporaries and as Elizabeth's eyes roved across the faces of the children of her nobles, watching them enjoying the freedom of the day, she realised she was seeing the future. Was this the precursor of the next Tudor court? she wondered, then shook her head to clear herself of such unnerving thoughts. Arbella was standing and waving, indicating she was ready for the knights to enter. Elizabeth clapped along with the throng for a few moments before turning back to her cousin.

"Yes, Kate, I do," she sighed, "but we will wait until we have heard from Mignonne. We have heard these rumours before and they have been nothing but gossip and scaremongering."

"Yet this time you believe there is substance?"

"Calypso would never correspond in such a way unless she was certain. You know how circumspect she is, particularly now she is married. Her nature is so different from the other women in her family. Her great-grandmother and her mother are both such determined women who would stop at nothing to follow their hearts and protect their families. Calypso is more like her grandmother, Lady Kathryn Knollys. Her nature was gentler and she battled shyness all her life."

"Have we heard anything from our She-Wolf to corroborate this tale?"

"Not yet," confessed Elizabeth. "She is much preoccupied with running her estates. When Katherine returns, I will request she writes to Lettice and asks her to join us at court. She will be safer here."

"And Calypso?"

"We will await word, but it is no longer safe for her to remain in Pembrokeshire," said Elizabeth. "However, I fear she will not wish to leave her beloved husband."

Kate opened her mouth to respond but her voice was drowned by the huge roar of excitement from the crowd as the trumpets sounded and the knights, the stars of the day, galloped into the arena. The huge destriers neighed and whinnied, their enormous hooves thudding on the ground like thunder. The armour of their riders dazzled in the sun and the silken banners declaring mottos of love, family allegiances and puns on names, flowed through the air like a magical rainbow, as the cream of the nobility readied themselves for the joust, the highlight of the festivities. Elizabeth's attention was drawn to the spectacle, her eyes noting each family banner, each crest and each rider.

"There is nothing we can do about this today, Kate," said Elizabeth, her eyes fixed on the young men of the court as they pranced and paraded, playing at war in their polished finery. "We should enjoy the festivities. There will be time for frowns and concerns if these rumours should prove to be true but, for now, let us revel in this day and the sunshine."

A week later, Elizabeth sat in her privy chamber, reading the report prepared by her leading spymaster, Sir Francis Walsingham. In stark contrast to the May Day celebrations, the weather had taken a grim turn and rain beat against the windows while a wind scattered the spring blossom across the sodden grounds of Nonsuch Palace, her father's confection of a hunting lodge in Surrey.

While she perused the document, Elizabeth left Walsingham standing by the fire. His three assistants, sitting at small tables at the far end of the room, kept exchanging uncertain looks, wondering why the spymaster had not been invited to sit in his usual place at the table to the left of Elizabeth's raised chair. Oblivious to their scandalised looks, Elizabeth continued to read. In reality, her refusal to offer Walsingham a seat was a face-saving exercise on her spymaster's behalf. His back was paining him again and standing was far more comfortable than perching on a wooden chair at the low table. The warmth of the flames would also soothe Walsingham's aches.

Finishing her spymaster's report on the situation in the Spanish Netherlands, she held the parchment aloft for one of his assistants. The man hurried forward and bowed, exchanging it for a second document, before backing away, still crouched in supplication. Elizabeth swallowed her sigh of irritation. The endless bowing and scraping bored her — all it did was get in the way of the business.

"And you are sure this is the most up-to-date information we have?" she asked.

Walsingham nodded. "It is a difficult situation, Your Majesty. The earl is having a great deal of trouble bringing the various states together."

Elizabeth wrinkled her nose in annoyance. The war in the Netherlands had been causing her difficulties for a long time. The previous year, she had signed The Treaty of Nonsuch at this very palace, agreeing to assist the United Provinces of the Netherlands in their war against Spanish occupation. Her part was to send a nobleman of rank and reputation to lead an army, as well as bank-rolling the invasion. Immediately, the Spanish had put a trade embargo on English and Dutch ships, costing the country a vast amount of money.

Since then, she had been treading a difficult path as she tried to keep her kingdom safe, while also helping her Protestant allies. Her favourite courtier and closest friend, Robert Dudley, Earl of Leicester, was her representative and leader of her troops. Her eyes, she thought. It was the nickname she had given him when she was first made queen and had made Robert her Master of the Horse. His loyalty was something she trusted implicitly and it was under her instructions he had accepted the title of Governor-General of the Netherlands. She believed it was the only way he would be able to achieve the necessary authority required to create any form of cohesion among the warring states. Yet this shrewd suggestion that Robert should rule in her place also gave her the opportunity to disassociate herself from any bad decisions he might make. The instruction for Robert to accept this role had been hers alone; taken without the usual consultations with her Privy Councillors, whom she had felt would only have delayed her intentions, as they had so often in the past.

"Wise men who are here to help you make such decisions," her most senior minister and Lord High Treasurer, William Cecil, Lord Burghley had exclaimed in fury when he had discovered the truth.

"And yet you think you are more able than I, the Queen of England, to rule my realm as I see fit. Would you have spoken to my father, Henry VIII, in such a manner? What annoys you more: that I made a wise decision or that I made it without consulting you?" she had retorted. "You forget, Lord Burghley, I am Queen. The decisions are mine."

He had glared at her mutinously. "Let us hope none of us live to regret your 'wise' decision," he had muttered, storming out in high dudgeon.

Elizabeth sighed as she remembered his outburst. She and Lord Burghley had been friends for years. He had worked alongside her throughout the difficult years of her house arrest when her half-sister, Mary, had been queen. When Elizabeth had ascended to the throne on 17 November 1558, Burghley had been the first person she had appointed to her privy council. She still trusted him, but recently she had noticed his tendency to push his own agenda above her own.

Burghley was not at court today, but Elizabeth knew he often colluded with Walsingham to manipulate her. Their schemes, which always claimed to have Elizabeth's safety at heart, were often tinged with agendas peculiar to the two men and their political leanings, rather than her own views on what was right for herself and her nation.

The second of Walsingham's reports concerned a plot on Elizabeth's life. His vast spy network had supplied a list of known plotters and high-ranking members of local boroughs who were considered to be of interest or who had pro-Catholic leanings. Reading each name and the attached list of possible misdemeanours against them, Elizabeth searched for anything that might corroborate the unsettling information she had received during the May Day celebrations. She felt sure Walsingham would have included the rumours had he heard of anything unusual. Yet there was nothing new on this list and, according to Walsingham's intelligence, there were no obvious threats, something which concerned Elizabeth. Once again, she held out the document and a scribe scurried forward, rat-like, to relieve her of it.

"What news of the Pembrokeshire coast?" Her tone was casual but Walsingham was not fooled. "There is nothing in the report concerning that area, yet it is a vast seaward-facing county with great potential for mischief."

"Your Majesty, at present I have no new intelligence from that area…"

"And yet a known felon who is on one of your 'watch lists' has recently been released from the Fleet Prison and is known to have travelled to Pembrokeshire?"

"Who?" asked Walsingham, taken aback.

"A former mayor of Tenby named Erasmus Sanders."

Walsingham beckoned to an assistant and issued an instruction to make notes.

"There is also the Barlow family, who have known Catholic leanings," continued Elizabeth. "Not to mention Charles Paget and Thomas Morgan, two more men of interest. You have no new information on these people and their potential plots?"

"No, Your Majesty."

Walsingham's assistants exchanged amused glances at what they perceived as the weakness of the female brain and its inability to grasp the complexities of politics.

"Perhaps you should check again," she said. "I have received information from a source I trust that suggests there are plans afoot for a Spanish invasion on the Welsh coast."

"It is an unlikely route, Your Majesty," said Walsingham, looking startled, "but we should never underestimate Philip II."

The assistants stifled their giggles of disbelief at such a ridiculous suggestion.

"What precautions have you taken to secure the Welsh borders?" Elizabeth asked.

"No new precautions, Your Majesty, but they are well protected. At present, Sir Thomas Perrot has returned from Sir Robert's campaign in the Netherlands to Carew Castle in Pembrokeshire where he would be available to muster the region, should it be necessary. If there were to be an invasion, the most likely landing place would be the harbour of Milford Haven because of its depth and size. Other potential landing points are Haverfordwest and possibly Pembroke itself. As you are aware, Your Majesty, there is a proliferation of castles along the Welsh coast. At present, Perrot, his uncle-in-law, George Devereux at Lamphey and Morgan Philipps of Picton Castle are all in residence. The marshal of Pembroke Castle, the duke of Hereford, has also recently returned with his son from the Netherlands, although he has not yet travelled west. There is no cause for concern." Walsingham gave Elizabeth a searching look.

"Check again, Sir Francis. I would like to know the whereabouts of Sanders and whether there are any fresh threats in this area. Begin by contacting Sir Thomas Perrot with the utmost urgency."

Walsingham gave his small, tight smile.

"You may leave me now," said Elizabeth.

Bowing, Walsingham indicated for his scribes and assistants to gather their materials and ushered them towards the door.

"One last thing before you leave, Francis," called Elizabeth. "Never bring those particular scribes with you again. I'd prefer to have men around who do not giggle like imbeciles."

The three men looked horrified and glanced at Walsingham, who cast them a black look before they filed out.

As the door clicked shut behind them, Kate Howard and Elizabeth Talbot, Countess of Shrewsbury, affectionately referred to as Bess of Hardwick, emerged from their position in the shadows at the back of the room.

"Walsingham hasn't heard the rumours then?" mused Kate as she cleared away the debris of ink, quill and discarded paper from around Elizabeth, while Bess poured her a goblet of hot wine.

"No, it appears not," said Elizabeth, stretching her arms out in front of her, before walking down the two steps of the dais and moving towards the fireplace. "Unless he is lying."

"Why would he?" asked Bess.

"In order to try and quell the issue," replied Elizabeth. "He has done it in the past when there have been wild rumours about invasion. To give credence to such rumours can build a momentum of its own and before you can stop it, the country is in a state of panic. Behaviour such as this only plays into our enemies' hands."

Swaying on the spot to relieve her stiff hips and back, Elizabeth stretched again, trying to revive her limbs after a morning of having to bear the weight, not only of the business of state as it was laid at her feet, but also of her restrictive, bejewelled, formal court dress.

"But, Elizabeth, what if…?"

Elizabeth shook her head. "Not here, Bess, too many ears. Has there been word from Lady Newton?"

"Yes, she has returned to her rooms. Her headache has passed."

Elizabeth smiled. "Very well, then I must pay her a visit to ensure her health is fully restored," she said. "Her handwriting is so beautiful; I may request she writes a short note to a friend. Would you inform her maid that I will visit soon? You will bring the alum, Bess," Elizabeth instructed. "We do not wish to have prying eyes on our words."

Bess curtseyed and hurried from the room.

Elizabeth stared into the roaring fire, lost in thought. She had been Queen of England for 28 years. Her reign had so far outstripped all the previous Tudor monarchs, except her father, Henry VIII, who had been king for 38 years. Before him, her grandfather, Henry VII, had reigned for 24. Her younger brother, Edward VI, had ruled for six years and her elder sister, Mary, only five. Her cousin, Lady Jane Grey, had been queen for only nine days and Elizabeth still shuddered over her grisly end. Beheaded for being a pawn in someone else's political ambition — a fate Elizabeth's own mother, Anne Boleyn, had also suffered.

Yet Jane's fate could so easily have been mine, too, she thought, *if my sister Mary and her husband, Philip II of Spain, had followed through with their plan. Now, this troublesome man is threatening my country and my throne again. A man who glories in war and bloodshed, firm in his belief that he fights for the purity and will of God.*

"What ails you, cousin?" asked Kate, breaking into her thoughts.

"These wars," sighed Elizabeth, returning to her raised chair, "these senseless games played by these tedious men."

The golden goblet sat on a table beside her seat and she sipped its fragrant contents.

"What would men do all day if they didn't have battles to plan?" said Kate, her eyes sparkling with mischief. "You have bestowed the honour of Lord High Admiral upon my husband and he now plays at war with his fleet. Like a small boy with a flotilla of toy boats he plans imaginary battle after imaginary battle, all in the name of protecting the realm."

Elizabeth laughed, despite her concern. Kate's verbal image was amusing.

"You're quite right. Women run the homes, bear the children, deal with the details of life, while men stomp about, arguing over religion and squabbling about borders. Then, if they can't use one of their daughters, sisters, cousins or aunts to secure the land they've taken a fancy to via a marriage treaty, they start a fight. It's all so much posturing. Even as Queen, I witness the patronising looks and arrows of despair from my privy councillors. They all believe they are my superior in intelligence, yet I was educated by my father as he would have educated a prince. My knowledge far outstrips theirs."

"But in most areas of life, men hold the positions of power. Despite the fact you prove them incorrect on a daily basis, men

— even the stupid ones — believe it is their right to govern women."

"Yet I am Queen."

"Exactly," said Kate, "you are Queen."

They exchanged a smile.

"And," continued Elizabeth, "there is another queen residing on our shores: Mary, Queen of Scots."

"Who also won't be held in check by the rules of men," said Kate.

"No, she won't."

The two women fell silent for a moment. Elizabeth spoke first.

"Burghley and Walsingham offer me good advice and yet their own agendas can't help but blur their vision. Burghley and his religious intolerance concerns me. As my late sister, Mary Tudor, pursued Catholics, his extreme Protestant leanings are evident in all the legislation he places before me. It tinges everything and his beliefs are becoming increasingly alarming." Draining the golden goblet, Elizabeth rose and walked towards the doors at the rear of the chamber. "Let us visit Katherine," she said, beckoning to her cousin. "The court can survive without me for an hour and she may have news of our She-Wolf or of Calypso."

Pressing the mechanism to release the panel that concealed a secret door, Elizabeth led the way into the narrow tunnel. Kate collected two candles from the table and followed. Moments later, the two women were weaving their way through the labyrinth of passages buried within the heart of the palace, making their way to the rooms of Lady Katherine Newton, the central meeting place for the Ladies of Melusine.

When Elizabeth's father, Henry VIII, had built Nonsuch Palace, he had incorporated a network of interior passages.

These were partly for practicality, making it easier for staff to move around with efficiency but there was another, less palatable reason. It had given the king the opportunity to traverse his palace unseen. He had instigated a spyhole here, a false window there, a hidden entrance in an unexpected place to enable him to listen, to watch, to peep; to spy on his courtiers without their knowledge as they went about their daily business. The corridors were a maze of wonder that both increased his sense of omnipotence and his raging paranoia that everyone was plotting to steal his throne.

When Elizabeth had discovered this hidden interior, she had seen more dangers than opportunities, knowing it presented an ideal cover for assassins, so she had created a small, elite guard to patrol these passageways, ensuring they were used by only a select few. As she and Kate hurried to Katherine Newton's rooms, passing two of these guards, they remained silent, ever conscious that the bustle of the palace was taking place only a heartbeat away from the path they trod. The last thing Elizabeth wanted was to have this private walkway discovered.

When they arrived at their destination, Kate beat out a pattern of low knocks. Moments later, there was a click and the secret door leading into the inner sanctum of the Ladies of Melusine opened to admit Elizabeth and her cousin.

"Your Majesty, how wonderful to see you," said Katherine. "Please make yourself comfortable by the fire — it is a miserable day."

Bess was already there, sitting to one side, preparing the alum that Elizabeth had requested. The women used it as invisible ink, writing a message between the lines of a note, doubling the security of the information. Any letter with hidden information would be marked with a small image of a rose in the corner, so the recipient was aware there was an invisible message within.

As she settled by the fire, Elizabeth relaxed, gazing around the room. It was one of her favourites, not only for its quirky shape but because she felt safe within its confines. It was octagonal and had windows on two sides. A door opened on to Katherine's private solar in the suite of rooms she shared with her husband, Henry. Shelves lined one wall, which were filled with books, rolls of parchment and an array of writing paraphernalia. The light was mellow and the atmosphere calm. A fireplace was opposite the door and the remaining walls were panelled wood, hung with tapestries. These served the dual purpose of keeping the room warm and disguising the hidden entrance. It was a small chamber, more of an annexe to the main living space, and it was for Katherine's own use.

For those within the palace who questioned the size and superiority of the rooms issued to Katherine and her husband, neither of whom were of noble birth, the answer was always the same: Katherine Newton shared the same blood as Catherine Howard, the former stepmother of Elizabeth and also the cousin of her mother, Anne Boleyn. Although Catherine Howard had vanished from court in February 1542, suffering from a dangerous fever, from which her uncle, Thomas Howard, the duke of Norfolk, had announced she had died some months later, there were those who suspected her end had not been so peaceful — especially when a rumour began to circulate that she might have been executed along with her lady-in-waiting, Jane Boleyn. Elizabeth denied such suggestions but this only added to the heated whispering. In the twisted web that was the Tudor court, somehow Katherine's mother, Agnes Leigh and subsequently, Katherine herself, had become suggested as being part of this conspiracy. As it suited Elizabeth, Katherine was encouraged to fan the flames of such rumblings, feeling it led people away from their true purpose.

As Elizabeth and Kate settled by the fire, Katherine gathered a sheaf of papers and joined them.

"You seem to have been busy, my dear," said Elizabeth, glancing at the pieces of parchment Katherine was shuffling into order.

"There has been an influx of letters," Katherine confirmed. "The Ladies of Melusine have been hearing rumours the length and breadth of the country. It amazes me that Sir Francis and Lord Burghley haven't informed you that there is something afoot."

"Neither of them seem to think the whispers are anything unusual," said Elizabeth. "Yet you do?"

Katherine nodded. "Unfortunately, I think this could be serious," she sighed. "Late last night, I received a note from Mignonne. It was quite complex and has taken me some time to translate but it appears there is a new Catholic plot being planned by a young man named Anthony Babington."

Bess looked up in surprise. "Anthony Babington — are you sure?"

"Mignonne named him in her letter," replied Katherine, checking her translation.

"Do you know him, Bess?" asked Elizabeth.

"Yes, he was a page in our household for some years," she replied. "He was a difficult boy, very easily led and had a vivid imagination."

"Was he trustworthy?" asked Kate. The length of pause Bess left before she responded answered the question.

"He was biddable," she said at last. "He was born into the Darcy family, although to the granddaughter of Thomas Darcy, 1st Baron Darcy de Darcy and was the third child, so he had no claims to any title. This made him bitter, even from a young age, and he seemed determined to make a name for himself elsewhere. Unfortunately, he rather expected the world to bend to his will and if it didn't, he tried to find someone else to blame."

"You're being very kind in your description," sighed Elizabeth. "Was he also lazy and expected everyone to clear a path for him so he could arrive at the last moment and try to take credit for someone else's hard work?"

"Well, yes…"

"Like so many men, younger sons in particular; rather than work for their rewards, they try to cheat their way to the top."

"Have you met him, Elizabeth?" asked Kate.

"Perhaps, when he was younger, but there have been so many men who could fit this category, they rather blur into one."

Katherine Newton stifled her derisive snort.

"What else did Mignonne divulge?" asked Elizabeth.

"She has once again been approached by Catholic supporters who wish to remove you from the throne, Your Majesty, and replace you with the Scottish queen," continued Katherine.

"Do these people never bore of repeating this same tedious plot?" asked Elizabeth in disgust.

"This one is a little different," said Katherine and the strained tone in her voice sent a cold shiver down Elizabeth's spine.

"What is it?"

"When Babington approached the household, looking for a safe person with whom to correspond, Mignonne stepped forward, as she always does, so she could intercept the letters. Babington is not working alone, neither is he working with the usual rag-tag chancers. His strings are being pulled by one of the men on Walsingham's watch-list, Thomas Morgan. He has moved to France and is a known Catholic sympathiser. Babington could not help but boast to Mignonne that they were being financed by someone even more important."

"Philip II of Spain?" questioned Elizabeth and Katherine nodded. "This is not unusual Katherine — he has funded other plots."

"It isn't that, Your Majesty. Mignonne is distressed for other reasons. The first is the deterioration in the health of the Scottish queen and the other is the fact that Babington said something which she understood, even if he didn't."

"Tell me," whispered Elizabeth.

"She said that Babington claims Philip informed him that he knows about the missing children. Babington did not understand but he seemed to sense it was important."

The silence that greeted this pronouncement was dense with fear.

"Impossible," breathed Kate Howard. "How could Philip know?"

"Perhaps he has turned one of our ladies," said Elizabeth in icy tones.

"Never," replied Katherine. "The Ladies of Melusine are loyal to you and you alone. I don't believe anyone would betray you."

Elizabeth closed her eyes as she composed herself.

"Would you like my view on this matter, Elizabeth?" continued Katherine. Elizabeth's eyes met hers and she gave a small, jerky nod. "The King of Spain has heard the same rumours that circulate this court — that you are not the only heir of your father, Henry VIII. Remember, as far as the Catholics are concerned your parents were not legally married because your father was not technically divorced from his first wife, Katherine of Aragon. We all know this is untrue but by suggesting you are illegitimate, it's easier for the Spanish to stir up trouble. Your father acknowledged a number of his illegitimate children." She paused and cast a glance at Kate Howard who smiled.

Kate's father was Henry Carey, Baron Hunsdon, the son of Mary Boleyn, and like his sister, Kathy Knollys, the identity of his true father had always been cloudy. Mary's husband, William Carey, had given both children a name but there were many who assumed they were both Henry VIII's offspring.

"I won't be offended," Kate murmured and Katherine shot her a grateful smile.

"Your Majesty, you know yourself you have a number of half-siblings, some of whom your father acknowledged, some of whom he didn't; I think Philip is using the knowledge that there are other half-Tudors to create unrest. It adds credence to his ludicrous claim that he is the rightful King of England."

Elizabeth gazed into Katherine's open, honest face. "You could be correct, Katherine, but it isn't a risk we can afford to take. You say there has been a flurry of correspondence? Please, tell me what my ladies have discovered."

For the next hour, Katherine talked Elizabeth through the salient points of the letters she had received from the network of noblewomen who made up the Ladies of Melusine. Rumours abounded of ships being sighted off various headlands along the west coast; some as far away as Cornwall, others along the Welsh cliffs, with more glimpses near Liverpool. The letters also reported gossip from their staff suggesting a proliferation of strangers being seen in towns and villagers with increasing regularity — unknown men who then seemed to vanish without trace. Yet the menfolk of the letter writers remained oblivious to these strange goings-on.

"My husband claimed they were pirates and would be dealt with by the Navy", wrote one correspondent.

"My son, the new earl, suggests they are smugglers", wrote another.

"My nephew told me to stop interfering but I saw the men with my own eyes. Two days later, they had vanished from their lodgings without a trace", claimed a trusted source from the Welsh heartlands.

"But where are they coming from?" asked Bess.

"It's unclear," replied Katherine, "it seems some are sailing in from the Irish waters. These were reported by Calypso and the information came directly from her father-in-law, Sir John Perrot, who regularly patrols that section of coastline."

"If these vessels are coming from Ireland, how can we prove they are funded by the Spanish?" said Kate. "Perhaps they *are* simply merchant ships."

"Perhaps," replied Katherine.

"If Philip is behind this, why would he send his men on such a circuitous route?" asked Bess.

"He wants to attack from both coasts," replied Elizabeth. "There is still a strong Catholic allegiance in Ireland: it is another war we have been fighting for decades. If he positions ships there and uses the Netherlands as another launching point, the two coasts will suffer simultaneous invasion, dividing my troops and making his victory certain."

"Which is a good idea in theory," said Katherine, "but he doesn't have control of the Netherlands. He is unable to berth his fleet there because of Sir Robert and his army. The same is true for Ireland — Sir John Perrot leads your troops there. The Spanish have no foothold."

Elizabeth considered Katherine's words. "You're quite correct," she mused. "So, what are these ships doing? If they don't plan to invade as an armada…" Then her face paled as a new thought occurred to her.

"What is it, Elizabeth?" asked Kate.

"This is only a suggestion, but it bears the cunning of Philip," said Elizabeth. "Perhaps he isn't planning a full-scale invasion. Perhaps his plan is subtler. What if he's slowly delivering men favourable to his cause along the coastline, leaving them to work their way inland? What if he is placing a silent army across my realm who will wait and watch until the signal is given, then attack from within?"

"Is that possible?" asked Katherine, horrified.

"Not only possible but probable," replied Elizabeth. "Katherine, we must write today to warn everyone of what might be about to envelope us. I will also speak to Walsingham and Burghley; our fox and wolfhound must make further investigations. One more thing, Katherine, you must write to both my She-Wolf and her cub, Calypso. They must go immediately to Kenilworth Castle and remain there until I give them further orders. I had planned to insist they come here to London but Lettice's castle is well-protected and it would be more prudent. Dorothy's home at Carew Castle is too near to the coast. I will not take unnecessary risks with the lives of those I love."

"Of course, Your Majesty," replied Katherine.

Elizabeth drummed her fingers on the arm of her chair as she considered the possibility of such a coup. Would it be possible or would the natural wariness of her subjects make this an impossible task?

"Does our information help you, Elizabeth, or does it bring you more heartache?" asked Kate, watching her cousin. "Do we offer you any comfort?"

"Oh yes, my dear, you make me feel safe," she said, patting Kate's knee in a reassuring manner. "Walsingham and Burghley deal with the treacherous spies in the male world but, as has been proved once again, they miss so much information because they regard the chatter of women to be nothing more than pleasant background noise. Yet we hear so much more than they realise."

The women exchanged knowing looks.

"We are the keepers of a shattering secret: the survival of my half-brother and half-sister. I wasn't told about them for many years, but when I was, I knew the information was passed on as an act of love, and it was my duty to protect them both."

"But, a brother?" said Katherine, voicing a question she had long since burned to ask. "A legitimate heir — should he not be king?"

"He should but, remember, he doesn't know his true identity. Thomas Howard, 3rd Duke of Norfolk was always wary of revealing such a secret. My brother has always assumed he is the illegitimate heir of Thomas. Despite the fact my half-brother has always shown a wisdom beyond his years, the prospect of power has overwhelmed even the calmest, most reasonable of men and I would not wish to risk the peace of the realm by revealing the truth to him. Until such time as I think he should know his true heritage, he will remain one of my closest friends and confidants. Why do you think I have yet to name an heir? Until I have explained the situation to the heir himself, how can I announce it to the nation?"

There was also the problem that should she name an heir, the many discontented nobles who loathed being subjugated by a female monarch might seize the opportunity to replace her with an English King. Her half-brother, a mild man, who was content with the position of power she had bestowed upon him, lived with his wife and son, ever ready to defend her crown. It was a situation Elizabeth was not yet ready to change.

"Neither of Catherine's children will ever challenge my throne, but one day I may have to name one of them as my heir and then we will need all our strength to withstand the chaos that such an announcement will unleash. Today, however, I must send word to both Walsingham and Burghley. It is time they investigated these rumours or it may be that no amount of legitimate heirs will be able to rescue our nation from the Spanish."

Chapter Two

A grey, cloudy sky gazed gloomily through the windows. It did nothing to improve Elizabeth's mood. There had been only a few good days of weather in a sea of spring storms and the entire court was feeling cooped up and restless. Elizabeth longed to ride out with the hunt, to breathe the fresh country air, but the terrible weather was holding them all hostage. Elizabeth wondered whether time itself had slowed down, an emotion that was exacerbated by the longer than usual wait for a response to their letters.

Katherine Newton had followed her instructions to write to the Ladies of Melusine a week ago and, so far, there were no replies. This was not unusual for the missives that had been sent further afield, but for those closer to London, it was concerning and it made Elizabeth nervous.

She had been awake since the early morning but her toilette took several hours. The preparations to make her ready to meet her ministers was, she believed, time wasted when there were important matters of state to discuss, yet, without the regalia of monarchy, her task of ruling would be rendered even more difficult. Despite her years on the throne, she knew her privy council still viewed her with derision, doubting her intelligence, waiting for her to prove herself to be too weak, too feminine, to continue to carry the mantle of monarchy. Her frustration with their constant antagonism often manifested itself as short-temperedness, a petty emotion she hated displaying.

This morning, she had insisted on meeting Burghley in her private solar, so it would not appear strange for her women to be present. Although she trusted him, Elizabeth was keen to have other ears listening to their conversation in case she missed a nuance. Gathered by the fire were her closest companions: Bess of Hardwick; her daughter, Mary Talbot; Kate Howard; her cousin, Anne West; Katherine Newton and Lady Penelope Rich, the eldest daughter of Lettice Knollys, the 'She-Wolf'. As she entered, Elizabeth noticed that Katherine's eyes were red-rimmed with tiredness and she felt a pang of guilt. This was due to Elizabeth's request to transcribe some of the messages of warning that had been sent by the Ladies of Melusine over the past weeks, a task that would have taken Katherine most of the night. Her intention was to show these to Burghley should he continue to deny the rumours of unrest.

Elizabeth glanced towards Katherine, who was staring out of the window at the heavy grey skies. Earlier that morning, while Katherine had been helping to prepare Elizabeth for her day ahead, Elizabeth had informed her that she did not intend to ask Lord Burghley outright about the possible threat but would instead lead the conversation to see what information he offered. She had asked Katherine to make particular note if she felt the man was dissembling.

Katherine had her bible open on her lap as she pretended to study the text, while underneath was a sheet of paper and beside her was a stylus and ink. If anyone asked what she was writing, she would say it was a moving passage and she was making a copy for Elizabeth. As Katherine was renowned for her elegant penmanship, no one would question her motives.

The trumpet fanfare announcing Lord Burghley sent a ripple of unease through the women. Moments later, he swept into the room, followed by his train of pages, who scattered themselves to the far corner of the room and prepared their papers and portable writing desks, throwing scandalised looks at the women.

"Good morning, Your Majesty," Burghley said, bowing to Elizabeth. "You requested a private meeting…"

"Yes, I have issues to discuss with you first, then Sir Francis Walsingham will be joining us," Elizabeth interrupted, settling herself more comfortably in her chair and smiling at her Lord High Treasurer.

"Yes, he told me earlier," confirmed Burghley, as though the suggestion had been his, rather than an order from his queen. Elizabeth gritted her teeth. She must not lose her temper so early in proceedings — not only was it exhausting, it gave the moral high ground to her advisors and she had no intention of allowing them to occupy such territory.

"Mary, Queen of Scots," began Burghley in his timorous voice.

"What about her?" asked Elizabeth, surprised by this unexpected opening stance.

"We must increase her guard. She is presently under the care of Amyas Paulet and remains at Chartley Manor in Stafford but there are rumours of another plot."

Burghley, a staunch Protestant who bordered on Puritanism, disliked Mary Stuart because she was a Catholic. He knew Elizabeth and Mary enjoyed a cordial friendship but he felt the threat of her religion, a situation that was made worse by the fact Mary had a strong claim to Elizabeth's throne.

"Would this be the rumours concerning Anthony Babington?" asked Elizabeth.

"Yes, Your Majesty," he replied, failing to hide the surprise in his voice. "How did you hear about that? Did Sir Francis mention it?"

"No, I have another source who told me of this plot some weeks ago. In your opinion, do you believe this is a Catholic threat?" she prompted.

"Yes."

"And, do you believe there is any truth in the rumours?" asked Elizabeth, shooting a glance at Katherine, who was busily writing.

"We think not at present," said Burghley, scratching his nose. "However, it is always wise to make arrangements should the threat prove to be real. I would suggest we move the Scottish queen to a more secure house. For her own safety, you understand."

Elizabeth narrowed her eyes at Burghley. He was walking a fine line, something of which he was aware. Ever since her cousin, Mary, Queen of Scots had been forced by her Protestant nobles to abdicate her throne in favour of her infant son, James VI and flee her own country, Burghley had wanted to treat her as a political prisoner. There had been suggestions that she had been involved in a plot to murder her second husband, Henry Stuart, Lord Darnley. Despite a trial and the desperate attempts of her ministers to use false evidence, it was apparent Mary had not been involved. However, her misjudged marriage to the unpopular James Hepburn, 4th Earl of Bothwell, had made it impossible for her to return to her homeland and try to regain her throne. Instead she had thrown herself upon Elizabeth's mercy. She had been a royal guest ever since.

"Her safety is of the utmost importance," agreed Elizabeth. "How is Mary's health?"

"She remains unwell," replied Burghley.

"In that case is Chartley the best house for her? From what I remember, it can be a draughty old place," said Elizabeth. "She has been in our care for nearly 18 years — I don't want anything to happen to her."

"Shall I send your physician?"

"Yes," said Elizabeth. "Tell him it is of the utmost importance to me that the Scottish queen is restored to health. I will pay for whatever she needs."

Burghley wrote a short note, then beckoned a page to deliver it. He rifled through his pile of paper and removed one from partway down, but before he could continue there was the sound of running feet and a woman's urgent voice. Moments later, the herald at the door announced the arrival of Lady Dorothy Perrot and all eyes turned as she burst through the doors, her hair flying and her face ashen.

"What is the meaning of this?" snarled Burghley, his tone cold, his eyes narrowed in fury at being interrupted by a woman.

"I have a message for the queen," said Dorothy.

Her chest heaved in her tight riding habit as she struggled to catch her breath. From the mud on the hem of her dress and her boots, it was clear she had come straight from the stables. Elizabeth rose to her feet in astonishment, hurrying towards the exhausted woman. Burghley raised his hand, meaning to take whatever message she was delivering but Dorothy stepped away from him, her eyes on Elizabeth.

"Why are you here?" demanded Elizabeth, sweeping past Burghley and taking Dorothy's arm. "You were told to go to Kenilworth with your mother."

"I'm sorry Aunt Elizabeth," she gasped. "The message must have passed me while I was en route. My husband sent the children and me to London when he realised the extent of the danger he was facing in Carew."

"What danger?" barked Burghley. "There has been no word of risk in Pembrokeshire."

"My husband, Sir Thomas Perrot, claims differently, sir," replied Dorothy.

"You must have misheard. You women are always confused by such things. This is why you should never meddle in the affairs of men..."

"Sir, I am not mistaken," interrupted Dorothy, her voice sharp and angry. "My husband sent us away because he has heard audacious whispers suggesting the King of Spain is planning a silent coup on the west coast. With the help of Erasmus Sanders, Philip II has been secreting men into the country for weeks and Thomas believes an attempt to take Carew Castle is imminent."

"Your Majesty," laughed Burghley, his smile indulgent, "it is impossible that such an attack could take place..." Burghley took Elizabeth by the hand as though she were a querulous toddler, making to lead her back to her seat, while ignoring Dorothy. Elizabeth shook him away, recoiling in disgust, fury rising like a phoenix from the flames.

"You dare to speak to me so?" she hissed. "If my father had presented you with such information, would you have told him he was mistaken?"

There was another fanfare and Sir Francis Walsingham crashed through the door.

"What's going on?" he demanded.

Elizabeth turned away from her two most trusted advisors, guiding Dorothy to the seat between Katherine Newton and Lady Penelope. Swinging back around she caught the look of amused exasperation being exchanged by the two men. Narrowing her eyes, she stalked towards Walsingham and Burghley.

"Before you dismiss this information as hysterical female nonsense, I suggest you both consult your own confidants and discover how much truth is in this rumour," she snarled. "If we have been misinformed, then there is no need for us to be concerned. If, however, a Spanish threat is silently creeping across Wales towards us, then we must warn the duke of Hereford, who will soon be setting out for Pembroke Castle."

She climbed the steps of her dais and stood before her ornately carved chair, glaring down at Burghley. In an instant, she saw his true nature — self-serving, sly, controlling and stubborn. The man on whom she had relied for years, whose judgement she had sought above all others, was now old and tired from his years of service. Despite a lifetime of working together, she understood that he remained dismissive of her ability to rule, as were so many of the other male courtiers in her privy council. As long as she agreed with his suggestions, he would treat her as an equal — the moment she crossed him, like now, he showed his true colours and treated her as though she were less intelligent than even the stupidest of men.

"I am a Tudor monarch," she said, glaring at the two men. "You will send riders to Carew at once. You will also send reinforcements to Chartley to protect the Queen of Scots, Amyas Paulet and his family. Until we know whether there is truth in this rumour or not, we will take no chances."

Walsingham shifted from foot to foot. "Your Majesty — could this be a feint?"

"Why do you say this?"

"We have recently discovered there is a spy, codenamed Julius, operating out of court. Could he have falsified this information in order to scare you?"

"A spy, and he is within the court?"

"It's not the first time, Your Majesty."

"Neither will it be the last. I trust my source," replied Elizabeth. "Send your men, Walsingham. We need to know what is happening."

Turning abruptly, Elizabeth dismissed the men with a curt nod. Walsingham did not move.

"There is one more thing, Your Majesty," he said, as Burghley and his scribes stalked out in disgust.

"What is it, Francis?"

"The spy, Julius — we believe his wife is a someone close to you, so please be sure that all correspondence you send is through a trusted advisor."

Elizabeth spun around, facing Walsingham. "Do you know the identity of these traitors?" she asked.

"Soon, my lady, soon. Until then, please tread cautiously."

Elizabeth paced her solar. On the table under the window a pile of letters fluttered gently in the breeze created by the swishing of her wide skirts. She was informally attired, her dress made from a soft green wool embroidered with Tudor roses and, she noticed with a smile, a row of tiny mermaids. Lettice, or one of her daughters, must have worked on the dress at some point — they were known for always using a mermaid emblem, sometimes in plain sight, sometimes hidden in the pattern.

She was awaiting the one person whom she knew would offer her comfort and would be able to deal with the stupidity of both Walsingham and Burghley: Ralph Fitzalan, Duke of Hereford.

Although several years her junior, Ralph was wise beyond his years and with his wife, Mary Seymour, the daughter of the late queen, Katheryn Parr and her fourth husband, Thomas Seymour, had always been a trusted confidant, a welcome member of her inner circle. Ralph was recently returned from the Netherlands and she planned to commission him to muster a force to secure the border between Wales and England. Her concern was that, should the worst happen and the Spanish invade via the Pembrokeshire coast, they might follow the route her grandfather, Henry VII had taken when he had marched to Bosworth to fight for his crown against the usurper, Richard III. It would not take much to vary this path and head towards Chartley Manor in Staffordshire, a property that belonged to Robert Devereux, the earl of Essex, and at present, the home of Mary, Queen of Scots.

While Elizabeth had no suspicion that Mary was involved in the plot, it did not stop her becoming a figurehead for fanatics, therefore putting her life in danger. Securing an area as vast as the Welsh borders was a huge task but she felt Ralph was ready to prove himself as a military leader.

The trumpet sounded outside her doors and her herald shouted the duke's name. Elizabeth beamed — Ralph Fitzalan was always a reassuring presence, whether it was his deep measured voice or his air of quiet confidence, he was a man to whom others naturally turned for advice, for comfort and for friendship. Orphaned as a child, he had been brought up among the Devereux clan, his wardship bought by Sir Richard Devereux of Lamphey Hall in Pembrokeshire, so his connections with the elite of Elizabeth's court had never been in question.

"Your Majesty," Ralph said, taking Elizabeth's proffered hand, "it's good to see you looking so well."

"Thank you, Ralph. How was Robert when you left the Netherlands?"

"He was coping. I think he's missing England, though. For all his experience and his loyalty to you, he is a man who thrives better in his home environment. Have you spoken to the countess?"

"She is currently at Kenilworth," replied Elizabeth. "We have not spoken for a few weeks, but from all I've heard, she is dealing stoically with his absence."

"Your messenger expounded that I visit with the utmost urgency. What couldn't wait, Elizabeth?"

She slid into the chair by the fire and indicated he take the seat opposite.

"The Spanish rumours," she said.

Ralph raised an eyebrow. "Which ones? During my journey back I heard a wide and varying array of tittle-tattle."

"Such as?"

"The usual ones: replacing you with Mary or Philip claiming the throne," he said, a wave of his hand dismissing them as worthless, idle gossip.

"Anything else?"

"You obviously suspect something," he said. "Why don't you tell me, rather than us playing cat-and-mouse for hours?"

"Walsingham claims there is a spy, codenamed Julius, who is giving information to the Spanish and that his wife is part of my court," she stated.

"Do you know his true identity?"

"Sadly, no, although Walsingham and his spy network have a few ideas. What concerns me is whether his wife is part of the collusion or whether she is innocent of his crime but has been forced to do his dirty work."

"That isn't something we can answer," replied Ralph, "therefore for now, you must set it to one side, Elizabeth. If anyone begins acting suspiciously, then we will pass this information on to Walsingham and his men. I know you have a number of sources of information — do any of these offer any clues to the identity of the spy?"

"Not yet, but we have only recently sent out word, so it's too soon to comment with any certainty."

"Anything else?" asked Ralph.

"Philip is delivering an army of Catholic soldiers into Wales in a bid to invade by stealth."

"Elizabeth, we've faced rumours like this before," said Ralph, trying to offer some reassurance. "What new proof do you have that an invasion is imminent?"

"Sir Thomas Perrot has sent word confirming sightings of unusual ships and a rise in the number of strangers."

"They could be innocent people trying to escape persecution."

"I have considered that, but this influx of strangers has been reported by a wide range of other informants whom I trust," she said, before walking towards the table and extracting a short note from the sheaf of papers, which she handed to Ralph. "There is also this. It was intercepted by one of Walsingham's men."

"I see," murmured Ralph. "This claims that Philip intends to activate those loyal to Spain once his fleet has invaded the Milford Haven coastline. They will then raise loyal Catholic subjects to assassinate you and place Mary, Queen of Scots on the throne in your place."

Elizabeth nodded, once more pacing around the room.

"Does the Scottish queen know of this plan?" asked Ralph.

"She was informed today."

"And have the Perrots raised armies along the Pembrokeshire coastline?"

"Yes, there is a muster as we speak. Sir Thomas Perrot has galvanised regiments as far up as Cardigan. He has also sent messengers into North Wales and towards the Marches."

"In that case, at first light, I will take my leave of you and head for my home in Herefordshire. From there, I'll be able to coordinate with Perrot and we can secure both the coastline and the borders. On my way, I will visit the Scottish queen."

For the first time since she had received Walsingham's intelligence, Elizabeth smiled.

"Ralph, thank you," she said. "Your father would have been so proud of you and your military prowess."

Ralph raised an eyebrow. He was always intrigued when Elizabeth made references to his father. "You knew him better than most," he murmured. "I'm honoured that you think I'm a credit to his memory. I've often wondered whether he would have been disappointed by my decisions."

"Never," said Elizabeth. "He was a man of great wisdom."

Ralph acknowledged her words with a swift bow. "Now, Your Majesty, if you can spare me, I'd like to return to my chambers and write to the Scottish queen advising her of my impending visit."

"Of course," replied Elizabeth, taking both his hands and looking into his unusual grey-green eyes. "May angels watch over you in your endeavours."

He squeezed her hands. "Don't worry," he said, kissing her cheek, "we've faced worse than this and survived. Philip will never steal your throne, not while you have your loyal friends and family around you." Bowing deeply from the waist, he swept from the room.

Elizabeth flinched as the door slammed shut behind him. In all her years, facing the constant threat of plot, treason and execution, she had never once felt she would fail, but this time, for reasons she could not explain, tears welled in her eyes as she watched storm clouds gathering on the horizon.

Chapter Three

Ever loving Venus, your physician was gratefully received. Mine seems to have nothing further to suggest than leeches! When I suggested some herbal assistance he crossed himself like a small child at a first communion and hurried to the confessional. Are foolish men to surround us always?

Your time sounds busy and I grieve that you feel melancholic. Do you sleep well? My concern is always that you do not rest enough. Let the others take the weight of your Haven for a while. It is summer, your favourite time of year, rest and enjoy the sunshine.

As you so rightly say, we are older ladies now, no longer can we dance the masque with such vigour but we can watch and remember. The thoughts of the past lifted me to smile.

Indeed we continue but, my friend the nun, for how much longer? The weight of illness lies upon me and my vision of the future is clouded.

Send me word if the troubles have been resolved.

Semper sorores, Artemis

Elizabeth looked up from the note from her half-sister, written under her codename of Artemis, as a white greyhound emerged from the bank of ferns with a leap and a bark of excitement, wagging her long tail. Elizabeth bent to stroke the dog's velvet muzzle.

"Hello Star," she said, "have you been having fun exploring?"

The greyhound leant against Elizabeth's legs, enjoying the attention and the soft swift strokes of her long slim fingers.

"Lead the way, sweet thing," said Elizabeth and Star gave a happy bark, trotting down the gentle slope towards the distant voices.

Katherine Newton fell into step beside Elizabeth, taking the note the queen had been reading and folding it into a long, narrow roll which she slid into a hidden pocket in the sleeve of her dress.

"Star is a gentle soul," said Elizabeth, watching the dog streak ahead of them across the grass towards the gathering of silken tents and her mistress who had whistled for her. "And this letter arrived late last night?"

"Yes, Your Majesty," replied Katherine. "It was approaching midnight when Lettice received this note on your behalf. We felt it would be prudent to translate it and only disturb you if it was urgent. I hope we made the correct choice."

"You did, my dear. There is nothing that needs immediate action," said Elizabeth. "It concerns me that Artemis is still unwell but I must take comfort from the fact she is at least well enough to write again. You say the original note was in her own handwriting?"

"Yes, and it was in code," confirmed Katherine, "which is the first time for some months. It must mean her strength is returning."

They were strolling through the woods of Kenilworth Castle in Warwickshire, the beautiful home belonging to Robert Dudley, Earl of Leicester and his wife, Lettice. The red-haired countess was yet another member of the extended Tudor clan — the second daughter of Lady Kathryn Knollys — and, although ten years younger than Elizabeth, was striking in her similarity to the monarch.

In the distance there was a sudden splash and the sound of laughter by the ornamental lake drew their attention. Elizabeth and her party had been at Kenilworth Castle for four days and, despite the constant stream of discreet messengers updating her on the situation in Pembrokeshire, Elizabeth and her trusted inner circle were attempting to present the usual lively face of the court while they were in public. They were not yet ready for the panic that would ensue were it to become known that a suspected Spanish invasion might be creeping forward from the west.

Star yapped, having returned to her side, bringing Elizabeth's attention back to the present.

"You're so impatient, little lady," laughed Elizabeth, kissing the top of the dog's head before she raced away. "Let us go and join the merry making," she continued, leading Katherine down the hill in Star's wake. "Until we have confirmation of danger, we are allowed some relaxation. It may be the last we have for some time."

As they followed the shaded walkway that led to the banks of the lake, Elizabeth breathed in the fresh, metallic smell of the water, feeling her lungs fill with its clean scent. They strolled towards the gathering of silken tents that had been set up on a temporary wooden balcony overlooking the water.

"Elizabeth," Lettice called, walking towards her and embracing her. When she was here, Elizabeth insisted her trusted inner circle dispense with the formal etiquette of the court. "Star found you in the woods, then?"

"No matter how well we were hidden, your little girl was on our trail," replied Elizabeth.

"I'm glad," and although Lettice's tone was light, there was concern in her wide brown eyes.

Elizabeth gazed at her cousin and considered again how their mixed Tudor and Boleyn blood had created them in each other's image. They had the same vivid colouring with their vibrant red hair, translucent skin and brown eyes and they were also of similar stature and shared many character traits, including a short temper. The major difference between them, apart from the crown, was the fact Lettice had married and was now a mother, something Elizabeth now knew she would never experience.

Lettice had married in her early teens to Walter Devereux and the union had been a happy one, producing five children: Penelope, Dorothy, Robert, Young Walter and Francis. Walter's death in 1576 had left Lettice a widow and after a mourning period of two years, she had married Elizabeth's favourite, Robert Dudley. Lettice had insisted it be a quiet ceremony because she knew the furore it would cause. Many courtiers had still believed Elizabeth and Robert would one day marry but the two women knew differently.

A week before the clandestine nuptials, Elizabeth and Lettice had discussed the matter one final time.

"You are sure, Elizabeth," Lettice had asked. "If you have any feelings for Robert, I will stop this wedding now. I would never wish to hurt you."

Elizabeth had reached for her cousin's hand and squeezed it. "Robert and I have always been star-crossed, but now the idea of being in love with him makes me laugh. You and he are so well suited, Lettice, I'm delighted that my most loyal companions have fallen in love. My best friend and my favourite cousin, your happiness makes me happy."

"Aunt Elizabeth, Aunt Katherine, Aunt Lettice!" came the breathless voice of the 11-year-old Arbella Stuart as she raced towards them. "Quickly, we're going out on the mermaid boat to do some fishing in the middle of the lake. You must come!"

Arbella's golden-red hair streamed out behind her like a silken banner, her curls catching the dancing sunbeams as the three women turned towards her.

"Grandmamma is waiting for me by the water," she squealed, pointing towards Bess, who was trying to smile encouragement rather than display her fear of water.

A long pontoon led out into the middle of lake and fastened to it was a selection of decorated boats. One bore a swan, another a mermaid and a third a golden fish with jewelled eyes. Along the bank were jugglers and tumblers from Elizabeth's own personal players, entertaining the glamorous guests invited by Lettice to enjoy Kenilworth Castle's legendary summer entertainments. A large flat barge was attached to the other side of the pontoon, where Elizabeth's musicians sat, their lilting tunes floating across the waves, giving the dappled midday light a magical feel.

"Arbella, my little May Queen, it sounds wonderful but I'm not really dressed for boating," laughed Elizabeth.

"Neither am I, my dear," said Katherine, glancing down at her silk dress.

"Although, I'm very happy to launch the ship for you," added Elizabeth.

"Really?" squealed the delighted child. "I'll run down and tell them to wait."

Elizabeth laughed and as Lettice waved them away, she and Katherine followed Arbella down the gentle slope to the shores of the lake. Arbella's grandmother, Bess, who cared for the orphaned child, was trying and failing to calm her down. One of the earl's household staff, Humphrey Cole, grinned as he lifted Arbella into the boat. His brother, Thomas, was already in the vessel and settled Arbella on one of the wooden benches, placing a fishing rod in her eager hand.

"Don't worry, your ladyship," Humphrey said to Bess, springing into the small boat. "We'll ensure she comes to no harm."

"Aunt Elizabeth, Aunt Elizabeth, are you ready to send us off?"

Bess turned, surprised to find Elizabeth and Katherine by her side.

"Of course, Arbella," Elizabeth called, "but only if you promise to stop wriggling. You'll all end up in the water at this rate."

Wide-eyed and breathless, Arbella stopped twisting and turning in her seat as the boat was launched into the rippling water.

"I name this ship The Kenilworth Mermaid," said Elizabeth. "May God bless all who sail in her."

Bess and Katherine clapped while the orchestra and jugglers cheered. Arbella beamed, then as a small ripple caught the boat and as it rocked wildly she shot an anxious glance at her grandmother.

"Enjoy yourself, Arbella," called Bess. "Humphrey and Thomas will keep you safe."

The women watched for a few minutes then turned, walking towards the shade of the vivid silken tents where Lettice and Kate Howard were seated in the pavilion nearest to the water's edge. From here it would be possible to watch Arbella's antics. As Elizabeth approached, they rose in a graceful duet, making way for the monarch. Once Elizabeth was comfortable and had waved to Arbella, she turned to Lettice.

"Has Dampard returned yet?" she asked.

"Not yet, Elizabeth," replied Lettice. "Dorothy is in the castle waiting. She is not coping well with the idea that her husband may be about to quell an invasion. It has taken Penelope all morning to persuade her to remain here and not to rush to her Uncle George at Lamphey Hall, which is only a few leagues away from Carew Castle. She seems to think she'll be able to help."

"Our treasured Calypso must not leave," said Elizabeth, aware her voice sounded harsh but it was concern that laced her tone.

"I have positioned one of the household guards outside her door and another at the foot of the stairs leading to her quarters. She won't be able to go anywhere without our knowledge."

Elizabeth accepted a goblet of cool wine, before shielding her eyes against the bright sun, searching the vessels on the lake until she identified Arbella. It was with relief that she noticed the Cole brothers had rowed only a few strokes away from shore before dropping their lines over the edge. If anything happened and the boat capsized, there would be no danger of drowning, as Arbella would be able to stand in the shallow water.

"You have many guests, Lettice," murmured Elizabeth, her eyes drifting over the laughing, colourful swathe of courtiers wafting around the grounds, enjoying the countess's hospitality.

"It's always easier to hide in a crowd," she replied, "and while it's well known you often stay here, I didn't want you to be too easy to identify."

"Is this the reason Bess has brought Arbella here?"

"Our security is extremely strong. There are many who think Arbella will one day be named as your heir, especially after your comment in May, and it's imperative she is kept from danger."

Elizabeth nodded. It was true that under different circumstances Arbella would have had the strongest dynastic claim to the throne.

"Now, if you will excuse me, Your Majesty, ladies, I must ensure things are progressing for this evening's entertainment, as well as checking on Dorothy," Lettice said. "I will inform you the moment Dampard returns."

With a curtsey, Lettice glided away. Her footman, Dampard, was loyal to Lettice alone. He had served her for years and the women knew he would lay down his life for the countess and her children. Elizabeth watched her cousin out of sight, then beckoned to Katherine to sit beside her.

"I would like you to reply to Artemis," she murmured. "There is so much going on, no one will hear me while I dictate my message. Bess, Kate, would you please ensure we aren't disturbed."

The two women moved forward so Elizabeth was obscured from sight, their eyes glued on the lake and Arbella. As Elizabeth whispered, Katherine scribbled down her words.

Sweet Artemis, your health continues to concern me, but my melancholic state lifts as my thoughts are drawn to our past. Oh sweet sister, what times! But as you say, we are now older ladies with grave responsibilities.

We have many to lavish affection upon us but I thank sweet God every day for you, my friend the nun, who can understand in a word what would take another a lifetime. This is why it is imperative that you watch those close to you, send word if you have even the smallest hint at subterfuge. These are dark days.

Sweet Artemis until we meet again, iuncta sanguine, Venus.

Folding the parchment and concealing it in her palm, Elizabeth watched Katherine Newton as she hurried back to the castle where she would translate the words into code. Until a response came to one of their missives, there was nothing Elizabeth could do, so she abandoned herself to the velvet rays of the sun upon her face, the company of her closest friends and the spectacle of the afternoon as it unfolded before her.

There were games and music, dancing and at one point an impromptu swimming race among the young men. She noticed Bess's eyes barely left her granddaughter and her activities. As the afternoon curved around them, lengthening their shadows and taking the sting from heat of the sun, her thoughts turned to the entertainments Lettice had planned. *Soon, we will retire and this evening will enjoy a performance from my players, who have travelled with us from London*, she thought. She hoped it would be a light-hearted comedy as, with all the unrest around her, she did not think she would be able to concentrate on anything more complicated.

Suddenly, Kate Howard was at her side.

"Elizabeth, Lettice wanted you to know that her man, Dampard, has returned," she murmured.

Elizabeth turned to face her cousin and from the extreme pallor on Kate's beautiful face she knew the news was the worst they could expect.

"Tell me," Elizabeth demanded.

"He comes direct from the duke of Hereford; all the rumours are true."

"They've discovered men loyal to Philip of Spain?"

"Worse," said Kate, tears filling her eyes. "Carew Castle has fallen to the Spanish and Dorothy's husband is being held hostage."

"No," Elizabeth breathed. "No, this cannot be."

Her instinct was to rise, to run, to act, but Kate's restraining hand kept her in her chair.

"There is other news, too. We have had word from Henry Herbert; Pembroke Castle has so far resisted any attempt to be taken. The duke of Hereford has sent word that Ludlow and

Cardiff Castles stand secure, as do Llansteffan, Picton and Manorbier. However, he fears that Tenby, Llawhaden and Haverfordwest Castles have fallen in a similar manner to Carew."

Elizabeth felt the world tilt. She grasped the air as though trying to gain her balance and Kate took her hand. "Where is Lettice?" she gasped.

"She's with Dorothy."

"We must go to her."

Elizabeth swept from her seat and set out across the undulating lawns towards the magnificent castle. Ignoring everyone, she marched through the entrance hall and up the curving staircase to the rooms occupied by the family when they were in residence.

"Where is Lady Perrot?" she demanded of the footman in Leicester livery at the top of the stairs. "I demand to see her at once."

"Elizabeth, we're here!" called Lettice's voice as she flung open a door halfway down the corridor.

Elizabeth pushed past the guard, hurrying towards her cousin. "Kate has told me — is it true? Thomas has been captured?"

Dorothy lay on the bed, red-eyed from crying. On hearing Elizabeth's voice she scrambled up to a sitting position. "Aunt Elizabeth, what shall we do?" she howled.

"Tell me everything you know," said Elizabeth, perching beside Dorothy on the bed but looking at Lettice. "What did Dampard say?"

"One of Thomas's servants managed to escape and made it to Lamphey Hall. He's confirmed that there were many loyal to the old faith working in the castle. All had seemed like good honest fellows but they have apparently been in the pay of the

Spanish all along," she said, her voice faltering as the horror of the situation began to sink in. "Late last night, a ship made its way through the estuary from Neyland, along the Cleddau river to the mill pond by the castle. From there it's only a short walk to the side entrance. It was cloudy, so they were unseen and their footsteps were silent. Their spies inside the castle opened the gates to admit them. Similar stories have come to Dampard from the other stricken castles. Haverfordwest is the worst. The captives are being treated roughly and the occupiers are threatening to burn anyone who is Protestant."

Elizabeth felt bile rise in her throat. The stench of her sister's vicious bonfires was one which would remain with her for life. Controlling her desire to retch, she asked, "And Thomas?"

"He was taken at knifepoint from his bed."

"Is he alive?" whispered Penelope, Dorothy's elder sister, who was hovering by the window.

"Dampard said the servant claimed he is being treated well but he is a hostage," replied Dorothy.

Elizabeth turned away. She twisted her ruby ring around her finger, an unconscious gesture as her quicksilver mind made decision after decision, weighing the possibility of success or failure and honing her options for survival for herself, her realm and those she loved. "I will order Walsingham to send men to assess the situation," she said. "If the Spanish are operating in such a clandestine manner and are not crowing over their victory, then we must be as circumspect. This may only be the first wave of their plan and if we can operate as swiftly and silently as them, we may catch the ringleaders before they are able to progress any further."

"But we will help them at Carew, won't we?" demanded Dorothy. "Thomas is my husband and…"

On a furious glare from her mother, Dorothy swallowed the end of her sentence. Her tone stopped short of being accusatory but Elizabeth was no fool — she knew Dorothy had been about to remind her that Thomas had put himself at risk on her orders.

"Of course, we will help them," murmured Elizabeth. "However, charging the castle with 200 horse will not solve this problem. We must be as cunning as the Spanish."

"But Aunt Elizabeth, what are you going to do?"

Elizabeth turned to the trembling young woman. Taking her hand, she squeezed it, trying to impart strength and reassurance.

"Do not fear, little Calypso," she said. "All is not lost; I will write to my brother — he will rescue your husband."

Never had Elizabeth sat through a longer, more tense evening. Despite sending the fastest messengers available at Kenilworth, their requests for help would not reach their destinations for many hours. Walsingham was at his home, Barn Elms, near Richmond Palace in Surrey, while Lord Burghley remained at his vast estate of Theobalds in Cheshunt, Hertfordshire. They were at least a day's ride away from where she waited in Warwickshire. The letter she had sent to the man she knew to be her brother did not have so far to travel but even he had not yet responded.

Her intention was to return to London as soon as possible in order to be at the heart of things. Being stuck away from the action was unbearable. She was Queen — she needed to rule, to assert her authority in case there were those who tried to steal it from her.

The following morning as her ladies helped her to dress, Elizabeth whispered her intentions to Lettice.

"It would be unsafe to return," Lettice replied, her tone firm. "Apart from this new threat, there has been word that the summer's plague has begun earlier than usual and is virulent in the City. You must not risk your health."

"But to be here, so far away from the centre of events, is also dangerous," Elizabeth hissed.

"And if you were to contract the Black Death, you would be handing your throne to Philip," snapped Lettice.

"I am the Queen of England," roared Elizabeth, her nerves stretched to the limit. "How dare you speak to me in such a manner?"

"Because I'm trying to make you see sense!"

Elizabeth drew herself up to her full height, her frown deadly and intimidating as she glared at Lettice. Around the room there was a stunned silence. Kate hovered ready to step into the gap between her two cousins, Bess edged towards the door, in a position to run for help if necessary, while Penelope was ready to spring into action, no matter what course it might take.

The two slender red-haired women stared at each other, so alike they could be sisters; defiance, fear and determination emanating from their rigid postures, their eyes flashing, their faces flushed. Elizabeth opened her mouth to speak, then as suddenly as her temper flared, her rigid posture slumped and tears sprang to her eyes.

"Oh Lettice," she wailed, and threw herself into the younger woman's arms. "You're right, you're right. I'm so sorry but it was the dream. The dream of my grandfather. Last night when we were under the blackness of the witches moon."

The women exchanged nervous glances.

"You think it was prophetic?"

Elizabeth nodded. Her fear of witchcraft was great and she lived in terror that an enchanter would place a curse upon her. She prayed for protection against evil magic every morning. Dreams, she knew, were often the prompt for supernatural arts and the previous night, she had visited a dark place. "My grandfather, Henry VII, came to me," said Elizabeth. "He reminded me of his own journey to the throne. How he landed at Mill Bay near Milford Haven, Pembrokeshire, which is not many leagues from Carew."

"But his journey ended in triumph," reassured Lettice. "He reclaimed the throne of England that was his by right of blood and created the noble house of Tudor. You are the glorious result of the blood of kings."

"And what if it is to end the same way?" said Elizabeth. "What if his appearance was a warning that another King, who has a claim to my throne through his ancient blood, marches on the same path? Are we to meet again in warfare? Is history to repeat itself as we are ill-met by witch-light? Will I be the last Tudor monarch, losing my crown in the mud and blood of a battlefield? A circle completed; a dynasty destroyed?"

The women stared at Elizabeth, none dared to contradict her and from their silence she knew they, too, could not deflect the darkness of this strange and unusual dream.

"But you are not the last Tudor," whispered Lettice into the growing silence. "You know there are others. We know you have heirs."

"Who languish in secret," Elizabeth retorted. "My half-brother, who is unaware of his true destiny. His son, a prince, whose identity can never be revealed. Another princess, my half-sister, who has been draped in mystery and danger throughout her life. Are our secrets, which have been kept for the best reasons, about to be our undoing? If what Mignonne told us is true, then it appears that the King of Spain might know our secret. Is this what my grandfather warns against?"

Only a select few knew about the twins and their true identities. These were the members of her inner court, the ones she would trust with her life and whom she would protect with her own. The people who knew all her secrets. Was it really possible one of them had been careless and this greatest of secrets had been leaked to Philip II? Is this why her grandfather had visited her in the dark of the witch's moon, to tell her to prepare, to reach for arms and defend this fair land?

"No, Elizabeth, no," said Lettice. "If you need them, they will step forward and fight by your side, like the true Tudors they are in their hearts and blood. King Philip's claim to your throne is unfounded — a work of nonsense and propaganda created when he was married to Mary. He will never command the love and support of your people. Any battle Philip might try to instigate will be crushed by your subjects. Your reign, should it ever end, will be in glory and love, not in the destruction and fear of a battlefield."

Elizabeth reached out to Lettice and, taking her hand, she squeezed it. "You're right, sweet cousin, but I won't rest easy until we have beaten Philip back to Spain. Even now his fleet might be gathering off Mill Bay."

Elizabeth allowed Lettice and Kate to guide her to a carved wooden chair that was lined with cushions. Leaning back, she closed her eyes and composed herself. Shouting at Lettice had been a foolish loss of control. No matter how she truly felt, showing such weakness, even among her loyal Ladies of Melusine, was potentially suicidal. She trusted everyone here but her greatest fear was always that their trust in *her* would be lost, that they would give up on her and begin to doubt her judgement. If she lost their love and trust, then to whom would she turn?

Throughout her life, she had chosen her friends carefully, taking her time before allowing them to become close. Yet, whenever her mood was dark, she saw subterfuge everywhere, even among those she loved. *It is my weakness,* she thought, *and it must be overcome.*

The familiar feeling of desolation engulfed her; it was an echo from her childhood, from the day she had learned it was her father who had ordered the death of her mother, Anne Boleyn. This had been two years after the event but the reality that the enormous King, her father, could order their lives to be snuffed out with one blow of the executioner's axe — or in her mother's case, a sword — was a terrifying truth. From then on, she had watched her father closely, learning to gauge his moods, to stay dutiful, to win his praise and to ensure her behaviour never aroused his anger.

"Elizabeth, please, drink this," said Lettice. "It will soothe your nerves." Lettice offered her a pewter cup. From inside came the scent of summertime. "It's chamomile and lavender infused in sweet wine and honey."

Elizabeth took the cup and sipped, enjoying the herbal flavours. Over the years, Lettice and Kate had perfected this particular drink and Elizabeth suspected there was a pinch of poppy seeds in it too; a known relaxant. She drained her cup and handed it to Lettice. "I must finish dressing. If word comes from Walsingham or Burghley, I must be prepared."

Elizabeth took a moment to compose herself, then returned to her place in front of the looking glass and allowed the work of creating a Tudor queen from a slight, 52-year-old woman to continue. She would be 53 in September. A rare age indeed, but she felt she had survived the ravages of time better than some. During the day, she was forced to wear the white make-up that was so fashionable. It had also become a mask to hide behind as she performed her duty as monarch.

Quick, light footsteps behind her startled her.

"Your Majesty, I have news," said Katherine Newton. "It's from Lady Fortune."

Elizabeth read the short note from her half-brother's wife and turned away. She felt as though a cold hand had squeezed her heart. Using the codenames for her brother and sister, she said, "Artemis has contacted Apollo and says she fears her household has been compromised."

"By whom?" gasped Kate.

"A priest called John Ballard," said Elizabeth. "Artemis claims this man's knowledge of the area around Carew is far too detailed. She has heard him discussing things with his clerk…"

"But this doesn't prove she's been compromised," said Lettice, fear making her irrational.

"There is also a note from Mignonne," said Katherine, "and she corroborates the words of Artemis. The information was passed to Mignonne by her betrothed."

Bess gasped. Mignonne was her granddaughter and a trusted member of the Ladies of Melusine. Her betrothed, Claude Nau, was one of Walsingham's agents and operated as a double agent for the Scottish.

"Katherine, what does Artemis say was overheard?" Elizabeth's interruption was sharp, urgent. "She would not write if she were not concerned."

"Late last night, Mignonne went to the kitchen to fetch some herbs she required for a sleeping draught for Artemis. On her return, she encountered Artemis who was trying to walk off cramp in her legs — you know how she suffers — and as they returned to their rooms, they overheard two men discussing our secret."

"The missing heirs?" asked Elizabeth, her face ashen.

"It seems the Spanish king knows there are two more Tudor heirs and has details of the identity of your hidden sister, even though at present, he doesn't know the identity of your brother. This plot, this invasion, it is in order to target your sister."

Elizabeth stared at Katherine in horror. "How could he know? How could he possibly have discovered this secret?"

"We know our household has been compromised, too. In her letter, Lady Fortune claims that Apollo has discovered the spy."

Elizabeth shut her eyes, acid bile rising in her throat as fear swept through her. "Who?" she gasped.

"Douglas Sheffield and her husband, Edward Stafford," whispered Kate. "They know the truth about your sister and, now, thanks to them, so does King Philip II of Spain."

Douglas Sheffield. It did not seem possible. How could sweet Douglas Sheffield be a spy?

Elizabeth paced the room, wringing her hands. Douglas was a Howard girl; she was part of the family. Would she betray her country to the Spanish? Elizabeth could feel panic welling inside her again. All her life she had lived with the uneasy prospect of family subterfuge. When she had barely been out of her teens her own sister, Mary, had wanted to execute her. It was why she was so careful when it came to choosing the people around her.

"Surely, Douglas must have been forced into this situation," said Kate, giving voice to Elizabeth's thoughts.

Lettice gave a harsh laugh. "Douglas is not as sweet and innocent as she appears," she snapped, her arms folded, her body rigid with fury. "She was Robert's lover before we were married and claims to have borne him at least one son. Don't let her pretty face and dimples fool you."

Elizabeth did not reply. The animosity between Lettice and Robert's former mistress was well known — it was the reason Elizabeth had never given Douglas a position within her inner circle. There was also Douglas's unnerving similarity to Elizabeth's former stepmother, Catherine Howard, who, along with Elizabeth's mother, Anne Boleyn, had both been Douglas's first cousins.

Walking to the ornate stained-glass windows that took up half the wall of the solar, Elizabeth unhooked the central panels that were cleverly disguised doors. Stepping out on to the stone balcony she gazed over the magnificent gardens to where the silvery water of the lake glinted in the distance. Beyond this was the magnificent Warwickshire countryside, ancient, beautiful, hers. This was her land, her realm, her kingdom, bequeathed to her through her father's will. Hers by right of blood and birth. Would she really let a silly girl like Douglas Sheffield try to steal it all away?

In an instant, Elizabeth's nerves vanished. Calmness suffused her, both body and mind. It was often the way when she was facing a crisis. Her initial reaction would be anxiety, but once her mind focused, her Tudor courage and her Boleyn and Howard cunning would rise up and fortify her. She would not let Douglas and her scheming husband, Edward Stafford, sell her realm to Spain and the Catholics. She was Queen of England and a Tudor queen at that. She would show those who doubted or challenged her that she would stand victorious. No one would steal her throne.

"We must question Douglas," she said. "Lettice, have one of your men discover where she is staying and invite her to meet me in London when we return. I will suggest that now her mother-in-law, Lady Dorothy Stafford, is becoming frailer, there might be a position available as Lady of the Bedchamber."

"Elizabeth, are you insane?" exclaimed Katherine, then covered her mouth with her hand afraid her outburst would anger the queen.

Spinning around, a determined look on her face, Elizabeth grinned at Katherine.

"Do not fear, Katherine," murmured Elizabeth, "I have not lost my wits. We need to discover whether Douglas is complicit in this plan or whether her bully of a husband has coerced her. If she has intentionally betrayed me, then this is treason and I will set Walsingham to arrest her. However, if her husband has forced these confessions from her — which is what I suspect — we may be able to persuade her to spy for us and see what other information he has passed on to the Spanish. We will promise to spirit her away and protect her should he ever suspect her role but it may yet pay greater dividends to leave Douglas with her husband."

"Of course," said Katherine, her eyes wide with awe.

"These are hard won lessons, my dear," murmured Elizabeth. "There have been many occasions when I have needed to rely on my intelligence, my nerves and my wits. Sometimes, you have to be as cunning and cruel as your enemies in order to protect yourself and those you love."

Katherine nodded but did not speak.

"Ladies, let us finish this ridiculous ritual of dressing me up as a Tudor queen, then Katherine, I'm afraid I will require your services again. We must reply to Lady Fortune, Artemis and Mignonne."

"Yes, Your Majesty."

In a flurry of pinning, painting and preening, Elizabeth watched in the mirror as she was transformed. Lettice departed in order to oversee the running of her great house. Kate, too, begged leave in order to see her husband who had arrived in the early hours of the morning, while Katherine, with Bess as her secretary, settled herself at the writing desk and waited for Elizabeth's dictation.

Twisting the ruby ring on her finger, Elizabeth forced herself to think rationally. The light from the morning sun flashed across the deep red stone. It was the jewel handed to her by her former stepmother, Lady Anne of Cleves — the gentle German woman who had been treated so appallingly by her father but who had found an unexpected friendship in her successor, young Catherine Howard.

It was Anne who had commissioned the two rings so she and Catherine could use them as a secret means of communicating. They had each owned a seemingly identical jewel and had used the secret chamber at the centre of the ring to pass the ciphers for their letter codes. The only difference in the two gems were the tiny levers that worked the mechanism to open the inner chamber. Catherine's had a sapphire clip and this she had given to her baby daughter. Anne's was set with an emerald and it was this ring that now adorned Elizabeth's elegant fingers.

Lady Anne was the first keeper of Catherine's secret, thought Elizabeth, and she passed the information to me. What a night that had been, she pondered, reliving the desperate night-time ride in her mind's eye. The air had been icy and they had all been aware of the terrible consequences had they been caught on the road so late at night. Lady Isabel Baynton; Isabel's eldest son, Henry Baynton and Robert Dudley had accompanied her as she answered the deathbed summons of the old queen. At the last moment, Robert had insisted two of the Dudley guards join them. For Elizabeth, there had also been the dreadful fear that she would not reach the Lady Cleves in time.

The night had held so many surprises. The first had been the ring; the second was the revelation of the other heirs; then there was the casket of letters and the surprising confessions. Elizabeth could see it clearly in her memories. Was it nearly 30 years since they had fled into the darkness?

Time, she thought, has woven its web around us. Elizabeth had been a child, only nine years old, when Catherine had been removed from the palace. Another step-mother taken from her, another mother-figure expunged by her father.

I made a promise to myself that night as we rode through the darkness, thought Elizabeth, *I promised that one day I would protect them all. I am Queen. It is my job to ensure the safety of my subjects, it is my job to protect my heirs.*

A small smile played around her lips; when they were younger, they had used other names. Secret names. The codenames Artemis and Apollo had come with adulthood. If they had indeed been compromised, then their aliases may also have been deciphered. Perhaps it was time to return to childhood, to allow her ladies to know this other name for her sister. The other name she once used. Clearing her throat and watching as Katherine placed her pen on the paper, ready to write, she began to dictate, confident that even if this note was intercepted, no one would know who had written it or where it was going:

My Dear Daisy, I write now as Lily, all other names forgotten, it is time for you to move to safety. You must prepare yourself for transportation to Tixall Castle...

PART THREE: November, 2018

Chapter One

Perdita padded along the corridor, a bottle of red wine in one hand, two glasses in the other, looking for her sister. Since the wedding, Piper had been using the algorithm she was writing to search for the missing ruby ring as an excuse to avoid everyone, including Perdita, working until late into the night and falling into bed as soon as she arrived back in the apartment. Perdita had decided enough was enough. She knew Piper had heard from Jeremy but once again she was bottling things up and Perdita was desperate to try and help her sister.

"Knock, knock!" she called as she entered the library.

Both twins loved this room, and even though it was smaller than their own library at Marquess House, it was well stocked and much quirkier. It was situated in the old dungeons but was far from gloomy and with a reinforced glass ceiling covering half of it to let in the mountain light, with the occasional transparent brick in the wall doing the same, it was a unique space. When she had first seen it, Perdita had wondered whether so much light would damage the rare books but Deborah had assured her that anything of value was stored well away from the sun's harsh rays.

Piper was in the far corner of the room, near the electric stove.

"Apparently, a real fire in a library is against insurance regulations," Kit had said when Perdita had lamented over the fake flames. She had had the grace to laugh.

Piper was so engrossed that she ignored Perdita's first call.

"Pipes?" said Perdita, approaching her sister but still Piper did not look up. Perdita put her hand on her sister's shoulder and Piper nearly leapt out of her seat.

"Oh my god, you shocked me!" she said, pulling out her earphones.

"Sorry, I hadn't realised you were plugged in," laughed Perdita. "What are you working on?"

"The algorithm still!" yawned Piper, stretching. "Oh, wine! What time is it?"

"Not late, 7.30, but we have a Mackensie-free evening ahead of us and I thought a glass of wine in our favourite room would be a good place to start. Deborah has even given us her permission, as long as we promise not to spill it over anything."

Piper grinned. "How wonderful," she said. "Let me save this, then I'm all yours."

While Perdita busied herself with the corkscrew, Piper turned back to her monitor and began saving the many pages she had scattered across the screen.

"How's the algorithm going?"

"Good, finally. It's taken a while because I've had to keep tinkering with it, eliminating certain search criteria and adding others. You wouldn't believe how huge the two databases are, Perds. Granny's collection of documents is vast but the Jerusalem archive is staggering. I think if we're going to find anything, it'll be in there." Piper paused and sipped her wine. "It's made me realise something though, Perds."

"What's that?"

"The Mackensies really are a force to be reckoned with."

"In what way?"

144

"The documents are all marked, so it's clear which collection they belong to, ours or theirs, and the Jerusalem logo pops up far more frequently than the Marquess House initials. Their database contains some incredibly rare documents from all around the world, not to mention a vast art catalogue, too. Did you know they owned a Picasso which is on permanent loan to the Reina Sofia in Madrid?"

"No," said Perdita, "but then to be honest, Pipes, I've had enough difficulty getting my head around our new wealth and all that goes with it, I haven't had time to contemplate anything else. I suppose it's obvious, though — you don't own a 12th century castle without having a lot of money, not to mention a house in London and other properties around the world."

"So, why do they work for us?"

"What do you mean?"

"Why do they run Marquess House for us? Why do they go out of their way to make our lives easier when they have more than enough to do with their own holdings?"

Perdita was about to respond that she had no idea when something Kit had said floated into her mind. "When Kit told me about MI1 and Mum's murder, the afternoon by the lake, he said the Mackensie family had always been the lord chamberlains to the women at Marquess House — that they were there to make our lives easier."

"But why?"

This time Perdita did shrug. "I've no idea, which makes me wonder about what Kit said to me on the night of the first party running up to the wedding."

"Which part?"

"The Suki Merriweather bit — how she wanted a rich husband. Kit must be loaded in his own right. She clearly fancies him and if she's after wealth, surely Kit would be a perfect choice."

"Maybe as the younger son, he isn't?" suggested Piper.

"Possibly."

"Would it bother you if she made a play for him?"

It was the first time Piper had broached the subject since Perdita had told her about Kit's unexpected revelation. Perdita took a glug of wine. "Honestly?" she asked and Piper nodded, although the teasing look was gone from her eyes. "Yes."

Piper allowed herself a small smile. "What's stopping you, then?"

Perdita put down her glass, suddenly restless — her intention had been to discuss Piper's love life, not her own. Although, now Piper had posed the question, she was secretly relieved to be able to discuss her feelings for Kit. She stood up, prowling up and down in front of the fire.

"I didn't tell you everything I discovered that night," she said at last.

"Do you mean there was more than the Suki Merriweather revelation?"

"Yes. I found out what really happened between Kit and Lydia, and why." The story was told within minutes and by the end, Piper's eyes were wide with surprise.

"Do you believe them?"

"Yes, I think I do," said Perdita. "The trouble is, I'm not sure how I feel about Kit. I like him a lot," she admitted, "but after what happened with Warren, I feel quite battered emotionally. I wouldn't want to start something with Kit, then have it fall apart."

Piper got up from her chair and crossed the space between them in a moment, giving Perdita a huge hug. "Want to talk about something else?"

Perdita hugged Piper back. "Definitely, but if I change my mind about Kit, I'll let you know."

"Good." Piper topped up their glasses then said, "How are the letters going?"

Sipping her wine, Perdita pulled a face. "The archive is fascinating but there are so many letters and we're nowhere near finishing transcribing them yet," she said. "In their raw state, they're not always coherent. Izabel and the Marquess House team have put them into chronological order but sometimes we only have an outward-going letter with no reply, so the questions within the letter remain unanswered. The same applies with letters received — sometimes they refer to things that haven't been mentioned before in any of the letters in our collection. There were obviously even more women involved in this writing circle than those we have correspondence for."

"What are the letters about?"

"A vast range of subjects. This afternoon, I finished reading a small collection between two women who sign themselves Lily and Daisy, which are probably codenames, and who were part of Elizabeth I's court. One was very ill — in fact, she was dying and wanted to be released from her pain — while the other, who's a relative, was devastated at the thought of being left alone. I think they were sisters but it's hard to tell."

"How interesting," mused Piper. "There are stories within the story. I thought it would be tedious court letters about the cost of servants with the odd coded message thrown in."

"The difficulty we have at the moment are the codenames they use for each other and for certain places," continued Perdita. "Although we have a number from a core group of women, until we can start cross-referencing these coded names with historical events and try to evaluate who might be whom, it doesn't make much sense. There's something else, too — the letters also share the most peculiar syntax, something which Granny Mary has suggested in her notes could be another aspect of the code."

"Wouldn't any irregularities be because of the writing style back then?"

"At first, I thought so, but after a while I realised it wasn't that. There are words and phrases that they use to describe things which feel odd, disjointed, and so I would have to agree with Granny that it's a form of code. You know, rather than me referring to you as my twin sister, I might use a euphemism like my Gemini or mirror image and it feels like that, as though they're deliberately disguising their real meaning with a series of riddles. The trouble is with any form of code, unless you have a cipher, they're difficult to break."

"If it's only word puzzles, though, we might stand a chance."

"True," said Perdita. Piper turned back to her keyboard. "Pipes, before we get on to the algorithm, do you mind if I ask you something?" Piper's shoulders tensed but she nodded. "Have you heard anything from Jeremy?"

Piper's sigh was resigned. "Yes," she said, spinning her chair around to face Perdita again. "I had an email today. He's left his job and decided to clear his head by going travelling with Kirstin. It seems she works on short-term contracts and her next job is at a tea plantation in India. Jeremy has decided to use *our* savings and take a year off to go with her because, in his words, he might as well spend it as I certainly won't need the money anymore."

Perdita was horrified. "Oh, Pipes, I'm so sorry," she gasped. "How can he have changed so much? This isn't the Jeremy we grew up with!"

"You'd be surprised, Perds — over the past few years he's become very materialistic and much harsher. I told Alistair about it this afternoon and he suspects Jeremy may file for divorce soon to try to claim some of my inheritance. Next week, he's going to put a team of London solicitors who specialise in big divorce cases on alert in case we need to move quickly."

"And is that what you want, too? A divorce?"

"Yes. Our marriage hadn't been great for a while and then Jeremy became obsessed with making money and it was a side to him I'd never seen and didn't like. He started being very controlling and argumentative. Then Kirstin popped up. OK, I know she deliberately targeted him, like Warren did with you and Rory, but it didn't take much to dislodge him, did it? I can understand why you're wary about getting involved again," said Piper. "Love is difficult enough to get right without interference from shadowy government departments."

"Put like that, you might have a point," smiled Perdita, although her mind flickered towards Kit and she checked her phone to see if he had sent a message. When there was nothing, she pushed these thoughts aside and turned back to her sister. "Tell me about the algorithm."

"Thanks Perds," said Piper. "Work is so much easier than messy emotions. Now, if I've got it right this time, which I think I have, it should work its way through the Jerusalem and Marquess House archives and match key words, you know, like a search engine but tailored to our needs. I've had a few trial runs and the first one was far too broad because it threw out 200,000 hits or something stupid, so I've been refining it to ensure the search is unique to our ring. Shape, size, the Latin quotation, and with luck, it'll show us if there is anything even vaguely similar."

"That sounds incredible, shall we give it a try?"

"We might as well, then if it doesn't work, I can tinker with it some more."

Piper wheeled her office chair back up to the desk and Perdita joined her. After a few moments of keying in passwords, Piper turned to her twin and grinned. "Here goes nothing." She clicked the mouse and they waited, barely breathing, then the screen displayed two hits.

"The first is dated August 1736, to the papers of an Elinor Bicton and the second February 1877, the diaries of Ada Winchester. Both in the Jerusalem collection. Pipes, you're a genius!"

Perdita was so excited she could not stand still. Piper's fingers flew over the keyboard as she accessed the digital archive, searching for the two entries so they could read them in their entirety.

"Ada Winchester's diaries are in the section that needs Deborah's ID to access."

"What? No!"

"It's because it's older and hasn't been requested for over ten years," explained Piper. "Let me try the other one first, then I'll find the code, Deborah gave it to me when she knew I was searching deep into the archives."

Perdita felt a wave of relief — to have been so close but to have been forced to wait would have been like torture.

"August 1736, the papers of Elinor Bicton, ruby ring with an engraving in the interior cavity, gold band and sapphire detail," read Perdita, more to herself than to Piper, as her sister typed in the details.

"I've found them," said Piper, her voice trembling with excitement.

Perdita leaned forward and after reading the document said, "It certainly matches the description. Listen to what she's written on page five: 'Today my father's present revealed its secret. If the tiny sapphire clip is moved, the body of the ring opens to reveal a Latin inscription, *Semper Sorores*, which I believe means Sisters Always. Within the base of the ring is another secret. If touched carefully, it opens to reveal a picture of a lady. She is very pretty; her hair is auburn and her eyes are blue. At her throat is the tiniest and most exquisite of necklaces, a silver locket, I think, and it is set with a real diamond. I suspect my father does not know the diamond is there or he would never have given me anything so valuable. The interior will remain my secret'. This one has a miniature inside it," said Perdita in surprise. "I wonder if ours has, too, and I didn't see the mechanism when I was examining it."

"Where's the ring?"

"In the vault where Alistair keeps all the valuables, so we'll have to wait until... Damn. Kit said his parents might not be back until tomorrow evening."

"Do you think the portrait is supposed to be Catherine Howard?" asked Piper.

"Almost certainly," replied Perdita. "It even references her wearing the locket with its diamond." She scanned through the document again, then asked, "Can you do another search on Elinor Bicton? We'll need to discover all we can about her to try and work out how she got the ring, what happened to it next and whether she has any connections with Ada Winchester."

Piper turned back to the screen and began typing. Perdita pulled her chair up next to Piper's as she tried as many variations of the name as possible but was frustrated at every turn. "Nothing, nothing," she murmured, then suddenly, "Oh, a copy of her will."

"Really? Can we access it?"

"Yes."

Pulling it up on the screen and enlarging it, the twins stared at the handwritten document. Perdita picked up Piper's notebook and began transcribing it, voicing her thoughts as they worked their way through it.

"Elinor Bicton was the daughter of Lazarus Bicton and she died in March 1789. With no children of her own, she left the ring to her goddaughter, Marianne Jefferson, the daughter of her best friend, Emma."

As Perdita wrote, Piper tapped a series of commands into the computer and nudged her sister.

"Look, an obituary of Lazarus Bicton, Elinor's father."

"Pipes, you're brilliant," Perdita exclaimed, before reading the short piece. "He was a well-respected, middle-ranking jeweller, no big aristocratic customers but plenty of wealthy captains of industry. I bet that's how he came across the ring, then he gave it to Elinor, who bequeathed it to Marianne Jefferson."

Using the secure IP address within the computer's library system Perdita and Piper sifted through marriage, birth and census records, tracing Marianne's family for the next hundred years and discovered she had had three children, the youngest a girl called Laura who had been born in 1790. Laura then married and gave birth to a daughter, Evangeline Barratt.

When Piper tapped in this new name, she discovered a newspaper cutting from July 1864, naming her as having helped to organise an exhibition of Tudor jewellery, including her own family heirloom, a ruby ring.

"Amazing work, Pipes," Perdita said. "If that's the missing ring, we now know it still existed in 1864. Only a few years separate Evangeline Barratt and Ada Winchester, so with luck, her diaries might close the gap. Shall we start on those next?"

Piper saved the link, then pushed herself away from the computer. "No, I think we should call it a night," she said. "I'm too tired. Let's come at it bright and early in the morning."

With a slightly disappointed expression, Perdita agreed. "OK, you're probably right," she said, stifling a yawn. "So much for our relaxed evening."

Piper grinned. "Incidentally, you didn't say where everyone had gone."

"Alistair and Susan are having dinner with the Merriweathers and will be staying over; Stuart is at a party and Kit's taken Callum to one of their old haunts."

"Didn't he invite us?" asked Piper, sounding hurt.

"Kit or Stuart?"

"Both."

"Stuart did, but without any real enthusiasm. Kit said there's a girl at this party that Stuart has been trying to impress for a while, so I think we'd have been a massive hindrance. Kit was a bit torn — he wanted to but I think he also wanted to have a boys' night, so I told him we didn't want to intrude," said Perdita.

Piper's faced cleared. "Fair enough. I wondered if Callum was avoiding me, you know, after the Kirstin incident."

"Kit did tell me Callum is nervous about upsetting you again," admitted Perdita.

"He has no need to be. I'll have to find him and explain. I should probably apologise for my crazy reaction, too," said Piper, then yawned again.

"Come on, let's go back to the tower," said Perdita. "When Alistair comes home tomorrow, I'll ask him for the ring."

"And maybe next week I'll sort myself out a new phone," sighed Piper, staring at the blank screen. "This one has been playing up for ages. It keeps vibrating and trying to charge itself even when it isn't plugged in. Stupid thing."

Perdita laughed, "It sounds as though it's possessed."

"It sounds as though it should be hit with a hammer," replied Piper.

Chapter Two

"Good morning, my dear," said Alistair, as he joined Perdita in her office. "Here's the ruby ring." He placed a long velvet jewellery box on the desk in front of her.

"Oh, Alistair, thank you," she said. Perdita cleared a space and reached into her drawer for her roll of jewellery-making tools and an eyeglass. Over Alistair's shoulder, she saw Kit arrive in his own office and beckoned to him.

"Morning Dad," he chirped, then grinned at Perdita. "Morning you." To her horror, Perdita blushed.

"Deborah showed me the extract from the papers describing the ruby ring we think might be the companion to our own. Do you think there could be a false bottom in this ring, too?" Alistair asked.

"In a few moments, we'll know," said Perdita as Piper joined them.

Pulling on a pair of protective gloves, Perdita flipped open the velvet box and gazed upon the beauty of the ancient ruby ring. Selecting the steel scribe from her tools, she turned the piece of jewellery over and, with great care, pushed the mechanism to release the catch. Shining a high-powered torch into the interior, she turned it around to face Piper, Alistair and Kit.

"Do you see the inscription in the top half?" she asked, pointing to the tiny letters.

"It's exquisite," said Alistair. "If only Mary could have seen it."

Perdita did not reply; it was a regret she, too, was still trying to come to terms with.

"The Bicton papers say Elinor pressed the bottom plate and it released," said Piper as Perdita inserted her eyeglass and placed the ring on the safe suede surface of the interior of the jewellery box. Once again, she noticed her hands were trembling with excitement and, had she been on her own, she would have savoured this moment of anticipation for longer but she could feel the desperate silence of the father and son opposite her, not to mention Piper's eagerness as she leant over Perdita's shoulder.

Taking a deep breath, she pressed the steel tip down into the base of the ring, applying gentle pressure. To her surprise, it moved and a line appeared down the middle of the golden base. Teasing the metal across with the narrow pointer, it gave easily and both sides slid into custom-made slots revealing an exquisite miniature portrait of a woman in a Tudor headdress, her dark hair visible at the front.

Perdita gasped, gazing at the woman's image. The dark eyes peered out across the centuries, deep, unfathomable, majestic against the paleness of her skin. The unique pendant around her neck marked her out but, if there was any doubt, at the base of the tiny painting were the initials AB.

Staring at the woman's face, Perdita felt humbled. She was so familiar from portraits, documentaries and years of studying history but here, seen in an original form, the woman's features were softer, prettier and her wide, dark eyes twinkled with mischief. Drinking in the beauty of the extraordinary piece of jewellery with its hidden secret, Perdita wiped away an unexpected tear.

"It's Anne Boleyn," she murmured and angled it so first Piper could see it, then Alistair and Kit.

"Are you certain?" asked Alistair, struggling to pull on a pair of protective gloves so he could take the ring.

"Look at her necklace," said Perdita. "It's the famous 'B' pendant that she wore so often in portraits."

Alistair handed the jewel to Kit, who peered at the minute image.

"Perds, this is unbelievable," he said, handing it back to her.

"This means the ring mentioned by Elinor Bicton could be the second ruby ring," said Piper. "It has the correct inscription and another hidden portrait, which proves that when these miniatures were added they were still being treated as a pair."

Perdita took the ring from Kit and once again placed it on the surface of the box, taking a series of photographs of the interior and uploading them on to her computer so they could see the images in greater detail.

"What do you think it means, Perds?" asked Kit.

"At this stage, I'm not sure. Who would have added pictures of Anne Boleyn and Catherine Howard? They were cousins but there was a significant age gap between them and I'm not sure if they ever even met."

"It's baffling," admitted Alistair. "I have another meeting so I'll leave this in your capable hands. Please be sure to return it to the vault each night. We never leave valuables lying around."

Perdita nodded and returned her gaze to the miniature.

"May I?" asked Kit, leaning over and pointing at the ring.

"Of course," she replied, placing it in his gloved palm.

Piper moved nearer the monitor and studied the image on the screen, her painter's eye looking for tell-tale clues as to the possible artist. Perdita moved away from the desk, her hands in the pockets of her short green skirt as she walked around the office, deep in thought.

"Elizabeth I," she said, after a long silence.

"What about her?" asked Piper, turning to meet her sister's gaze.

"She owned a very beautiful example of what was known as a Tudor locket ring, which contained dual portraits of herself and her mother, Anne Boleyn. It was mother-of-pearl and, like our rings, was set with rubies. On the top was a letter 'E' made from six diamonds, which was overset on a pale blue enamelled letter 'R' and there was a pearl on the side. It was hinged to open to reveal the pictures within; would it be beyond the realms of possibility that our ruby ring was the inspiration for the other locket ring?"

"It's possible," said Piper.

"But why would Elizabeth have what we now know is Anne of Cleves's ring?" queried Kit.

"I don't know," replied Perdita, "but I feel as though the answer is somewhere staring us in the face and we're missing it." Sweeping her hand through her hair, she turned away from Kit and Piper.

When they had found this ring, she had hoped it would provide answers but it had only delivered more questions, more mysteries to solve. Was this a ridiculous and impossible task? They were lucky that their ring had been hidden for centuries and lay undiscovered, but was it possible the second ring could also have survived? They could date it to 1864 but what had happened to it next? She knew Piper planned to work on the second series of documents they had located: the Ada Winchester diaries, but would they be lucky twice in finding these tiny pieces of ancient jewellery?

She wandered to the window and gazed out at the angry sky. How do the rings prove beyond all reasonable doubt that Catherine Howard was the mother of two legitimate Tudor heirs? she thought. Especially if one ring contains a portrait of

Anne Boleyn. How could the jewellery be anything other than another piece of interconnected information rather than a means of proof in its own right?

"Perds, what's wrong?" asked Piper. "I thought you'd be excited."

"I am," she said, turning back to look at her sister and Kit, both of whom were watching her with concern. "Very excited, but I'm also frustrated and confused. None of this makes any sense and I'm beginning to worry that it never will." Neither of them spoke and she understood that this was their concern, too. "Maybe we should give up and spend the rest of our lives in luxurious hiding," she sighed, staring back at the snow.

The phone on her desk rang and Kit answered it, his voice rising in excitement.

"Perds, we need to pack up the ring and give it to Dad for safekeeping," he said, his tone urgent.

"Why?"

"Izi and Eveie have found something they think might be important and they want us to meet them downstairs in the boardroom."

"Now?"

Perdita hurried back to the desk and with great care replaced the covering over the portrait, then clicked the secret compartment back into position before placing the ring back in its box.

"I'll take it. I'll see you downstairs in a minute," said Kit and dashed off.

"Hiya," said Izabel as Perdita and Piper hurried through the boardroom door. Perdita dumped her laptop bag on a chair. Izabel and Eveie, one of Deborah's assistants, were examining a spreadsheet that they had placed on the long polished table.

159

Next to this were photocopied pages, numbered like exhibits in a court case. Perdita recognised some of them as letters from the Lady Pamela archive but to her surprise there were others and these, too, were familiar.

"Are these from Lady Kathy Knollys's Book of Hours?" she asked, pointing to a selection of colour copies at the far end of the table.

"Yes," replied Eveie, "we wanted to double-check before we showed you what we'd discovered, then we hoped you might be able to explain it."

"What have I missed?"

Kit hurried through the door and his attention was also caught by the variety of pages the two women had selected.

"Nothing yet," said Izabel. "Eveie and I have been cross-referencing the data from the letters and we noticed something odd concerning the Book of Hours. Am I correct in thinking it was discovered in the box with the Lady Pamela letters?"

"Yes," confirmed Perdita. "Whether Granny had known it was part of the cache or whether it was a separate purchase added to the box at random at a later date, we have no idea. Jenny says there will be accounts and a receipt but we haven't checked it yet. I didn't think it was relevant."

"It might be," said Eveie. "We think the Book of Hours was put there deliberately because it's connected to the letters."

"How?" asked Kit. "I've spent a long time writing a report on the Book of Hours — did I miss something?"

"You didn't miss anything — your notes are where we think we've found the link," said Izabel. "It might be nothing but we thought we'd better check."

"Remind me about the Book of Hours," said Piper, sliding into the seat beside Izabel. Eveie was on her other side, Perdita and Kit sat opposite.

"The Book of Hours," supplied Kit, "was a devotional book, a prized object and one owned by women of rank. This one is a remarkable document, partly because of its age — 16th century — but also because of its provenance. It once belonged to Lady Kathryn Knollys, the daughter of Mary Boleyn."

"We then discovered Kathryn had been part of Catherine Howard's inner court and was privy to the secret of Catherine's children being born at the priory on the island of Marquess House's lake, Llyn Cel," continued Perdita.

"The book doesn't stop with Kathryn, though," added Kit. "She died on 15 January 1569 and her Book of Hours was passed to her second eldest daughter, the infamous Lettice Knollys."

"Why did it go to her and not the eldest daughter?" asked Piper.

"According to a note in the book, the eldest daughter, Mary Knollys was given a jewelled pendant, Lettice was the next oldest and she inherited her mother's book," replied Kit. He examined the pages on the table. "What have you discovered?" he asked.

Izabel pointed to one of the exquisitely illuminated pages, "This lettering," she said. "The image on the page is a standard depiction of the Virgin and Child, but this detail around the edge appears to have been added afterwards." She flicked up a hugely magnified image on to the screen at one end of the room and using a laser pen, traced the light down the decorative edging.

Perdita leaned forward to examine it. "I remember Kit telling me that the borders of swirling acanthus style leaves were typical of Ghent and Bruges decorations," she said, "while the stylised drawings of the figures leans to the Dutch style. I take it the lettering is an anomaly."

Eveie nodded. "We've checked it against as many examples as we've been able to find and no other Book of Hours from this period has lettering in the borders. This is why we think it was added later."

"I don't understand," said Piper.

Perdita, however, had moved towards the screen and was examining the tiny letters — with each revelation, her eyes widened in surprise. What she had taken to be unusually shaped flowers or stylised Mediaeval birds were all tiny letters, but rather than running from left to right, they ran from top to bottom. Yet if they were read in sequence, they spelled out a name.

"Artemis," said Perdita. "It's one of the codenames in the letters."

"One of the celestial twins," said Kit, comprehension dawning on his face.

"Twins?" questioned Piper, exchanging a look of understanding with Perdita. "Is Apollo mentioned anywhere? Artemis was the female deity of the moon and he was her twin, the god of the sun."

"Yes, here," said Perdita, tracing her finger along a row of letters that were intertwined with the name Artemis. "This must be a reference to Catherine's twins: Nicholas and Elizabeth Tudor."

A shiver of excitement ran down her spine.

"Do you think they would have used such obvious names?" asked Piper.

"They're not that obvious, though," responded Kit. "If you put the codenames in the context of the period, only those of noble rank would be educated enough to have knowledge of mythology. There were very few people who would have understood the reference."

"For us, it means we have another record of them," said Perdita as she continued to examine the image. "This shows both twins had survived, for a while, at least. Why are there only letters on one side of the image?" She turned back to Izabel and Eveie, "Are there any more of the codenames hidden in the Book of Hours?"

"We think so," replied Eveie, grinning.

"We've made a list of what we've found so far," said Izabel pointing to a folder, "but we thought you'd want to continue from here."

"Thank you," said Perdita. "We will, although you're very welcome to stay."

"I'd love to but I'm heading home today," replied Izabel. "We wanted to show you this before we left. Elliot is flying me home this afternoon." She nodded towards the suitcases standing by the door.

"And I'm going, too," added Eveie. "I haven't seen Nan for a while."

Piper looked confused.

"We're cousins," explained Eveie.

"It really is a family business, isn't it?" said Piper.

"This was our last task and now we really do have to dash," said Izabel, pulling on her coat.

"Please send everyone our love," said Perdita, hugging them, one after the other. "We hope to be home soon."

"Good luck with this," said Izabel.

"Give us a call when you're back and we'll update you," called Kit, who had remained by the screen and waved goodbye. "Ring Perds, she's in charge," he added with a wink in Perdita's direction. She raised her eyebrows at him and he laughed.

"All right you two, get a room," sighed Piper.

"I wish," murmured Kit.

"And returning to the matter in hand…" said Perdita, her cheeks flaming. Pulling her laptop on to the table, she flicked it open and brought up a document. "This is the list of all the codenames Izabel and the Marquess House team have come across as they've been digitising the Lady Pamela letters they've worked on so far. Some are classical with Greek references: Astraea — the star maiden; Hebe — the goddess of youth and cupbearer to the gods and goddesses on Olympus; Clio — the muse of history, Artemis and Apollo — the celestial twins — which must be a reference to the missing heirs. While others are more baffling and, I would guess, give a clue to the person they are supposed to represent: Lady Glass; Lady Holbein, Lady Griffin and one that combines the two: Lady Venus. There are flower names, too."

"Did you notice these when you were studying the book, Kit?" asked Piper.

"Yes, but to be honest, with everything else that's been going on, I hadn't yet made the connection. I thought they were odd — it's why I made a note of them."

"Which must have been why Izi and Eveie made the link," said Piper.

"From what I remember, the names are scattered throughout the text, but why?" said Kit. "I'm going upstairs to grab my laptop, too — it's got all my rough drafts on it for my report on the Book of Hours. Be back in a bit."

Perdita and Piper gazed down at the list.

"These are the codenames of people and, possibly, places," said Perdita, running her finger down one column, "which means if they're written in the letters and in the book and we know it passed from Kathy Knollys to her daughter, Lettice, then we must assume at some point both of them were involved in the letter-writing group who referred to themselves as the Ladies of Melusine, whose letters were possibly compiled by Katherine Newton and have passed down the years to Lady Pamela."

"But how did Lady Pamela get such an expensive heirloom from a different family? Wasn't she descended from the Bayntons?" questioned Piper.

"I don't know. Someone must have bequeathed it to her at some point, either that or the final compiler of the letters had it. Remember, the last date we have on the Lady Pamela letters is 12 December 1662, so it could have been given to whoever was still compiling them at that point."

Kit hurried back in; his face serious. "Did you say there were flower names?" he asked.

"Yes, and last week I read a set of exchanges between two women calling themselves Lily and Daisy. There were only a few, so I'm not sure how they're connected to the rest of the letters."

"Lily and Daisy? Are you sure?"

"Positive, why?"

Kit attached his laptop to the screen and flipped up another page he had scanned from the Book of Hours. It was festooned with wreaths of highly coloured vines, leaves and flowers and worked into the Mediaeval bouquet were the words: honeysuckle, sunflower, rose, iris and hyacinth.

"Interesting, but no lilies or daisies," said Piper.

"Look at this," said Kit and directed his laser pen to the top right-hand corner of the page garlanded with flower names. The clear shape of two flowers were lit by the laser's glowing red fire: a lily and a daisy, curled around each other forming a circle. At the bottom of this floral wreath were two interlinked rings, each bearing a heavy red-coloured jewel, while in the centre two tiny golden crowns were linked together by a delicate but melancholy mermaid.

"Lily and Daisy?" whispered Perdita. "Crowned and accompanied by a mermaid?"

"And the rings," added Kit.

This was a vital piece of evidence but as Perdita stared at it, she did not seem to be able to process the information. Instead panic and distress were rising in her but she could not explain why. Kit grinned at her, exuding excitement, delighted for finding such an important clue. Then, she remembered something and, at last, her excitement began to build, replacing the unexplained panic. Rifling through her computer bag, she extracted her own notes.

"Look!"

It was a photocopied page from the back of the Ladies of Melusine manuscript and showed a small blurred photograph of a section of the carved wooden frieze that decorated the older sections of Marquess House. There was the same circle of flowers and, in the centre, two crowns linked by a rudimentary mermaid.

"I don't remember ever seeing that," said Kit. "Is it at Marquess House?"

"Granny states in her notes that this was once part of the frieze but because it was in a very poor state of repair when our ancestor Lettice Lakeby bought the house, she had it removed," said Perdita. "Granny found the photograph and some sketches stored with the architect's plans that were used to renovate Marquess House. Perhaps Lettice or Granny had intended to have it recreated but never got around to it."

"And we're back to mermaids," said Kit. "How does this help us, though?"

Perdita stood in front of the screen, staring up at the beautiful illumination.

"Why have they written the names in the book?" she mused. "To keep a record, perhaps? To pass the information on to the next generation?"

"Both are possible," said Kit.

"But the information would be useless without a key, a cipher to the names?" And then she saw it. "I need a mirror," she said.

Hurrying back to the table she scrabbled for her make-up bag. Pulling out a small compact mirror, she sorted through the pages on the table and found the print-out of the page displayed on the screen. "I knew it was something obvious — look. There's a line down the middle and the image is the same on both sides." She pointed and both Piper and Kit leaned over, nodding in agreement. "Except, it isn't," said Perdita, triumph ringing in her voice. "Look." She placed the mirror on the line facing away from the side where the letters were woven into the image. The other side also had strange markings but it was not until Perdita held the mirror up to them that they made sense.

"They were written backwards," said Kit. "Are they women's names?"

"Yes," breathed Perdita. "Kathy, Mary, Lettice, Elizabeth, Anne, Catherine, Maud…"

"Who were they?" asked Piper.

"I think they're Kathy Knollys and her daughters," said Perdita.

"Why is Lettice written in a different colour?"

Perdita felt a cold shiver run down her spine as an idea floated to the surface of her mind. A thought so staggering, she doubted herself.

"No," she whispered. "It can't be…"

"What?" asked Kit.

"Lettice Knollys was born in November 1543," she said.

"And?" said Piper.

"That's a year after Catherine gave birth to her twins at Marquess House," said Perdita.

"Although birth dates back then are always questionable," added Kit, picking on her train of thought.

"What if the date has been altered? What if she was born in November 1542?"

"Because we know Kathy Knollys was there," said Kit, his face ashen as he realised what Perdita was saying. "We have written proof that she was with Catherine Howard at Marquess House."

"And we know she left shortly afterwards because she's back in the court records in London," said Perdita. "She could have taken the baby with her."

"Are you saying what I think you're saying?" asked Piper.

"Yes," whispered Perdita. "We may have found the first heir. What if Lettice Knollys wasn't Kathryn Knollys's child, but was, in fact, Catherine Howard's missing daughter, the unacknowledged Tudor princess, baby Elizabeth, renamed Laetitia when she was hidden in the household of Kathryn and Francis Knollys. Kathryn was an unacknowledged daughter of King Henry VIII — would it be too much of a leap to suppose she would give a home to her half-sister?"

"Lettice Knollys," she continued. "I don't know — could it be her?"

Despite her excitement, Perdita was unsure whether to commit to this theory yet. *Follow the evidence*, she told herself. *Let it lead you.*

"For those of us without an advanced knowledge of history," said Piper, "who was Lettice Knollys?"

"Lettice Knollys was, as we've said, the second daughter of Lady Kathryn Knollys and Sir Francis Knollys. While Edward VI was on the throne, her parents enjoyed good positions at court because they were Protestants but, like many of the noble Protestant families, they fled into exile when Catholic Mary I took the throne. Lettice was thought to have been left in the care of sympathetic friends and family in England, along with her siblings, while Kathryn and Francis fled to Germany. When Elizabeth became queen, Kathryn, who was related to her officially through her Boleyn blood — her mother was Mary Boleyn — was immediately made a Lady of the Bedchamber."

"And Lettice?"

"She was created a Maid of the Privy Chamber. In July, 1560, she married Walter Devereux, Viscount Hereford and they stayed at court for about a year before heading to the seat of Walter's power in Carmarthen, and from there, they continued to Lamphey Hall in Pembrokeshire."

Piper's eyes were wide with surprise. "Pembrokeshire?" she said. "All roads lead to Marquess House."

"Well, certainly neighbours of Marquess House," said Kit.

"It's strange, though, isn't it?" said Perdita. "Lettice married a man with Welsh heritage, like the Tudors. They were reputedly very happy and had five children. Lettice was also supposed to be a favourite of Elizabeth. However, things went awry after Walter died on 22 September 1576 from dysentery. Almost two years to the day, which was the period of official

169

mourning, Lettice secretly married Robert Dudley, Earl of Leicester, who was Elizabeth's favourite. It has always been claimed that Elizabeth was furious with them both, but it was her cousin, Lettice, who was banished from court and never forgiven. Eventually, Dudley was given back all his privileges and Elizabeth forgave him. Lettice was branded a she-wolf from then on and never allowed to return to court."

Kit spun around and flipped through some images on his laptop before opening it on the enormous screen.

"Look at the corner section with the animals," he said. "There's a she-wolf and around the edge the letters spell out Laetitia Devereux. Lettice's full name was Laetitia and her married name during her first marriage was Devereux."

"Which is odd," said Piper. "If the name 'She-wolf' was supposed to be an insult, why would it appear in the Book of Hours?"

"You're forgetting something," said Perdita. "The brief outline I've given you refers to the official view of history. Isn't it possible the she-wolf name could have been one of affection? It could easily be misconstrued as a negative name or even rebranded as such when history was being muddied in order to put forward the new view."

"It's possible," Kit agreed. "If we take a step back and look at this from another angle, suddenly the derogatory name given to Lettice Knollys all these years might not have been that at all. It could have been an affectionate nickname, a joke perhaps."

"It would seem an odd thing for her to put in her Book of Hours if it was an insult," said Piper.

Perdita twirled her hair around her finger as she considered this new information. Lettice Knollys was the correct age, she was famous for her physical similarity to Queen Elizabeth and rather like her, had lived to a great age — an extremely unusual feat in Tudor England. Elizabeth had died in her seventieth year, Lettice had been recorded as being 91 when she passed away at her family home, Drayton Bassett, near Chartley in Staffordshire, on Christmas Day, 1634. Was longevity another Tudor trait shared by the two women?

Perdita's thoughts returned to Kathryn Knollys. She was a woman whose true parentage still caused debate. There were those who believed she was the illegitimate daughter of Henry VIII, the issue of his affair with Mary Boleyn, and there were those who rubbished the suggestion. Perdita considered the implications of both scenarios.

If Kathryn had been an illegitimate Tudor, would it be so strange to conceal another hidden princess with one who had grown up already keeping a similar secret? The difference, though, was that Kathryn had been illegitimate, therefore she had no claim to the Tudor crown. If Lettice was really Catherine Howard's missing child, she was legitimate and had a very strong right to the throne. On the other hand, if Kathryn Carey had been the daughter of Mary Boleyn and her husband, William Carey, why would she have taken the child? Out of loyalty to her cousin Catherine Howard? If so, this would have put Kathryn and her young family in considerable danger.

Piper stood up. "I'm going to leave you two to wrestle this one out," she said. "Since we've discovered that our ring and the one mentioned in the Bicton papers could indeed be the missing jewellery, I'm going to head back to the library and see if I can find a link between the Bicton papers and the Ada Winchester diaries."

"Cal said he'd be happy to help if you need it," called Kit as Piper reached the door. "He's not strong enough to go back to work full-time yet but he's bored doing nothing."

"I'll give him a shout," said Piper.

Perdita sat down and contemplated the pages strewn across the table. Kit rang through to Deborah and asked if she had any reference books on Lettice Knollys.

"There's only one biography of Lettice," he said. "Deborah says she appears in other people's biographies but the information on her is quite limited. However, she does have a copy of Robert Dudley's account books, and Lettice might be mentioned in them."

"They're worth a look," said Perdita. "We need to either find more evidence to prove the theory that Lettice is the missing princess, or, if she isn't, eliminate her."

After an hour in the boardroom, Perdita and Kit had returned to their separate offices to trawl through as much information as possible on Lettice Knollys before comparing notes.

Due to the lack of direct information about Lettice, Perdita had deduced that the most obvious place to start was with Lettice's more famous husband: Queen Elizabeth's favourite, the charismatic, Robert Dudley, Earl of Leicester. Perdita had diligently worked her way through the bound copy of the earl of Leicester's accounts, searching for mentions of Lettice, but the comments about her were few and far between. This was explained away by a footnote stating most of Lettice's household expenses would have been detailed in a separate set of ledgers, all of which had mysteriously disappeared.

"Convenient," muttered Perdita, before returning to the list of page numbers she had collated.

Opening the book to a section near the back she read another reference to Lettice, then ran her eyes to the bottom of the page where the compiler had pointed out short periods of time when it was difficult to pinpoint Robert Dudley's movements because many letters had been lost. Then another comment caught her eye and she shivered. The compiler stated, "It might be noted that all his correspondence with his wife has disappeared."

All his correspondence? All the letters that Robert had written to Lettice over the ten years of their marriage, not to mention their correspondence before this when they had been friends? It seemed unlikely that this had happened by mistake; for all their letters to have vanished felt as though it had been done deliberately.

Once more Perdita felt the pangs of frustration. Would she ever make sense of all this information? Glancing at her notes, she pulled a dismissive face. Was Lettice or was she not the missing heir? The argument had been persuasive and in the heat of the first moments of revelation, Perdita had thought it was likely but now she felt less certain. She needed solid evidence and the best place to discover that was in the vast cache of Lady Pamela letters. She also found it difficult to dismiss the two women signing themselves Lily and Daisy. Who were they and why was there a flower motive joined to a mermaid and the two rings in an old image from Marquess House?

Deciding she had done enough for one day, Perdita began shutting down her computer when her door was flung open and Piper appeared, followed by Callum and Kit.

Piper was brimming over with excitement and clutching an iPad to her chest as though it were her new-born child.

"What's happened?" Perdita asked, on her feet, immediately infected with their enthusiasm. "The ring?"

"Yes, the ring…" began Piper.

"Your sister is a genius," butted in Callum.

"Something I already knew," smiled Perdita.

"I've been doing more research on Ada Winchester," said Piper, "while Cal's been creating a family tree for Elinor Bicton and filling in the gaps between her and the date we know Ada had the ring."

"What is it? What have you found?"

"A direct living descendant of Ada Winchester," said Piper, her green eyes sparkling in a way Perdita had not seen for months.

"And?"

"Her name is Hannah White and we have a positive picture identification from one of her social media accounts."

"What do you mean?" Perdita was gazing at Piper, aware that Kit and Callum were watching her, waiting for her reaction. Piper tapped the screen of her tablet, refreshing the image.

"Look at the chain around her neck," said Piper.

Perdita gazed down at the image of the tall, slim, dark-haired girl in a white dress, laughing as she held up a vast multi-coloured cocktail to the camera. Around her neck was a long golden chain and hanging from it, like a pendant, glittering in the light of the camera flash was a ruby ring identical to the one they had found in the tunnel under Marquess House.

"No!" Perdita stared at Piper, all thoughts of her own research into Lettice Knollys pushed aside.

"Yes!" squealed Piper. "Yes! Yes! Yes! And, if the ring still exists, the locket might still be out there somewhere, too!"

"Piper, you're amazing!" stuttered Perdita. "How?"

Piper flipped the image away and brought up a series of family tree diagrams.

"Alistair gave us a secure, encrypted IP address to use so we could search present day records," she explained. "All the genealogy websites take you backwards to the census records but present-day Births, Deaths and Marriages records are only available if you have the right passwords. Ada Winchester née Fraser, our last recorded owner of the ring, was an heiress in her own right. In her diaries she explains that she bought the ring from her friend, Emerald Lester, who was selling some of her jewellery. There were no other mentions of the ring in the diary but we found her will. It listed a bequest to her daughter-in-law, Mildred Winchester née Harrison, of 'an antique ruby ring with inner cavity'."

"No!" gasped Perdita.

Piper giggled. "Yes!" she responded, then continued, "Mildred had married Edgar, who was the only child and heir of Ada and her husband, John. They had two children: Ralph, born 1919 and Honor, born 1921. Ralph was killed during the Second World War, but Honor married a man called Stanley Westcote and they had one daughter, Lucy, who married a Mark White, and they had a daughter, Hannah, who has obviously inherited the ring."

"Unbelievable," breathed Perdita, enlarging the photograph of Hannah White in order to take a closer look at the ring.

"Do you think that's it, Perds?" asked Kit.

Perdita examined it with her expert's eye. "It certainly looks the same," she said. "Do we have an address for Hannah White?"

"Not yet," admitted Piper, "but we're going downstairs to discuss it with Alistair. We thought you'd want to be there, too."

"Lead the way!"

The four of them clattered down the stairs, talking excitedly. *The issue we now face*, thought Perdita, as they almost ran down the corridor to Alistair's suite of offices, *is finding Hannah White and seeing if we can persuade her to sell us the ring.*

PART FOUR: July, 1586

Chapter One

"Pembroke Castle has fallen."

Elizabeth stared at Walsingham; her face livid with terror. "The birthplace of my grandfather," she gasped. "When?"

"In the early hours of this morning," said the spymaster. "My messenger informed me only moments ago. Once again, it was silent and bloodless. Men loyal to Philip have been disguising themselves as soldiers and servants, infiltrating the castle over the past few months. With all eyes on the sieges of Carew, Tenby, Llawhaden and Haverfordwest, they timed their attack well, waiting until the garrison led by the duke of Hereford had left to add their support at Carew, then those left behind took control."

"And where is the duke?" asked Elizabeth.

"He is at Lamphey Hall with George Devereux. They're planning their next assault from there."

"And the duchess and their son, William?"

"His wife and son didn't accompany him; they're safe at the duke's country seat, Orleton Hall in Leominster."

Elizabeth felt a flutter of relief amidst the turmoil of emotions racing through her but it was quickly engulfed by the danger of the situation. The king of Spain had now successfully taken five of her Welsh strongholds. Each one may have been centuries old but these buildings were still solid, defendable lines of protection. A wall of grey stone that Elizabeth had always thought was impenetrable, a barrier between the sea and the broad Welsh coast. It was the first line of defence and this ancient barrier was falling to the Catholics.

"Walsingham, we must stop this invasion," said Elizabeth. "We can't allow the Spanish to gain any more of a foothold. I always thought Pembroke Castle was the strongest and safest of all the coastal defences — it's the heart of the Tudor dynasty. This is a devastating blow."

She turned away from the men around the table. Her privy councillors exchanged nervous glances. For weeks she had been pressing Walsingham and Burghley to take her suspicions of strangers fanning out across the Pembrokeshire coast towards the border with England seriously; yet none of them had heeded her words of warning. Without fail, they had dismissed her questions as the nervousness of a woman trying to rule when she was incapable. Elizabeth had once again been underestimated by her privy council. When the threat was dealt with — if it could be resolved in their favour — she would make them pay for their transgressions and they were aware this punishment would follow.

"What is your plan, Walsingham?" Elizabeth demanded, taking her position on the great chair of office under her cloth of state, her brown eyes staring across the room, the fire within them a malediction all of its own.

All eyes turned to the spymaster; no one else dared to speak.

"We are awaiting more news from the duke of Hereford," he said. "Until we know the position of his men and the numbers we can muster, we must proceed with caution…"

"Caution?!" Elizabeth bellowed, rising to her feet. "It was caution that allowed this disaster to develop! This is the time for action, Walsingham. When I warned you about this growing threat, you dismissed me. Perhaps if you had heeded my words we would not be having this discussion."

Lord Burghley cleared his throat as though to speak but Elizabeth flashed him a furious look at his interruption and he subsided.

"You will send your fastest men to discover exactly what is happening. I suggest you begin with Morgan Philipps of Picton Castle, Thomas Revell of Forest, the Wogan brothers: Morris and William of Wiston, Alban Stepney of Prendergast and, with utmost urgency, John Howell, Mayor of Tenby. You may or may not be aware but there is a network of tunnels running down to the harbour…"

"Your Majesty, this is a legend…" began William Paulet, 3rd Marquess of Winchester, his tone dismissive.

"Do not speak unless you are able to improve the silence," growled Elizabeth. "These tunnels exist as certainly as I stand before you. It was thanks to these passageways that my grandfather, Henry VII, and his uncle Jasper Tudor were able to escape from Tenby when they had been routed by the York king, Edward IV. Do you understand now why it's imperative to send word to the mayor of Tenby? These tunnels must be blocked up. I will not have Philip of Spain or his men using them to either escape from our troops or to try and smuggle more men into my realm." Seating herself again, she glared at each member of her privy council in turn, her sweeping look of contempt scorching them. "Why are you all still here?" she asked after a long moment of tense silence, her voice ringing with sarcasm. "You are needed to save my realm. Why are you not hurrying to muster your men?"

She watched as they scrambled to leave, a few trying to retain their dignity, most wishing to be away from her. *The feeling is mutual,* she thought. *If these are the great men of my realm, thank goodness for my women.*

"Walsingham, Burghley and Sir Francis Knollys, you will remain," she called.

Her three most senior councillors paused and she sighed inwardly as they exchanged looks of satisfaction. Did they really think they were staying because she wanted their advice? The men returned to their seats and waited while the hall emptied. Elizabeth rang a bell and four women entered. Elizabeth rose from her chair on the dais and beckoned to the women to join the three elder statesmen at the table.

Kate Howard, Lettice Dudley, Katherine Newton and Bess of Hardwick sat two on either side of Elizabeth, facing the three men. Sir Francis was in the middle, flanked by Walsingham and Burghley. Lettice nodded to her father, Sir Francis Knollys.

"Gentlemen, there is something else of importance that we wish to divulge," said Elizabeth and indicated to Katherine Newton who placed a pile of paper on the table. She selected the top document and passed it to Elizabeth. "This quiet Spanish invasion is a smoke screen," said Elizabeth. "It is taking place in order to distract us from Philip's true plan."

"Which is what?" blustered Burghley.

"An attack that would give him the excuse he needs to launch a full-scale invasion of my realm," Elizabeth continued. "As you are aware, I take information from those close to me very seriously and Bess's granddaughter, Elizabeth Pierrepont, the daughter of Bess's eldest child, Frances Cavendish and her husband, the MP, Sir Henry Pierrepont, has sent disturbing news. She is betrothed to Claude Nau, one of your most trusted double-agents, Walsingham."

Elizabeth pushed the paper towards Walsingham. His face curious, he reached out and taking the parchment, he read the short note.

"And you say this is from someone you trust?" he confirmed.

Elizabeth nodded. "This states that the Spanish sympathisers and their masters plan to kidnap the Scottish queen but to stage the crime so it looks as though it is on my orders," Elizabeth said. "So it is my soldiers, my men, who will appear to hold her hostage. They have said to make it brutal, to harm her."

"But for what purpose?" asked Lettice, sickened by the words.

"Don't you see, Lettice? It is very simple but very clever. Mary is a Catholic and I'm a Protestant. If I am seen to be ill-treating her, Philip has the perfect excuse to ride into my country on a Holy War," said Elizabeth. "He will be one Catholic monarch rescuing another. It's possible this is another reason why he has been placing those sympathetic to Spain across the land."

"Your men have been following the traitor, Anthony Babington," said Sir Francis Knollys to Walsingham. "What have you discovered? If this information is indeed true, then we are dealing with a far more complex plot than we first expected."

Walsingham shuffled the pile of documents in front of him and removed a lengthy scroll. He hesitated, unsure whether to pass it to Elizabeth or Katherine Newton who had reached towards him. Elizabeth nodded to Katherine and with a disgruntled snort, Walsingham handed it her. She unrolled the parchment and held it close while she read.

"Explain in brief, Walsingham, while Katherine absorbs the details," said Elizabeth.

With a scowl, the spymaster spoke: "Through the efforts of my trusted agents, Thomas Phelippes, Gilbert Gifford and

Robert Poley, we have been able to ascertain the names of the ringleaders of the Catholic plan to kidnap the queen of Scots on behalf of the Spanish king, however, we were not aware this assault would be made to look as though it was a direct order from yourself, Your Majesty."

Elizabeth shifted. Mignonne's note had named one man, a young, easily led scholar, Chidiock Tichbourne, as being one of Babington's loyal men.

"I may be able to persuade him to tell me their secrets," she had written in her last note to her grandmother, Bess. Walsingham, it seemed, may have discovered others.

"Tell me their names," demanded Elizabeth, wondering which of her subjects had once again betrayed her.

"John Ballard, a Jesuit priest who has long been under our observation, has been trying to recruit young scholars, through his links with Caius College, Cambridge. He has already recruited Chidiock Tichbourne and has also approached Charles Paget," began Walsingham.

"Approached?" asked Burghley. "What do you mean by approached, Walsingham? Speak clearly man, you're not among your spies and thieves now."

"Charles Paget has not taken Ballard's bait but came to me with the information that Ballard, who sometimes goes under the name Black Fortescue, is using his position to smuggle Jesuit priests from the school at Douai into the country to help him carry out Philip's schemes."

Elizabeth drummed her fingers on the table and stared at Walsingham.

"Who else?" she snapped.

"Your Majesty, the spy Julius is involved but he works alone — those around him have no knowledge of his association with the Catholics and the Spanish," said Walsingham.

"Julius and his wife, Douglas, are in France," she informed the men. "As far as we know they are in the court of the de Medici's."

"And while they are there, they are unable to hurt you, my dear," said Sir Francis Knollys. "If they have fled, let us leave them where they are. It is only if they return we need to deal with them."

Elizabeth was about to protest but his experience and wisdom had highlighted the truth. Her troops were spread thin: the bulk of her men were in Holland with Robert Dudley, Earl of Leicester. There were more riding to support the duke of Hereford in the defence of the Welsh coast — he also had a battalion mustering men along the border between England and Wales in order to delay or stop any other invaders. To send men to pursue Edward and Douglas Stafford in France would be a waste of resources.

Elizabeth gazed into the elderly man's gentle blue eyes — his words were wise and she heeded them. Giving a small nod of understanding, she returned her gaze to Walsingham and Burghley.

"For now, then, Your Majesty, we will set men to watch the Staffords but we will focus our attention elsewhere," said Burghley.

"Others under observation," continued Walsingham, "are the Welsh Roman Catholic priest, Owen Lewis, along with known Catholic sympathisers James Beaton and Thomas Morgan. Both Claude Nau and Gilbert Curle, the two secretaries to the Scottish queen, are in my pay. Of the lords, it is more difficult, as most claim to be Protestant, although the earls of Westmorland and Northumberland are suspected Catholics, as are Baron Vaux and his family, and also Baron Ughtred. They are all in contact with the Welsh cleric, Richard

White, but as yet I have no firm intelligence on their involvement in the coup. My men Nicholas Berden and Francis Mylles continue to work to place these traitors at the heart of the conspiracy. We do know that the Spanish ambassador in Paris, Bernadino de Mendoza is providing a safe house for anyone of noble birth fleeing from this country."

He paused and Burghley butted in. "Your Majesty, considering the religion of the Scottish queen, do you not think she could also be involved in this treasonous plot?"

Elizabeth glared Lord Burghley into silence. "The Scottish queen is our guest and remains under our protection," she said, her voice calm. "I assume the guard around Mary has been increased."

"Yes, Your Majesty. She is currently at Chartley Manor and has guards watching her day and night. However, if we need a dwelling with stronger fortifications, she has suggested a move to Tixall Castle."

Elizabeth gave a small smile of acknowledgement. "And are there updates on Babington? I understand he has fled now that his name and his involvement in this plot have been made public?"

"He is still at large," replied Walsingham. "However, we are tracking his movements and at present, it is more conducive for us to have him free. He thinks his contact with the Scottish queen is going unwatched but we are reading every communication he sends. We are also checking Mary's responses, which are being written under our instructions in order to lure Babington further into the plot. He is a dangerous man, though, Your Majesty, and we will not allow him to continue this endeavour for too much longer."

His tone was light but his eyes were cold. If even half the rumours about Babington's vile behaviour were true then the man was a monster. The sooner they had him locked in the Tower of London the better.

Suddenly, there was a loud knocking. Elizabeth started and looked to Walsingham in astonishment. The door was flung open and Lord Zouche, another member of the privy council, entered.

"What is it?" asked Elizabeth, her voice urgent.

"A note from my wife," he said, looking puzzled. "She insisted I bring it to you at once."

Burghley began to bluster but Lettice was already on her feet and hurrying towards Lord Zouche. The remains of red wax were on the outside and Elizabeth saw the outline of the mermaid seal used by the Ladies of Melusine.

"What does it say?" she asked.

"She has overheard a conversation suggesting there is 'hunting afoot'," said Lettice.

"I have had the same from Richard Bagot," confirmed Walsingham. "He heard it from my man, Phelippes, but we didn't think it could be true. Do you trust this source, Your Majesty?" He nodded towards the letter and encompassed Lord Zouche into the question, who looked affronted at the accusation.

"It is well known that Lord Zouche and his wife Lady Eleanor Zouche are estranged — why would she write to him?" whispered Burghley.

"Because he is at court and can pass the information straight to the queen," snapped Katherine. Burghley glared at her but before he could retort, Elizabeth spoke over him.

"What is 'hunting afoot'? Walsingham, tell us."

"This is the worst news, Your Majesty."

Elizabeth stared at him, baffled, awaiting an explanation. She noted the whiteness of his knuckles as he gripped the edge of the table. Her heart thundered in her chest; she could feel the icy grip of fear enveloping her as she strained forward, wanting but also not wanting to hear the terrible meaning behind the two seemingly innocent words.

"What does it mean, Francis?" she urged him.

With great reluctance, Walsingham met her agitated brown gaze. "It means, Your Majesty, that the plans to take the Scottish queen have advanced and the Spanish are ready to act. Her life hangs in the balance and we must move immediately if we are to save her."

Chapter Two

Hunting afoot.

Two small words, yet they spelled disaster, possibly death. Cold fury rose in Elizabeth as once again she cursed the men of her privy council for not heeding her warning sooner.

Pacing her private chamber in Oatlands Palace, Elizabeth tried to control the rising tide of anger and panic. Despite the fact she was Queen, in this escalating situation she knew her age and her gender worked against her. At almost 53 years old, she remained fit and healthy, thanks to her love of hunting and other outdoor pursuits, but even she had to admit that the three-day hunts she used to partake in during her youth were past forever. These days, she could manage a few hours, maybe a day of riding, but any more would leave her tired and in need of a longer recovery time. Being a woman in a position of power was a daily battle to assert herself over the men who believed her incapable. As her fears escalated for the silent invasion, her dread also grew that in not being a man and therefore able to ride at the head of an army, she might prove her doubters correct. How, as a woman, could she defeat this threat?

Pausing by the window, she shut her eyes, rolling the problem around in her mind, searching for a solution, but she had barely begun to tease apart the nest of thorns when there was a tentative knock on the door.

"Your Majesty?" came Katherine's quiet voice. "Are you well? I have a note for you."

From her tone, Elizabeth knew she was about to be served another devastating blow. Holding out her hand, she took the square of parchment and read Katherine's beautiful flowing script. Elizabeth felt tears spring to her eyes. At such a time, when there were so many upheavals, to hear such news.

"This cannot be so," she snapped, despair making her voice sound harsh, thrusting the letter back into Katherine Newton's hand. "You must have mistranslated it. Check it again."

"I'm sorry, Your Majesty," said Katherine, her eyes lowered, "the content was so shocking, that I checked and re-checked. Bess, Lettice and Kate drew the same conclusions when they translated the words, too."

"But this..." Elizabeth waved towards the piece of parchment. "How is this possible?"

"Elizabeth, you've known for some months that Artemis was ailing," said Lettice.

Elizabeth walked away and stared out of the window at the unbearable, mocking beauty of an English summer's day. Behind her, the loyal four ladies on whom she always relied exchanged a concerned glance. Kate, Lettice, Bess and Katherine: the core of Elizabeth's inner court, her most reliable and trustworthy Ladies of Melusine.

"Read it to me again," Elizabeth demanded, her shoulders shaking with grief.

Katherine glanced at Bess, Kate and Lettice who nodded encouragement, and clearing her throat, she began to read aloud:

"Beloved Lily, I am dying. There is no hope for me but there is still hope for you. This plot must be taken seriously; as should every attempt on your precious soul. You must take care. An idea has been growing in my heart but your reaction, I fear, will be anger. While I live, there will always be danger. If I were to die, the threat would be no more. My death is inevitable, my pain is unbearable, my sweet friend the nun, help me to die quickly. Allow a plot to lead to me, end my pain with a swift swing of the axe. Anything will be better than this slow rotting, living-death I am being forced to endure. If allowing these men to take me will relieve you from danger, then please, do not stop them.

"Remember what we were told of the sweet calm of the Welsh lady when the Judas's worked their evil intent. In my death there will be confession and my beautiful ached for end will let us correct the damage. We will be able to speak with truthful tongues, allowing me to rest in peace. Jezebel and Cassandra will no longer be able to hide their harlotry and wantonness with their dry signature, while our lineage is sullied by their devilish work.

"Help me to die, sweet Lily. Help me to claim my rightful place by your side. I am a legitimate heir, a true Tudor. Help me, my sweet elder sister. Your loving, Daisy."

Elizabeth wiped her eyes. If this letter was in earnest, then there was soon to be another death, another loss. It was not unexpected — the reports had been growing more devastating with each visit of the physician — but she had hoped, prayed, wished for a different outcome. Yet she could not condone the plan that was being suggested. Her mother had died in this shocking and barbarous manner, with every fibre of her being she would resist the same end for another beloved relative.

"I must reply to Daisy," said Elizabeth. "She has been careless with her revelations and if there are spies in our midst who know something of our secret, she may have revealed too much. I can't allow what she suggests to take place but I must impress upon her that she must remain circumspect in her correspondence."

"Her words were hidden. Her reference to your mother as the Welsh Lady will not be understood. Neither will the coded names of your father's later queens — Jane Seymour and Katherine Parr — as Jezebel and Cassandra," said Katherine. "She had drawn a rose on the corner of the letter to indicate there are clandestine words within the lines. Her message was written in lemon juice and woven between a secondary message from Mignonne."

"Was there anything in Mignonne's note that I should know about?"

"Nothing new," said Bess. "The traitor Babington continues to use the barrel method to correspond with the Scottish queen but, at your order and the suggestion of Walsingham, she pretends to be supportive of the plot in order to discover what else the Spanish king plans. Babington has confirmed he is recruiting a group of six men to assassinate you, then Mary will replace you as Queen."

"Yet this is not the plan we have unearthed," said Lettice, in confusion.

"This is Philip's method," sighed Elizabeth. "When he was married to my half-sister, Mary, he would create endless machinations. Each one twisting and turning, like strangling weeds, as he caught us all up in his web. However, in those days, when he would flirt with me, trying to win me over so he could marry me once my sister was dead and continue as king consort, I noticed his terrible flaws."

"And what were they?" asked Kate.

"His arrogance and his laziness," she said. "In his conceit, he believes he alone is more intelligent than those around him and no one but he will ever be able to see through his Machiavellian schemes. Unlike Niccolò Machiavelli who was the consummate politician and ruthless diplomat, never leaving anything to chance, Philip's laziness, his lack of attention to detail and his belief he is untouchable and unstoppable, usually leads to the failure of the majority of his schemes. He relies on friends with similar attributes to himself or men who are not as clever as either he or they believe. I suspect these convoluted intrigues of the king of Spain are built on foundations of sand and will fall away the moment they are hit by our storms of good men. As it says in the Bible, in the book of Matthew: 'And what a terrible fall that was!'." Elizabeth paced restlessly around the room, feeling cooped up and trapped.

"Do you think it's possible anyone could have discovered the truth, Your Majesty? We've always been so careful."

"My fears are that Douglas Stafford has revealed this secret," sighed Elizabeth. "The fact she and her husband have fled convinces me further, though I don't believe it was done maliciously. Edward Stafford is a bully and Douglas has never been strong. I suspect she was tricked into giving this information. She may never have been a member of our writing circle but she is a Howard and this secret has a Howard girl at its heart."

"Your former step-mother, Catherine Howard?" asked Katherine. "My great-aunt."

"Yes, my dear," said Elizabeth. "You weren't born when my father was alive, so let me explain. He was a large and often terrible man and when Catherine's children were born, it was essential he never discovered the truth. My younger half-sister, whom Catherine named Elizabeth, like me, was destined for a special role. Even before her birth, Catherine's uncle, Thomas Howard had been scheming with his brother who had contacts in foreign courts.

"Children were often born unexpectedly and out of wedlock to high-ranking members of society and Thomas Howard was well-versed in placing illegitimate children in places of safety, where their true identities could be disguised until such time as he might need them for one of his schemes. The hiding of a royal princess took all his skills, yet the home he found for her was truly remarkable. Her life has been similarly so, but now we must ensure her death is not on our consciences, for that I could not bear." Elizabeth came to abrupt halt. "I am ready to reply to Daisy's letter," she announced and Katherine hurried over to the writing desk. Opening the drawer at the front, she clicked the mechanism to release the false bottom, revealing a secret chamber where she kept the codes and ciphers most often used by their group. When she was ready she glanced over at Elizabeth and nodded.

Elizabeth thought for a moment, then began to dictate:

"My dear Daisy, you are correct, my response is anger. This idea is a blasphemy. You cannot think this will be the answer to any of our myriad problems. To die a common criminal? You, who has been chosen. This can never be. What precedent would this set? One who is chosen condoning the death of another. My life would be in greater danger.

"We are depicted as women who are enemies; yet we know this could not be further from the truth. We have guarded this dangerous secret in our hearts all our lives and yet you reveal too much, madam, in your latest correspondence. The truth will be revealed when we are both safe and not before.

"This is your illness, your delirium speaking. You cannot mean to follow the path taken by my mother. Reconsider. Do not leave me as the others have, my sweet Daisy. Ever loving, your Lily.

"I must walk in the gardens," Elizabeth said, her voice breaking with emotion as Katherine finished writing. "This room is too small, too dark. I must be outside. There are games taking place and the day is too fine for being indoors."

"But Elizabeth," said Lettice, "is this wise?"

"I am surrounded by guards," snapped Elizabeth. "We will walk and we will partake of some exercise. It will do us all good."

As the women gathered Elizabeth's cloak and sunshade, readying to visit the gardens, Katherine said, "Your Majesty, if you are willing, I will remain here to translate your message to Daisy."

"Of course, Katherine," smiled Elizabeth. "I will tell people your pesky headache has returned."

Katherine Newton gave Elizabeth a brief smile, then turned her eyes back to the note, eager to translate it and send it on its way.

The heralds announced the queen as the doors to her chamber were thrown open. Processing through the palace, Elizabeth glanced around, aware of who was in court and who had fled, wondering whose Catholic allegiances had made them nervous for their positions and their lives. *Oh, these tiresome wars over religion*, she thought as she led the way to the large formal gardens.

It is the same God whether we speak to him in our own tongue or in Latin, she thought, *these men who dictate the terms of the Lord's word, they are the only people who benefit from the wars. If God was a woman, we would have far fewer problems.* Surrounded by her ladies, Elizabeth walked to her favourite part of the Oatlands gardens, the rolling lawns that led down to the wide and majestic beauty of the river Thames. The lifeblood of her capital city, London, and the heart of her England. This was where she felt alive.

A vigorous game of bowls was taking place. Cones had been positioned at either end of the bowling green, with the object being for players to roll their round wooden bowls as close to their opponents cone as possible. Around the two teams of competitors, a laughing crowd had gathered.

Katherine's husband, Henry Newton and his brother-in-law, Sir Ambrose Coppinger, who was married to Katherine's half-sister, Lettice Fitzgerald, and Francis Aungier, who was married to another of Katherine's sisters, Douglas, formed one team. While the opposing team was named The Three Thomases — Thomas West, 2nd Baron De La Warr who was married to Anne, one of Elizabeth's cousins and the sister of Lettice Dudley; Sir Thomas Leighton, who was married to another Knollys sister, Elizabeth, and finally, Thomas Scrope, 10th Baron Scrope of Bolton, who was the husband of Philadelphia Carey, Kate Howard's younger sister. Watching from the sidelines were Lord Robert Rich and his wife Penelope, beside them was Lady Dorothy Perrot, who still looked pale and tired with worry.

They are all my family, thought Elizabeth, as the game halted and she was welcomed into their midst. Cousins everywhere I turn, she thought, but no siblings, not here. They are both far away and, despite my best efforts to keep them safe, both are in danger.

"Your Majesty, would you like to bowl?" called Lord Rich.

Elizabeth waved away his request with a smile and instead made for the arrangement of chairs at the top of the bowling rink. "Not while there is a game in progress," she replied. "I will watch my cousins and have a wager as to the winner."

It felt good to be outside, she thought, as the breeze brushed her face and the laughing, cheering voices resumed as the game began again. In a world of constant threat, Elizabeth felt that the fate of the Welsh coast seemed distant as she sat here, enjoying the sport taking place in front of her. At this moment, her concern was the health of the Scottish queen. When Mary had thrown herself upon Elizabeth's mercy in May 1568, there had been no question about helping her. Although, Elizabeth's ministers had been furious, Elizabeth had immediately placed Mary under the care of her most trusted and close advisor, Sir Francis Knollys.

Part of the reason Mary had fled from her own country and been forced from her throne in favour of her Protestant son, James, was because her second husband, Henry, Lord Darnley had been murdered. Although she had not been involved, Elizabeth's ministers insisted there was a trial in order to clear the Scottish queen's name before she was welcomed into the country. Once again, her privy council feared retribution from outsiders and the excuse for an invasion.

Despite her irritation at these requests, Elizabeth had agreed to a trial and Mary's nobles had fabricated the evidence of the Casket Letters, suggesting Mary was complicit with the plotters of her husband's death, while choosing to ignore the evidence gathered which exonerated her from all crimes. Although, it was all in the past now. Mary had lived in England for 18 years, while her son, James VI of Scotland, who was now 20, ruled in his own right. Yet for most of that time there had been a stubborn silence between the two.

The previous summer, Elizabeth had decided it was time to be the bridge between mother and son. She had begun bombarding James with presents, including, in June 1585, a gift of horses organised by Robert Dudley, which had been the grandest of all. Since then, she and her privy council had been negotiating a league of agreement to win James over. If all went well, then this treaty would be ratified in the next few days and James would be in the pay of English, with Elizabeth giving him an annual pension of £5,000 — a fortune even for a king. The treaty would also recognise him as the rightful King of Scotland. When in earshot of her privy council, Elizabeth had explained that she would need a Protestant heir. James was a Protestant and she hinted if he behaved, he might be the next King of England.

The pension would also buy his silence.

Away from her privy council, Elizabeth had told James the entire story of her half-siblings, so he, too, was a keeper of the secret of the ruby rings. When she had finished, issuing commands of her own, James had knelt fealty to her and promised he would do all he could to uphold her decisions and defend her realm. Three days later, he had visited his mother and their feud had ended in forgiveness and understanding.

But for what purpose if Philip is trying to win my kingdom by stealth? thought Elizabeth, then she shook herself. Although she might not reveal her plans to those around her, Elizabeth was very clear of who she would name as an heir and how she wished her kingdom to be ruled. None of her plans involved an invasion from Philip of Spain.

I cannot let that man steal all I have worked to achieve in the kingdom I inherited from my father. I may have the body of a weak and feeble woman, she thought, *but I have the heart of a king and a king of England, too. I am a Tudor. I will win any battle thrown at me by the Habsburgs. They will never take my throne.*

"Your Majesty…" an urgent voice interrupted her musings.

"William?" she murmured, bemused. He was supposed to be in Herefordshire. "William Fitzalan, Viscount Rutland… Why are you here? Where is your father?"

William was hot, red-faced and covered in dust from the road, yet he beamed when he saw Elizabeth and kissed her hand.

"He is at Lamphey with Sir George," said William. "He and mother insisted I come to you."

"Do you bring news of the siege?"

"Yes," gasped William, whose eyes scanned the crowd, all of whom were staring at him in surprise. "Where's Dorothy?"

On hearing her name, Lady Perrot pushed her way through the crowd, her skirts caught up in her hand as she ran towards them.

"Is there news of my husband?" she asked, reaching her hand out towards William. Lettice and Elizabeth moved closer to her, ready to catch her if the news was bad but William's smile became even wider.

"Sir Thomas Perrot has escaped his Spanish captors," he said. Dorothy shrieked, then her legs sagged and both William and Lettice reached forward to grab her. Moments later, with the help of Penelope Rich and her husband, Robert, Dorothy was seated in the shade, her eyes sparkling with tears of relief.

"William, this is wonderful news," said Elizabeth. "How?"

"He disguised himself as a miller and hid with the other workers when they traversed the mill stream," said William. "Once free from Carew Castle, he sailed around the estuary and using backwaters made his way to Lamphey Hall."

"And he is well and safe?" Lettice interrupted, eager to hear news of her son-in-law.

"Yes, my lady."

"William, this is wonderful news," exclaimed Elizabeth. "Does he have intelligence of the Spanish?"

"He says their hold on the castle is loosening," he reported. "The Catholic nobles who were working with the Spanish are beginning to fear for their lives. They have heard nothing from Philip or his generals since the fall of Pembroke Castle — many are unsure whether the Spanish king will send the support he first promised. With each passing day, the Spanish sympathisers are becoming disillusioned and are beginning to desert. Aunt Elizabeth, I think the siege is breaking. I think we will be able to beat Philip."

Elizabeth gazed into his smiling face but, despite the happiness and delight at his words, she could not rejoice. If Philip was letting the castles slip away from him, then had he succeeded with the other part of his plan? Forcing a smile, Elizabeth turned away, summoning Bess.

"Go to Walsingham," she said, her voice choked with fear. "Tell him we must bring Mary to London; she'll be safer here."

Bess curtseyed then hurried away, while Elizabeth closed her eyes and prayed they were not too late.

Chapter Three

Elizabeth threw the long, velvet cape around her shoulders and fastened it at her neck. She toyed with the cowl hood, trying it in various ways, deciding which would be the most useful for disguising her identity. There were quick, light footsteps as Kate entered, followed by Lady Katherine Newton. Both carried capes similar to Elizabeth's.

"The barge is ready," Kate said in a low voice. "Lettice has sent it from Leicester House. Two of her servants are with it, so we will be safe."

Katherine arranged Elizabeth's hood, obscuring as much of her face as possible. Despite the seriousness of the task ahead, Elizabeth could not help but give Kate a small, nostalgic smile.

"This reminds me of the old days," she said. "Do you remember the day I disguised myself as your maid, Kate?"

"I'll never forget it," Kate replied. "You wore that terrible brown cloak so we could sneak out of the palace unnoticed to watch the boys have their archery contest at Windsor Castle. One boy in particular, if I'm not mistaken."

"Oh yes, back then I had eyes only for Robert Dudley," she admitted. "He was so glamorous."

"And forbidden!" said Kate. "He was married to Amy Robsart."

"He never strayed," sighed Elizabeth.

"Then you met Alencon," Kate reminded her.

Elizabeth paused for a moment as she remembered the young French duke who had wooed her so well. He, like so many others, was dead now but she had mourned him, wearing widows' weeds for six months. It had surprised the French ambassador, Castlenau, when he had visited her to watch the hunt from the newly-built terrace at Windsor Castle a few months after Anjou's demise. It had been a crisp September day and she had still been wearing a long black dress and a diaphanous veil that reached the floor. Without doubt her heart had been broken at the unexpected loss of the man she had always called her 'little frog'. If she was honest, she had never stopped missing him. Shaking her head to clear these sad thoughts, she brought herself back to the present.

"Where are Burghley and Walsingham this evening?" she asked.

"Burghley is at his country estate, Theobalds, for a few days and Walsingham is in Paris," replied Katherine.

"Paris?"

"He had a lead to follow up and he trusted no one but himself with the task," Katherine said. "He wouldn't believe that Edward Stafford was the spy 'Julius' because the intelligence came from a woman. He's gone to confirm it for himself. He also intends to discover what secrets Douglas may have been forced to spill."

Elizabeth frowned. "Walsingham is a good man," she said, "but he has missed so many details of this plot because he's allowed his prejudices to cloud his judgement. I hope he has learned his lesson. However, it doesn't matter — if they are both away, there is nobody to stop us with what we must do this evening."

Kate glanced out into the solar. "Why are there so many of your court here this evening?" she asked, closing the door and leaning on it.

"Probably at Walsingham's order," sighed Elizabeth. "He's trying to make amends for doubting us. Katherine, would you tell the ladies out in the solar that I feel like some fresh air and we will be taking a walk in the gardens. They're not to worry if we're gone a while and they're definitely not to tell anyone. Demand that they retire in an hour as I will go straight to bed upon my return."

Katherine Newton nodded and slid through the doors. Elizabeth knew her women were loyal and no one would gossip about her sudden disappearance but she did not want to give any would-be assassins the opportunity to quietly kill her while she was on one of these night-time jaunts. This was not the first time she had disappeared from the palace and she doubted it would be the last. Not when there was so much at stake.

Elizabeth, Kate and Katherine scurried through the dark passages of Whitehall Palace, following the servants' route to the river below. Elizabeth paced behind the sure-footed Katherine Newton down the steps to the wharf and Lettice's awaiting barge; the Leicester colours, covered with a wooden board in order to disguise it. Throughout her life she had enjoyed moments of subterfuge like this, escaping from her palaces and manor houses in order to spend a few hours away from the trappings of the oppressive Tudor court, to relax with her friends and family, to be, simply, Elizabeth. Tonight though, there were important events to discuss and she doubted there would be much time for leisure.

Two men were waiting: Lettice's trusty footman Thomas Dampard, who was never far from the countess's side, especially when Robert was away from home, and, beside him, the Leicesters' bargeman, Jolyon Gillions. Another trusted member of the earl's staff. He had been with Robert for many years and his wife, Joan, was the chief laundress at Leicester House.

"This way, my Lady Venus," murmured Dampard, helping Elizabeth into the barge. Immediately, Gillions stepped forward and settled Elizabeth on the cushions Lettice had placed in the covered section at the centre of the boat. A moment later, Kate was by her side, tucking a blanket around their legs to keep off the chill of the river. Katherine joined them and, once the women were seated, they heard the soft plash of oars and the barge moved out into the choppy tidal flow of the river Thames.

Crafts of all shapes and sizes filled the wide river on the balmy July evening and the shouts of water boatmen carried over the grey waves, as the sun sank into the gathering clouds. None were aware their beloved queen was among them on the river. As the summer twilight drained the colour from Elizabeth's vibrant capital city, she breathed in the multitude of smells on the busy waterway. Everything from the pleasant scent of the woodsmoke from the brazier on the barge, to the dubious odours of rotting food, dead rats and more besides.

The river was bustling and chaotic, especially as The Queen's Players were opening a new play at one of the theatres in Shoreditch that night. The excitable crowd was heading through the swirling river mist, chattering and laughing in anticipation of a night of riotous entertainment. Elizabeth smiled and settled back against the cushions breathing in her London, her home, her heartland.

"Elizabeth, how wonderful! Come and sit by the fire. The evening has turned unexpectedly cool."

Lettice hurried forward, as ever the gracious hostess.

"My little She-wolf," Elizabeth smiled, forgetting all court etiquette and hugging her cousin. "What news from Robert?"

Lettice indicated to her page to pour wine and arrange refreshments near the chairs that had been set by the fire before taking the seat opposite her cousin.

"A letter arrived this afternoon," she said. "Things continue to flounder but he hopes that now more of his trusted guard has arrived, he will have a proper council of war and his plans will finally come to fruition. I also had a short note from my son, Robert, who is with him. He said that there are good men advising my Lord Leicester — Philip Sidney, Sir John Norris, William Stanley — and Robert's brother, Ambrose, too. He won't fail you Elizabeth."

"I know, my dear," she said.

Kate, Katherine and Dorothy Perrot entered. Dorothy was smiling.

"Aunt Elizabeth," she exclaimed.

"How is Thomas?"

"Exhausted but he asked to be woken when you arrived," she said. "I'll fetch him."

Dorothy hurried from the room.

"And William is here, too?" Elizabeth turned to Lettice as she asked the question, referring to the duke of Hereford's son.

"He is in the games room, playing cards with Penelope. I believe she is relieving him of some of his fortune."

"Good," said Elizabeth, smiling. For the first time in weeks, she felt relief. This evening, at least, she was among friends, safe from spies and able to speak without the fear of being overheard. Usually, these visits were times of laughter and fun but tonight her active mind continued to ponder the problem that would arise every time she was left with a moment to herself: Philip of Spain. He did not scare her but he was an irritant and she was eager to see him vanquished, but to her frustration she had still not divined a way to make this possible.

The door opened, bringing her thoughts back to the present, and Dorothy entered with her husband, Sir Thomas Perrot. He was a tall man, handsome and modest, usually brimming with laughter but this evening he was pale and one side of his face was blackened with bruises. His walk was cautious and he winced when Dorothy accidentally brushed his side. Following traditional etiquette he began to bow but Elizabeth hurried forward and instead led him to her chair by the fireside.

"No formalities tonight, Thomas," she said, passing him a goblet of wine. "You have travelled many miles to bring me news and I appreciate your efforts."

"Thank you, Your Majesty…"

"Aunt Elizabeth," she interrupted, correcting him.

"Aunt Elizabeth," he said and took a sip from his drink, flinching in pain as he manoeuvred himself into a more comfortable position. Dorothy rushed forward with a cushion, fluttering around him until he placed his hand on hers to calm her and indicate he was settled, then he spoke, "Has Babington been apprehended yet?"

"Babington?" asked Kate, taken by surprise. "Why do you ask about him?"

"He is key to this convoluted plot of Philip's," said Thomas, contempt lacing his voice. "Babington has been loyal to the king of Spain for many years. From listening to the soldiers at Carew, he is much admired for his unflinching questioning of non-believers to the Catholic faith, not to mention his methods of persuading them to confess to their sins."

Elizabeth was appalled. "Not the Spanish Inquisition?" she said, disgust rounding out every vowel.

"Yes," said Thomas, "Babington is one of their most-admired men."

And he is at the heart of the plot spun around the Scottish queen, thought Elizabeth. "But what has this to do with the coup in Pembrokeshire?" asked Elizabeth.

"There are so many plans, Aunt Elizabeth, each one overlapping with the next. The king of Spain is determined to try and capture this land so he can return it to what he sees as the true faith. He has attacked the castles on the Welsh coast to try and shore up a base to march his troops across from the west. He also thought it would draw your armies away from London, leaving the Thames estuary unguarded and open to potential invasion. He believes he will soon have victory in the Netherlands, then he will have a base to invade from the east coast, after which he intends to march towards Scotland. He is confident that if he offers King James your crown, then the young monarch will join forces with him and march on England from the north."

Elizabeth turned away. She knew the others thought she would be upset by these revelations of Philip's plans but her overriding emotion was annoyance. Wars and more wars, battles, invasions — why were men obsessed with such tedious issues? These schemes and skirmishes were the result of ego, posturing, pomp and stupidity. Each raid would cost thousands of marks, the country would be stripped of its young men, there would be famine, there would be fear as foreign soldiers looted and raped their way across her land and all for what? The right to say the mass in Latin rather than English.

"Thank you for this information, Thomas," she sighed. "While the cost and thought of such a prolonged campaign disgusts me when the money could be used more wisely, the idea doesn't surprise me. It was one Philip would ruminate upon when he was married to my sister, Mary. After several glasses of wine he would bore us with his battle strategies. My sister would smile at what she perceived to be his worldly wisdom. I would pretend not to have understood but I did and I listened hard. It seems this attentiveness has served me well. Until then, I had not realised the Thames estuary could be a weak point and ever since my reign began I have ensured it is never left unguarded. The Netherlands are holding firm, thanks to Robert, and loyal Protestant, King James has signed a Treaty putting him in my pay. He will not take Philip's grubby coin or convert to Catholicism."

Thomas winced again and Elizabeth felt sorrow for the young man. These injuries had been inflicted when he had been fighting for her.

"Did you discover anything else?" she asked. "Other than his grandiose plans for invasion."

"He is planning a sea battle, too," said Thomas and Elizabeth spun around to face him, her attention caught at last. This was new. "A fleet is currently being assembled by Alvaro de Bazan, 1st Marquis of Santa Cruz de Mudela. He alone believes the sea is the best place to fight and win this country. The king, however, hesitates, as he thinks a land battle will be more successful. Santa Cruz is frustrated by this as he believes the king's prevarication causes many embarrassing political and financial mistakes. He thinks this disjointed attack on the Welsh coast is one such example. However, from what I heard one man saying, Santa Cruz is preparing to fit out his fleet in Lisbon, where Philip has claimed the crown for himself."

Light sparkled in Elizabeth's eyes. This was fortuitous news indeed, especially if Philip felt this was a waste of time. The security around the Spanish fleet would be minimal. Beckoning to Katherine, she asked her to write down all Thomas had said as she wanted a record, not only for herself, but to show to Walsingham and Burghley when they were back at court.

"There was one more thing, Aunt Elizabeth," he said, his face drawn and parchment yellow with exhaustion.

"Only one more thing, Thomas, then you must return to bed — anything else can wait until you've slept," she said, concerned by his colour.

"Yes, Aunt Elizabeth, this may not mean anything but I know Dorothy has a number of secret names for you all and I wondered if this would make sense."

The atmosphere in the room changed, when Thomas had been speaking of war and invasion, the women had not been surprised, now however, they exchanged sharp, nervous glances.

"What is it?"

"A few days before I was able to escape a letter arrived from Babington. It was addressed to the Welsh traitor, Erasmus Sanders, who was often at Carew, strutting around as though he were the rightful heir to the castle, not I, and it stated that Artemis was being chased into their trap and he was confident Apollo would follow. Soon, only Venus would remain, but she would be easily removed."

Elizabeth did not sleep well that night. The words, which had meant nothing to Thomas, held huge significance for the Ladies of Melusine. Elizabeth's sister and brother were both in immediate danger, and she herself would be the next target. What trap did Philip mean, though? Even now, Artemis was travelling to safety. Each night, she moved to another safe house, wending her way across the country on a path devised by Walsingham and his extensive spy network. Her core of ladies were with her, as was an elite force of guards. How did Philip hope to force her into a trap when, as far as the outside world was concerned, she languished, too ill to be moved, at Tixall Castle? Apollo was also far away and safe from the Spanish forces.

She twisted the ruby ring on her finger. Could it be that her information was old? The network of ladies wrote each day but was it possible, even with their constant updates, they had missed some vital piece of news. Elizabeth glanced around. She was surrounded by women but her closest confidants were not in their midst. Elizabeth beckoned Philadelphia Scrope to her side and whispered, "Where is Kate?"

"My sister is with her husband and children," Philadelphia replied. "They will return to court this evening."

"Of course," murmured Elizabeth. Kate had sought her permission the previous night when they had returned from their sojourn with Lettice. With the sudden threat of invasion her need to see her children had been overwhelming. As had her desire to impart the information about Santa Cruz and his plans for a Spanish Armada to her husband, Charles, the Lord High Admiral of Elizabeth's fleet, even if Philip was hesitating. "And Bess?"

"Her husband arrived late last night and is ailing. I believe she is nursing him. She sent word, apologising for her delay."

Elizabeth dismissed Philadelphia with a wave. Lettice was in Dudley's town house where she was playing to host to William Fitzalan, Viscount Rutland, the son of Ralph. Only Katherine was at court this morning but, on the queen's instructions, she was writing urgent messages to key members of the Ladies of Melusine, asking if they had heard anything that could confirm the rumours Thomas had reported from Carew Castle. The thought that Anthony Babington and his men were working under the auspices of both Philip II of Spain and the Spanish Inquisition was a terrifying and unexpected development.

A fanfare announced both the countess of Shrewsbury and the countess of Leicester. A smile bloomed on Elizabeth's face. At last, the two people she most needed on this unnerving morning. The two women curtseyed to the floor and Elizabeth stalked towards them.

"Where have you been?" she snapped. "Neither of you had my permission to be late. I will speak with you in my private chamber."

Marching across the room to her solar, Elizabeth beckoned to the two countesses to follow. The doors were flung open and Elizabeth stormed in, walking towards the window, where she turned to face them, her expression softening the moment the door was shut and they were alone.

"Was there any more news last night?" she asked, her voice urgent.

"Nothing more from Thomas or William," said Lettice. "Both were still sleeping when I left an hour ago. Penelope and Dorothy are in residence to ensure no one enters who is unwelcome."

"Good, thank you, Lettice," said Elizabeth, walking forward and taking her cousin's hands, squeezing them in thanks.

"And Arbella, Bess. Where is she?"

"She's with her Talbot cousins and my daughter, Mary, at our London house. Shall I send for her?"

"Yes. We need her at court as quickly as Mary can arrange it, please."

Bess nodded her understanding and left. Elizabeth waited until the door had shut behind the countess and her footsteps had receded, then she turned to Lettice.

"I'm sorry Lettice — last night, we decided to recall Robert from the Netherlands but I've realised, at the moment, this would be a disastrous move…"

"Why?" interrupted Lettice.

"Because I need you to leave the dangers of this court and go to the alternative court Robert has created for me in Holland."

"What?" Lettice sounded horrified.

"You are to take Arbella Stuart, as well as your own daughters and their children. The duke of Hereford's son, William Fitzalan, will also accompany you."

Lettice's eyes were wide with fury. "And if I refuse to go?"

"Please don't make this any more difficult, Lettice," snapped Elizabeth. "You knew this day might come; your family and the Devereuxs all knew it could come to this. You are my best hope for the future, all our planning, all our scheming, your mother, you, your sisters, your cousins, your daughters have all been at the heart of it and you know the reason why." Elizabeth glared at Lettice as she turned away, aware she had a mercurial temper to match her own.

"I won't leave you, Elizabeth," she replied. "My place is here and you know it."

"You have no choice," said Elizabeth. "My actions are designed to make my country and the succession safe. If I am killed, by any means — assassination, murder, in battle — I must know that my heirs are safe."

"But..."

"Lettice, please, you know this is the only way. You have known since you were a young girl and you came to live in my household that you were chosen to play this role. Your father prepared and trained you from childhood for such a situation as this. You knew, one day, I might have to call upon you. I know what I'm asking could put you in danger but you were always so sure, so proud of this heritage." Elizabeth stared into her cousin's face, features so similar to her own, their colouring identical, her voice imploring, her eyes pleading.

"It isn't the danger to myself," said Lettice, reaching up and placing her hand on Elizabeth's cheek. "It's the thought of leaving you here to face a potential invasion without me to take care of you."

"I'll have Kate, Bess and Katherine, as well as the cousins, but knowing that you are fulfilling your part of the agreement with Robert will make it easier for me to face whatever happens here."

"Must we play it out as Father planned?" asked Lettice.

"His plan is good," sighed Elizabeth, "even if it will cause us to part."

The cousins stared at each other, their identical brown eyes reflecting the other's sorrow at what was to come.

"Very well," said Lettice, reluctance lacing her words, "as my father planned, we will begin the rumour that you hate me, that you have never forgiven my marriage to Robert and that I am preparing to leave for the Netherlands."

"And between you, will you and Robert be able to keep the children safe?"

"We have an army at our disposal — no harm will come to the heirs."

"Thank you, Lettice, thank you. I know this will put you in great danger…"

"But do you think it will work, Elizabeth? If Philip really has discovered Artemis and Apollo's true identities, will he be fooled?"

"I will ensure he, at least, doubts his information," said Elizabeth. "Nobody looking at us would think otherwise once they have the barest facts and have heard the rumour that there is a secret princess hidden in the midst of my court."

"In that case, Elizabeth, I am pleased to lead the trail away from you and your sister, while you and your brother do whatever is necessary to save this beloved realm of yours."

The two women gazed at each other for a long moment, then threw themselves in each other's arms, embracing with all their might, clinging on as though this was their final farewell.

Chapter Four

"Babington has been caught."

Elizabeth spun around; her eyes wide with surprise. She thrust her bow into the hands of one of her stewards and walked to meet Katherine and Kate who were hurrying towards her. Ignoring the looks from the assembled courtiers, Elizabeth positioned herself between her two friends and slipped her arms through theirs.

"Where? When?" she asked, drawing them away to a secluded bower where they would not be overheard. A stone seat followed the curve of the yew hedge while in the centre of the secluded grove a fountain decorated with a small, smiling, naked cupid played.

Elizabeth and her entourage were in the gardens at Oatlands Palace in Surrey. Despite her wish to remain in the capital at either Whitehall or Richmond, the summer plague was so virulent it was considered wiser to depart to the countryside. The archery practice and subsequent competition that would be taking place during the afternoon had been at her suggestion. She felt it was wise for everyone to have recently brushed up on their skills, including herself.

"He fled London a few days ago, aware he was being pursued by Walsingham's men. He was hiding in a barn in Harrow when they cornered him. Walsingham has him in the Tower."

"What did Walsingham say?"

"He hasn't," muttered Kate, "the information is from Mignonne. Claude Nau heard the news while they were at an inn near Fotheringhay Castle."

Elizabeth narrowed her eyes in fury. "Thank goodness for Mignonne," she said. She reached out her hand to take the translation of the coded note. "Babington suspected his part in the plot had been discovered and he tried to flee to the coast. Do we know anything else?"

"I've had a number of letters from our ladies," whispered Katherine, "but the tales they tell are very different from the plans we know Walsingham has constructed. My husband and brothers-in-law are well-informed men, Your Majesty, and I make a point of being in our chambers when they are discussing Walsingham's latest escapades."

"And yet, Walsingham claims to tell me everything," sighed Elizabeth. "Even after all these years he doubts my intelligence and my ability. It is a curse to be surrounded by idiot men."

Kate smothered a laugh.

"Tell me, Katherine, what does Walsingham keep from me?"

"He has men searching for the Catholic priest, John Ballard, who also uses the name Black Fortescue. Walsingham's man, Nicholas Berden, has been watching him and claims both Ballard and Babington are in London with another man who is supposedly in the spymaster's pay — Robert or Robin Poley..."

"I know these names," interrupted Kate. "Thomas Phelippes has contacted my husband in order to obtain arrest warrants for these men. Although, curiously, rather than fill in the paperwork with the names, he asked for them to be left blank, merely signed by my husband to make them legal and valid."

"Yet Mignonne and Apollo have both sent word saying Ballard has left London and is heading towards

Northamptonshire. The men who have been left behind in London are decoys. They are being used to distract Walsingham and his men. Babington was trying to lead the spymaster away from Ballard."

"Northamptonshire?" queried Elizabeth. "Are you sure?"

"It's what Katherine Hastings, the earl of Leicester's sister, wrote," said Katherine. "On your orders, Artemis is making her clandestine trip across the country and she stayed for three nights at Hill Hall, near Abbot's Bromley. The countess was the only member of the family in residence, as you know — her husband Henry Hastings is with Lord Leicester in the Netherlands."

"And from whom did the countess hear this information?"

"One of her footmen. He is very loyal and has been in her service for many years. He had been on a journey to deliver alms and he overheard the conversation between two men wearing the livery of William Vaux, 3rd Baron Vaux of Harrowden. Vaux has known Catholic leanings and is descended from the Parr family. He was committed to the Fleet prison after being found guilty of recusancy on a number of occasions and, after that, he was tried in the Star Chamber in 1581, along with his brother-in-law, Sir Thomas Tresham, and charged with harbouring a known Jesuit named Edward Campion. He was imprisoned in the Fleet again and fined £1,000 and we know he has connections with Babington. The men were heading to Little Harrowden in Northamptonshire and they were planning to meet a hunting party somewhere between Rugeley and Leicester."

"Hunting?" said Elizabeth. "What were the exact words?"

Katherine paused while she thought. "There have been so many letters but I believe the phrase they used, as reported by the countess was, 'they had heard there was hunting afoot and

they would make merry with such sport'. Oh, Your Majesty…"
gasped Katherine as she realised the turn of phrase was
deliberate. "'Hunting afoot' is the code for the plot concerning
Artemis."

Elizabeth knew the time had come to make a stand. "Kate,
Katherine, prepare something suitable for me to wear to visit
the Tower," she said. "It's time our spymaster listened to the
clamouring voices from the Ladies of Melusine. We have
wasted enough time in this dance of game and counter-game.
If we are to prevent Philip from succeeding, we must put all
our information together."

"But Elizabeth, I don't understand…" began Kate.

"Someone within Artemis's household has betrayed her,"
said Elizabeth. "As far as the world knows, she lies too ill to be
moved at Tixall Castle. Only a few know that she has been
wending her way through the country heading for safety at the
Tower of London. If Ballard and Vaux's men are heading
towards Northamptonshire, they must have been told that
within a few days Artemis will arrive in the village of
Fotheringhay. I suspect they plan to intercept her somewhere
along the route."

"Oh, Elizabeth, no," gasped Kate but Elizabeth had no time
for emotion, not when so much was at stake.

"Babington must be made to tell us what he knows. He has
put my sister's life in danger. I want to be there while they
question him. The plague be damned, I've had enough of
hiding here playing silly games. It's time to be at the heart of
the matter."

"I'll arrange for the barge," Kate muttered and hurried away.

"Katherine, would you ask Burghley to meet us there, too?
It's time we called the privy council together again and not
only to discuss the Irish and Dutch issues. I must take control

of this ridiculous situation; I am sick of this silence and subterfuge. Katherine, while we travel, I will need you to write to my brother. I'm sorry that so much of the burden always falls to you, my dear."

"Elizabeth, it's no burden," said Katherine. "Artemis and Apollo are my family, too."

Elizabeth squeezed Katherine's hand. Twisting the ruby ring around her finger, Elizabeth beckoned to her other women and they processed back to the palace to prepare for their journey.

The Tower of London held many memories for Elizabeth, most of them tinged with fear. Her mother had died here, executed on trumped-up charges on her father's order, and it was here she had been held while her older sister decided whether or not she was guilty of treason. Yet it was also the place Elizabeth had spent the nights leading up to her coronation. Even when held as a prisoner, her accommodation had always been in the sumptuous royal apartments. Babington would be given no such consideration. Deep in the bowels of the Tower were the dungeons: the cold, rat-infested cells where those who had committed treason and murder were held. She knew that it was down here Walsingham and his men used all manner of methods to extract information.

"You don't have to do this, Elizabeth," said Kate, a few hours later as they made their way along the damp, dripping passageway.

The journey on the Royal barge had been tense as Elizabeth and Katherine had written to the members of the Ladies of Melusine whose homes were situated along the route Walsingham had devised, convinced no one would ever discover their subterfuge, something which had been proved wrong. Each household was warned to be on alert for strangers and any whispers of unexpected 'hunting parties'. They had also devised letters to the men leading the battle on the Pembrokeshire coast and to both Robert and Lettice Dudley informing them of the new threat and putting them both on their guard. As soon as they arrived at the Tower of London, Katherine had hurried away to despatch trusted messengers.

"Walsingham's men are sometimes overenthusiastic," she said. "If they are aware I am in residence, they will temper their methods for fear of being punished themselves. We need information but he is not to be killed."

Turning a corner, two guards crossed their pikestaffs in front of the queen, barring her entrance.

"How dare you?" roared Elizabeth, her nerves already stretched. "Move aside! I am Queen of England. You do not block my path."

"Orders of the spymaster, Sir Francis Walsingham. No one enters."

"You dare…" began Elizabeth but at that moment Thomas Phelippes, one of Walsingham's most trusted codebreakers appeared out of the gloom.

"What is the meaning of this noise?" he barked, then he saw Elizabeth and flew forward, pushing the two soldiers aside and dropping to his knees. "Your Majesty," he gulped, "this is an unexpected visit."

"Get up, you stupid man," snapped Elizabeth. "Where is Walsingham?"

"He is otherwise engaged…" began Phelippes.

"You mean he is torturing Anthony Babington?"

"Questioning the prisoner, Your Majesty," he replied. "Interrogating…"

"Take me to him at once."

Elizabeth strode past him and Phelippes had no choice but to hurry along beside her. The two women walked with him further into the bowels of the Tower, where the walls were thick, the rooms were dark and the dampness of the river Thames oozed down the ancient bricks, clammy and cold, like the hands of the dead. At last, they reached a narrow corridor with a thick, scarred wooden door at the end.

"He is here, madam," said Phelippes. He shot a helpless look at Kate who shrugged. "Are you sure, Your Majesty? This is an unpleasant place."

Elizabeth pushed him aside and walked towards the door, banging on it three times. She waited, and when Walsingham opened it, she pushed past him into the stinking filth of the torture chamber.

The man strung up high from manacles was younger than Elizabeth had expected. He had probably once been good-looking but now his head lolled forward, his chin rested on his chest; his brown hair was stiff and matted with sweat and blood.

"He was hiding in a barn," said Walsingham. "He fled his town house in London when he suspected it was being watched. He knew my men were looking for the Catholic priest and his conspirator, John Ballard, but when we realised we had been tricked and Ballard wasn't there, Babington disappeared. Once he was out of the city, he changed into peasant clothes, cut his hair and smeared his face with mud in an attempt to disguise himself. My men caught up with him early yesterday morning when they were given a tip-off that a stranger with a 'posh London accent' was hiding on a nearby farm."

"What has he told you?" asked Elizabeth, her eyes fixed on the pitiful figure. "Can't you let him down, Walsingham?"

Her spymaster gave her a curious look. "This man was planning to assassinate you," he said, "yet you wish to show him compassion? He has tortured countless men, women and children because they are not as devout as he would choose and you suggest mercy?"

Elizabeth gave him a cold look. "Let him down, Walsingham," she repeated. "I want the information he gives us to be the truth. I do not want him pushed so far beyond the limits of human endurance that he merely tells us what we want to hear in order to stop his own suffering. I believe this man to be a vile specimen of humanity and, in the end, he will be punished as such, but for now we need him alive and able to speak. Only use your most violent methods when you have no other option."

Walsingham glowered but did not dare to disobey a direct order from the monarch. He indicated to one of his men, who with a great clanking of keys released the semi-conscious man, helping him to the pile of sacks in the corner that served for a bed. Satisfied, Elizabeth turned away from the prisoner and focussed on Walsingham.

"Has he told you anything new?" she asked.

"He confirmed a few things," began Walsingham.

"Such as?"

"That Philip II of Spain has been planning an invasion for some years and this is only the beginning of his battle to win the English throne."

"Was he able to confirm any names?" she asked, pushing aside her visceral fear of invasion.

"No, all we managed to get him to tell us was that he and six other gentlemen had been specifically chosen as…" he paused, looking uncomfortable.

"Tell me," commanded Elizabeth, preferring to hear the worst from someone she trusted.

"Six gentlemen who are still practising Catholics charged with your assassination."

"But we don't know the names?"

Walsingham shook his head. "Apparently, the final six were never decided upon."

"Convenient," snapped Elizabeth. Standing over the wrecked body that had once been a man, she considered her next move. "Keep questioning him, Walsingham. We need names and details but leave enough of him to stand trial. I will see justice served and he'll pay for his crimes."

Elizabeth turned away. She had no desire to watch Babington being tortured but her message had been delivered: Walsingham would do what was necessary but nothing more. She looked around at the implements of torture: the rack, the manacles, the cabinet in the corner known as the Little Ease, where a man could not stand upright and the Scavenger's Daughter which was an ingenious system of compressing all the limbs in iron bands. She knew an official order had to be given to authorise the use of these contraptions and as she had not given it, she could only assume either Burghley or Kate's husband, Lord Effingham had signed the order. Men, she thought, conspiring among themselves to do what they feel is necessary.

"Sir, I've found something…"

Nicholas Berden raced into the dungeon then halted when he saw Queen Elizabeth and Lady Howard.

"Show me," commanded Walsingham, holding out his hand.

"It was found sewn into the lining of his coat and it's addressed to Her Majesty," Berden said, his voice tremulous.

Walsingham scanned the message, the colour draining from his face.

"Show me," demanded Elizabeth.

"Your Majesty, no..." began Walsingham but Elizabeth had snatched the tattered, mud-stained piece of parchment. With each word she read, the room reeled.

Kate ran to her side and took her arm, holding her steady.

"This note is to me and it's from John Ballard on behalf of His Majesty, King Philip II of Spain."

"Let me read it, Elizabeth," said Kate, taking the note from Elizabeth's shaking hand. "To The Imposter Queen, Elizabeth Tudor, heretic and usurper. His Royal Highness, Philip Habsburg, King of Spain, sends word that he holds the twins: Elizabeth and her brother, Nicholas, the children of Henry VIII and his fifth wife. Unless you abdicate and declare Philip II your heir, neither twin will be shown mercy."

PART FIVE: December, 2018

Chapter One

Christmas was fast approaching and Perdita and Piper had decided to drive to the capital, Andorra La Vella, for some last-minute Christmas shopping.

In the past few weeks, liaising with their godmother, Sarah Eve, who was also the housekeeper at Marquess House, they had followed her advice about how Mary had always organised presents and bonuses for everyone who lived or worked at the ancient manor. Now they were working through a list of gifts for the Mackensies and each other, including collecting a surprise present for Susan from Alistair, which meant when his name flashed up on Perdita's phone, they were amused.

"Hi Alistair," she said, putting him on loudspeaker, "do you have more things to add to the shopping list?"

"Not at present," he replied. "I was calling to let Piper know she dropped her phone. Cal found it in our car park and I didn't want her panicking."

"Thanks, Alistair," said Piper, "that's thoughtful. Has it smashed?"

"No, it's perfectly intact."

"What a shame! It hasn't been working properly for ages. I've been meaning to get a new one and if it had properly broken I'd have run out of excuses. Do me a favour and stamp on it, Alistair!"

They laughed but when Alistair next spoke, all the amusement had faded from his voice. "When did it begin playing up, Piper?" he asked, his tone sharp.

"A few months ago," she replied. "When I left America, I think."

There was silence.

"Alistair, are you still there?" asked Perdita.

"Yes," he said, but his voice was serious. "Piper, would you mind if I examined your phone in more detail?"

"If you like," she said, sounding perplexed. "Why?"

"I think it may have been tampered with."

"What?" spluttered Perdita. "By whom?"

"Kirstin Chaplin," replied Alistair. "For a while now, I've been wondering if our security has been breached but I couldn't work out how. Perhaps your handset was the cause, though the bug seems to have damaged the operating system, hence the reason the phone has been malfunctioning. This has worked in our favour because it's meant Connors and Chaplin won't have heard as much as they would have hoped."

"Alistair, do you want us to come back to the castle?" asked Perdita, exchanging a horrified look with Piper.

"No, you'll be safe in town but if you wouldn't mind coming home before it's dark, it would ease my nerves."

"We'll be back by early afternoon," Perdita assured him.

"See you later then."

The line went dead.

"Do you think he's being paranoid?" said Piper into the stunned silence.

"I hope so," replied Perdita, but the excited anticipation they had been sharing melted away.

"So much for a relaxing day shopping," Piper sighed.

"Let's do what we have to and get back," said Perdita.

"Definitely," agreed Piper, pulling into a parking space.

Perdita climbed out of the car and looked around at the smiling faces of the Christmas shoppers. She felt twitchy and unnerved by Alistair's revelation and as distant from the festive crowd as if she were on a different planet. Slipping her arm through Piper's as they headed into the throng she wondered if they would ever be free from the looming danger of both MI1 and Randolph Connors.

"What is it?" asked Kit later, as they stared at the tiny metallic device.

"A listening bug," replied Callum, "but it's been disabled now."

"And it was in Piper's phone?" checked Perdita.

"Yes. It was inexpertly fitted, as though it had been done in a hurry, which is rather a relief for us because it means it has never transmitted properly," said Alistair.

Piper stared at the grey metal square with fury on her face. "Isn't it bad enough that she trashed my marriage without spying on us, too?"

All eyes turned to her and Perdita moved to her sister's side but she could tell from the set line of Piper's mouth that she was in no mood to be comforted.

"I'm sorry, Alistair," said Piper. "It appears I allowed Randolph Connors into the heart of Jerusalem."

"Piper, this isn't your fault," said Susan, stepping forward. "You are not to blame in any way. Thankfully, the bug caused your phone to malfunction so the transmission was probably unclear for most of the time."

"But they will have heard how much we've discovered with the letters and the ring," Piper said.

"As to that, there's nothing we can do about it," said Alistair, his tone calm. "The leak has been plugged and until we can safely reactivate your phone number, I have this pay-as-you-go handset for you to use."

He slid an expensive looking Smartphone towards her but Piper did not pick it up. Instead she walked to the windows and stared out at the cold, clear evening. They were in the cosy sitting room, off the Grande Hall, but the tense atmosphere was at odds with the roaring fire and the twinkling lights on the large Christmas trees.

Perdita watched her sister for a few moments, then turned back to Alistair.

"Is Connors interested in uncovering the historical mystery?" she asked. "You've told us the reasons why he wants access to the house and our titles but is he actively searching, as we are?"

Alistair considered her, then choosing his words with great care, said, "Connors would like the mystery to be solved for him so he can use it as a tool to blackmail as many governments as he feels is viable. It would put him in a position of even greater power than he presently commands."

"And he was hoping that by bugging Piper's phone he would have been able to eavesdrop on our discoveries and use the information?" clarified Perdita.

"I don't know, but that would be my assumption."

To break the tension, Kit and Callum busied themselves pouring drinks for everyone. Before the discovery of the bug, the plan had been to meet for a glass of wine in the sitting room, then head down to the local bar, The Terrace, for the evening, but none of them were in the mood any longer. Perdita took the glass of Prosecco he offered her and sipped the cold bubbles.

"Alistair, what happened to Randolph's mother?" she asked.

He turned to her in surprise. "You mean, Cecily, Mary's younger sister?"

"Yes, our great-aunt."

"Why do you ask?"

"I'm curious, but I also want to try and understand why someone who has so much can't be satisfied. Why must he

227

strive for more and use such underhand methods to achieve his ends?"

"Goodness, Perdita, those are huge questions," said Susan.

"He's a psycho?" suggested Kit. Callum grinned as he walked over to hand Piper a glass of Prosecco. She turned away from the window, her face calmer and joined Callum on the sofa.

"You said Cecily died young," said Piper, glancing at Alistair as they all settled in the assorted chairs around the fire. "Please, Alistair, even if Granny left a hundred letters requesting you spare us the gory details, I think it's important we know. There seems to be danger coming at us from every angle and Cecily's death may have some relevance on Randolph's determination to steal our inheritance."

Alistair looked at Susan, who nodded and with obvious reluctance, he conceded to her request.

"I may not be correct in all the dates, as I don't have the paperwork in front of me, but I can give you an outline," he said and Perdita noticed a hint of anxiety in his voice. "As you know, Mary had a younger sister, Cecily. She was born in 1940 and very sadly, your great-grandmother, Eleanor Fitzroy died not long after from a haemorrhage. From what I've been told, she had never been a strong woman and her pregnancy with Cecily had been a difficult one. Mary and Cecily's father, David Fitzroy, your great-grandfather, were abroad when Eleanor died."

"Why?" asked Piper.

"It was 1940, the Second World War was raging and he was an officer in the RAF," said Susan.

"David came home on compassionate leave," continued Alistair, "and, a few months after Cecily's birth, Mary was sent to a boarding school that had been evacuated to Welshpool, while Cecily was cared for by David's younger sister, Tabitha."

"What?" said Perdita, sitting upright. "We have another great-aunt? Why did no one ever tell us?"

"There are Fitzroy cousins, too," admitted Alistair. "You weren't told for the same reasons you were cut off from us. Fear that you would be murdered while you were children by MI1 Elite. I believe there is a full family tree in the Marquess House library. Those members of the family who are best avoided I'll ink in red," he said, with an attempt at a joke, but Perdita and Piper stared at him, aghast. "However, the family who interest us at present is Cecily and her offspring. After the war, David bought a house near to his sister and her family…"

"Where was that?" asked Perdita. She and Piper had grown up thinking they were alone in the world — these casual revelations of cousins, aunts and uncles were more unsettling and painful than she could ever begin to explain to Alistair. She understood her grandmother's desire to keep them safe but she could not help feeling that in isolating them so completely, Mary had denied them so much.

"They lived in Cornwall, so quite a long way from Marquess House," said Alistair. "Are you sure you want to do this now, Perdita? It's a lot to suddenly divulge."

"Yes, Alistair," she said. "We want to know everything. So, David Fitzroy?" she prompted.

"He had been a similar age to your great-grandmother and worked as an accountant in London, however, when war broke out, as Susan said, he enlisted in the RAF. At first, Eleanor planned to stay in London during the war but shortly after David was posted, she discovered she was unexpectedly pregnant. It was then Eleanor and David decided it would be safer for her to return to the family home that she had inherited from her mother…"

"Marquess House?" asked Perdita.

"Yes," replied Alistair. "David survived the war and on his return, as I said, moved to be nearer to Tabitha and her husband Michael. Eventually, Cecily followed your grandmother to boarding school. Mary had excelled there and gone on to study at Cambridge University, where she met her future husband, your grandfather, Hector Woodville.

"Cecily was the complete opposite — she wasn't interested in schoolwork and once she discovered she would inherit a sizeable trust fund on her 21st birthday, she threw herself into the fun of post-war London. Mary once told me how she dreaded Friday afternoons as there was inevitably an irate telephone call from the school saying Cecily had run away again to attend a party somewhere. She avoided being expelled because Mary and her father managed to persuade the headmistress to keep her there with a sizeable donation to the school. Once she was 18 and had left school, Cecily spent a few months at Marquess House with Mary, which is when they must have hatched a plan. There was a seven-year age gap between them, so Mary had already come into her inheritance, but Cecily, bored with the remoteness of Pembrokeshire, needed distraction, so Mary gifted her one of their London properties and gave her an allowance until she would receive an income of her own. Cecily had a few months of hi-jinks with the jet-set and was beginning to become a staple of the tabloid press, when she surprised everyone by eloping with businessman, Albert Connors, who was 19 years her senior."

"Was he rich?" asked Perdita.

"Excessively, but then, so was she, so perhaps it was a love match," replied Alistair. "A year later, she gave birth to Randolph. He was six months younger than your mother, Louisa. After Cecily came into her inheritance, she and Mary only really kept in touch via Christmas and birthday cards.

There was no rift, despite what many gossipmongers have stated — they were simply two very different women. Then, in 1974, Cecily and Albert were on holiday in Monte Carlo. They had hired a yacht and were entertaining an array of minor European royalty, Hollywood stars and musicians, when Cecily disappeared. She had been complaining of a headache and had told Albert she was going to lie down but when he went to check on her an hour later her bed hadn't been slept in.

"The yacht was searched and one of the crew found a damaged railing. Cecily's Pucci silk scarf was caught on the side of the boat — it had snagged on a rusty bolt below a porthole, according to the official inquest. The police were called, a huge rescue mission was launched, funded by both Mary and Albert, but Cecily's body was never found. The coroner concluded accidental death by drowning. Cecily had suffered from intense migraines all her life and they often caused her to faint. The inquest stated it was possible Cecily had fainted and fallen overboard. Albert found it very difficult to come to terms with her death — he blamed himself for not escorting her to their bedroom."

"How awful," gasped Perdita.

"Mary was devastated," he said. "Their father, David, was still alive and after Cecily's death, he dissolved his accountancy practice in Cornwall and moved in with Mary at Marquess House. He lived there until he died."

"What happened to her husband and son?" Piper asked.

"Randolph was at boarding school, where he remained, coming home in the holidays," said Alistair. "Albert Connors moved first to Africa, where I believe he had an older spinster sister, Dorothy, who had a farm. Although when they say farm, it was thousands and thousands of acres of wildlife reserve. When she died a year later, he moved to India and increased his fortune by buying a string of tea plantations. He was a very able businessman and exceptionally good at predicting trends. His tea business boomed and when Albert died five years after Cecily, Randolph inherited everything. It transpired he had also inherited his father's business acumen and with the fortune left to him by both his parents, he has made himself a powerful player in the world's commodity markets. He has houses all around the world, and, although he was born in the UK, he spends most of his time on his tea plantation in Darjeeling." Alistair drained his glass and smiled at Perdita. "I can only apologise for not telling you both this tale sooner but with Mary's instructions and the years we've all spent protecting you, it felt strange and uncomfortable to be revealing so much. However, you're right — you do need to know everything."

To Perdita's surprise, Piper jumped to her feet and enveloped Alistair in a hug.

"And you did keep us alive," she said. "Now that we know more about Cecily and Connors, hopefully, we'll be able to contribute to our continuing existence."

Perdita could not help but laugh.

"Now, weren't you going to The Terrace?" asked Susan.

"Yes," said Kit, "but this rather took precedent."

"It's only 8pm," continued his mother, "why don't you go now? I think after these revelations you should go and let off steam."

Having grown up with only their father, who had always been very protective of them, it felt peculiar to Perdita to hear a parental figure suggesting they go out and have fun. Susan's words fell into silence, before Perdita realised Piper, Kit and Callum were all looking at her. *When did I become the leader of the gang?* she wondered.

"Perds?" questioned Kit.

"You're right, Susan," she said, knocking back the rest of her Prosecco. "We need a night out. This is ancient history and we can't change it — we also shouldn't be afraid of it. Would you be able to order us a car to take us to The Terrace in half an hour, please?"

"Of course," replied Susan, beaming.

Piper nodded her agreement, while Kit and Callum grinned and hurried off to get changed. Perdita was the last of the four of them to leave the room. She turned to Alistair and Susan.

"Thank you for telling us all this," she said. "I feel better equipped to deal with Connors now. Incidentally, has Piper told you that Jeremy and Kirstin are travelling to India?"

"She hadn't, no," replied Alistair.

"Even though she's angry with him, Piper still cares about her husband and wouldn't want anything untoward to happen. Would we be able to have someone tail him for his own safety?"

"Of course, my dear, consider it done."

"And," continued Perdita, "even though it makes me uncomfortable because I don't like keeping secrets; at this stage, it would be preferable if Piper didn't know — I wouldn't want to worry her."

A rueful smile spread across Alistair's face as he nodded his agreement.

"Welcome to my world, Perdita," he sighed.

Chapter Two

"The trouble is, Kit," said Perdita, her tone hesitant. "I'm not sure Lettice is the missing heir."

"Why not?"

"Lots of things. For instance, there is no record of her travelling to the north as a child and we have a comment about the baby girl being sent there — it's in the account books. If she was the heir and she was living with Kathy Knollys as one of her family, would they really have allowed her to marry into a family with Welsh connections, who lived so near to Marquess House that Lettice might discover the truth?" she said.

They were in Kit's office where he was creating an illustrated family tree of the Tudors and Stuarts, showing the potential missing heirs. Prominent in this vast and eccentric collage was a picture of Lettice Knollys. There was no denying Kit's endeavour was packed full of relevant information, but if Perdita was honest, it was also hilariously funny and even Kit had consented to admit that it was reminiscent of a school project he had completed when he was ten years old.

"But it's useful," he had laughed. "We won't have to keep double-checking dates and it shows the links between the families very clearly."

Which was something Perdita could not deny as her eyes followed one particular line. It began with Mary Boleyn and swept down to Lady Kathryn Carey, who had married Sir Francis Knollys and produced up to 15 children, with at least 12 surviving into adulthood. No wonder poor Kathy died so young, thought Perdita. Only 45 and probably pregnant for most of her married life. Her body must have been exhausted.

Perdita's eye flickered to the window where a grey sky glowered, threatening another snowfall.

"Why are you uncertain?" he asked.

"I've finished reading all the Lady Pamela letters that Jenny and Izabel have compiled," she replied.

"Me too," Kit said.

"And?" prompted Perdita.

"They're an odd mix," he hedged.

"Odd mix?" she snorted. "Kit, that's a huge understatement. I know they're still working on the later letters, so we only have until June 1586, but the story they tell is so vastly different from 'historical truth' I'm beginning to wonder if they're fakes."

Kit threw the ball of red wool he had been using to create the lines on the wall to join the varying members of the family tree together on to his sofa and moved away from his masterpiece to sit at his desk. Perdita flopped into the chair opposite him.

"I thought so, too," he admitted.

"Why didn't you say…" began Perdita, but Kit interrupted her.

"But rather than throw my doubts at you like I kept doing before, I decided to do some digging and see if I could discover anything useful before we both sat down in despair." He pulled out a folder from his desk and pushed it towards Perdita. She was touched by his consideration.

Perdita flicked through the pages of emails, noticing they included messages from the Pembrokeshire Archive, Pembroke Castle Trust, Dyfed Archaeology, Picton Castle,

Carew Castle, Haverfordwest Castle and various other contacts of Kit's from his years of working for Jerusalem.

"The Lady Pamela letters claim there was an invasion of the Welsh coast by the Spanish in 1586," she said, thinking aloud, "yet no history book anywhere even hints at such a thing. The only vague suggestion was in January or February 1587, when Burghley told Elizabeth that the Spanish Armada had landed on the Welsh coast, terrifying her into signing the death warrant for the execution of Mary, Queen of Scots. Historians have always stated Burghley fabricated this in order to manipulate the queen — in other words, he lied."

"Except, maybe he didn't," said Kit, "but because it was such a bizarre idea and there was no other paperwork to confirm this, historians have created their own neat version: Burghley lied as a means to an end to achieve his main objective, the death of Mary, Queen of Scots and with her demise, the elimination of the Catholic threat to Elizabeth's Protestant throne. Burghley was a staunch Protestant. But, having lived in and around the Pembrokeshire coastline for most of my life, something struck me, hence my quiet investigation so I could speak with some authority."

"Come on then, Smug-Mackensie-Kid," said Perdita, placing the file on the desk. "You've obviously discovered something, so spit it out."

"In all the years I've been visiting the castles along the Welsh coast, and trust me, when we were kids, Mary took us to them a lot. I think she liked to pretend you and Piper were there, too," he added, looking at her white face. "Anyway, for years it had never struck me, but after reading this, I had an epiphany."

"Which is, what?"

"All the castle tours tell the visitors about very early history: William Marshall, Princess Nest, the Normans, and then there's a leap to the late 17th century and the Civil War."

"What are you saying?" asked Perdita, sitting forward, urging Kit to reach the point.

"There is practically no information for any of these castles for the time period covered by the Lady Pamela letters. The records at Picton Castle were destroyed in a fire. Carew mentions the Perrot family very briefly and the fact the castle was modernised in Elizabethan times, but nothing else, and, most staggering of all, Pembroke Castle, that has hugely detailed timelines skips the Tudor period altogether, except for a small mention of Henry VII being born there and how he and his uncle, Jasper Tudor, escaped during the Wars of the Roses using secret passages under Tenby that led down to the harbour. I contacted a mate at the Pembrokeshire Archives to see if they had anything that could fill in the blanks but there was nothing."

"But that's impossible," said Perdita.

"There was one guidebook entitled, *A Short History and Guide to Pembroke Castle*, which was published in the mid-1970s. It skipped from 1536 to James I's rule, stating the castle remained as crown property until the young Scottish king, who was now King of England and Wales, gifted it to a private individual: Major General Sir Ivor Philipps, KSB DSO, whose family kept ownership until 1928."

"But James didn't come to the throne until 1603," said Perdita, "that's a huge leap of 67 years!"

"Exactly. There was also a very small booklet called, *A Guide to Pembroke Castle*, priced at one shilling, that claimed there were no records for Pembroke Castle from 1595 until the Civil War in 1642 and all that could be found for the 1595 date was a record that stated, 'all the walls of Pembroke Castle are standing very strong, without decay, only the roofs and leads have been taken down'. There is discussion of a new dig taking place there soon to open up a search from the 1930s, when it was suggested there could have been a manor house within the walls of the castle, but it's ongoing."

"Within the walls?" queried Perdita. "I've never heard of that before. It would be a unique discovery."

"It might also explain where all the Tudor history has disappeared to," said Kit. "The only reference to Henry VII's birth is from John Leland, the poet and antiquarian who describes a fireplace in the room where Henry was born. It was always thought to be one of the larger towers but it could have been a room in this mysterious manor."

"As you say, it would explain the lack of information from the Tudor period," she agreed. "And Haverfordwest Castle?"

"Nothing firm for the Tudor period there either, only references to later on. There's certainly nothing for the times these letters covers."

A smile was breaking over Perdita's face. "Then the letters must be genuine," she said. "If you, with all your contacts and research capability can't find official records for any of these castles at the time we now have correspondence suggesting there was a coup, the real records must have been deliberately destroyed in order to hide something enormous."

"And an invasion, even a failed one, is pretty huge."

"Oh Kit, I could kiss you!" exclaimed Perdita, leaping from her seat.

"I'm not stopping you," he said and smiled at her.

Perdita shot him a flirtatious look and tried to control her racing heart before continuing. "I'd almost convinced myself these letters were a fabrication but it seems they're not. They're the only surviving records of what really happened in the summer of 1586 on the Pembrokeshire coast," she said and marched over to Kit's wallchart. "Although, I do still wonder if Lettice is the missing heir?"

"All the evidence points that way…" began Kit, then understanding flooded his face. "Very clever," he said, almost to himself. "Whoever this person, The Scribe, was, he or she was remarkably good at distraction."

Perdita turned back to him and grinned. "My thoughts, exactly," she said, relieved. "When I was going through the notes, it kept reminding me of Catherine Howard and how the only evidence ever 'found' concerning her supposed affair with Thomas Culpepper was information that incriminated her. The only details we have left about Lettice Knollys are sketchy and with only a few definitive dates: her marriages, her children and her death, but there are no letters concerning one of the most tempestuous of those relationships — her marriage to Robert Dudley — and it's suspicious. It's as though she's been set up as a decoy."

"Would it have been deliberate?"

"I'm not sure," admitted Perdita. "There is one letter that intrigues me because it's from She-Wolf to Lady Griffin, saying the plan put in place by She-Wolf's father is working. If we're taking it that She-Wolf is Lettice, her father is Sir Francis Knollys, another man who was part of the Catherine Howard conspiracy, so it wouldn't be beyond him to create a smokescreen again to protect the real heir."

"Using his daughter?" asked Kit, sounding uncertain.

"She must have agreed."

"It's possible, Perds," he said, his eyes thoughtful, "but if we're suggesting Lettice isn't the heir, do you have any thoughts about who it could be?"

"No, not yet, but there is another section I want to check. There are a few miscellaneous letters that Jenny couldn't identify. She emailed them last night — you were copied in on the message."

Kit glanced at his inbox and gave her a thumbs up. "Do you want some help?" he asked, his eyes straying back to his wallchart.

"No, I wouldn't want to come between a man and his ball of red wool," said Perdita. "I'll be across the corridor if you need any help unravelling yourself."

Reinvigorated by Kit's findings, Perdita hurried back into her own office, flipped open her laptop and printed out Jenny's email. Within minutes, she was engrossed in the detailed document.

Perdita, there are a number of letters here that are unsigned but by studying the writing we've tried to identify the correct authors and place similar letters together, however, these are not definitive and are only our best guesses. The oddest is note 12678b. It is something of an anomaly, the handwriting is unique in this collection and there is no date to help us to identify the writer. However, Izabel and I both think there might be a small similarity in the formation of the letters 'a', 'z' and 'M' to those of the letters attributed to Lettice Knollys, so for now, we've included it with these.'

Looking at the scan of the short letter, Perdita understood why they were unsure. It was only a few lines long and could barely be classed as a note, let alone a letter, and it was written in French. She wondered if it had been part of another piece of correspondence that had been lost over time.

Baby Elizabeth arrived with a ring on the Feast of the Immaculate Conception of the blessed Virgin Mary. She is now our beloved daughter, Mary.

Perdita read it through a number of times. It did not make sense. Perhaps it was the translation, she thought, returning to the copy of the original, but however she translated it herself, and no matter how many language programs she used online, the meaning did not alter.

"What's up, Perds?" asked Kit, when she beckoned him over half an hour later.

"This," she said, glaring down at the note in frustration before pushing the paperwork towards him. "What do you think it means?"

Kit considered it, then gave it back to her. "Don't know. There were so many Elizabeths and Marys, it's hard to say who it's even referring to."

"Elizabeth and Mary," mused Perdita. "The Tudor queens, or two of Lettice Knollys's sisters were called Elizabeth and Mary."

"And two of Arbella Stuart's cousins were Elizabeth and Mary," said Kit. "Every time you turn around in the Tudor court you trip over an Elizabeth or a Mary."

"Elizabeth and Mary, Elizabeth and Mary." Perdita muttered it under breath like an incantation, staring at the note. Kit wandered across the room and sat on the sofa. She could feel his eyes upon her but she could not break away and speak to him yet. An idea was forming in her mind, as insubstantial as morning mist but there was a thread there and she could not afford to lose it.

She continued to run through Elizabeths and Marys who were high status enough to be important. Elizabeth. Mary. Elizabeth. Mary. *Elizabeth is now our beloved daughter, Mary…*

"Baby Elizabeth Tudor," she said aloud, while a thought took shape, "Catherine Howard's graffiti in Marquess House — the two names: Elizabeth and Nicholas."

"Baby Elizabeth is now our beloved daughter, Mary," quoted Kit.

Perdita was on her feet, utter certainty driving her as clarity overtook doubt: this letter was referring to the missing female child. Catherine's daughter. Elizabeth…

"With a ring," she said, her voice stronger now, as she pulled her theory together. "It must be the ruby ring. We know Catherine sent hers with her daughter. It was probably the only personal item she had to give to the child to remember her by."

"When's the Feast of the Immaculate Conception of the Virgin Mary?" asked Kit.

"The eighth of December."

"Are you sure?"

"Yes, definitely."

"Then we need to find girls called Mary who were born on or around that date," said Kit.

Perdita turned away in order to hide her confusion and excitement. There was someone who had been born on that date and she had been called Mary. Perdita remembered learning about her at school — it was this woman's story that had prompted Perdita's burgeoning interest in history, but it was impossible. It could not be. She shook her head, clearing the thought from her mind. She must be mistaken.

Let the evidence lead you, she reminded herself, *let the facts prove themselves. Don't try to force the facts to fit your theory.*

"We need to go to the library," she said. "There's something we need to check."

Grabbing his hand, Perdita dragged Kit behind her, wondering if she dared believe in the hypothesis she was forming. If she was correct, then discovering Catherine Howard had not been executed seemed almost trivial because, in comparison, this secret was enormous and the ramifications could be shattering.

Perdita tore through the castle, her mind in constant motion. She was aware of the warmth of Kit's palm against her own, his closeness as he hurried along beside her. Never before had she realised quite how much of a partnership they had formed. Even his quiet investigations into the history of the Pembrokeshire castles showed how much he trusted her judgement. During their quest for Catherine Howard's true story he had doubted and questioned her, waiting for her to prove herself correct before he would add his own intellectual weight to her theories. Now, he was following her lead and helping her to prove her ideas. He was truly by her side, in every sense. The thought made Perdita feel unexpectedly content.

But would he believe what she was about to suggest? She could be wrong, but it would explain why an elite force of spies had been charged with protecting this secret — why the mysterious character that Alistair's great-great-grandfather, Douglas Mackensie had dubbed The Scribe was also written from history and why there was still an armed, military section of the Secret Services whose sole purpose was to stop this information becoming public knowledge.

The Watchers did not know the full details, either. The secret had been buried so deeply that they too had lost sight of the truth — Alistair had explained this much to them in the summer. They must have an idea though, thought Perdita, as she ran towards the library, and that's why they are so diligent about retaining the structure of Tudor history. If one thread unravelled, the entire fabrication could tumble down. The Watchers must have access to more secret documents than anyone else and she found it hard to believe that the government did not know the truth.

Then another thought struck her and the readings that both her father and her grandmother had chosen at their funerals made sense. Piper had said the identical choices suggested the two passages might mean something about their mother, Louisa, but Perdita realised it was not that at all. Not only had they been clues used by Granny Mary to guide Perdita to the letters she had written for the twins, they were also warnings about what was to come. Had they chosen the readings together as their last chance to alert Perdita and Piper to the dangers they faced?

The first reading had been a short excerpt from George Orwell's classic book *1984* with its creepy vision of a society whose every move was monitored by the state. The main character, Winston Smith, worked for the Ministry of Truth, in a job that involved altering history on a daily basis in order to fit with the current propaganda of the government.

The second reading was from the book of Susannah, no longer in the main Bible but in the Apocrypha and it told the tale of a woman who nearly died due to the false testament of powerful men. The key was not the ultimate ending, it was the first line, Perdita now realised, the line 'and God knowest the secrets'.

The secrets.

Everywhere she turned there were secrets. And this one, if she were able to prove it, was the greatest of all. If she was right and the story she had been taught at school, the universally accepted version of these events, was in fact a fabrication, then how could any part of history be trusted? No wonder Randolph Connors had bugged them while they did the hard work for him. If he had this information he could use it to blackmail governments and seize who knew what level of extraordinary power? Her mind began to whirl with fear.

Follow the facts, she told herself, *there's no point panicking — you might be wrong. Follow the facts.*

To her relief, the library was deserted as she and Kit barged through the door. Dropping his hand, she began searching the shelves. There were a number of books she needed, all of which she had in her own bookcase back at Marquess House. They were popular biographies and she was confident there would be copies of them in such a well-stocked library.

"Bingo," she murmured.

"Are you going to tell me what we're looking for?" asked Kit, standing in the middle of the room while she gathered her armful of books.

"One minute," she said. "I need to check something because this theory is a bit wild."

Piling the books on to one of the long library tables, Perdita began to sift through her treasure. If it was here and there was a reference leading her to the primary source, then she might have some evidence.

Five minutes later, her face white, she looked up at Kit from her growing pile of open reference books.

"Perds, what is it?"

"I'm scared, Kit," she whispered and the voice she used did not sound like her own.

"Why? What have you found?"

"I think I've found the female heir," she said, "and it changes everything."

"More than discovering Catherine Howard wasn't executed?" Kit was incredulous.

Perdita bit her lip and nodded.

"Let me see," he insisted and Perdita passed over the brief series of notes she had scribbled. Kit stared down, recoiled as he read her suggestion, then reached across and checked a few things. Perdita watched him, trying to read his expression as she waited for his verdict.

"What do you think?" she asked. "I'd prefer it if you could have a Smug-Mackensie-Kid moment and tell me I'm wrong."

But when Kit turned around, his face was as pale and shocked as her own.

"And you worked this out from those few lines of text?"

"From the date. I wanted to check before I said anything."

Kit ran his hands through his hair as he always did when he was thinking.

"And you think she's Artemis?"

"Yes, I also think she's Daisy, which is very old familiar version of her name."

"Daisy?" asked Kit, confused.

"There are a few letters between Lily and Daisy discussing Daisy's illness and how she wanted to die to save herself any more pain..." Perdita paused, as another truth revealed itself. "Lily? Lady Venus, of course, of course. Lily was Elizabeth I and Lady Venus was her other codename, the one Lady Penelope Rich used..."

"But you said you thought Lily had been married," said Kit.

Perdita pushed another book towards him. "Perhaps she was," said Perdita and Kit's eyes widened in horror, "look, here, here, here and this too." She pointed at lines of text that she had highlighted. She did not think Deborah would mind her defacing library books under these extraordinary circumstances. "It's thin, I admit but it fits."

"It does fit," replied Kit. "Let the evidence lead us — they were your words and this evidence has definitely led us."

They stared at each other, uncertain how to proceed.

"But Lady Venus — what did you mean about Lady Penelope Rich using the name?"

"Penelope Rich was Lettice Knollys's eldest daughter from her marriage to Walter Devereux. In her adult years, Penelope was quite a woman. After enduring an unhappy marriage to Lord Robert Rich and providing the required heir and spare, she had a long-running and very public affair with Charles Blount, 8th Baron Mountjoy and had a number of children with him. She was also something of a political mover and shaker and was very focussed on the next monarch, James I, so much so, that she and her brother, Robert Devereux, Earl of Essex began a secret correspondence with James before Elizabeth's death, using codenames. These were intercepted by Thomas Fowler in 1598. He was one of Burghley's men, and the codename used for Queen Elizabeth was Venus. Penelope was Rialta and King James was Victor. The most interesting, though, was the name they used for Robert Dudley, which was The Weary Knight. All these codenames appear in our letters."

"But how do you know this?" asked Kit astounded.

"This is why I've been so frustrated," said Perdita, "because I knew I'd read these names before. I studied Penelope Rich at university and her involvement in espionage but it was only for one essay. The names have been nudging me for weeks but I couldn't remember where from. Reading all this has finally made me see what I've been missing. It's as though I was trying too hard and the answer wouldn't reveal itself but, today, suddenly, it's come back to me. The letters intercepted by Burghley are in the public domain — well, they were. The Watchers may have since removed them."

Between them, they found, catalogued and printed the letters. Staring down at their evidence, Perdita felt a huge shudder run through her.

"We need to tell your dad," said Perdita.

Kit began shutting the books and piling them into the battered Fred Perry sports holdall he used as a computer bag. Perdita followed suit and moments later the desks were clear. Kit wiped his search history from the terminal he had used and with great reluctance, Perdita did the same.

"We'll do it together."

He took her hand and after a moment's hesitation, Perdita let him lead the way to his father.

Chapter Three

"All electronic devices off, please," said Alistair. "We're doing this the old-fashioned way: pens, papers and, if necessary, an overhead projector. The information we're about to impart is so sensitive I can't risk any security breaches."

Around the table Piper, Callum, Stuart, Deborah and Susan exchanged bemused glances but complied with Alistair's orders. He was at the head of the long boardroom table with Perdita and Kit seated on either side. They had been closeted in Alistair's office for the past hour, discussing Perdita's discovery, and had decided the others needed to be appraised of their suspicions.

Alistair waited until everyone was settled, then stood, his movement drawing everyone's attention.

"As you may have gathered, Perdita has made a rather startling breakthrough and we need to discuss it."

"What's going on, Alistair?" asked Piper. "The three of you look as though someone has died."

Alistair shuddered at her comment but forced his usual calm, reassuring smile to his face even if, this time, it did not quite reach his blue eyes.

"No one has died," he said, "but if what Perdita has discovered can be proven, then the repercussions could be extreme."

The alert and expectant atmosphere around the table shifted to an uneasy silence.

"As it's quite a complex, I'll let Perdita, with Kit's assistance, lead you through her evidence, then after she has finished, we can discuss her findings and add our own thoughts."

He sat down and turned to Perdita, who looked around the table. The nervous faces of the people she loved best gazed back at her and a sharp pang of guilt shot through her. Once she had told them, they too would be involved in this dangerous discovery and they would be in even more peril than they were at present. She knew that was not her fault but delivering bad news was always a thankless task. Shaking back her dark hair, she forced a small, professional smile to her lips as though she were about to begin a university lecture.

"I'm going to start a bit further back than is probably necessary," she explained, "but it's important in order to frame this in the proper context."

They all continued to stare, her nervousness adding to the tension in the room.

"Despite what is stated in our history books, we have discovered that Catherine Howard gave birth to twins, a girl and a boy." There was nodding around the table as everyone acknowledged this information. "Catherine was still married to Henry VIII, so these children were legitimate Tudor heirs. We know the boy ailed but from other information we have gathered, we're certain he survived. His name, as given to him by his mother, was Nicholas. Her daughter also lived and we know this child's birth name was Elizabeth. These children were royal Tudor heirs, so their correct titles should have been Prince Nicholas Tudor, Duke of York, as this was the title given to the 'spare', while the heir was always the Prince of Wales. The little girl would have been Princess Elizabeth Tudor, however, as there was already a Princess Elizabeth, it's unlikely this child would have remained being called by her birth name."

Perdita sipped some water, using the pause as an excuse to gather herself before continuing.

"After we arrived here, with the help of our brilliant library teams, we began studying Granny's second unpublished manuscript, which we've named *The Ladies of Melusine*. We have also been transcribing the primary source material for this work, which are the letters she bought from her friend, Lady Pamela Johnson. As we are all aware, these were sent between a group of women covering the dates 1541 until 12 December 1662. They used codenames and a form of secret language to communicate, but the main correspondence centres around 'Artemis' and 'Apollo' — who we think are the missing twin heirs, thanks to Izabel and Eveie's work on Lady Kathy Knollys's Book of Hours. There is also a woman named 'Venus'. Kit and I have deduced that a short series of letters between 'Lily' and 'Daisy' are connected, too. We think 'Lily' and 'Venus' are the same person, likewise 'Artemis' and 'Daisy'..."

"And, 'Apollo'?" asked Susan.

"Nicholas Tudor, the lost Duke of York," said Kit. "Although, we're certain his name was changed and we are yet to identify this new title in historical records. For now, we've concentrated on the women, particularly as Piper has found a lead for the second ruby ring — the piece of jewellery we know was given to Catherine's daughter shortly after her birth."

"Let's focus, please," called Alistair. "There's a lot to get through and we need to be methodical."

Perdita checked her notes, her hands trembling and continued, "What you may not be aware of is that Lily is a familiar name for Elizabeth and Daisy is a very old 'shortened' version of Mary..."

"Those two names again," interrupted Callum. "Elizabeth and Mary."

"Exactly. All roads seem to lead us back to two women called Elizabeth and Mary," agreed Perdita. "For a while, I wondered if these were rare, newly-discovered letters written by Queen Elizabeth I and her half-sister, Mary Tudor, daughter of Henry VIII and his first wife, Katherine of Aragon. However, as 'Lily' discussed her marriage, I dismissed this idea. Elizabeth was famously The Virgin Queen.

"Yet it would have been foolish to dismiss the hypothesis without discussing their relationship. These two women have been described as being friends in childhood but as having an uneasy relationship once Mary ascended to the throne on 19 July 1553. In fact, it became so fraught Elizabeth was imprisoned in the Tower of London and had to beg for her life. On 17 November 1558, Elizabeth heard the news that her sister Mary Tudor was dead and she was now Queen of England.

"Reading the letters, which were warm and funny and discussed 'Lily' and 'Daisy's' hopes, fears and love lives, none of the dates or conversations tallied with those that would be expected between Elizabeth and Mary Tudor. I know we're dealing with shifting sands here because things have been changed but the Mary in the letters spoke about her late French husband, who had been the elder brother of Lily's husband. Mary Tudor was married to Philip II of Spain — she did not have any links with the French court. So I dismissed both Elizabeth I and Mary Tudor as potential corresponders and decided the Lily and Daisy letters, while interesting, were unconnected with our search for Catherine's missing daughter."

"What changed your mind?" asked Stuart.

"The note we found this morning," she replied.

To her surprise, Kit produced photocopied sheets of the short note and handed them around the table.

"Baby Elizabeth arrived with a ring on the Feast of the Immaculate Conception of the blessed Virgin Mary. She is now our beloved daughter, Mary," Deborah read aloud. "This was the odd one out in the letters that Jenny Procter and I discussed at length," she explained. "It was tucked in with some that we've since translated and are signed by Lady Margaret Douglas, the Countess of Lennox, but at the time, we thought the handwriting was similar to that of Lettice Knollys, Countess of Leicester, which is why we included it with hers."

"I'm glad you did," said Kit. "It sparked something in Perdita's memory and stopped us from going too far wrong. Before we read this, we thought Lettice Knollys was the heir."

"But she isn't?" clarified Susan.

"No," replied Kit.

"What did you recall, Perds?" asked Piper.

Perdita turned to look at her sister. "You must remember, Piper, I have a favourite person in Tudor history."

Piper's eyes were wide. "But how…?" She shook her head, waiting for her sister to continue, her face blanched white at the implication of Perdita's words.

"When I read the note: 'Baby Elizabeth arrived with a ring on the Feast of the Immaculate Conception of the blessed Virgin Mary. She is now our beloved daughter, Mary', it reminded me of something. I needed to be sure because it had been so long ago, I couldn't remember clearly. This morning in the library I checked the reference to the Hamilton Papers, which were published in Edinburgh in 1890 and were a history of Scotland in the sixteenth century. In them, it states that 'The daughter and only surviving child of King James V of Scotland was baptised at the palace of Linlithgow, West Lothian, on the

Feast of the Immaculate Conception of the Virgin Mary on 8 December 1542. She was baptised, Mary. Although, one rumour stated that she had been named Elizabeth'."

There was a collective gasp but Perdita continued: "This is compounded by the fact that there has always been a question over Mary, Queen of Scots's true date of birth. You see, prior to this, her mother had been under huge stress and was thought to have had the baby prematurely. A contemporary report to Henry VIII from one of his informants, Lisle, stated: 'The queen was delivered before her time of a daughter, a very weak child, who is not expected to survive'. That was followed by another report which claimed this baby was 'a weak child named Elizabeth'. There was then a sudden change of tone, when on 19 December 1542, Lisle reported; 'the princess lately born is alive and good-looking'. The child in question was from then on known by her official title."

Perdita paused, looking around at the intent faces of those she loved, aware she was about to deliver a theory that would put them all in even more danger if it were proved to be true. As she spoke, her voice was low and tense.

"I think Catherine Howard's daughter, baby Elizabeth Tudor, was swapped for the daughter of James V of Scotland and Mary of Guise, and her new name was Mary, Queen of Scots."

"But that's impossible!"

It was Deborah's voice that cut through the uneasy silence.

"We thought that, too," replied Perdita, "but no matter how I look at it or how I try to rearrange the evidence, these are the comments that crop up again and again."

"If she was swapped, surely someone would have noticed?" said Callum.

"Not necessarily," replied Kit. "Would you be able to tell the difference between one new-born baby and another if you'd only seen it for a few moments?"

Perdita looked over at her sister. "What do you think, Pipes?" she asked.

"It's persuasive," she admitted. "My main issue, though, is why would the king of Scotland and his wife agree to such a swap?"

"The king probably didn't know," said Perdita. "He was ill and died on 14 December 1542. He had been fighting Henry VIII's army at the Battle of Solway Moss but had taken heavy losses. The Scottish army was in disarray and the king had retreated to Falkland Palace in Fife. He died not long afterwards from a fever. Shortly before this, his wife had given birth to a daughter. This child was the only surviving heir to the Scottish crown. It's possible Mary of Guise was aware her daughter was unlikely to live, so she was looking for anything that might help her."

"But, Perds, how did Mary of Guise know about Catherine Howard's baby?" asked Piper. "If you remember, Catherine was supposed to be dead. And, even if you push that to one side, Catherine was in the depths of Pembrokeshire while Mary of Guise was in Scotland. It's a huge distance."

"Lady Margaret Douglas," replied Perdita. "She was James V of Scotland's half-sister. They had the same mother: Margaret Tudor, older sister of Henry VIII. We know Margaret Douglas was part of Catherine's inner circle and we can place her at Marquess House at the time Catherine gave birth. She was engaged to Catherine's brother, Charles Howard. She gives us a direct link to the Scottish court. In *The Catherine Howard Codex* there is a short letter suggesting she planned to travel to

Scotland, although we don't have written corroboration yet to say whether she made the journey —"

"We do!" interrupted Deborah. "Lady Margaret Douglas had already organised safe passage for herself and any other members of Catherine's entourage who wished to escape to the Scottish court."

"What?" Perdita was startled.

"It's in one of her letters," Deborah said. "We haven't finished translating and transcribing all Lady Margaret's letters from The Lady Pamela Collection but of the few we've completed, there was one referring to the king of Scotland's generous offer of protection."

"So, we have a definite link," said Perdita, a thrill of fear in her voice.

"Why would Mary of Guise agree to this madness, though?" asked Stuart.

"She didn't have an alternative. If her daughter died, there would be no heir to the throne, which would have led to civil war, to invasions from England, possibly Spain. James V, with Mary of Guise by his side, had worked hard to stabilise Scotland and under his reign it was beginning to prosper. With James suddenly dead, Mary was in danger. Yet, if she was the mother of the monarch, no one would be able to disregard her power as regent. So, if her daughter was ailing and Lady Margaret Douglas had told her about another royal baby who needed a safe place to hide, preferably with other royal children, there's a strong chance Mary of Guise would have agreed to take her in. I would also suspect the wily duke of Norfolk was involved somewhere, too. His brother, George Howard, was an envoy at the court of King James V and apparently, George's daughter, Douglas, was with him."

"And we know," said Kit, "Douglas went on to marry Edward Stafford, who was eventually uncovered as the spy 'Julius'. Douglas may well have heard her father discussing the moving of baby Elizabeth Tudor and this is how, in later years, the secret reached the ears of Philip II of Spain."

There was silence as the group processed the information that Perdita had drawn together from her many sources in order to make a coherent whole.

"It would explain why Mary of Guise was so resistant to the idea of Mary, Queen of Scots marrying Prince Edward Tudor, heir to the English throne, and uniting the two countries," mused Deborah, breaking the silence. "Only she and a select few knew that the two children weren't cousins but were half-brother and half-sister."

Susan turned to her husband. "Alistair, you're very quiet, what do you think?"

"I think it's possible to argue this from many angles," he said, his tone reflective, "but, ludicrous though it seems at first sight, the more you examine the evidence, the more convincing this version of events seems. However, Perdita has more to explain."

Perdita was still standing, staring down at her scrawled notes. "Lily and Daisy," she said, "constantly refer to each other as 'my friend the nun' — another word for nun is 'sister'."

A wave of understanding rippled around the table.

"Elizabeth and Mary," continued Perdita. "When I was checking this morning, there was something else I needed to confirm. History tells us that Elizabeth I never married, however, she came close to it a number of times. There was one man in particular who bounced backward and forwards into her life…"

"Robert Dudley, Earl of Leicester…" began Susan, but Perdita shook her head.

"No, I think he has always been the red herring, rather like Lettice Knollys," she said. "There was someone else, a French duke."

"Who?" asked Callum.

"Francis, the count of Alencon, who later inherited the title, Duke of Anjou," explained Perdita. "He was the youngest son of Henry II of France and Catherine de' Medici. This made him the younger brother of Francis II of France, who when he was the Dauphin, was married to Mary, Queen of Scots."

"But Elizabeth didn't marry Alencon," said Stuart. "She remained single throughout her life."

Perdita lifted a book from the stack in front of her and flicked through to a page she had marked earlier.

"The duke of Anjou died in June 1584," said Perdita. "Elizabeth was said to have been devastated, but what is rarely reported is that she went into mourning for six months. When the French ambassador, Castelnau, visited her in September 1584 at Windsor Castle, he was invited to watch the hunt in the park from a newly built terrace that was on the walls of Windsor Castle at Berkshire. What's remarkable is, when the queen finally appeared, she was wearing a black dress and a veil that fell to the ground. Castelnau was shocked and later wrote that Elizabeth's attire was akin to that worn by a widow."

"There's also testimony that she wrote poetry about the loss of her love at this time and some of it specifically names Anjou as the recipient of her feelings," added Kit, passing around photocopies of the poem, alleged to have been written by the queen.

"Not to mention a large collection of jewellery all featuring frogs," added Perdita.

"You're suggesting Elizabeth actually married Anjou?" asked Piper.

"Yes," said Perdita. "Despite the age gap — he was 24 and she was 49 — there are numerous comments scattered throughout her biographies saying she referred to him as her 'beloved frog', gave him jewels and even funded his, admittedly rather disastrous, invasion of the Netherlands. But if Elizabeth did marry the duke of Anjou, why was it written out of history? There were no children from the union, so why pretend it was yet another disastrous engagement rather than a barren, short-lived marriage?"

"To discredit Elizabeth," suggested Deborah. "To continue with the popular theme among male historians that because she couldn't hold on to a man, there must have been something fundamentally wrong with her."

"Excellent reasoning," murmured Susan, exchanging a complicit look with Deborah.

"For our purposes, it also muddies the issue," said Perdita. "If we assume Elizabeth was married, then this new evidence when brought together with their letters confirms it, because the letter writers discuss their husbands and Lily's loss. It also suggests that the two monarchs knew of their real connection, that Mary was aware she was the daughter of, at least, Henry VIII — we don't know if she knew her mother's identity. However, throughout Elizabeth and Mary's surviving official correspondence there are endless references to each other as 'sister', but this has always been considered to be an affectation, as they were accepted as being second cousins."

"There's something else, though," said Kit, his face unusually sombre. "Remember how Mary, Queen of Scots died? She was executed on the orders of Elizabeth I."

"You're saying Elizabeth knew Mary was her half-sister but she signed her death warrant anyway?" asked Susan, shocked.

"No, Susan," said Perdita. "Why would Elizabeth execute the mother and then anoint the son? Mary, Queen of Scots's son, James VI of Scotland became James I of England, uniting the two warring countries for the first time. Yet, under the terms of Henry VIII's will concerning the succession, no one born outside England was eligible to ascend to its throne. If Elizabeth had followed this law, then James VI could not have become her heir because he was born in Scotland.

"It begs the question: if she had really authorised Mary's death surely it would have been the obvious thing to invoke this law and keep Mary's line of descent away from the English throne, yet she didn't. Under the terms of Henry VIII's will, Arbella Stuart should have been Elizabeth's heir. Unless, of course, Elizabeth knew that James was the grandson rather than the great-nephew of Henry VIII and therefore was the legitimate heir.

"There's something else, too," Perdita continued. "Remember how in our research on Catherine Howard, we discovered the Bill of Attainder colloquially known as her 'death warrant' was never signed by King Henry VIII but was signed 'in absentia'? According to one of Mary's most respected and renowned biographers, Mary's 'death warrant' or the legal document signed by Elizabeth I authorising the Scottish queen's execution has vanished from the official records. All that remains are a few hastily made draft copies that have never been signed by Elizabeth and don't bear the official seal of England that should have been attached by the Lord Chancellor."

Around the table, all eyes were upon Perdita, each face registering intense shock. The revelations about Catherine

Howard seemed minor in comparison with this new version of events, yet Catherine was the key to it all. The silence continued until, with a certain amount of apprehension, Deborah cleared her throat.

"Perdita, I concur with all you've said, but may I play devil's advocate for a moment?"

"Of course," said Perdita.

"How did Elizabeth and Mary discover the truth? If you say they wrote warmly to each other, who would have told them and wouldn't Elizabeth have been wary of having other Tudor heirs around?"

Perdita flipped through her notes and spread a few pages in front of her.

"Izabel has been concentrating on the early letters, the ones written around the time Mary, Queen of Scots was a baby," said Perdita. "These letters were mostly written in French or Latin but, for some reason, not code, and there are only a few from that period," she said, sorting through the printed sheets in front of her. "This is the list of letters from 1542 and 1543."

Kit read Izabel's notes aloud: "Letters from Lady Margaret Douglas, Lady Isabel Baynton, Lady Margaret Arundell, Lady Kathryn Knollys, Lady Anne of Cleves, a woman signing herself Catalus and another signing herself Marie. In total, there are only 38 letters from the period of 1541 to 1552."

"The heavily coded correspondence begins in 1557," Perdita continued. "There are a few before then, but this is the year when the pseudonyms replace real names and the strange syntax appears with more regularity, as though a new generation of writers has taken over and they have begun developing their own system of elaborate codes."

"Mary Tudor was on the throne in 1557," said Deborah. "Elizabeth and her women were under house arrest at Hatfield

House, although she was occasionally allowed trips to Brockett Hall — in fact, some historians believe she may have been there when she heard the news she was Queen. Right up until Mary Tudor's death, there was a great deal of uncertainty as to whom she would name as heir. In early 1558, it was recorded she thought she was pregnant, but again it turned out to be a false alarm. Also, in April 1558, Mary, Queen of Scots married Francis, the Dauphin of France."

"There was one other significant event," said Perdita. "The death of Anne of Cleves on 15 July 1557."

"Would that be relevant?" asked Susan.

"Possibly," said Perdita. "We know she was at the heart of the secret from the beginning and then there's the mystery of Anne of Cleves's baby."

"What?" and this time it was Alistair who sounded startled. He had been so quiet, allowing them to reason things out, Perdita had forgotten he was in the room. "She had a baby?"

"No, Alistair, but there are historical records stating that Anne of Cleves was accused of having the king's child. However, when the house was searched and her women questioned she was exonerated because there was no trace of an infant. Kit and I think the rumour was probably started when she looked after baby Elizabeth Tudor at some point during the journey from Pembrokeshire to Linlithgow. We can corroborate this because there is a reference in the Marquess House account books stating that Catherine sent Anne a gift of linen as a thank you for her help."

"Fascinating," said Alistair. "Mary would have been so proud of you."

Perdita swallowed the unexpected lump that rose in her throat and continued, "In the accepted version of events the year is slightly out but we know how many things have been changed, so it's likely this is the link we need.

"As for the rest of Catherine's inner circle, we know that Lady Kathy Knollys returned to court in London," said Perdita, reading from the summary prepared by Izabel. "She'd given birth to her son Henry in early 1542, then in November 1543 she gave birth to Lettice Knollys. Lady Isabel Baynton remained with Catherine until June 1543, when she returned to court to support her husband Edward. Lady Margaret Arundell stayed on, though, and in the middle of 1554, she and Catherine were joined by their younger sister, Mary."

"Where's Lady Margaret Douglas?" asked Piper.

"Not at Marquess House and neither is Charles Howard, which means they could have been on their way to Linlithgow with baby Elizabeth Tudor. The next definite date we have for Margaret Douglas is the announcement of her engagement to Matthew Stewart, the earl of Lennox, on 25 June 1544."

"And what happened to Charles Howard?"

Perdita shrugged. "It's another one of those historical mysteries. He disappears from the records in 1544 and nothing is ever heard about him again."

"Do you think he died?" asked Callum.

"Possibly or was murdered," Perdita replied.

"So, most of her women dispersed and left Catherine with the remaining child," confirmed Susan.

"Yes, Nicholas Tudor, who should have been the duke of York."

Perdita watched Kit as he flicked through the transcripts. Once again, there were scans of the originals alongside the new translations. Perdita felt the hairs on the back of her neck stand up as she watched the words sliding in front of her eyes. Words written so many years ago, holding the voices of women, long dead, many forgotten, who back then were as vital and full of life as she and Piper were now. She could not explain the strength of the link she felt with Catherine and the story that was unfolding around her.

Then, as Kit turned another page, reaching the item he was searching for, she felt a cold tingle run the length of her spine. Once more all eyes were on her and Kit gave her a reassuring smile as she placed the letter on the old-fashioned overhead projector, flipping it on so everyone could read it. The letter was addressed to someone called Catalus and was brief but she could still feel the impact of the words resonating through time like the ripples on a lake.

Chere Catalus, your gift has been our salvation, to offer salve to your broken heart, take solace in the knowledge the beautiful child is crowned. Our ruby is safe in the land of the thistle, one day she will know. I promise, when the time is right, I will tell her. Lady Holbein.

"Catalus is Latin for kitten, which is a very old-fashioned diminutive of Catherine and one that is used throughout the Catherine Howard codex," said Perdita. "I think this is a message to Catherine Howard. The ruby is the ring and the crowned child is baby Elizabeth. 'Lady Holbein' was confirming that Catherine's daughter was safely in Scotland, 'the land of the thistle', and had been crowned Queen. If you take this with the other note about Elizabeth becoming Mary, this takes us a step further."

"But who is Lady Holbein?" asked Stuart. "While it's interesting, it still doesn't explain how Elizabeth I and Mary, Queen of Scots discovered they were half-sisters and not cousins."

Perdita turned back to the letters and Izabel's list of codenames searching for the final piece of the puzzle: a letter dated July 1584.

My sweet Daisy, news comes to me today from the Fens, where the watches have been increased due to the threat of the old. Oh, that we should be free of the troublesome wars of God, so that we could show our true loyalty to one another. When the Lady Holbein summoned me that dark night to tell me the secret she had kept for so many years, I had never imagined we would ever be this close because of our opposing beliefs. You who were raised in the old and myself in the new. Did you find solace in your prayers when you were widowed? My mourning is hard to bear, being a widow of only one month. How did you cope? You have been in this position three times? Such strength. Like the Lady Holbein, you were resilient in the face of cruel and powerful men. She was wise and beautiful in every way. Despite what my father said. Semper sorores, sweet sister.

Everyone looked at Perdita, awaiting an explanation.

"When we discovered the Catherine Howard codex, there were snatches of letters to the only other person who could fully appreciate what Catherine had been through during her marriage to Henry."

"You mean Anne of Cleves?" confirmed Piper.

"Yes," replied Perdita. "When she was first betrothed to Henry VIII it was on the strength of a portrait painted by Holbein."

"So, you think Lady Holbein was Anne of Cleves?" asked Callum.

"Why not?" said Kit, his voice defensive. "It would show Anne's sense of humour."

"You think Anne of Cleves told Elizabeth the truth about her younger half-brother and sister?" confirmed Deborah.

"Yes," she replied, but before she could elucidate, Susan interrupted.

"Perdita, what does the rest of the letter mean?" she asked, gazing at the text as it floated on the screen in front of them.

"As I've been going through the letters, I've been making guesses as to the meanings of certain words and I think 'old' referred to Catholicism, as is the old religion versus the 'new', which was Protestantism. Is it possible that when Anne of Cleves knew she was dying, she summoned Elizabeth to tell her the truth. I think the revelation of the secret had to come from someone with authority and Anne was a former Queen Consort. Anne commissioned the ruby rings, she was at the heart of the subterfuge — if she had kept these secrets all this time, don't you think it's likely that when she knew death was approaching she passed the information about Mary's true identity on to Elizabeth as she had promised her old friend, Catherine Howard? There is a line in Anne's will bequeathing Elizabeth a 'jewel', which could have been her ruby ring, the one with the emerald clip. The ring currently downstairs in the vault."

Once again, silence greeted this pronouncement.

"If you're correct, and I think you are, Anne took a huge risk," said Deborah in awe. "So did Elizabeth."

"Perhaps she was hoping Elizabeth would find solace in the fact that she had a sister who was connected to her through her Howard as well as her Tudor blood — remember Anne Boleyn and Catherine Howard were first cousins. It would also explain the upsurge in letters and the development of the new codes and hidden words around this time."

"You can understand why they didn't advertise the fact Mary was a Tudor — it would have caused civil war, again. Do you think they knew about the boy, Nicholas?" asked Piper.

"Difficult to gauge," replied Perdita. "I can imagine knowledge of his existence would have made them both edgy. If there was a male Tudor heir lurking in the background, not only would his claim to the English throne have been superior to Elizabeth's, he would also be a key focal point for rebellions."

"However, there is the issue of Mary, Queen of Scots' execution," said Deborah.

"Which we don't think Elizabeth sanctioned," Kit interjected, glancing at Perdita who nodded her agreement.

"No, I don't think she did," said Perdita. "I think that was a tale created in the aftermath, rather like the legend of Anne Boleyn's supposedly monstrous last miscarriage, the one that 'proved' she was a witch and drove Henry into the arms of Jane Seymour. The tale of the misshapen child was actually proposed 40 years later by Nicholas Sander, a Catholic propagandist and there was no contemporary evidence."

"Another clue pointing to changes in real events," said Kit.

"Which brings me to the question: was Mary actually executed?" asked Perdita.

Once again, a lengthy silence grew around the table. It was Kit who spoke first.

"My doctorate was on the manipulation of legislation for the preservation of national security," he said. "I used the Babington Plot as my opening argument."

"Exactly, the Babington Plot," she said, nodding to Kit, stepping back to allow him to take up the explanation.

"It was created and controlled by Elizabeth's spymaster Sir Francis Walsingham to catch Mary, Queen of Scots in the act of treason against the English monarch," Kit continued. "Elizabeth's lord chancellor, Lord Burghley, told the queen that Spanish ships had been spotted off the Welsh coast and an invasion was imminent. This was two years before Philip II of Spain launched the Armada, but apparently the queen was so terrified by the prospect of an invasion, she signed the death warrant and gave permission for Mary to be executed, believing the Scottish queen was in cahoots with Philip of Spain."

"So, what are you saying?" asked Alistair, leaning forwards, his face tense.

"After reading all the new evidence in the letters," said Perdita, "we're suggesting that the ships were really there but that they weren't part of the Armada as Burghley supposedly claimed. We think they were part of this invasion force that has been written out of history. The Babington Plot is one of the oddest entrapment stories in our past, yet it is studied endlessly and never changes, despite the fact it's littered with anomalies — the most obvious being that a consummate survivor like Mary, Queen of Scots would never have been careless enough to incriminate herself on paper. Do you think it's possible that the reason the Spanish invasion has been expunged from the records is because they were the ones responsible for the death of Mary, Queen of Scots, and not Elizabeth and her Privy Councillors? Maybe the death of the Scottish queen was the first move Philip II made as part of his plans to invade England but it was rewritten by The Scribe in order to discredit Queen Elizabeth."

PART SIX: September, 1586

Chapter One

To dress a queen was a work of art. Each layer had meaning, each jewel was a message. Nothing was there by chance. Every expensive and exquisite detail was part of the trappings of war.

The chemise came first: linen as pale and pure as moonbeams on a clear winter night, embroidered with shimmering white silk, the contrasting fabrics catching the light with every movement. Next were the stockings, delicately woven silk that whispered on the skin, coloured the freshest rose pink, hinting at spring, youth and beauty.

The pair of bodies followed, made from the finest golden cambric, patterned with mythical creatures — mermaids, unicorns and, flying majestically across the back, the glorious phoenix. The Spanish farthingale, a cone-shaped frame of wire and whalebone was tied to the corset, poised and waiting, ready to receive the weight of the heavy skirts.

A rowle was attached to this, crescent-shaped and snug around Elizabeth's waist, gentled in against her back, another layer of support before the triangular stomacher was laced into place. Its shimmering silver thread was another hint of the intensity still to come. The twinkling precious metal was her talisman of femininity, her reminder of the moon, the celestial sister who hung in the night sky. The kirtle was laced around her, fitting over the farthingale, its white silk the perfect foil for the splendour of the forepart: bedecked and bejewelled with intricate patterns of lace cutwork, accented with gems of coral, green and purple — coral for protection against evil, emeralds for love and amethysts for devotion — it rested like a shield, awaiting the battle to come.

The cloth-of-silver partlet was tied under her arms to fill in the low neckline of her gown, its delicate ruffles patterned with golden thread and rows of seed pearls glinting in the light. Gold for the masculinity of the sun, for power, for success, juxtaposed against the dainty pearls; the representatives of tears, of purity and of peace. The snowy white ruff was attached to this, the frame for her flaming red hair but, before this, was the majesty of the cloth-of-gold gown. Breath-taking in its beauty and so heavy it required two of her women to fit it to her slender frame.

The women fluttered around her, their delicate but firm fingers lacing and patting the spectacular gown into place, their touch offering familiarity and comfort. They were her army of helpful hands, of soothing voices and determined companions, ever her supporters and her soldiers in this interminable war. Turning in the early morning light, amber gems flared like flames within the dense golden fabric, adding lustre to the metallic sheen of the skirt. Amber was for drawing out impurities and offering healing, a potent fire from the dawn of time, offering endings and beginnings.

The matching sleeves were tied into place, slashed to reveal the cloth-of-silver lining and, in each delicate opening, an embroidered mermaid peeped out, the outlines captured in shimmering greens, blues and purples. As they caught the light they appeared to swim — sensuous and mysterious — like a woman's heart.

On Elizabeth's feet were placed golden slippers, the latchet style with two side flaps that fastened over a central tongue. The soles were thin, supple leather and the uppers were the same embroidered cloth-of-gold as her gown. On each instep flew a phoenix surrounded by flames. She would walk on fire today as she fought to save her realm.

Seated before an oval looking glass, her favourite wig was placed over her own red hair. Its vermillion brilliance dazzled against the starched white ruff with its intricate cut work. A string of deep, twinkling emeralds were woven through her curls. Around her neck and shoulders were draped strings of matchless creamy white pearls and nestled at her throat was the fabulous phoenix pendant given to her one Christmas by her younger half-sister. On her pale white fingers were the ruby ring given to her by Anne of Cleves, the locket ring containing the miniature of her mother, Anne Boleyn, and on her little finger, the golden signet ring worn by all the Ladies of Melusine, the top embossed with the mermaid they used to imprint their seal.

White make-up was smoothed across her skin, the herb eyebright was dripped into her eyes to add extra sparkle, rouge was dabbed on to her cheeks, while a perfect cupid's bow was painted around her lips and delicate perfumed oils were applied to her wrists. Finally, her women fell away, one by one, forming a circle around her as they checked their handiwork, allowing no errors to mar the importance of their mission and, as an appreciative silence fell, Gloriana rose from the chair in the centre of the hushed room: like Venus from the foaming waves, she was complete, perfect, formidable.

"Leave me," she said, her voice low. "I would like some time alone with my thoughts before we descend to the hell that awaits us below."

With a rustling and murmuring like the breeze through the autumn leaves, her women gathered the paraphernalia required for dressing a monarch and walked noiselessly through the doors, their departure leaving an eerie silence in the brightly painted chamber.

Time had passed since they had found the shocking letter sewn into the lining of Babington's coat. The man had confessed, and the following day a horseman had arrived in the Habsburg livery to deliver a sealed scroll to Elizabeth, and this time she knew Mary was in terrible danger. It was the reason why she was now in this room in Boughton Hall in Northamptonshire. It was the home of Sir Edward Montagu and his wife, Elizabeth, daughter of James Harington of Exton in Rutland. Both were wealthy men, dependable Protestants and staunch supporters of Elizabeth, yet neither usually moved in the high-status, high-glamour and high-stakes world of the inner court. Today, though, Boughton Hall was the centre of power.

Soon to arrive in the presence chamber below was the envoy from Philip II of Spain. Within the hour, Elizabeth would be bargaining not only for her own life but for that of her sister too, and, more importantly, for her crown and kingdom.

Her privy council, including George Talbot, Earl of Shrewsbury, in his capacity as her Earl Marshal of England; his son, Henry Talbot; Sir Francis Walsingham; Sir William Cecil; Sir James Croft; Sir Christopher Hatton and a solid wall of support from her remaining council members, including 26 earls, barons and senior justices, were all filling the hall as she waited for the allotted hour when she would descend to Hades.

Mr Edward Barker would act as registrar of events — he was Robert Dudley's lawyer and had been responsible for notarising the depositions made in 1582 by the witnesses at Lettice and Robert's wedding. He was another man loyal to her, to the crown and to justice. Even Robert Dudley and his men were poised in the Netherlands to return and fight for Elizabeth, should she send word.

Outside the window, the September sky was clear. No clouds marred the dome of blue as it stretched upwards towards the sun. A swirl of leaves floated past the window, red and yellow, full of glee at being sent on a final adventure. Elizabeth watched as one danced and whirled on the golden eddies of the breeze, following its progress while it skipped and hopped across the ancient landscape of her kingdom. In the distance she could hear shouts from the fields as the final harvests were gathered, birds sang for the pure pleasure of being alive and the world shimmered in the flawlessness of an English day. Yet it sickened Elizabeth and, shuddering, she turned away from the bucolic perfection.

A casket sat on the small table beside the bed. When the word had come to request a parley at Boughton House, Elizabeth had insisted this unassuming wooden chest was included in the heavily guarded and securely padlocked strongbox containing her jewels. Alone now, she sat on the embroidered counterpane with its pattern of swirling Tudor roses weaving its way across the bed. Removing a key from a small pouch secreted under her pillow, she unlocked the box for the first time in nearly 30 years. With fear and uncertainty now enveloping her reign, the time had come to ensure all was in place in the event that her successor might need her help, even if was from beyond the grave.

On the night her former stepmother, Anne of Cleves, had given her this box, she had clutched it on her knees, transfixed, as Lady Isabel Baynton had told her the tale of Catherine Howard, but even she had not known everything, and Elizabeth had been certain the remaining answers lay in the casket. When, at last, she had climbed into bed that fateful night, she had waited until those around her had fallen asleep before scurrying to sit by the fire, to use its light to read the contents of the box, to understand what it had been so vital for the Lady Anne to pass on.

Inside had been a series of letters between Anne and Catherine, discussing their fear and heartbreak as they tried to find a path of safety through their lives and their shared experience of being married to Elizabeth's violent father. Folded neatly below these, she discovered a full confession written by Anne, explaining her part in Catherine's disappearance and the assistance she had given with moving Catherine's daughter, Elizabeth, to be hidden in the Scottish court with Mary of Guise. To her surprise, the young princess had discovered that it was Lady Margaret Douglas and her fiancé, Charles Howard, who had volunteered to take the little girl on her dangerous journey the length of the country. The Lady Anne had placed her official seal on the document to add gravitas to its words.

However, the most surprising piece of parchment had been a similar confession written and sealed by the all-powerful Thomas Howard, 3rd Duke of Norfolk. He had died on 25 August 1554 and the letter was dated a week earlier. Like the Lady Anne, the duke had given a detailed account of his involvement in events, including the alteration he had made on the death warrant of Katherine Tilney and Joan Bulmer and the new identity given to Catherine's son, the Howard heir to the throne, who when Catherine had died in 1552, had been made his ward. A year later, the duke had placed the boy with the Devereux family in Lamphey, Pembrokeshire.

Elizabeth had been both scared and delighted at the prospect of two more legitimate siblings and while, over the years, she had slowly forged a strong bond with her sister, her fear of what might happen if a male heir emerged had left her wary of revealing the truth to her brother. And yet, she knew him, liked him, loved him even, and, in adulthood, had often relied upon him. As a small child, the boy who should have been king revealed himself to Elizabeth, even though she had not understood it at the time.

Closing her eyes and looking back down the years, she saw the scene playing out in her mind as though it were yesterday. It was 1547, her father, Henry VIII, had recently died and she was living with her final stepmother, Katheryn Parr, at her manor in Hanworth, Middlesex. The dowager queen had surprised the court by marrying the handsome, dashing rogue, Sir Thomas Seymour, very soon after she was widowed. Thomas, who was uncle to the new king, the nine-year-old Edward VI, had acquired a number of wardships in order to bolster his income, one of which belonged to Elizabeth's cousin, Lady Jane Grey.

One morning, Thomas Howard had arrived with a small boy, whom he introduced as Nicholas, although he claimed this was a familiar name and not the boy's full title. Howard was reasserting his power, having only narrowly escaped an untimely death at the hands of the executioner's axe. To his relief, the old king had died before the sentence he had bestowed could be carried out and the new king, wishing to begin his reign on a positive note, had pardoned him. Thomas Howard had swept the country, assuring all who would listen that he was still powerful and influential.

While he and Thomas Seymour had enjoyed wine and victuals with the former queen; Elizabeth, Jane and young Nicholas had been left to their own devices. Jane had offered to read a passage from the bible to them, but when Elizabeth and Nicholas had declined she had flounced away. Her irritation had been so over-dramatized it had made Elizabeth and Nicholas laugh and from here they had begun to form a friendship. In fact, the boy had been so taken with Elizabeth he had confided to her his greatest secret about his most precious treasure.

"My mother has given me a locket," he had whispered to the young princess.

"A locket?"

"Yes, it's silver and it has a diamond in its centre. Inside she has put a lock of her hair, so I will never forget her, but what makes it mine are the secret words on the inside."

"Can you tell me?" Elizabeth had asked and the little boy had nodded, his face solemn.

"*Spe et nereidum*," he whispered. "It's Latin, it means 'Hope and mermaids'."

It was many years before Elizabeth read those words again in Anne of Cleves's confession and she realised the small, serious child who had confided in her had been her half-brother. After the death of Catherine Howard, Thomas Howard had bought the boy's wardship and the boy was no longer known as Nicholas. When Thomas died two years later, following instructions in a codicil added to his will from his deathbed, the child was placed in the care of the Devereux family at Lamphey and from there, he had flourished.

Even now, though, this man assumed he was the son of Thomas Howard, Duke of Norfolk and some unnamed highborn lady of rank, but with danger creeping across the kingdom towards her and in the knowledge that her sister would not survive this fight due to the severity of her illness, Elizabeth realised the time had come to add her own signed and sealed document to the cache of secrets. It was also the moment to tell her brother the truth and leave him this casket as the proof he would need to follow her on to the throne and continue the Tudor line.

Chapter Two

"We will be waiting in the ante-chamber," Kate Howard assured her cousin.

"You may not be able to see us but we will be nearby," added Lady Katherine Newton.

Elizabeth blinked back the sudden rush of unexpected tears. This day was extraordinary and emotions were taut.

"Thank you, my dears," she said, forcing a confidant smile. "We go into battle as surely as if I were seated on a great destrier and bedecked with armour instead of cloth-of-gold. We work to save my kingdom and to save a life. One that is so very precious."

Elizabeth and her ladies processed into the Great Hall at Boughton House, making it clear this was no ordinary meeting. The circumstances might be denying her the beauty of Westminster Hall but Elizabeth needed her privy council to understand that this gathering was as important as any that took place in the hallowed halls of Parliament. Lives were at stake and one life in particular. Out of the corner of her eye she noticed Bess's husband, George Talbot struggling to stand. His newly frail appearance was shocking.

Reaching the carved chair that Sir Edward Montagu had placed on a hastily built dais, surrounded by her cloth of state, Elizabeth seated herself, then waited while her ladies melted away into the shadows. There was a soft click and she knew they had departed to the ante room where they would wait until summoned. Sweeping her eyes around the room, she felt heartened as she saw her councillors, all dressed as she was in their finest attire: velvets and silks rippled in the September air.

Jewels twinkled on every doublet producing a dazzling show, a line of defiance. This was England — no foreign invader had any right to try and call the terms of war. Elizabeth was fierce, brittle and majestic in her golden dress — her court exuded power.

The door opened to admit a tall, thin man in dull brown ecclesiastic robes, with sallow skin, mousy hair and grey eyes. He marched into the room, tailed by two more clerics, their eyes downcast, who hovered in the shadows at the back of the hall. The man made no deference to the crown, no humility, no awe at Elizabeth's splendour as God's representative on earth, instead he fixed his gaze on her and paused in the centre of the room, his expression mocking.

"You will bow!" thundered Sir Francis Walsingham but the man stood his ground, gazing at Elizabeth. "Sir, you will kneel!"

The shout was taken up by the surrounding courtiers, each one taking a step forward, but the man, who wore the robes of a Jesuit priest, was not intimidated. His glance encompassed the furious men and, after a moment of consideration, he smiled, his head unbending. Lord Zouche raised his hand to summon the guard to force the man to his knees but Elizabeth stayed him.

"No, Lord Zouche," she said, her voice quiet, calm, controlled. "Do not allow this man to toy with your sensibilities. Let us hear what he has to say, then we can throw him from the building."

Lord Burghley stepped forward and scowled at the man. "You are John Ballard," he said, his voice cold as he glared at the priest, "also known as Black Fortescue. A Catholic sympathiser and spy who has spent time at Cambridge University, trying to recruit men to betray their country. You are here today under the laws of parley and, unless you break these, you will be given safe passage to deliver your message and leave. However, if you break these agreements, your head will be in danger."

Elizabeth's glittering brown eyes turned back to the priest. "Speak," she ordered.

Ballard smiled, then beckoned to one of his assistants. A young man emerged from the shadows, his rough brown robes designed to match those of his superior. The contrast to the glittering splendour of Elizabeth and her court was stark. He bowed and handed Ballard a scroll of parchment before scurrying away, his eyes flickering from side to side as though trying to locate a face in the crowd.

"I have a decree from His Supreme Majesty, Philip II of Spain," the man said.

He was English, his voice tinged with a northern accent. Elizabeth noticed his hands were soft, he had lived a privileged existence. The parchment crackled as he shot a look of pure malevolence at the queen.

"Walsingham," said Elizabeth in a bored tone. "You read the decree. I'm not sure this man will stick to the words written by Philip."

Ballard looked furious but two guards had already moved forward and taken the document, handing it to Walsingham. Elizabeth turned to look at her chief spymaster, ignoring the priest who stood, his hauteur dented, with eyes narrowed in the middle of the room. As though following a pre-planned cue, Elizabeth's ministers also turned their eyes from Ballard to Walsingham, who clearing his throat, began to read:

"In the year of our lord, fifteen hundred and eighty-six, in the month of September, I, Philip Habsburg, do offer you clemency. If you will abdicate the throne of England that you usurped from me, the rightful heir, my mercy will be made manifest. You shall be allowed to live in exile abroad. My throne will be taken by my daughter, the Infanta Isabella Clara Eugenia…"

Elizabeth laughed, a reaction that was echoed by her court.

"There is more, Your Majesty," said Walsingham, his voice grim. Elizabeth indicated for him to continue. "My graciousness will spread to your heir, your younger sister, as long as you comply with my decree…" Relief flooded through Elizabeth but Walsingham continued: "She is held by my representatives and, due to her other crimes, she will be tried under the law of the Inquisition. If she is found guilty, her punishment will be severe."

Elizabeth waited as Walsingham's eyes widened and he read the remaining few lines: "To your brother, I will show no mercy. My men will move forward from your western coast and will route him. His head will adorn the Tower of London."

White-faced, Elizabeth and Walsingham locked eyes. Her spymaster gave a small shake of his head but Elizabeth had never needed his guidance less. Ignoring the gasp of confusion that had skittered around her ministers at the mention of a brother, she turned to stare at the priest in the centre of the room, who was watching her with growing triumph in his eyes.

"This is nonsense," snapped Elizabeth. "Your decree is not even signed or sealed by Philip. You are a troublemaker and if you leave here today with your life you will consider yourself lucky. As if you would dare to apprehend any member of my court and hold them against their will. You are a charlatan and a monster. Yet you seem to think this decree is genuine. How is it possible to issue threats that are so ill-informed? It is laughable that you suggest I have siblings. Tudor heirs? If I had a brother, then I would not be Queen, he would be King…"

She forced a peel of derisive laughter. Her courtiers followed suit, the sneering brays filling the room. "As for a sister, to whom do you refer?"

Her heart pounded as she posed this question. Only a select chosen few knew the truth. Philip may have threatened her with the name "Baby Elizabeth" but this rumour had been mooted before and quashed. When Mary of Guise had given birth, there had been many conflicting accounts of the true name and birth date of her child. The duke of Norfolk had taken full advantage of this confusion and had muddied all suggestions even further.

Very few people knew the truth about what had really happened in those desperate and dark days, when two royal female children had been born. Two princesses, from opposing countries, with warring parents, yet both carrying Tudor blood. Both were briefly in the royal Scottish nursery until the real Scottish princess had died — the tiny infant, born prematurely, had lost her battle to survive. It was then that baby Elizabeth Tudor, the daughter of Catherine Howard and Henry VIII, had been baptised into the Catholic faith, named for the day she was christened, the Ascension of the Virgin. The child known forever more as Mary, Queen of Scots.

Yet, even with information from that stupid woman, Douglas Stafford, could Philip really have discovered the truth? thought Elizabeth in desperation. *Or was this a bluff? As for the name of her brother, this was impossible, even he did not know his true identity.*

"Would you like me to say her name?" asked Ballard in a quiet, sly voice, bringing Elizabeth back to the present. "To reveal the lies you have told to those around you. Why, even the suggestion of another Tudor princess would be enough for many to place your neck on the block as your father once placed your mother's."

Casting an uneasy glance around the room, she saw her guards were blocking every exit — the three priests were captive in this hall and Elizabeth was reaching the end of her ability to remain calm. One look to Sir Christopher Hatton and her bodyguard would swoop. The priests could be in the Tower of London in Walsingham's torture chamber within hours.

"There is no name to repeat," said Elizabeth, "because I have no sister."

"You deny her?"

"How can I deny a person who does not exist?"

The priest waved to his second assistant, who hurried forward and placed something in his hand.

"Perhaps you might wish to reconsider your words, Your Majesty," said Ballard, his tone silken with hatred.

Walsingham hurried forward and took the velvet pouch from the man, nodding to the guards to surround the three priests, before delivering it into the outstretched hand of Elizabeth. With trembling fingers, she opened the drawstring and upended the bag. The room swayed as pure, cold terror filled her heart. Emerald clip for Lady Anne. Sapphire for Queen Catherine. The token given to her daughter when the child set off on her epic journey to the north. A symbol of love and also of recognition. Lying in Elizabeth's palm was a ruby ring, identical in every way to the one she wore on the middle finger of her left hand, except for one tiny detail: while Elizabeth's ring held a minute emerald on the side, this one glimmered blue from a sapphire.

Elizabeth's fingers curled around the ring. It took every ounce of her self-control not to cry out. The Catholic priest had indeed taken control of Mary and her household. There was no other way he would have been able to secure this ring, this most precious of items. This was Mary's message to Elizabeth and she suspected the cavity of the ring held more words sent by her sister.

The ruby in her palm seemed to pulse with life as she considered all this ring represented: the friendship of women, the trust they had placed in each other and the discovery of a sister. After the midnight ride to see the Lady Anne of Cleves and the revelation that she was not the last Tudor heir, Elizabeth and Lady Isabel Baynton had discussed her next course of action. It had taken her many months to summon the courage but eventually Elizabeth had contacted the young Scottish queen, who by then was living at the French court with the family of her betrothed, Francis, the dauphin.

Mary's immediate reaction was to reject Elizabeth's suggestions as a cruel joke, a way to diminish her claim to the Scottish throne, but Elizabeth had persevered and in one letter she had sketched her ruby ring, explaining it had been bequeathed to her by the Lady Anne, describing the small emerald underneath, she mentioned that it was a clip that could be moved to open the hidden cavity. Elizabeth had continued that Mary's ring was decorated with a sapphire clip and if she were to open it, she would find the space that Catherine and Anne had used to send messages.

Silence had followed this letter and Elizabeth became worried it had been intercepted, even though she had sent it through a trusted source. Worse, she was concerned that Mary still did not believe that her offer of friendship was genuine.

Then one day a letter arrived from Mary and the royal child, who had thought herself alone in the world, had embraced her older half-sister. She knew the ring, she had written, it had been in her possession since she was a child and she had always been curious about it. She had written to Mary of

Guise, the woman whom she had assumed was her real mother and to her amazement, Mary of Guise had confirmed Elizabeth's story.

After the death of Mary of Guise in 1560, Mary, now Queen of France, had turned to Elizabeth, who had ascended to the throne of England and the two had slowly built a relationship of love, trust and emotional support as they battled their separate paths in the world of men. It had been a source of succour and relief to them both as they discussed the limitations they felt were thrust upon them by the stubbornness of men to believe that women were their intellectual equals and could govern as well as any man.

Now, as Elizabeth stared at the ring resting in her hand, her heart breaking as she feared the loss of another of her close female companions, this time her beloved and ailing younger sister, the silence in the room unfolded in a dense, suffocating wave. All eyes rested on Elizabeth as she considered everything that the small insignificant piece of jewellery meant to her, to the country and to the possible succession. Without thinking, her thumb found the clip and clicked it back, causing the top to move. A glimpse of parchment confirmed what Elizabeth hoped — a note.

"Take these men to the dungeon," Elizabeth announced into the tense air of the chamber. "Search them and when we are confident they will take nothing from here but their own sorry selves, eject them."

"Do you have a message for the king of Spain?" hissed John Ballard as the guards seized his arms.

"If I wish to speak to Philip, I will do so," said Elizabeth. "I don't need a grubby little go-between like you."

The two assistants submitted to the guards without a murmur. The taller of the two was still searching the faces in the crowd, his eyes becoming frantic as he seemed unable to locate the correct person, then the door to the ante-chamber opened and Elizabeth's women entered. Kate led the way, Bess was one step behind her with Katherine following. The young priest struggled free of his guard and threw himself in front of Bess.

"Mercy, lady, mercy," he cried, reaching out to her and pushing something into her hand. Moments later, he was dragged away but there was relief on his face.

"Quickly, Katherine, translate it," demanded Elizabeth, pushing the small roll of parchment into her hand. "What does she say?"

Katherine scanned the note. It was a simple letter code, the most basic of their repertoire and took her only moments to translate. With tears in her eyes, she handed it to Elizabeth.

"No," whimpered Elizabeth as she read it. "No, this cannot be."

The piece of parchment fluttered from Elizabeth's trembling fingers, floating to the floor, where Bess snatched it up and read aloud:

"We have been intercepted and are en route to Fotheringhay Castle. They plan to try me in an Inquisition court. It will find me guilty and charge me with high treason towards the Catholic church. The penalty will be death. I am dying. Nothing can prevent this outcome. My dearest sister, if you love me, you will leave me be. I will negotiate the safe release of my women and of your life and then I will die, happily, willingly knowing that in my death, your life will be preserved. Please, sweet sister, do not fight this decree for I do issue it as a Tudor princess and as a queen of Scotland. *Semper Sorores* my sweet Lily-Venus."

On the reverse she had written: "In my end is my beginning" and the basic outline of a bird with flames around it.

"A phoenix," said Bess, "but what does she mean?"

"She means that once she is dead, I will be able to reveal her true identity. So, as Mary, Queen of Scots dies, the true Tudor princess can be revealed."

There was silence as the impact of the words ebbed and flowed around the room like a curse.

"And your message, Bess, what did it say?" asked Elizabeth.

"The note is from Mignonne," she said, "I think that's why the young priest was searching for me, she's my granddaughter, after all."

"We must inform Walsingham to isolate this young man and question him alone. Keeping him in a single cell may also be necessary for his own safety. Tell me, Bess," said Elizabeth, her voice gentle. "Whatever it is, we must know so we can work on a counterattack."

"An elite force of Spanish soldiers has been despatched from Carew Castle," Bess said, her voice trembling at the enormity of the information she was about to impart. "They are a royal bodyguard for Gaspar de Quiroga y Vela…"

"No!" The exclamation was from Katherine Newton, guttural, fearful. "He's one of the most senior officials of the Spanish Inquisition."

Bess nodded. "He is being escorted to Fotheringhay Castle."

Elizabeth stared out of the window, her shoulders shaking as she sobbed, allowing herself this small indulgence for a few moments, before forcing herself once more under her usual icy control.

"What shall we do, Elizabeth?" asked Kate, wiping the back of her hand across her face to try and stem the tears that were streaming down her cheeks. "Shall we send men to rescue her?"

"For now, we will do as she requests," said Elizabeth, even though each word was akin to a knife through her heart.

"What?" said Kate, horrified. "We will allow her to die?"

"She has issued a decree under her seal, look, in the corner, a tiny drawing of it and next to it, our mermaid. As a fellow monarch, I must respect her wishes…"

"But, Elizabeth," gasped Kate, "she is dying. This is her illness speaking. We must rescue her and offer comfort for her final days. We can't abandon her, not now. We've worked all our lives to keep her safe."

"Mary has been weakening for months, she has begged me to leave her be," said Elizabeth. "For now, we must let this plan unfold while we decide how best to resolve Philip's terrible plot."

There was no denying the terrible truth but Elizabeth could not look into the eyes of any of her women. Without doubt she would read shock, anger and betrayal. Only Katherine knew about Mary's last letter, written while she was clandestinely being brought from Chartley Manor across the country in gentle stages to London where Elizabeth felt she would have been safer and, also, where she could have visited her without arousing suspicion. Throughout the journey, Mary had been growing weaker, until she had written to Elizabeth requesting that they pause a while in their travail because she did not have the strength to continue. Elizabeth had agreed but before the letter could be dispatched, Babington had been caught and Mary had been apprehended. This last note from her sister at least gave them her definite whereabouts.

"And your brother?" asked Kate, fury in her voice. "Will you finally tell him the truth."

Elizabeth looked up, her brown eyes locking with Kate's blue. "Yes," she said. "Summon Walsingham, Burghley, Hatton and Francis Knollys — their task must be to secure my brother's safety. They will need to send men to update us on the Spanish position. We must also recall Robert, Lettice and the children."

"Won't they be safer away from the turmoil?" said Katherine.

"Not anymore," replied Elizabeth. "Philip has many cruel men in the Netherlands. As we are refusing to submit to his ludicrous plans, he will be vicious in his slaughter of my men. Walsingham will warn Robert immediately but we must write to Lettice."

Katherine bobbed a curtsey and left the room to assemble her writing implements.

"Where is Ballard?" asked Elizabeth, her strength returning as she began to evolve a plan of action.

"In the dungeon, as you commanded," replied Bess. "Although, my husband, as Earl Marshall of England, claims we can't hold him for more than a few days. Under the laws of parley, he must be released unharmed."

The usual commotion ensued as Walsingham, Burghley, Sir Christopher Hatton and Sir Francis Knollys entered. Elizabeth remained seated, waiting while they jostled for position in front of her, like schoolboys visiting the headmistress.

"Burghley, we will release Ballard and his men immediately," she announced without preamble, "but, Walsingham, ensure they are followed. The young man who gave us the note..."

"Chidiock Tichbourne," supplied Walsingham.

"Be gentle with him — he has supplied us with a great deal of information. It is worth considering releasing him with the others as he may consent to continue to spy from the heart of this nest of vipers," instructed Elizabeth. She waved Bess forward to hand Walsingham the note. "Mary is being held at Fotheringhay Castle, not far from here. No doubt, Philip is enjoying a little joke by taking over this old fortress. The castle has ancient links to the kings of Scotland. After the original Norman lord, Simon de Senlis, Earl of Huntingdon-Northamptonshire died, his widow, Maud married David I in December 1113, who became king of Scots. It's also in the middle of a marsh, so it will be difficult for us to stage any kind of attack."

Walsingham finished reading the short note, hardly hearing Elizabeth's words. "Where did you get this?" he asked, astounded.

"Hidden within the cavity of the ring," replied Elizabeth. "Mary and I have used these as methods to pass messages for many years. Your men will follow these priests and when they arrive at Fotheringhay they will assess the health and welfare of the Scottish queen."

"But, Your Majesty," spluttered Burghley, "how can we be sure the Scottish queen is trustworthy? She might be in league with the traitor Babington."

"Oh, for goodness sake, William!" exclaimed Elizabeth. "Mary is not in league with anyone and she doesn't want my throne. She is dying and she is trying to protect the realm by offering herself as a sacrifice. Her proposal is to allow herself to be found guilty of a false crime..."

"This could be a disaster, Your Majesty," said Sir Francis Knollys. "If Mary is executed, it would give Philip the perfect excuse to invade. The whole of Catholic Europe would rise up to support him. We know he has already given the word that the men who were supposed to kidnap Mary would do so disguised as your soldiers. Do you honestly think he will hold a court under the Spanish Inquisition's banner? He will twist it to make it look as though you have sanctioned her death."

"If only she could die naturally..." began Sir Christopher Hatton but recoiled at the gasp of horror this statement created.

Elizabeth turned away from her courtiers and rising gracefully, she walked to the window. "Whatever we do, Mary will not live for more than six months," she said, her voice calm. "Yet we can't leave her at the mercy of these men. We must act. Walsingham, bring me the necessary warrants — let us execute Babington and his supposed accomplices. It will send a clear message to Philip that we won't be intimidated."

"Your Majesty," said Walsingham with a deep bow of acquiescence, then hurried from the room.

"What news on the Welsh invasion?" Elizabeth asked. "When he escaped, Sir Thomas Perrot claimed the Spanish were becoming disillusioned. Is this still the case?"

Burghley cleared his throat, threw a smug glance at the remaining two men, then spoke, "Recently, I received a message from the duke of Hereford. He claims that the Spanish are indeed retreating. More ships have been spotted off the headlands but they do not seem to be approaching — it's as though they've come to collect their men. Each morning, more of the invading forces have left the strongholds. However, what these Spaniards have not communicated to each other is that the duke of Hereford and George Devereux have positioned their own forces to gather these men up as they try to flee through the night. The Spanish soldiers are currently being held at Pembroke Castle, which we have liberated and is once again our most secure garrison."

Elizabeth stared at him aghast. "How long have you known about this?" she asked, furious that he had been keeping such vital information from her.

"A few days, Your Majesty," he said.

"A few days?" She turned away from him, appalled. "What have these men confessed? You have questioned them?"

"Yes, they claim that Philip has changed their plans. He is no longer interested in taking the castles, not now his elite force is working their way across the country…"

"Burghley!" The exclamation came from Sir Francis Knollys. "There are Spanish soldiers here?"

"The duke of Hereford and his men are in pursuit," said Burghley. "He has assured me he will keep us informed but I am confident he will resolve the issue."

"The soldiers are escorting Gaspar de Quiroga y Vela to Fotheringhay Castle to try Mary," stated Elizabeth, gratified at the shocked expression on Burghley's face. "We don't have much time. It's imperative we discover the truth about what's going on within the confines of the castle. Once we have a true picture, we will be able to plan."

The three men stared at her, dumbstruck.

"Christopher, take Lord Burghley back to the great hall, gather my privy councillors — we need to assemble a war office in order to deal with this threat and offer support to the duke of Hereford. Sir Francis, remain here."

Bowing, the two men left, shouting instructions to their attendants as they hurried down the wide staircase. Even Burghley, she noticed, was following her directives without argument, understanding the true danger of the situation.

"Kate, you will organise my rooms. We must return to London, immediately, and when you are done, you must write to the duchess of Hereford. Insist she joins us there. I will have all those around me who are important for the succession and she is one of the few who knows the truth. Bess, you will accompany Kate and you will write to Mignonne — we need to be kept updated as often as she is able to get word to us."

The women curtseyed and hurried from the room, leaving Elizabeth alone with her old friend and confidant, Sir Francis Knollys, who lowered himself into the nearest chair and gave her a paternal smile.

"You have recalled Lettice?"

"Yes," she said, sitting opposite him, biting her lip. "It's the only way."

"I understand," he said, but he sounded weary. "When her mother and I suggested the plan, we knew it would be dangerous but from the moment Lettice was old enough we explained the role she had to play in the Tudor court."

Elizabeth did not speak. The emotion of the day had taken her beyond words, instead she listened to Sir Francis's soothing voice as it recapped their complex and convoluted history.

"She was a similar age to Catherine Howard's daughter," he continued. "We always thought she would be a suitable substitute or decoy, should the need ever arise."

"It was a brave decision," murmured Elizabeth, "but then, our little She-Wolf has always been fierce and protective of those she loves."

"And she loves you very much," said Francis, "even though in recent months we have released gossip suggesting you loathe her."

"It is the best ammunition we have to protect her," said Elizabeth. "If I push her aside and make it clear she is nothing but an irritant, she will never be a target for plotters. It will ensure her safety and that of her children."

"And now, she returns?"

"Yes, with Robert," said Elizabeth. "There is a task she must perform; one she has succeeded in before. Dorothy and Penelope will remain at court, Sir Thomas Perrot continues to recover, Penelope's husband is in London, making more money, Lettice's son is with Robert, leading the charge at Zutphen on a supply convoy for Philip's garrisons. Her other boys are safely studying at Cambridge. Since the death of Lord Denbigh, her son with Robert, two years ago, she has been more cautious but now we have reached this crisis, I know she will agree to my request."

Sir Francis gave her sorrowful smile but he nodded his head, confirming that his daughter would not flinch from any task requested of her by Queen Elizabeth.

"And your brother?" he asked. "What of him?"

Elizabeth rose and swept to her inner chamber, returning moments later with the wooden box given to her by Anne of Cleves.

"This will remain in my strong room," she said. "The key will be in the charge of Katherine Newton, who is the great-niece of Catherine Howard. She has been one of my secret keepers ever since she came to me as a maid of honour. On our return journey to London, I will dictate my confession to Katherine and when it is finished, I will place my seal and my signature upon it. This document will be placed with the others in this box. If Philip should succeed with any of his plans and both Mary and I meet an untimely end, I charge you, Sir Francis Knollys, to open this casket and use it to prove the validity of my heir apparent, my half-brother and the man, who should be king."

"But Elizabeth, he doesn't know..." began Francis.

"He will, when you have sent men to find and support him as he chases across the Welsh heartlands in pursuit of the Spanish soldiers. You will take whomever you need and you will search my realm until you find him, then you will bring Ralph Fitzalan, Duke of Hereford to me at Westminster. I will inform him of his true parentage and will promise to name his as my heir."

"What about James VI, waiting in Scotland, assuming he will one day be King of England?"

"I made no promises. Ralph has the strongest claim, followed by his son, William. They will make the Tudor line secure."

"My dear, I am unsure. This could begin another Civil War."

"Then let us hope Philip fails and I remain on the throne for the foreseeable future," said Elizabeth, placing the casket on a table near the window and folding her arms across her chest. "If I am murdered by the Spanish, my realm will need a strong king to lead them into war against Philip II. Ralph Fitzalan is the son of my father, Henry VIII and his fifth wife, Catherine Howard. He is the twin brother of Mary, Queen of Scots, who was born Princess Elizabeth at Marquess House in Pembrokeshire. He is the best hope we have and I am prepared to risk naming him as my successor should the necessity arise."

The setting sun in the window behind her lit Elizabeth's red hair so it glowed with otherworldly intensity. Her determination radiated from her like a beacon, her brown eyes glinting with power, every inch the personification of God's representative on earth, the true Queen of England.

Sir Francis Knollys stared at her, feeling the power emanating from her and gave the smallest nod of his head.

"Thank you, Francis," said Elizabeth, her relief palpable. "Now I have your word, I can turn my attention to other matters of importance."

"Such as?"

"Saving my realm from the Spanish, freeing my sister and ensuring she does not die alone."

Chapter Three

The late autumn winds rattled the windows at Westminster Palace. Icy blasts threw hail and wet leaves at the diamond-shaped panes. Fires blazed in every hearth and Elizabeth stalked through her corridors of power, barking commands as she fought her way through the tumultuous treachery that threatened her realm.

"The earl of Leicester will return within the week," said Walsingham as he walked beside Elizabeth. "Sir Peregrine Bertie, Lord Willoughby, will replace him as leader of your troops in the Netherlands."

"Yes, my eyes will be home at last," said Elizabeth, lapsing into the nickname she had bestowed upon Robert Dudley in their youth.

"The news of the death of the young poet, Sir Philip Sidney, is tragic," said Walsingham.

"Indeed, he is the best friend of Robert Devereux, the eldest son of Lettice Dudley from her first marriage. The two young men have been inseparable since childhood. He returns with his stepfather, Leicester, intent on accompanying his friend's body on its last journey…" Elizabeth allowed the sentence to trail away as she continued to stride towards the Star Chamber. *So much loss,* she thought, *endless deaths and for what purpose?* Once again they would reconvene to discuss the torturous happenings at Fotheringhay Castle. Each day brought a flurry of fresh information, keeping the privy council hard at work as it sifted through the endless stream of messages flooding into Walsingham's den of spies and cryptographers. Walsingham had finally understood the importance of the news sent by the

Ladies of Melusine and how, in this war against the creeping shadow of Spain, the smallest detail could make a difference, even that supplied by a woman.

It was from a meeting with Katherine Newton, Bess of Hardwick, Kate Howard and Philadelphia Scrope that the two had come. Walsingham had read the assembled letters from the Ladies of Melusine as translated by Katherine and added their information to the intelligence his own men had gathered. The news was not good.

"Could we rewrite the Bond of Association to include the Habsburgs?" Elizabeth asked as they walked. "We might not be able to implement it but it would prove to Philip he is not the only one who is able to indulge in flights of fancy when it comes to passing laws in someone else's country."

"Burghley could certainly draft an amendment," said Walsingham. "As you say, we would never be able to press the sentence but it would irritate Philip."

"Which is always a good thing," mused Elizabeth.

"Her Majesty, Queen Elizabeth!" shouted the herald as the doors were thrown open and she swept into the Star Chamber, the centre of government, where her full privy council was gathered. Unlike the usual relaxed atmosphere of the chamber, where the noble men of the realm often viewed these meetings as a social event as much as a legal obligation, there was a buzz of raw energy coupled with an underlying hum of fear and tension; with the country on a war footing all men knew their duty. As Elizabeth entered her councillors bowed, each relieved to see her but also quietly wishing she were her father, as they all felt they needed a man to guide them through these troubled times.

"Rise, rise," she called, her voice, as ever, tinged with impatience at the obsequious bowing. "Walsingham, update the chamber on the news from Fotheringhay," she barked, settling herself on her raised chair under her cloth of state.

Sir Francis Walsingham bowed to Elizabeth, then took his position in the centre of the room.

"Our informers have sent word that for the last two days, Gaspar de Quiroga y Vela, supported by John Ballard, hereafter known as Black Fortescue, have been conducting an illegal court under the auspices of the Spanish Inquisition in which he has tried Mary Stuart, Queen of Scotland and the Isles, Dowager Queen of France for crimes against the Catholic church."

"And what are these charges?" demanded Sir Christopher Hatton.

Elizabeth, who knew what was coming, closed her eyes and gripped the arms of her chair until her knuckles were white, listening with increasing horror as Sir Francis Walsingham delivered the report sent to him by Ralph Fitzalan and confirmed by Mignonne.

"But how is this possible?" exclaimed Lord Zouche. "Mary has never denied her faith. She has remained a true Catholic."

"The charge was that she has not tried to assassinate Her Majesty, Queen Elizabeth, which under the papal bull issued by Pope Pius V in 1580 was the objective of every practising Catholic in this realm. As you remember, this edict excommunicated the queen and encouraged her Catholic subjects in this heinous act," said Walsingham. "It is nonsense but de Quiroga y Vela and Fortescue are about to pronounce the sentence under the law of Spain. Our fear is that should the worst happen, any act of violence will be made to look as though it has been sanctioned and carried out under the orders

299

of Queen Elizabeth. The prospect of one anointed monarch sentencing another to death, if this is indeed what they plan, it could be enough to begin a war supported by all the Catholic nations in Europe."

"And yet," snapped Elizabeth, "it is acceptable for Philip to constantly threaten me and my realm and for the Vatican to pronounce a death sentence over my head because they are men and Catholics, therefore they presume they are above God and the law, when, in fact, nothing could be further from the truth."

Silence greeted this pronouncement. Elizabeth could feel bile rising in her stomach, not only with fear for Mary but also with fury for Philip. How dare he and these upstart priests attempt to pass laws in her realm? What right did they have to threaten her? The men around the chamber stared at her, but no one spoke — they did not dare disagree with their queen.

"Do we know when they will deliver their decision?" Elizabeth asked, after a few moments, spitting out the words, each as distasteful as the next.

"No, not yet," replied Walsingham, relieved to be back on safer ground. "Mignonne has managed to get word to us that the Scottish queen is coping well, although her health continues to fail. It's possible the Spanish are hoping she will die naturally and then they can add her neglect to the many crimes they are already trying to place at your feet, Your Majesty."

Elizabeth shook her head in annoyance. Philip had been a constant irritant for years, costing her money, men and time. As she considered the many wrongs he had dealt her, even before she became Queen, she felt power rising within her heart.

"Walsingham, would his abortive attempt to take my country by trying to invade from the Welsh coast make the rest of Europe, as well as our allies, realise that Philip is duplicitous?"

"Very few know about his failed attack on Carew and his brief occupation of the other castles," Walsingham reminded her. "The duke of Hereford and I have discussed this and we think it's probably the reason Philip allowed that first plan to falter."

"Explain yourself, Walsingham," bellowed Christopher Hatton. "Why do you make such a statement?"

"The duke and I believe Philip was playing several plots at once," said Walsingham, addressing the entire chamber. "He enthralled Babington and his group of Catholic traitors in order to discover the whereabouts of the Scottish queen. By convincing these foolish young men that his plan was to save Mary and place her on the throne once they had assassinated Elizabeth, he created the necessary diversion to slowly deliver a Spanish force on to one of the more remote coastlines of our realm. He seemed to imagine the Welsh would respond to his call, rising against the monarchy, but he forgot that the Tudors are Welsh, and when men are asked to take up arms, it is rarely against one of their own.

"It was one of Philip's biggest mistakes. It didn't take him long to realise that a land battle across the width of the country would be prohibitively expensive. By then, he'd also discovered Mary's weakened state of health and realised she would never be able to be his puppet monarch. I believe this was when he decided his daughter would be a suitable regent and he would murder Queen Elizabeth, while trying Mary under the laws of the Inquisition and freeing himself of both, as he thinks, 'troublesome queens'."

"But is he really willing to sacrifice Mary? Another Catholic monarch? It would make more sense if he were to try me, a heretic," said Elizabeth.

"He will do whatever is necessary and if that means sacrificing Mary in order to give him a reason to invade England and steal your throne, then, yes, I have no doubt."

"This is monstrous," exclaimed Lord Zouche.

Elizabeth glared around the room. Until now, she had allowed Philip's plot to unfold, she had taken Mary's request to be allowed to die into consideration but things were becoming ludicrous and she refused to be in this position any longer. The time had come to act rather than react, despite the instructions Mary had decreed in her letter to Elizabeth.

"Enough," she said and turned abruptly to Walsingham. "The sentence on Mary has not yet been passed. Until this happens, we must consider all possible outcomes. Know this, though — Philip will confound me no longer. The duke of Hereford resides, at my request, at Boughton Hall, not many miles from Fotheringhay Castle. When the sentence is passed, whatever verdict is delivered, the duke must be in a position of strength, with men and arms, prepared and ready to storm the castle and put an end to this ridiculous dance with Spain. There is no other way. We will rescue Mary and her women, then these Catholic traitors will be put to their deaths."

There was uproar. Male voices clamoured, each shouting their view, most disagreeing with Queen Elizabeth's unexpected change of plan. Until now, they had been advising her to proceed with caution, to advance at a gentle pace in order to allow them to sift through the information available, but now her Tudor blood was rising and she was suspicious of their endless words of warning. Elizabeth stood. She had listened to their pronouncements of tremulous fear for too long. The time was now; they must act.

A shout from outside drew all their attention to the doors as they were thrown open by the heralds.

"The countess of Shrewsbury, Lady Newton and Lady Effingham," came the cry as the three women tumbled through the door.

"What's happened?" asked Elizabeth, already halfway across the chamber to meet them.

"This, from Mignonne," said Katherine, pushing a leather scroll into Elizabeth's hand. Unfurling it and stretching it out across the table, Elizabeth began to read.

"This is the deciphered and translated version, madam," explained Bess, approaching the table. "It arrived only moments after you left for this meeting. We decoded it as quickly as possible."

Elizabeth was too intent on reading to reply. When she had finished, she turned away, her face blanched white. She thrust the scroll at her spymaster, who scanned the text before handing it to the other members of the privy council to read.

"Do you think it's genuine?" asked Sir Francis Knollys.

"Who but the king of Spain would have the audacity to put something like this in writing?" snapped Elizabeth. "This proclamation states that there is a way to save Mary. If I am prepared to stand aside and give her my throne then Philip claims he will let me live quietly until my death, which would probably be shortly afterwards. Once again, he throws in a counterplot. This man is infuriating."

"And if you refuse?" asked Burghley from the shadows.

"Mary will be executed," said Elizabeth, her voice icy cold.

Walsingham continued to study the scroll; his brow furrowed. "But why would he offer the throne to Mary when he knows she's dying?" he asked. "It makes no sense."

"She is a Catholic. I'm sure he believes it is better to have a dying Papist on the throne than a healthy heretic," Elizabeth replied. "He is playing us; he is seeing how far I am prepared to go to save my sister … Queen." Aware of who surrounded her, Elizabeth covered her small slip.

"Elizabeth, this is ridiculous," came a voice and all heads turned towards Kate Howard. "This ludicrous situation has gone on long enough. At the centre of all this egotistical plotting is a sick woman. It doesn't matter about her religion — she is dying and while she languishes alone and in pain, held on false charges, you all quibble and posture as you try to appear the most intelligent while pushing your own political agendas."

The silence was eloquent and Elizabeth caught Kate's eye, giving her permission to continue her impassioned speech, even though the assembled men were staring at her in transfixed horror.

"The Welsh border is now safe," continued Kate. "The Spanish coup has been quelled as easily as the Ridolfi Plot. It's the same with most of Philip's plots — he has an idea but then doesn't properly commit money or men, hoping they will work out of their own accord. He might think he is a great military strategist but his plans are based on the boasts of his oldest friends and his own delusions of grandeur. He seems to think God will intervene, yet strangely, *He* never does. This plot is the same. The duke of Hereford and his men must set up camp near Fotheringhay Castle. Our informers tell us it's possible to smuggle people in and out because of the laxness of Philip's guards. If we had the Scottish queen here, under our protection, it would render Philip's insane plan null and void."

"You are quite correct, Kate," said Elizabeth.

Around her, the great men of the land exchanged nervous glances.

"Such strategies as men like Philip devise will never work because they are careless with the detail," said Elizabeth. "The earl of Leicester returns within the week. We begin to plan our invasion and when our weary knight is home, he and the duke of Hereford will lead the charge to remove the Scottish queen from the clutches of the Spanish. Until then, we must hope we're not too late."

PART SEVEN: January, 2019

Chapter One

It was Monday morning and Perdita pushed her chair back from her desk, wandering over to stare out of the window as she considered all she had read in the past few days. She was still reeling over the possibility that Elizabeth I did not sanction Mary, Queen of Scots' execution and the suggestion that it was an unknown Spanish invasion that had been the true cause of her death, but, to her, all this paled into insignificance in the face of her theory that Mary, Queen of Scots was in fact the missing princess; daughter of Henry VIII and Catherine Howard, rather than the daughter of James V and Mary of Guise. It was an idea that continued to send shivers down her spine.

As ever, Kit was by her side, assuring her the information was all there to back up their new theory. Today, he was going to talk her through the Babington Plot to see what anomalies they could spot. He had sent her a copy of his thesis and, although she had not yet told him, she had read it over the weekend and found it fascinating. Despite his obvious intelligence and his natural sharpness when it came to dealing with his role within Jerusalem, Perdita had never given much thought to Kit's academic background but now she realised he was bordering on a genius.

As though her thoughts had summoned him, Kit crashed through the door with his usual exuberance. His hair was standing on end and his battered Fred Perry computer bag was slung across his chest.

"Is it just us?" he asked, dumping his bag on the sofa.

"Yep, Piper and your dad are discussing her divorce," said Perdita.

"Oh, I'm so sorry. Poor Piper."

"Jeremy has emailed to say he wants to begin proceedings," she continued. "He's being very aggressive and threatening. Your dad has had divorce lawyers on hand for a while but Piper was reluctant to go ahead — now, though, she's furious and that's driving her."

"Breaking off a relationship is hard enough," he said. "Filing for divorce must be gut-wrenching."

The distress in his voice was genuine and Perdita wondered if he was remembering the pain he had inflicted on Lydia when he had ended their relationship. Although, thought Perdita, he had done it with tact, consideration and decency, trying to soften the blow as much as possible, not like Jeremy, who had been flaunting his new relationship in Piper's face.

"Exactly — the end of a marriage seems so sad," she sighed. "Especially as we've known Jeremy since we were children and we've always been close to his parents, too. They were Dad's best friends from his art college days. Your dad and Piper are going to have an update on the ruby ring, too. Alistair has been tracing the current owner, Hannah White."

"Didn't you want to be there?"

"No, it's her inheritance, too; she's allowed to make decisions. Anyway, she found the ring."

Kit took some papers out of his bag. "I've been refreshing my knowledge of the Babington Plot. I did study it for my doctorate but it was a while ago..."

"I read your thesis," she said, waving it at him, as he had once done to her with her grandmother's unpublished Catherine Howard manuscript.

"All of it?" asked Kit, a hint of doubt tingeing the question.

"Yes," she replied. "Once I got started, it was impossible to put it down. Your writing style carries the argument so well, it's engrossing."

For a moment Kit looked unsure, then he grinned.

"Thanks Perds, I think you're probably the only person outside of my tutors and Dad, who's ever read it."

Their eyes met and Perdita found it difficult to tear her gaze away.

"The Babington Plot," she stammered, forcing herself to look down.

"Yes, one of the oddest entrapment schemes in British history," said Kit and Perdita was pleased to see he was flustered, too.

"From what you state," she said, "the Babington Plot was manipulated by Elizabeth I's chief spymaster, Sir Francis Walsingham, in order to implicate Mary, Queen of Scots in a plot to suggest she sanctioned the assassination of Queen Elizabeth."

"Very succinct," said Kit, dropping into the seat beside her. "Walsingham's plan was in response to the Bond of Association; the law Burghley had created which stated that should an attempt be made on Elizabeth's life in favour of the Stuart succession then both Mary and James VI could be executed."

"Was that even legal?" asked Perdita.

"I shouldn't think so, which was why Elizabeth was furious. She viewed it as a lynch law that would undermine her sovereignty, so she changed the wording. Instead, any claimant or pretender to the throne who stood to benefit from a plot to assassinate the queen would be tried in a special court. Even if a guilty verdict was reached, nothing could be done until Elizabeth declared it so and signed a proclamation under the

Great Seal of England, which tied Burghley's hands."

"And it was with this in mind that Walsingham formed the Babington Plot," said Perdita.

"Yes," said Kit. "Burghley had set up the legal framework, now Walsingham used his spy network to lead Mary into their web."

"So far, so believable," said Perdita, "but only if you take the view that Elizabeth hated Mary and saw her as a potential threat."

"Something we now know to be incorrect, thanks to the Lady Pamela letters."

"Exactly," said Perdita. "What happened next in the 'history-book version'?"

"Sir Francis Walsingham used his double-agents to encourage a young, rather boastful, Catholic nobleman called Anthony Babington to approach Mary and open lines of communication. She was said to have begun a correspondence with him. Babington passed his messages to the queen using 'The Barrel Method'. With the help of a friendly brewer, he would seal a letter in a water-tight casket and hide it in the stopper of the barrels of beer that were sent to Mary's home. This would then be delivered to Mary and she would reply using the same method," explained Kit. "Unbeknown to Babington, the brewer was a spy in Walsingham's pay. All his letters were being passed to Walsingham first. They were deciphered and read, then replaced in the barrels and passed on to Mary. In one case, Pheilippes, Walsingham's double agent, even added information to a note for Mary in order to incriminate her further. Interestingly, Mary's secretaries, Claude Nau and Gilbert Curle admitted, under torture, that these fabricated documents were the real letters that they had written and not Walsingham's fakes."

"Do you think that was the case or was it added by The Scribe later?" asked Perdita.

"As we have no evidence in the Lady Pamela letters to suggest either man was ever arrested, I would suspect The Scribe," replied Kit. "Against the advice of her secretaries, Mary allegedly wrote to Babington agreeing to support the plot. This incriminating document became known as 'The Bloody Letter'."

"Walsingham now had enough evidence to incriminate Mary," Perdita said, and Kit nodded.

"But," he added, "in order to be sure he had a water-tight case, he wanted to catch Babington and force a confession out of him to corroborate this supposed written evidence from the Queen of Scots in order to convince Elizabeth.

"Babington was caught on 14 August 1586 and was taken to the Tower of London. After intense interrogation, on 18 August he confessed all he knew about the plot and implicated Mary, Queen of Scots. Elizabeth was said to be unconvinced but allowed Walsingham to continue his investigation. Now it gets really odd; according to official records, at this point, Mary was then tricked into leaving Chartley Manor where she was under house arrest and was forced to stay at Tixall Castle while Chartley was searched. All her letters and money were seized."

"Meanwhile, according to the timeline I've been creating from the Lady Pamela letters," Perdita added, "there was upheaval in Pembrokeshire and the rumours that Carew, Tenby, Llawhaden and Haverfordwest castles had been captured by Spanish soldiers."

"Something which isn't evident in any records except ours," said Kit.

"Convenient, wouldn't you say?"

"Especially as at that point, Burghley is reported to have approached Elizabeth demanding that now she has this information from the Babington interrogation, she must act swiftly, brutally and without mercy."

Perdita looked appalled. "Whoever The Scribe was," she said, "he or she was either completely ruthless or so scared of what they had been commissioned to do, they were writing for their life."

Kit gave Perdita an appraising look. "Do you know, I've never thought about it like that before," he said. "I always assumed The Scribe was in cahoots with whoever ordered this widespread changing of history. Perhaps it was fear motivating them rather than agreement with what was being done because to alter events to this level is enormous. Do you think it was done deliberately to smear Elizabeth?"

"Possibly," said Perdita, "but I think it's bigger than that."

"Bigger than executing a monarch?"

"She wasn't the only one though, was she? There was Charles I — he was beheaded outside the Banqueting House in London on 30 January 1649. For The Scribe to suggest that Mary, Queen of Scots was also executed, a monarch of the blood royal rather than a consort like Anne Boleyn, then there is precedent and English law is based on that rather than a constitution, which would have made the decision over Charles I's death easier."

"Really?"

"Oh yes, we have a constitutional monarchy which was introduced in 1689, entitled the Bill of Rights, when William and Mary were crowned but we don't have a written constitution like they do in America. Our law has been built up over years of Parliamentary Acts and in the case of the legal system and the law courts, we follow precedents…" she broke off, her face immobile as another possibility occurred to her.

"What?" prompted Kit.

"Of course; the swapping of the royal baby," she said. "There was something nagging me but I couldn't remember what — hang on a sec, Kit, let me check something."

She flicked through a few pages on a search engine and after a moment, grinned up at Kit.

"On 10 June 1688, King James II and his second wife, Mary of Modena, had a son who was christened James Francis Edward, however, there has always been a rumour that the baby was stillborn and another child was smuggled into the queen's chamber inside a bed warming pan in order to replace the royal heir."

"And James II was a Stuart?" confirmed Kit.

"Yes, he was a direct descendant from Mary, Queen of Scots — she would have been his great-grandmother. In 1688, he was deposed and replaced by his daughter, Mary II, who incidentally was named after Mary, Queen of Scots, and her Dutch husband, William III. This was what prompted the Bill of Rights."

"Why?"

"Mostly to do with religion," said Perdita. "It came after a law was passed saying no Catholic could sit on the British throne. Don't you think it's odd that considering what we've discovered that there's another well-known rumour concerning a royal baby being swapped, but many years later?"

Perdita watched Kit considering this new piece of information. He ran his fingers through his hair, screwing up his face in concentration.

"It's definitely curious," admitted Kit, "but we can't connect it."

"Not yet, anyway," said Perdita.

"OK," Kit said, "going back to the Babington Plot. On Tuesday 20 September 1586, Anthony Babington was taken from the Tower of London to St Giles's Field near Holborn on a horse-drawn sledge where he and six accomplices were hanged, drawn and quartered on the charge of treason."

"Nasty," said Perdita, the words horrific enough, the thought of the deed still shocking. "But strange that there is no record of who the other six were, seeing as they were executed alongside Babington. You'd think someone would have written their names down?"

"You would, considering how evil their punishment was in connection with the crime," agreed Kit. "However, the next day, Mary was moved to Fotheringhay Castle via Hill Hall to await trial."

"And that's another weird thing," said Perdita. "My geography isn't great, so while I was reading this, I looked up the houses on a map. Chartley Manor is in Rugeley near Stafford, and Tixall, the other place Mary was placed, is also near Stafford. So, why move her to Fotheringhay Castle in order to make her stand trial — it's over 90 miles away near Oundle, Northamptonshire. If Mary was so ill, wouldn't Walsingham, Burghley and Elizabeth suggest she was held and tried somewhere closer to where she was already staying?"

Kit looked at her in surprise. "I've never noticed that before," he admitted. "Although, if you add in the extra information that we have from the Lady Pamela letters, we now know that Mary was making her way gradually towards London. Perhaps she was near Fotheringhay when the Spanish caught up with her."

"Deborah said she'll have the next section of letters for us later today, so we might find something relevant there," said Perdita.

"Great — in that case, we'll keep going," said Kit. "On 25 September, Elizabeth continued to refuse to send Mary to trial, despite the fact there seemed to be incontrovertible evidence of her involvement in the plot. On 1 October, Amyus Paulet, Mary's gaoler, told the Scottish queen she was to be interrogated and advised her to confess but she refused.

"On 8 October, the Commissioners gathered at Westminster and agreed to try Mary under the Bond of Association. They arrived at Fotheringhay on 11 October. Meanwhile, Elizabeth had written to Mary advising her that it would be in her best interests to appear in person at the trial. Mary agreed but only to answer the single charge of plotting Elizabeth's assassination, which she denied."

"And this is when the supposed trial took place?" asked Perdita.

"Yes," replied Kit. "On 15 October 1586, Mary entered the Great Hall at Fotheringhay Castle to be confronted by the earl of Shrewsbury, who was also Earl Marshal of England and had been her gaoler or carer — depending on how you view her stay in England — for over 25 years; Sir Francis Walsingham; William Cecil, Lord Burghley; Sir James Croft, Sir Christopher Hatton and the bulk of the privy council. Mary was supposed to defend herself with no idea about the case against her. She denied writing the letters but the council quickly overturned this claim.

"Mary defended herself for two days, then at the end of the second day, Elizabeth ordered the trial to be prorogued, pending her decision. The judges returned to London to debate their findings in the Star Chamber. Only Shrewsbury remained behind because he was too ill to travel."

"And wasn't that when the Commissioners found Mary guilty of treason?" asked Perdita, consulting the timeline she had made from the facts they had gleaned from the Lady Pamela letters.

"Yes, what do you have as happening then?"

"We have 'Mignonne' sending letters to 'Lady Venus', voicing her concerns about the health of Artemis — who we assume is Mary — saying that if their captors move them again, she is unsure Artemis will survive because she's so weak. She names someone called Black Fortescue being in charge and asks for clemency for Chidiock Tichbourne who has been doing his best to help them. Shortly after that, she mentions a Gaspar de Quiroga y Vela."

"No, that isn't possible," Kit said, his eyes wide.

"Why? Who's Gaspar de Quiroga y Vela?"

"He was a Catholic official who was an important and very senior General Inquisitor of Spain."

"Oh my goodness, Kit, that must have been Philip's real plan. To smuggle a member of the Inquisition in during the coup in Pembrokeshire. It was a distraction to get one of his top torturers into the country to fight from within." Perdita walked to the desk and, perching on the edge, facing Kit. "What happened next?"

"On 25 October 1586, the Commissioners reconvened in the Star Chamber in Westminster and declared Mary guilty of plotting to assassinate the queen, which was treason. One man, Lord Zouche, stated he wasn't happy with the result and despite the fact the council found Mary guilty, Elizabeth refused to agree to the execution of her 'sister Queen'," said Kit. "And from here it becomes increasingly murky."

"Go on," said Perdita. "We need as much detail as possible from the 'accepted version' so we can compare it with the details in the letters. According to our sources, the Spanish threat had fizzled out, largely due to Philip's lack of planning and his arrogant assumption that the Catholic people of England and, particularly Wales, would rise up for him against Elizabeth."

"Despite Elizabeth refusing to sanction the execution, on 19 November 1586," Kit continued, "Lord Brockhurst told Mary she has been found guilty of treason and she would be executed. He asked for a confession, which Mary, understandably, refused to give."

"Which seems awfully presumptuous of the Privy Council."

"Yes, although they seemed to think Elizabeth was persuadable and began a massive push to make her agree to Mary's death. Robert Dudley returned to England on 24 November and was replaced by Peregrine Bertie, Lord Willoughby in the Netherlands. Philip Sidney, the poet and Robert's nephew, had died from his battle injuries and Robert brought his body back. The court was devastated and went into mourning, then on 27 November Robert re-joined the court at Richmond. There are very few records of him trying to persuade Elizabeth to execute Mary — mostly the documents from around then say that she was giving him hell about spending vast sums of money on entertaining in the Netherlands when he should have been fighting."

"So, despite what should have been a pressing time concerning her safety and the safety of her realm, Elizabeth is quibbling over money?"

"Apparently."

"But it doesn't make sense. Not if what you put next is correct, that throughout December, Burghley was putting

317

intense pressure on the queen to acknowledge Mary's guilty sentence. So much so that Elizabeth supposedly agreed and Parliament obtained a declaration confirming the guilty verdict. Suddenly, in the run-up to Christmas, with festivities in full swing, she's bowing to persuasion from Burghley and arguing with Robert Dudley, whereas a few weeks earlier she was fighting her Commissioners against a guilty verdict. What changed her mind?"

"Maybe nothing," said Kit. "Maybe it was changed after the event and that's why it doesn't really follow any trail of logic because, after this, it becomes even more peculiar."

"How so?"

"On 15 December 1586, Mary wrote a farewell letter to Elizabeth, asking her to speed her to execution but Paulet refused to send it, instead he kept it, only giving it to the queen after Mary's death. In it, Mary had asked to die."

"Mary asked to die?" said Perdita. "Why?"

"Up until now, it hasn't made any sense, but if you consider what Mignonne says in her letter that Mary was seriously ill, perhaps the Scottish queen had reached the end of her tether. She knew she was dying; she was in pain, and a quick death by the executioner's axe may have seemed a blessed release from her agony. A sort of Tudor elected euthanasia."

"But Paulet didn't send the letter," Perdita clarified.

"No, although, that's not to say that other people weren't aware of this strange new request from Mary because about then Walsingham is recorded as having something of a meltdown. He claimed Elizabeth had treated him appallingly, refusing to agree to Mary's execution, when he'd worked very hard to deliver Mary into her hands. He was so annoyed that the queen still refused to sign the Bill of Attainder that he flounced out, leaving the court to spend Christmas at home. In fact, he was so stressed about the situation, there are reports that he became ill."

"And where is Elizabeth in all this?"

"Suddenly, she does an about-turn and concludes that Mary must indeed die but rather than execute her, she begins dropping hints that she would prefer it if someone were to quietly assassinate her."

"What?"

"Weird, wouldn't you say?"

"Yes, very peculiar. Did she approach anyone in particular?" Perdita asked.

"Elizabeth supposedly asked her new secretary William Davison to write to Amyas Paulet and request he discreetly smother Mary in her sleep — an order Paulet chose to ignore because he didn't want to become the scapegoat for Mary's death."

"Very smart man," agreed Perdita. "Although, where did this sudden change of heart come from?"

"Who can say?" said Kit. "But by sometime around the January or February, this new secretary was making his mark. He and Burghley had hatched a plan — they had decided that the only way to convince Elizabeth to sign Mary's death warrant was to scare her into it."

"And these were supposedly her loyal council?" Perdita said.

"They were loyal as long as the queen was biddable, otherwise they were ruthless in pushing their own agendas and doing their utmost to play on the queen's fears and manipulate her."

"No wonder she had trust issues."

"Anyone would if they'd been through what she had," said Kit. "Cecil agreed with Davison and fabricated the lie that Spanish ships had been sighted off the coast of Wales.

However, with the evidence we have in the letters, it would seem that there might really have been ships off the Pembrokeshire coast as part of Philip's failed first invasion fleet and Burghley was merely embellishing the facts.

"To fully ensure Elizabeth capitulated, Walsingham, Leicester, Hatton and the new French Ambassador, Guillaume de l'Aubespine, Baron de Chateauneuf met at Burghley's house in Bishopsgate and conspired to 'discover' another assassination plot. The one they 'discovered' was actually two years old and had accounted to very little. It had focused on a man called Michael Moody who had planned to either leave barrels of gunpowder under Elizabeth's bedchamber and blow her up — sound familiar? — or to poison her shoe or stirrup."

Perdita gave Kit a quizzical look — the famous gunpowder plot had not taken place until 1605 and by then Elizabeth was dead and James I, Mary's son and the first Stuart king of England was on the throne.

"On Wednesday 1 February 1587, terrified by this new information and told to double her bodyguard, Elizabeth was at Greenwich, desperate and fearful," continued Kit. "She temporarily decided to give in and sign the warrant but she demanded that Davison did not let it out of his sight until it had been signed and sealed by the Lord Chancellor, Sir Thomas Bromley — who, rather conveniently, died three months after Mary, Queen of Scots was executed. Incidentally, he was the one who had first suggested they stage a special trial for Mary. She was not an English citizen, therefore, technically, she could not be tried under English law.

"Predictably, Davison didn't do as Elizabeth asked. As soon as he had it, he showed the warrant to Leicester and Burghley who pressed for it to be sealed that afternoon. The next day, when Elizabeth contacted Davison and told him to delay because she was still unsure, Davison confessed it was too late and the seal had been applied by the Lord Chancellor, Sir Thomas Bromley. Elizabeth questioned why it had been done in such haste, then apparently turned away, saying she wanted no more to do with it."

"She did what?" asked Perdita, outraged.

"I know, another peculiar anomaly," said Kit. "She should have been furious, so to not react is very suspicious. Anyway, to ensure the warrant's safe-keeping, Burghley insisted Davison give it to him. And, to add insult to injury, Burghley called a meeting of ten privy councillors in order to assess the queen's frame of mind."

"This is scandalous," exclaimed Perdita.

"It gets worse," said Kit, his expression grim. "Two days later, still worried that Elizabeth might change her mind, Burghley gathered the members of the Privy Chamber again. He already had a letter signed by them to authorise the earl of Shrewsbury and the Clerk of the Council, Robert Beale, to carry the warrant to Fotheringhay and ensure the execution was carried out immediately. The members of the council were sworn to secrecy until Mary was dead. Burghley claimed the need for secrecy was to spare Elizabeth's feelings. I suspect it's because he was still convinced he could manipulate the queen and that once he had executed Mary, Elizabeth would thank him whole-heartedly.

"But, that night, Elizabeth had a nightmare that Mary had been executed. Dorothy Stafford, who was sharing Elizabeth's bed, had the same terrible dream. At daybreak, Elizabeth sent for Davison and told him of this strange 'augury'. Davison remained loyal to Burghley and skirted the issue of the warrant. Elizabeth felt sure something was amiss and mentally prepared herself for bad news from Fotheringhay. She also became determined to show her councillors that they could not control her.

"On Tuesday 7 February 1587, two men arrived at Fotheringhay with the signed and sealed warrant. Mary had already retired to bed but on being told it was urgent she agreed to see them. She and her servants were informed that she was to die at 8am the next day. Worse, it was the ailing Earl of Shrewsbury who has to deliver the news. He had difficulty speaking — he had known and cared for Mary for nearly 25 years."

"But this is utterly barbaric," said Perdita, tears welling in her own eyes. "If there is any truth in this, Elizabeth was virtually tricked into signing the warrant. Why would anyone believe she would behave so appallingly towards a fellow queen? It's so inconsistent with her other documented behaviour."

"The thing is, Perds, people have pieced the story together from official documents, so they find a way to make it fit, even if sometimes you have to twist the facts almost to breaking point to make it believable," said Kit.

"This is *too* unbelievable, though," said Perdita. "It's a complete fabrication. Even other historians state that Walsingham invented and manipulated the plot to ensnare Mary."

"Remember, Perds, with every discovery we make, we're proving that the facts are wrong and when we have the second ring, we'll be in an even stronger position to prove we are correct and history is a lie."

"Yes, you're right," she said. "It's the injustice of this particular tale that's getting to me. Let's finish off: Mary has been told she is to die — what happens next?"

"The following morning, true to their word," continued Kit, "Mary, Queen of Scots was executed in the Great Hall at

Fotheringhay Castle. The earl of Shrewsbury and the earl of Kent were the official witnesses. Two of Mary's ladies and five of her gentlemen were allowed to accompany her. Shrewsbury had to give the command and his voice nearly failed him. It took two blows to kill her and Shrewsbury was so distressed he was unable to say Amen to the prayer afterwards.

"Shrewsbury's son, Henry Talbot, set off for London on Thursday 9 February 1587 to carry the news to Burghley. Burghley and Hatton received the news at dawn; Chateauneuf heard it at midday. Elizabeth was out riding with the Portuguese ambassador, so she was not told until the evening when Burghley confessed what he had done. Elizabeth was so stunned that she did not react and Burghley thought his gamble had been successful. However, the next day, the full horror of Mary's death hit Elizabeth and she became hysterical. Walsingham was absent from court, Leicester made himself scarce and Elizabeth would only speak to Burghley via Hatton. She blamed him and Davison entirely. She was furious they had acted without her express sanction, however, as the deed could not be undone, she resolved to make them suffer her wrath instead."

"And so she should — I hope she made them beg for forgiveness."

"She did. She summoned the Privy Councillors and was so terrible in her fury, they dropped to their knees, begging for mercy. Davison was sent to the Tower and a month later was tried in the Star Chamber and fined 10,000 marks, which would be about £6,000,000 today. He served a year in the Tower but the fine was never paid. Burghley was banished. Elizabeth wanted to humiliate him and prove she would no longer allow him to manipulate her, although he did write a couple of hasty official documents trying to blame everyone else and purged his own papers in order to remove anything incriminating."

"What an absolute coward," muttered Perdita.

"Yet he's remembered as a respected statesman and protector of the realm." Perdita tutted at these injustices and Kit continued, "Walsingham returned to court in March and was questioned as to the whereabouts of the Bill of Attainder. It appears the original that Beale delivered to Fotheringhay had mysteriously disappeared, which is why the only records we still have are two hastily written copies made by Beale shortly before he left for Fotheringhay Castle. And, finally, in the April of that year, Elizabeth allegedly wrote to Mary's son, James VI of Scotland, feigning innocence and brazening it out. She sent her cousin, Robert Carey, Lord Hunsdon's youngest son to report the 'miserable accident' because the two young men had met before and got on well. Carey, however, was advised to wait at the border, where he delivered the message to two of James' councillors instead of the king."

"And Mary was dead and Elizabeth was known from that day on as a murderer of monarchs," said Perdita. "Although, now we have the Lady Pamela letters, we can prove there is another version of events, one that makes more sense."

"Well, we have the letters, but at the moment we can't corroborate them," said Kit.

"There was something else I wanted to ask you," said Perdita, consulting her notes. "This states Philip Sidney was buried on 16 February 1587, eight days after Mary was executed. Another oddity, isn't it? A state funeral in all but name with over 700 mourners, eight days after the death of a queen?"

"But for a male courtier who didn't even have royal blood?" mused Kit.

"And, on 12 March 1587, a requiem mass was held for Mary in France, although she wasn't interred in Peterborough Cathedral until the 30 July 1587, when she was buried with full honours. It was also in July 1587 that the 11-year-old Arbella Stuart, potential heir to Elizabeth's throne, was officially presented to Elizabeth at court for the first time and, in Spain, Philip was beginning to amass the Armada."

"All in all, 1587 was a busy year."

"And one of huge contradictions," said Perdita.

They both lapsed into silence, which was broken by the door suddenly being thrown open and Piper rushing in, her face flushed with excitement.

"Piper, what's happened?" asked Perdita.

"Nothing bad — in fact, it's good news," she said, excitement radiating from her. "We've found Hannah White's address."

Chapter Two

"We know where Hannah is and she still has the ring," Piper exclaimed.

"What? How did you find her?" gasped Perdita.

"Alistair told me when we'd finished discussing the divorce — the contact details came through while we were talking. He's suggested he approaches Hannah to see if she would be willing to sell the ring. He's going to pose as an antiques dealer."

"Piper, that's a huge step forward," said Kit.

"Your dad has said we need to be circumspect," Piper told him, "as he doesn't want to alert MI1 to Hannah's presence or, in case he's still watching us, Randolph Connors either."

"And the divorce?" asked Perdita, her voice cautious.

"Going ahead," said Piper. "We'll offer Jeremy a one-off, very substantial, settlement and make it clear, if he accepts it, there won't be any more money. He will also be denied all access to Marquess House and has no claim on the property, something which is made easier because the house belongs to us jointly."

"And your house in Twickenham?"

"He can have it," she said. "I won't be going back there again."

As Perdita hugged her sister, there was a knock on the door and Alistair poked his head around the door.

"Dad," exclaimed Kit, beckoning his father inside. "This is unexpected news about Hannah White. Is it too soon for a response?"

"Unfortunately, yes — we need to give Ms White time to consider her options and check out the extensive antiques emporium website Cal has created for me to make the offer seem innocent..."

"He's done what?" asked Perdita.

"It's something we do when approaching people, Perdita — create a viable and searchable web history."

Perdita and Piper exchanged bemused glances, then a frightening thought occurred to Perdita. "Perhaps the reason she hasn't replied is because the Watchers have already found her," she said. "After all, we managed to. MI1 might have traced her first."

"It's possible but unlikely," replied Alistair. "Tracking people down isn't in their remit. They watch but they only act when it's necessary. I've also had word from the Home Secretary — he's assured me that Inigo Westbury has taken his team off our case at the moment."

"He's still in charge?" exclaimed Perdita.

"Not for much longer," Alistair reassured her. "The Home Secretary has informed me that the investigation into Inigo Westbury is concluding and once it is, he will be removed."

"But he isn't the only senior member of MI1 Elite," said Perdita, inexplicitly nervous at Alistair's trusting acceptance of the word of a government official. "What if someone else has been assigned and they're fobbing you off with this supposed inside information on Westbury?"

Alistair shook his head. "You're seeing things that aren't there, Perdita," he said, but his voice was calm and kind. "We have to choose whom we trust and, at present, I believe we can trust the word of the Home Secretary."

"Despite the fact he lied to you about The White List..." Perdita began, feeling the familiar wave of panic rising.

"Yes, Perdita, I do," said Alistair. He walked across the room and took her hand. "If I had a moment's doubt, please believe me, I would tell you."

His blue eyes, so similar to Kit's, were guileless but as she opened her mouth to protest, she saw Piper give a tiny shake of her head and swallowed her words.

"Very well, Alistair, I'll trust your judgement," she said.

"But Dad..."

"Kit, no." Alistair had released Perdita's hand and for the first time, he sounded angry. "When you become involved with the world of espionage, it's possible to drive yourself insane — you begin to see danger and spies everywhere. This is not the case. You have to keep perspective."

The force of his words left a resonant silence in the room. Alistair forced a smile and walked back to the door.

"My apologies for interrupting — see you for drinks later," he said and opened the office door.

"Let us know if you hear anything from Hannah White," Perdita called and Alistair waved acknowledgement of her words as he disappeared down the corridor.

The minute Perdita was sure Alistair was out of earshot, she turned to Piper.

"What is it Pipes?" she asked her sister. "What do you know?"

"I know why Hannah White hasn't replied to Alistair," she said, "and it isn't because the Watchers have got her. Hannah White is taking a sabbatical from her job."

"How do you know?"

"I've been following her on social media." She grinned. "Alistair isn't the only one who can play the subterfuge game. I'm using a false name. I've managed to trace her through her IP address. She's in Cornwall and from her social media profile, I know she's on a Reiki course."

"We should talk to her, Pipes, you and me," Perdita said. "She's a young woman, she's more likely to respond to us than to a middle-aged antiques dealer — no offence to your Dad."

"None taken but, Perds, you can't!" Kit replied.

"Why not?" she snapped. "We can't corroborate any of this — yet," she waved her hand, encompassing their work and discussions in her gesture, "but we know these letters cast enough doubt to make it worthwhile pursing the leads we have for the second ring."

"Yes, and what then? You let the Watchers murder you so the real truth is never revealed?" Kit sounded angry but when Perdita looked into his eyes, she realised it was not fury that had caused his outburst, it was fear. "Look what they did to your mother and your grandmother! Do you want that to be you or Piper?"

Perdita hesitated but then she forced herself to dismiss his words. Her own heart was beating with confusion and uncertainty and she could not deal with Kit's issues, too; the stakes were too high. She had to follow her instincts and these told her to keep going, to continue travelling on the path her grandmother had laid out for her when she had left the estate to her and Piper, and if that meant hunting down Hannah

White and the second ring by themselves, then that was what they would have to do.

"Kit, please, trust me on this," she implored, trying to take his hand but he shook her off. "Six months ago we had no idea there was even a suggestion that there could be another version of history. Now we've discovered enough anomalies to make even the most well-known historical events look as though they contain about as much fact as a fairy tale. We can't keep letting the Watchers bury the truth. We have to stand up to them."

"And what about Randolph Connors?"

They stared at each other, the air crackling with tension.

"What are you suggesting, Perds?" asked Piper, stepping forward, breaking the atmosphere and bringing them both back to the present.

"The Lady Pamela letters are an important find, probably as vital as the Paston letters," Perdita said. "It's an accepted academic fact that the Tudors and Stuarts were terrible record keepers. They might have passed endless statutes and bills and filed away court documents but they were left in mouldering piles to be eaten by mice and other vermin. It was the Victorians who began filing and compiling. They did their best, but so much has been listed incorrectly that it's not surprising that MI1 have been able to bury so much controversial information. In fact, considering what we've discovered, I'm amazed that a recent discovery about Mary, Queen of Scots was published a few years ago."

"What do you mean?" asked Kit.

"Records have been found in the last ten years that exonerate her from any involvement in the murder of her second husband, Lord Darnley."

"Really?"

"Yes, and the reason they had never been seen before was because they had been filed with other documents that had nothing to do with Mary or Darnley. It was a complete fluke that they were discovered at all."

"And they were published?" confirmed Piper.

"Yes."

"But that must mean MI1 has no idea about her true identity," Piper continued.

"Exactly!" said Perdita.

"How do you reach that conclusion?" Kit asked.

"If a book was published, suggesting a different version of events — that Mary was innocent of any involvement in Darnley's murder, which has always been implied by the Casket Letter trial — MI1 must have decided it was unimportant, otherwise I bet they would have pulled strings and the book would never have seen the light of day," said Perdita. "It's probably why the Armada letters haven't been removed from the public domain either."

"What Armada letters?" This time Piper was the one questioning her sister.

"A few years ago, there was a box of correspondence bought at auction containing letters written by Philip II of Spain during the Armada. They give a new perspective on his thoughts and actions and show that he was a terrible commander-in-chief. What I'm saying, Kit, is that these have been accepted and are available online. The Watchers have no idea that the anomaly they're trying to hide is linked to Mary, Queen of Scots or the Spanish invasion which followed her supposed execution. If they did, these new pieces of information would have vanished without trace…"

"Perdita," Kit interrupted, "do you really think the Watchers are going to allow you to release any of this and live?"

She turned away from him, her heart pounding. He was right, but she was frustrated with the endless caution, the waiting, the skulking in the shadows.

"Kit, if we can get the ring and use the jewellery to prove these letters are genuine, we might have some leverage against the Watchers. Rather than killing us, this might be the one thing we can use to save us. We need to speak to Hannah and it would have more impact if it was face-to-face."

Perdita and Piper stared at each other. Piper gave a short sharp nod.

"I'm in, we should go to Hannah White," she said.

They turned to Kit.

He hesitated but before he could speak there was an urgent knock and Deborah hurried in, carrying a folder. Her eyes were wide and her hands were trembling.

"What is it?" asked Perdita, immediately on her feet. "What have you found?"

"A series of letters from around the time of Mary, Queen of Scots' execution. Some are from Mignonne, the granddaughter of Bess of Hardwick, who was part of Mary Stuart's household, but there are others too — a whole series," Deborah said breathlessly, pale and scared. "We've only just finished translating them. Perdita, you must read them — if they're correct then this secret is even bigger than we anticipated."

Perdita opened the folder the woman had thrust into her hand. Removing the sheaf of papers, she spread them across the table, her eyes scanning them. Kit and Piper hurried over to stand beside her and together they read the letters. It took only a few moments for the impact of the words to make themselves felt. Piper recoiled first; her eyes wide with disbelief. Kit reached out and gripped Perdita's arm.

"Has Alistair seen these?" Perdita asked.

Deborah shook her head. "No. He instructed me to allow you first look at everything as we translated it. He trusts your judgement implicitly."

At any other time, Perdita would have been flattered by this comment but now the enormity of what they had uncovered fell fully on to her shoulders and she wondered if she would buckle under the weight.

"We need to show your dad," she said to Kit. "I'm out of my depth here. He's the only one who's going to be able to help us."

Gathering the letters together, she led the way out of the office and along the corridor to where Alistair was sitting behind his desk, waiting.

PART EIGHT: October, 1586

Chapter One

Elizabeth had never felt so alive. Draped in a drab cloak, her hair hidden under a simple scarf and with her face free from make-up, she was unrecognisable as she galloped through the cold night. The steady pounding of her horse's hooves beat in time with her heart. The wind whistled past her, ruffling the hem of her dress, stinging her cheeks, as she remembered another summons, another chase across the midnight landscape, another loss. Once again, she feared she would be too late and this was what drove her — the cause that had been motivating her for so many months.

Before, there had been only a few of them: Lady Isabel Baynton, Isabel's son Henry, Robert Dudley and two of Robert's men. Her eyes. Her best friend. Once again he had offered to accompany her but he had another task to perform while she was away, one that would keep her safer than if he rode at her side. On this moonlit race, her trusted guard of honour surrounded her and her few chosen companions. Each dressed, as she was, in dull clothes, their heads cloaked and their faces disguised with scarves. Even the white flash on her horse's forehead had been painted out so it would not shine in the dancing moonbeams.

They had left Boughton Hall as twilight fell, travelling stealthily through the night. Now they were within ten minute's ride of Fotheringhay Castle. While the others had murmured in relief, Elizabeth could not deny the stab of disappointment at the thought that their night-time adventures would soon be at an end. She had enjoyed the anonymity and the excitement of their clandestine gallop across her realm, even if the destination would be traumatic. In a life where she was always on show, it had been a gift to blend, unnoticed, into the background for a while.

Her fear about their arrival and all it entailed was also beginning to rise. For a moment, she wondered what would happen if she kept going, riding away into the darkness, vanishing from sight. It was a daydream she had often indulged but, in her heart, she knew she would never abandon her realm. As she pounded across the dark landscape, Queen Elizabeth and her favourite, Robert Dudley, Earl of Leicester, were causing a scandal as he insisted on spending the evening alone with her in her private chambers. As this thought rolled around her mind, unable to stop herself, Elizabeth laughed out loud. The gossip caused by the nights Robert was seen slipping into her chambers would create such a diversion that no one would ever guess the truth.

Once again, Lettice and Robert were prepared to continue the charade that their marriage was nothing more than a convenient cover for Robert to facilitate his long-term affair with Elizabeth, while it had been put about the court that Lettice had been banished to Wanstead, although, the rumours stated, the contrary duchess had decided to travel to Kenilworth Castle instead. When word had arrived from Mignonne that Mary's health was deteriorating further, Elizabeth had summoned Lettice to her chambers and explained her plan.

"Elizabeth, it isn't safe for you to visit Boughton Hall — it's not far from Fotheringhay and it certainly isn't viable for you to visit the castle," Lettice had spluttered.

"But I won't be going to Boughton Hall or Fotheringhay Castle, my dear," Elizabeth had replied, with a sly smile. "You will, as part of your journey to Kenilworth. Sadly, we will have rowed because I'm so jealous about your union with Robert, and in my temperamental female fury I will have banished you from court in disgrace. In the meantime, I, the queen, will remain here."

Kate and Lettice had exchanged a bemused glance.

"But you said…"

"Lettice," Elizabeth had snapped, her tone impatient as her cousin failed to grasp the subtleties of the plan, "*you* will be here disguised as me, while I travel to Northamptonshire as you. Who would dare challenge the snubbed and furious countess of Leicester en route to her favourite home, incandescent with rage over the stupidity of the queen's ridiculous jealousy? I know I am ten years older than you but we are the same height and build — with one of my simpler wigs my hair could pass for yours and in your clothes, with your litter and livery: who would question me?"

"And what about me? Left here pretending to be you — isn't that treason?"

"Of course not. I've given you permission. You will retire to your — my — bedchamber where you will complain of a headache and only come out when it's essential. In the meantime, you will allow Robert Dudley to attend you, sparking a flurry of rumours to distract everyone from what is really happening. Hidden in plain sight, my darling Lettice. Philadelphia, Katherine and Bess will be here to help, while Kate, I must ask you to risk even more and accompany me to Fotheringhay. With luck we will be gone a week at most."

"Elizabeth, this is reckless," Katherine Newton had whispered.

"Yes, Katherine, I know, but I must visit my sister. The months of her incarceration have passed slowly, I must go to her."

"Do you intend to rescue her?" There had been hope in Katherine's voice.

"No," Elizabeth had replied, in a voice laced with pain, "to say goodbye. She is too weak to be moved."

"You ask too much," Lettice had managed finally, her voice choked with sobs.

"I do," Elizabeth had agreed, taking her cousin in her arms and hugging her tightly, "but this is not the first time we have used this ploy. You have shown your courage in the past — please, Lettice, do not fail me now. You have played this role with such conviction, pretending to be me so I could move around my kingdom, unseen, and visit my sister. It was part of your promise to help us protect our dear Artemis."

"But, Elizabeth, you are going to the most dangerous place in the country," Lettice had said, her voice calm as though trying to make Elizabeth see reason. "What if something should happen to you?"

"You will continue as queen."

"No!"

Lettice had turned away, hot tears spilling down her cheeks.

"You always knew this was a possibility," Elizabeth had reminded her. "You accepted this role many years ago, my little She-Wolf. Don't fail me now, my dearest Lettice. I will return, I promise…"

"Not far now," said Kate in a low voice, breaking into Elizabeth's thoughts and bringing her back to the present.

Their horses were so close that they were almost touching but before she could reply, Elizabeth felt a hand on her reins and she was brought to a slow trot.

"What's the matter?" she hissed to the captain of her yeomen guards, who was now close on her other side, fear prickling down her spine.

"There is a horseman in those trees," he hissed. "It may be a bandit. Pause awhile, my lady — let my men ride ahead and deal with the ruffian."

Elizabeth and Kate did as they were asked and followed the captain into a shadowed copse, while two of the soldiers cantered towards the looming figure. As they neared him, the man turned his horse and flew down the slope, disappearing into the darkness. Elizabeth felt for Kate's hand, her joy at the midnight ride replaced by pure terror as the vulnerability of their situation struck her.

"Captain, what do you advise?" she asked.

"My objective, as always, is to keep you safe, Your Majesty," he replied. "If need be, you will join me on my horse and we will return to Boughton House, while my men deal with any rogues and thieves. Sergeant Abel will take care of your cousin but with luck, this threat will be nothing more than a startled poacher."

A twig cracked, echoing through the still night air and Elizabeth looked up. In the moments they had held their whispered conversation, twenty horsemen had picked their way through the trees and surrounded them.

"Captain Hynde, you have full command," she murmured, flinching as she heard Hynde unsheathe his sword.

"Force will not be necessary, Captain," said a calm voice and Elizabeth turned in surprise. "My apologies for causing alarm but we travel without livery in order to keep Her Majesty safe."

"Identify yourself, sir!" snapped Captain Hynde but Elizabeth had recognised him the moment he had spoken.

"Ralph Fitzalan, Duke of Hereford, I should have your head for this," Elizabeth gasped. "You, sir, are supposed to be surrounding Fotheringhay Castle with your men."

"We are, Your Majesty, but this is not the place to explain," he said and there was an urgency to his voice. Elizabeth noticed he was continuously scanning the area beyond their small copse. "We must escort you to safety at once. There are games afoot and until we have secured the area, you must remain hidden."

Elizabeth scowled but she nodded her head, acquiescing to his order. Ralph Fitzalan turned his horse and allowed Elizabeth to bring hers level with his own. There was a dark slope leading to the encampment of tents where Ralph had been holding the castle to siege conditions for the past four months.

"Do you see the large pavilion in the centre?" he murmured to her and Elizabeth nodded. "You might be my big sister and you might be queen but I bet I can beat you to flag outside my tent…"

He grinned through the darkness at Elizabeth and in the moment it took for her to process his words and their challenge he had taken off down the hill. Seconds later, she was fast behind him, laughing, exhilarated, high on the adrenalin of the moment as she chased her younger brother through the night.

"Things are becoming worse," said Ralph, as he guided Elizabeth to a chair and handed her a goblet of wine.

Elizabeth was thankful for the glowing stove in the centre of the luxuriously appointed pavilion. Frost was biting in the February air and, although the wild race had been a moment of excited fun bringing a flush to her pale cheeks, now she was cooling, the chill of the encampment was unpleasant. As she listened to Ralph's report, she understood his caution.

"Mary's belongings have been confiscated and they have taken her money," he continued. "There has been another development, too. In the past week, there have been hourly patrols sent from the castle."

"Have they tried to engage you again?" asked Elizabeth.

"No. In the first week when there were still soldiers at Fotheringhay, they sent a few squads out and there were skirmishes. However, we were able to repel them and since then, thanks to our spies within the walls, it has been apparent that there is a minimal military presence inside."

"Philip has no soldiers here?"

"None. The few who remain are English traitors — the Spanish have melted away."

"What do you think the patrols are about?"

"We think they're lookouts," said Ralph, and Elizabeth raised her eyebrows in surprise.

"For what?"

"A rescue force," he replied.

"To rescue Mary?" Elizabeth was bemused by this answer.

"No — to rescue Black Fortescue and his men," said Ralph with a grim smile. "The Welsh invasion has failed. We've had reports from Walsingham that there are still a few ships off the Pembrokeshire coast, but they're anchored away from shore and appear to be waiting, rather than coming closer. The soldiers Philip had thought he was spreading through the country have vanished — it seems they were not as loyal as he imagined, but then from the few pieces of information we've gleaned, it's probably because he was so careless of his men, treating them harshly and never paying them, so most of them have deserted at the first opportunity."

Elizabeth considered this information. It was typical of Philip to abandon a plot halfway through. His need to control every single detail was his biggest weakness, never allowing those he appointed to carry out the jobs he had given them. His arrogance drove him to assume he knew better, that he was the most experienced soldier, sailor, leader, and due to his constant interference his plans lost momentum — the lines became blurred as he issued constant conflicting, over-complicated advice which resulted in strategic disasters, wasted time and a loss of funds, loyalty, men and arms. Throughout her reign, she had witnessed the mistakes made by the king of Spain and she prayed that his grasp of this particular plot was also slipping away.

"Who has charge of Mary?" she asked. "Whoever it is, we must have leverage somewhere?"

"Most of the remaining men are Catholic or Jesuit preachers from the school of Douai," said Ralph. "Few have families, and those who do have been disowned. Gaspar de Quiroga y Vela hasn't been seen for some days. It's our belief he has left. We did not witness it but our most recent communiqué with Mignonne suggests this grim and cruel band of brothers is losing faith with one another. A message arrived last week and since then the men have become increasingly nervous. Black Fortescue, as his men call him, has no wife or siblings, neither does James Beaton, Owen Lewis, or Thomas Morgan — they are desperate men. Erasmus Saunders was here until a few days ago but he has also vanished. We think he may be trying to work his way across country back to Tenby."

"Could he have been given instructions in this letter?" asked Elizabeth.

"It's possible, but I think he left without the other's knowledge. There was a huge row the morning they discovered he was no longer in the castle. From this we've surmised he has abandoned them and their scheme. Mignonne is trying to persuade Chidiock to read the letter and reveal the contents to her but Fortescue has it locked away. We have concluded that either Philip has given the order to execute Mary, which they are loath to do without solid guarantees he will immediately send men to remove them to Spain, or Philip has abandoned them and they are considering their best move. The patrols are a way of checking to see whether there is a force of Spanish sympathisers preparing to swoop in and rescue them."

"And is there?"

"No," he replied, "and if there were, we would ensure they never reached the castle."

It was the first time Elizabeth had heard such bitterness in her half-brother's voice. He was usually the most optimistic of men but it seemed living in siege conditions for four months, in the constant shadow of looming death, his resilience had been dented. Although, she reasoned, his discovery of a twin sister at the point they were to be separated by Mary's illness could not be dismissed as a reason.

Elizabeth understood how he had felt — despite having siblings and cousins, her royal blood had always marked her as different and as such her childhood had been solitary. Ralph Fitzalan thought he had been orphaned at the age of ten and he had believed himself to be alone in the world. Yet the truth of his lineage had been revealed to him some months ago and with this, the discovery that he had a twin sister, who like him had been hidden. The fact he also had the other Tudors as family — Mary, Edward, Elizabeth and their string of illegitimate half-siblings, too, must have come as a strange new reality.

"And Mary, how is her health?" Elizabeth broke the silence that was growing between them.

"Her physician, Dominique Bourgoing, continues to do all he can to keep her pain at bay but she's bedridden. Her legs are so painful, it's impossible for her to stand for more than a few moments," said Ralph. "From what we've learned from Mignonne, the rest of Mary's staff remain loyal — Bastien Pagez, Andrew Melville and, her groom, Hannibal Stuart. Mignonne attends her, as do Mary Beaton, Jane Kennedy and Elizabeth Curle. Your emissary, Sir Thomas Gorge, was there until a few days ago, but he was forcibly ejected and has been living here with us ever since. He says the conditions within the castle are reasonable but they are not good."

Elizabeth shot Ralph a concerned glance. "Do they have food? You and your men have been holding them to siege conditions for many months now. Has this damaged Mary's health further?"

Ralph shook his head and joined Elizabeth by the small brazier in the centre of the pavilion, topping up her goblet with hot, spiced wine.

"We have ensured sustenance and medications have been passed to Mary. It's the men who are holding her whose supplies we have halted. Mignonne is truly Bess's granddaughter, she is indomitable. She is the one who has kept everything together inside the castle. It was also thanks to her that we were able to clear and reuse the passage through the walls. It was once part of a system of delivery tunnels to bring food up from the river. We'll use it to get inside tonight.

"Thanks to her grandmother, who has taught her how to read architects plans, Mignonne searched through the piles of paperwork in the library and discovered early drawings showing the first stages of the building works of the castle. It was she who sent men to search these tunnels out and cleared them, so we had a way in and, if necessary, they had a way out.

The only reason they have not fled is because Mary is too weak to endure such a journey. Even when Fortescue threatened Mignonne, demanding to know how she was smuggling in medication for Mary, she refused to tell him. She has been magnificent."

Elizabeth placed her goblet on the table and stood, reaching for her cloak. "I must see Mary," she said. "It concerns me that if we wait too long, the opportunity will be lost."

"Of course," said Ralph, "but Elizabeth, it will be dangerous. These are ruthless men, and if they discover you, they will have no compunction about killing you. If they can deliver you to Philip along with Mary, they will be feted as heroes."

Elizabeth swallowed. She was aware of the danger but fear would not stop this last visit to her sister.

There was a pause. Ralph looked at her.

"Sister," he began. "I still don't understand how this can be so. If I was the heir to the throne, would the duke of Norfolk not have proclaimed it to the world? He would have been in a powerful position to act as regent if he had been able to place me on to the throne after Edward died."

"Thomas Howard was a changed man from the moment he discovered your mother, Catherine Howard, in such a terrible state after the beating our father had administered," Elizabeth replied. "His ambitions were exposed in all their shallowness and cruelty. He saw his true self and he never recovered. Protection of Catherine's children became his objective.

"He knew your sister would be safest in the royal nursery in Scotland where she was re-christened Mary, while you, who were a smaller baby, were left with your mother until she, too, ailed. The life she had lived with our father had weakened her and in March 1552, she died from a fever and was buried in the Marquess House chapel. The Devereux's had been loyal

345

friends to Catherine and they took you into their household, even though they were aware of the risks.

"You may not have known then, Ralph, but the key to your identity was the locket, given to you by your mother. It had been a present to Catherine when she first arrived at court in December 1539 from Lady Isabel Baynton and her husband, Sir Edward. If anything should happen to me this evening, Sir Francis Knollys holds a casket which contains written testimonies from the Lady Anne of Cleves, Thomas Howard and myself, telling the whole story.

"Our cousin, Lettice, currently masquerades as me but she, too, knows of your existence and your claim to the throne. If our venture is unsuccessful this night, she will continue as 'queen' for six more months before 'dying'. In this period, you will take your position in court and when the day comes for her to name an heir, she will name you."

"No, Elizabeth, this is maudlin..." began Ralph, but Elizabeth simply smiled.

"No, it is practical and it is just," she said. "You should be king, Ralph. I should be your spinster sister, living quietly in the countryside somewhere."

Ralph's expression was one of grief as he hugged Elizabeth, squeezing her to him.

"We will keep you safe, this night," he said, as he released her, his unusual grey eyes staring deep into her brown ones. "You will return to London and we will never speak of this again. I do not want to be king."

Elizabeth shrugged. Walking to the entrance of the tent, she allowed Ralph to drape her dull brown cloak around her and pulled the hood over her bright hair.

"Come," she said, her voice low. "Let us visit our sister. For a few hours the three of us can be together."

Chapter Two

The icy February air bit into the delicate skin of her face as Elizabeth followed the broad-shouldered back of Ralph Fitzalan. The new watch from the castle had returned to the gatehouse only moments before and would not patrol again for another hour. This was their chance. Behind her were two guards and another led the way in front of Ralph.

Kate, exhausted and overwhelmed from the journey, had begged to be allowed to stay behind with Captain Hynde. He would assume responsibility for the camp while Ralph and his second-in-command, Golding, escorted Queen Elizabeth on her perilous quest, and had promised he would protect Kate with his life. Elizabeth, on seeing her exhausted cousin, had understood she had no choice but to agree, but it did not stop her from being nervous about venturing into the darkness without Kate's strength and support.

"Watch your footing, Elizabeth," murmured Ralph, "the castle is built on a marsh and the ground is boggy."

"Is it far to the tunnel entrance?" she asked, for the first time doubting the wisdom of her plan.

"Not far but the path is steep," he replied.

Gripping the hand he offered, Elizabeth steeled herself for the difficult descent. Clouds scudded across the moon, creating eerie silver shadows as they prowled the night-time world. The distant howling of nocturnal animals unnerved Elizabeth and unbidden, frightening thoughts of angry spirits, ghouls and witches filled her mind. The further they walked, the more the dense, strange night threatened to overwhelm her. Her nerve was at breaking point when Ralph pulled her towards an oddly positioned rock.

"Here," he whispered, "Golding will go first, you will follow, then I will be behind you. These two fellows, Merrick and Abel, will remain here to guard the entrance. Once inside, Mignonne will meet us and escort us to Mary's chamber. If we're lucky we will have 20 minutes to say our goodbyes, but no longer — the men check on her every half an hour."

Elizabeth bit her lip, unsure whether her courage would hold. Think of Mary, she told herself — this might be the last time you are able to be together.

The ground was slippery but she concentrated on placing one foot in front of the other. She knew if she focussed on simple things, it would keep fear and panic from consuming her. Feeling her way through the darkness, aware of Ralph behind her and the enormous figure of Golding prowling his way like a force of nature in front of her, she kept walking. Water dripped from the ceiling, glistening on the stone walls like poison, while under her feet loose stones and puddles caused the going to be slow. There was the occasional crunch as one of them crushed a mouse skeleton, sickening Elizabeth to the stomach. Each noise seemed to be magnified and with every step forward she felt sure that at any moment they would be captured by one of Philip's men.

Suddenly, Golding stopped.

"We're here, Your Majesty," he whispered. "Please stay in the shadows while I check all is well."

Ralph reached forward and pulled her behind him, sheltering her from the tunnel entrance. There was creaking and a sliver of light spilled into the blackness as Golding opened a thick wooden door, sliding through a gap Elizabeth felt was far too small for someone of his girth. In front of her, Ralph was silent, tense, his hand resting on his sword hilt. She shut her eyes, composing herself, checking the belt at her waist and ensuring the small leather pouch remained attached. Light flashed into the tunnel and a female voice hissed,

"Quickly, Your Majesty, we must hurry."

Ralph caught Elizabeth's hand and pulled her forward into the stone-floored corridor. The slim figure of Elizabeth Pierrepont — Mignonne — waited, a candle flickering, casting shadows of monstrous size up the walls.

"The Scottish queen is this way," said Mignonne and turned, walking swiftly into the gloom, her candle the only beacon of hope. Time and terror eradicated the need for the bowing and scraping Elizabeth so loathed and she hurried on silent feet behind Bess's granddaughter, braver now she was inside the castle, ready to fight to see her sister. It took only minutes to weave their way through the servants' passageways and up the winding staircase to Mary's room, but before they approached the door, Mignonne pushed them into a shadowy window alcove.

"Wait here," she hissed. "The guard sometimes come at unusual times."

Melting into the darkness, she left Elizabeth and Ralph helpless, pressed against the cold walls in the shadows.

"Your Majesty, Your Grace, this way!"

A door opened across the corridor, firelight flickered and the smell of burning sage wafted towards them.

"It's supposed to purify the air," explained Mignonne. "I dried it during the summer months. Quickly, before the guards return."

Summoning her courage, Elizabeth shook back her concealing hood and hurried into the room.

It was warm, dry and comfortable, which gave her great relief. A bed dominated the space, heaped with delicate embroidered throws and piled with soft cushions. Sitting up, her auburn hair now faded with illness and sorrow, caught in a loose bun at the nape of her neck, her face drawn and lined from years of pain, was Mary. Hints of her good looks remained around her eyes and in the elegance of her bone structure but her alabaster skin was now tinged a waxy yellow and the shimmering brown of her eyes was dulled. She was smiling, though, and in her joyous expression was her true beauty.

"Mary!" exclaimed Elizabeth, running across the room to embrace her sister.

"Elizabeth!"

The greeting was warm, heartfelt, full of love.

"Oh my sweet Artemis, together again at last." Tears of joy streamed down Elizabeth's pale cheeks.

"...and those days in Buxton, taking the waters with Bess, Lettice and Kate," laughed Mary. "Do you remember the day I engraved my name on the window in order to prove to Robert it was a real diamond in my ring from Bothwell and not glass as he insisted."

Elizabeth grinned in response. "He was terrible that year — he showed off all summer to impress Lettice," she said. "I was always amazed when our little She-Wolf agreed to marry him."

"I think she did it for you, Venus," sighed Mary. "She was keeping him close, just in case you ever changed your mind and decided you did like him after all."

"Really?" Elizabeth was astonished that Lettice would even consider making such a sacrifice. "But she does love him, doesn't she?"

"Oh yes, she adores him, but she is loyal to you and will always put your happiness first."

Elizabeth did not speak as she considered this unexpected and extraordinary idea. She was stretched out on the bed next to Mary, Ralph was in a chair beside them, and for those few minutes, it was as though they were ordinary siblings, reunited for a happy event, rather than three relative strangers who were joined by a twist of fate and their tainted royal blood. They knew the visit would be short but for those few precious moments, they were reliving shared memories and silly jokes, basking briefly in the glow of family love.

"And Ralph, do you remember Christmas night with the Shrewsbury's at Sheffield Castle?" said Mary. "Your son, William, was ten and there were so many children there that year. We played games with them for hours and in the end they were so overexcited, you suggested a competition to see who could stay quiet the longest."

Ralph laughed. "I hadn't imagined for one moment it would happen," he said, "but they sat there for nearly 15 minutes before Dorothy Devereux couldn't stand it any longer and began to giggle. It set them all off."

"Such simple pleasures," sighed Mary.

The stories came thick and fast. Elizabeth noticed the slight sorrow in Ralph's eyes. Although he had always been part of their inner circle, she could see he was curious as to how his status, had it been known, would have changed events. *The past is done*, thought Elizabeth, squashing the burning wave of guilt at keeping this from Ralph for so many years. *We have this moment, the three of us, siblings, we must take this small gift and remember it always.*

It was as Elizabeth began regaling a tale about Mary chasing Robert Dudley with a wooden practice sword during a visit to

Brocket Hall that she noticed the sudden change in her younger sister. Her jaundiced face contorted as pain engulfed her and in a moment, Mary's happy laughter turned without warning to a violent cough.

The sound of merriment was swallowed by a deep rasping noise that wracked her entire body, sending it into convulsions. Jane Kennedy and Mary Beaton, two of the Scottish queen's most loyal women, surged forward holding goblets containing soothing tinctures. Elizabeth scrabbled from the bed to allow them room to work, to calm Mary and make her comfortable, while Ralph stood so quickly to clear space that he sent his chair flying and it collided with a small table causing a huge crash.

Mignonne was on her feet — all this time she had been sitting with Elizabeth Curle, working on a detailed sampler of a mermaid and a hare, but her needlework had been thrust aside in her panic.

"Your Majesty, you must hide." Her voice was taut, urgent. "The guards will come to investigate the noise."

Elizabeth dragged her eyes from Mary, who lay ashen-faced on her pile of pillows, her eyes closed, her breathing shallow, her coughing fit soothed for the moment.

Mignonne took Elizabeth's hand and pulled her across the room.

"Your Grace," she called to Ralph, who stood frozen to the spot, staring down at his twin sister. "You must hurry."

The high-pitched tremor in her voice roused Ralph from his torpor.

"In here," said Mignonne, as she wrestled open a narrow door cut into the panelling. "I'm sorry, there isn't much space, but the guards don't know about this. We think it was once a servant's room but was turned into a priest's hole some years ago. We've been using it to keep the Queen's medications and food hidden from Fortescue and his men."

Elizabeth hesitated as the fetid air of the tiny chamber overwhelmed her but Mignonne ignored all protocol and gave her a hearty shove in the small of her back. Seconds later, Ralph was beside her and Mignonne had fitted the panel back in place, plunging them into darkness. There was barely room for the two of them and they stood with their backs against the stone wall, their faces so close to the door, they were almost touching the wood. Elizabeth opened her mouth to whisper to Ralph when there was a crash outside and the sound of heavy boots.

"What was that noise?" came an angry male voice.

"In my rush to attend the Scottish queen, my skirts knocked the chair and it overturned the table."

The heavy footsteps marched across the room and Elizabeth nearly jumped out of her skin when she heard the man speak again — he was inches from where they were hiding.

"Search the room," he shouted, his voice menacing, "and make sure you search the bed. I wouldn't put it past these bitches to hide someone in there."

It took every ounce of self-control for Elizabeth to remain quiet. Her eyes were wide with outrage and fury but she was also conscious of the fact that if she were discovered, she would never leave this castle alive. Ralph's reassuring hand slipped into hers and squeezed. Tears of fury, frustration and fear filled her eyes as she listened to the brutality with which the women on the other side were being treated as the men searched every inch of Mary's chamber. When they were back at court, she would ensure these men paid with their lives for their barbarous treatment of her sister and her subjects. Philip

II would learn that she was not to be underestimated merely because she was a woman.

"Check for priest holes," came a newer, softer, but more menacing voice. Elizabeth recognised it as belonging to Black Fortescue, the man who had tried to bully her during the meeting at Boughton Hall. "I have long suspected there of being at least one within these walls."

Elizabeth swallowed her gasp as someone began tapping the panelling. Beside her she felt Ralph reaching for his dagger. Closing her eyes, Elizabeth summoned all her courage, preparing herself for possible confrontation if they were discovered. The tapping came closer. Her only hope if they were found was to trust that these men would fail to recognise her without her finery. Stripped of her court elegance and the thick white make-up, she was almost unrecognisable from her painted images. Fortescue had only met her once — it was unlikely he would guess her true identity, not at first, anyway.

The tapping noise came again, on the panel nearly touching their noses. Neither of them moved. Elizabeth wondered if she would ever dare to draw breath again. Tap, tap, tap. Again, the enquiring noise and a long pause. She felt Ralph try to manoeuvre himself in front of her, then to her relief, the tapping came again but this time from a panel further away, until eventually, with much shouting and what sounded like someone being slapped, causing a female scream of pain, the men left the bedchamber with a ringing slam of the door.

Fury was overwhelming her when Mignonne finally released them from their dark prison.

"I'm sorry, Your Majesty," she whispered, white-faced as she pulled Elizabeth into the room, sinking into a curtsey, her head bowed.

"My dear, Mignonne, you saved our lives," Elizabeth whispered, raising the girl to standing. "I shall tell your grandmother — she'll be very proud of you. Will it be safe for us to leave or will they have positioned someone outside?"

"There aren't enough of them to keep a permanent watch on us," said Jane Kennedy. "Most of the Spaniards have left, either when they escorted de Quiroga y Vela away a few days ago or they've deserted, slipping away with the twilight and never returning. Black Fortescue is in a constant fury as he feels he has been betrayed by all sides: the Spanish, the Church and by the men who claimed to be loyal Catholics…"

"Your Majesty, I'm sorry to interrupt but we don't have long. It's time to say goodbye."

Ralph, who had been standing beside Mary's bed, staring down at her prone figure, reached down to her, whispering to his twin sister before placing a kiss on her forehead. When he turned away, tears filled his eyes. Elizabeth threw him a sorrowful smile, then fumbling with the pouch on her belt she removed the two ruby rings.

"Mary," she whispered, "do you have the strength to open your eyes?"

The eyelids of the Scottish queen flickered, then with a huge effort she looked up at her elder sister.

"Our rings," Elizabeth whispered, "can you see? I commissioned my royal jeweller to add embellishments so we have them as a constant reminder of each other and our shared past. Here is yours, the one that belonged to your mother Catherine Howard, it has the sapphire clip, the colour of her eyes, and inside I've had the words *Semper Sorores* inscribed, one of our codes and a phrase that is so very true — we will be sisters always. It is like my motto: *Semper Eadem*, Always the same."

Mary reached out her ghostly white hand and Elizabeth placed the ring on her palm so she could see the detail.

"In the bottom, I had her painted, your mother, an image of Catherine from the portrait my father had commissioned of her when they wed. She is wearing the silver locket which Ralph has as his memento of his true heritage."

From the corner of the room, Ralph gave a stifled sob but he turned to watch the scene on the bed.

"And this is mine," said Elizabeth, placing the second ruby ring into Mary's hand. "Mine reads: *iuncta sanguine*, as we said, we are joined in blood on both sides of our lineage, through our father and our mothers, Anne Boleyn and Catherine Howard who were cousins. In mine, I've put a picture of my mother."

"And here's mine," said Ralph, striding forward, allowing the locket to slide across the two rings, cold and slippery, completing the trio. "*Spe et nereidum*, hope and mermaids."

"Arbella," whispered Mary. "Give them all to Arbella. It is the women who will tell our tale and she must be the first of our secret keepers. She will always have hope and mermaids."

With a shudder, her hand slumped to the bed and Mary slid into unconsciousness.

"Mary, no," gasped Elizabeth but she was pushed aside by Mary's physician, Dominique Bourgoing.

"She is sleeping, Your Majesty," he reassured her, "but her time will not be long."

"Your Majesty, Your Grace, we must leave," said Mignonne, her voice tense and urgent. "The guards will return soon. I believe they may search the room again."

"But what about Mary?" said Elizabeth, tears welling in her eyes.

"There's nothing we can do for her now," said Ralph and gathering the three pieces of jewellery that had scattered across the bed, he tucked them into a leather pouch at his belt. "Come Elizabeth, we must take you to safety."

Elizabeth hesitated, not wanting to leave but then sense reasserted itself. Leaning over the bed, she hugged Mary's wasted body to her and kissed her sunken cheek, then with one last desperate look at her sister, she forced herself to turn from the prone figure in the bed to follow Ralph and Mignonne from the bedchamber and back into the gloom of the tunnel.

Once more Mignonne's candle led the way through the dark corridors. Every nerve in Elizabeth's body was alert as they crept through the shadows, until finally, they were by the concealed door.

"Hurry," whispered Mignonne. "I must return — it would be a disaster if they knew we have a key. Chidiock supplied it. Morgan thinks that once they've locked us in at night we're their prisoners. Stupid men." Her voice rang with contempt.

"Take care, my dear," said Elizabeth, hugging Mignonne. "Send word to Ralph if you need him."

"We shall — now, please, Your Majesty, be careful."

The concealed door creaked open and Golding peered out. Mignonne bobbed a curtsey then melted away into the darkness. Elizabeth hurried through the gap and into the dank tunnel, Ralph behind her. They paused as Golding shut the door, sliding it back into place with care so no unexpected noise would alert the prowling guards to their presence.

"We must hurry," said Ralph, and taking Elizabeth's hand, he pulled her along the slippery tunnel.

None of them spoke as they fled. Their footsteps seemed so loud to Elizabeth that she felt sure they would be heard inside the castle, but neither Ralph nor Golding showed any inclination to slow their pace. Elizabeth realised that the encounter with Black Fortescue had unnerved the usually calm duke. Perhaps he regretted allowing her access to the Scottish queen. Had they been found, she had no doubt she would be languishing in a dungeon now — if she had been allowed to live. The thought sent icy shivers down her spine.

"Stay here, Elizabeth," said Ralph, coming to an abrupt halt. "Golding, check the tunnel entrance, I will be right behind you."

Elizabeth, once again, stood shivering in the darkness with water sliding down the walls beside her, wondering what had possessed her to plan this night-time adventure. The visit with her younger sister had been both wonderful and devastating. For the brief period when she, Ralph and Mary had been laughing, she had glimpsed the lives they had all lost because of their royal blood. There were many who envied her the position of Queen, with its privilege, money and power. Yes, she was lucky but with the trappings of monarchy, which provided so much on a material level, it also destroyed personal relationships.

After watching Philip II try to steal the country from under her elder sister, Mary's nose when they had been married, Elizabeth had realised it would take a remarkable man whom she would trust enough not to be overwhelmed by the lure of the crown. Anjou had come close but their union had been short. It had barely been announced to the country before he had succumbed to the sweat — not syphilis, as his enemies were fond of suggesting. Perhaps, she thought, as she waited in the dank gloom, his early death spared me having to watch him being corrupted by power. Her mind flickered to Mary's second husband, Henry Stuart, Lord Darnley, cousin to them both through Lady Margaret Douglas. The Scottish crown had never rested easily on Darnley's handsome head, altering him almost the moment he was able to wield such power.

"Elizabeth, there is trouble afoot," came Ralph's voice through the darkness. "Merrick and Abel have been attacked. Merrick is dead, Abel is injured. Fortescue is not as useless as we thought — after searching Mary's room, he sent out the few soldiers he has left. Luckily, our men were able to move away from the tunnel entrance so it wasn't discovered, but I must be certain it is safe for you before you leave this place."

He slid his cloak from his shoulders and wrapped it around Elizabeth, then led her to a rocky ledge which was wide enough to use as a seat.

"I'm sorry," he whispered, his face white with fear, "but you will have to remain here for a few moments longer."

"Ralph, no," she responded.

"Trust me?" he asked and after a moment's hesitation, she nodded.

"I will return for you," he said, and leaning forward he kissed her forehead as he had Mary's earlier, then he was gone and Elizabeth was alone in the blackness.

Chapter Three

The queen of England was at her favourite palace of Richmond in Surrey. The letter was addressed to Bess because her granddaughter, the doubtless Mignonne, had, in her grief, reached out for her beloved grandmother. Katherine Newton had translated it and, after some consideration, the queen had gathered her most trusted group from the Ladies of Melusine around her — they had been by her side throughout her protection of Artemis. Reading the letter was the most difficult task she had ever performed but she would not fail. With tears in her eyes and pain in her soul, she delivered the final instalment of the eventful and extraordinary life of Mary Stuart, Queen of Scots.

My dearest Lady Glass, this is a day of great sadness. Our Lady Artemis has been taken from us in the most brutal way.

Two evenings ago, she weakened further and was unable to rise from her bed. Despite his cruelty, we knew the man they call Black Fortescue to be an ordained priest and I sent word, begging him to give Our Lady the blessing of the Last Rites. We had no response and I feared Artemis would die without hearing the sacrament that is of so much importance to those of her faith.

Early yesterday morning, there was a knock on the door and Black Fortescue entered, followed by two of his men. He administered the sacrament of the Last Rites to Her Majesty. We were all most humbly relieved and believed at last our captors were showing their compassion. The men left, assuring us they would return within the hour. This was when we understood we should fear their intentions. However, our beloved Artemis was unmoved. She sank back into her mound of pillows, calling us to her. Once more she requested her Book of Hours should be passed to Arbella, along with the gift of the ring, which Her Majesty, the Queen has in safekeeping.

Her breathing faltered and as we sat, weeping at our sadness, her face became radiant as the angels carried our beautiful Scottish queen to her final peace. As the pain left her, she sighed so happily, free at last from the torture of illness.

Oh Grandmamma, we were hugging and weeping, mourning our loss when the evil Fortescue processed into the room and read an official decree from the Spanish king, ordering her execution. Mary Beaton laughed in their faces and told the man he was too late before spitting at his feet. Screaming with rage, the evil Fortescue struck Mary Beaton to the floor, then ordered his men to lift the queen's body from her bed.

They carried her downstairs, ignoring our screams and protests. Her little dog, Otto, barked and growled but when one of the guards tried to kick him, I pulled him safely into my arms. The guards tried to hold us back but Mary Beaton and I managed to run after Our Lady.

She was wrapped in her beautiful red silk robe with its fine embroidery. The phoenix, which she had taken as her symbol so many years ago, flew boldly on her retreating back, her motto — In my end is my beginning — glinting gold in the torchlight. The guards carried her to the Great Hall and laid her on the raised dais, her head resting on a block. Mary Beaton screamed and, I could not help myself, I began to sob. I ran forward but a guard caught me around the waist and held me fast.

Death had not robbed the queen of beatific smile, her face was suffused with such radiance and peace, she could have been sleeping. We realised it did not matter what these men did now, they could no longer hurt our beautiful sister. Our tears dried on our cheeks and we hissed defiantly as the madman Black Fortescue gave his wicked order in the name of the Inquisition and King Philip II of Spain. In their pettiness and vileness, they beheaded her corpse, leaving the body on the dais as they fled, forgetting the duke of Hereford's men were waiting outside the castle to apprehend these cowardly curs.

Oh Grandmamma, we are lost without Our Lady. She who was so kind, so gentle and so caring. The duke of Hereford and his men arrived not long after and they carried her body to her chamber. We have prepared her with the love and reverence she deserves.

The duke was said to be much affected by the death of the Scottish queen and was brought in by his men. His injuries, sustained as he and Lady Venus left us two nights ago, have weakened him considerably. His leg and his arm are both most heinously damaged, however, he sat beside her with his head bowed, sobbing as though she had been his great love. His soldiers captured Black Fortescue and his men, they are held in the dungeons here and are chained most painfully. The duke was terrible in his fury and awaits Walsingham and his men.

As Her Majesty requested, I have kept her Book of Hours safe for my cousin Arbella.

The duke of Hereford will soon arrange for us to travel to his home and with our blessed Lady Venus will decide upon the correct treatment of our lady, Mary, the Queen of Scotland. However, he requested I send you this news now we are all safe.

May angels bless you, Grandmamma, I hope soon to be by your side and in your comforting embrace.

Mignonne

The queen turned away from her gathered crowd as each expressed grief in their own way. A few sobbed, some were white-faced with shock, others sagged into chairs. The queen walked to the enormous windows of her solar, looking out over the river Thames, the heart of her capital, her realm, her land. On her left hand she wore both ruby rings. *Semper Sorores. Iuncta Sanguine. Sisters Always. Joined in Blood.* Around her neck hung the silver locket, *spe et nereidum*, but she felt no hope today and no mermaids raised their beautiful heads from the flowing, choppy water below as she mourned her loss.

Behind her, she could hear the assembled women being ushered out by her closest confidants. It was not long before only Bess, Katherine and Kate remained. The letter she had read aloud was now a week old. She had paused before she had announced it to the wider circle of trusted women, wishing to evaluate the consequences before the shocking news was revealed.

Now, though, the death of the Scottish queen at the hands of Philip II and his Inquisition would become common knowledge. The country was on a war footing, prepared for the invasion fleet they knew he was amassing in Portugal. In the past few days, she had given her permission for Sir Francis Drake to carry out a clandestine visit on the Lisbon port, to see how many of the ships he might be able to destroy or steal in a smash and grab raid. This, however, was not what troubled her. Philip would always be there with a scheme and she would defeat him every time.

Her heart was breaking because of news brought to her concerning Ralph and his injuries. He had been so brave, fighting off the last of Fortescue's soldiers, keeping them at bay until Captain Hynde had arrived with reinforcements from the camp. Golding had been killed in the skirmish, as had Merrick and Abel. To her horror, Ralph had succumbed to his extensive wounds two days earlier.

They were dead, she thought, both the twins, Catherine's children, who we worked so hard to protect. One a crowned queen, the other a man of great character who had died trying to save his sister and his monarch.

"Your Majesty...?" Kate's voice was tentative as she approached her but the queen did not react until she felt Kate's hand on her arm.

"Yes, Kate," she said with a start.

"William Fitzalan, the 2nd Duke of Hereford has arrived for an audience, as you requested."

The queen's brown eyes filled with tears. "Should I tell him?" she asked. "Do we trust him enough to reveal the truth?"

In Kate's hesitation was her answer and the queen nodded, her worst suspicions confirmed.

"He has Henry's blood, Henry's temper and Henry's duplicitous nature," Kate whispered. "He must never know."

"And Arbella?"

"She is the next secret keeper." Kate turned to Bess. "The burden will rest on Arbella's shoulders, but you will train her, Bess, so she will be prepared."

Bess nodded, emotion making it impossible for her to speak.

"The funeral for the duke and his sister will be as planned," continued the queen. "Robert Dudley, the earl of Leicester, will be the chief mourner. Katherine, you will continue as my chief cryptographer. We will need the Ladies of Melusine as much now as before. Arbella must be protected."

Katherine bobbed a curtsey, her eyes red-rimmed from crying.

"And Kate, my dear, darling Kate, I will need you more than ever," the queen said, tears spilling from her eyes, sliding through the white make-up, revealing the smooth skin below, "but now, my dear friends, please leave me while I adjust to these terrible events."

Curtseying, Kate, Bess and Katherine swept from the room on silent feet.

Alone for the first time since the news had arrived, brought by a frantic Henry Talbot, Bess's stepson, the queen collapsed on to the ornately carved chair by the fire, her heart beating with fear and sorrow. A tentative knock on the door was followed by the dear, familiar voice of Robert Dudley, Earl of Leicester.

"Hello, my sweet," he said, his tone gentle, concerned, kneeling at her feet and looking up at her. "How are you bearing up?"

"Not well," she admitted.

"We must be strong." He took her hand and she gazed down at him.

"Oh Robert, what will I do without her? Without them? How will we cope?"

His eyes were full of sorrow and every word seemed to cost him dear as he put her hand against his cheek. "Because, my darling Lettice," he said in a voice choked with tears, "we have no choice."

Tears slid from her brown eyes and with a sob, the queen said a final farewell to her beautiful, troublesome, wonderful Tudor cousins.

PART NINE: January, 2019

Chapter One

"This is impossible," said Perdita, her voice shrill. "If these letters are correct, they claim that Elizabeth I was killed after a skirmish outside Fotheringhay Castle, while her cousin, Lettice Knollys, masqueraded as her on the throne of England."

The winter sun was setting over the Pyrenees, flooding the boardroom with a burning, ethereal glow. Perdita stared at Alistair who seemed equally as stunned by this new revelation. Beside her were Kit and Piper, their faces as white as Perdita's. Callum and Deborah were also there — Deborah in her capacity as chief librarian and Callum because Alistair had asked him to double-check the room and their electronic devices for anything suspect. After discovering the bug in Piper's handset, he was even more vigilant than usual on security.

"What are your thoughts, Kit?" he asked, turning to his youngest son.

"I want to say it's nonsense and these letters are forgeries but there's too much in them that explains the historical anomalies of the era," he replied, and Perdita shot him a grateful glance. Even if the content seemed unbelievable, she was relieved that Kit was giving her his full support.

"Such as?" asked Piper.

"The strangeness of the Babington Plot, the inability of historians to be able to present Elizabeth I as a more rounded personality. Of course, it comes down to the interpretation of the individual historian but she is credited with such a huge range of personal defects and contradictions, it's as though she was more than one person…"

"Which we now suspect might have been the case," said Perdita. "Not to mention the fact that there have always been rumours concerning the longevity of her reign."

"Wasn't there one suggesting she was a man?" asked Callum.

From her position behind him, his mother snorted in disgust.

"Cut me some slack, Mum," he muttered, "I'm here as IT support. The reason I said it is because if I've heard of it, being a non-historian, then it must be quite widespread."

"You're right, Cal," said Perdita. "There was a rumour that Elizabeth died young and was replaced with a man and this was why she never married, so the secret of her gender would never be discovered."

"Why a man, though?" asked Piper. "Why not another woman? Or why not let the next heir inherit the throne?"

"It's a misogynistic attack with no historical merit levied at one of the greatest female monarchs," said Perdita. "It's to discredit all she achieved — after all, how could a woman possibly defeat Philip II of Spain and his mighty Armada? Would a woman be capable of reigning for so long without a man to guide her while creating a prosperous country and resolving so many of its political issues? Elizabeth terrified most men of her era because she was strong, politically astute, clever and educated to a higher standard than most of her privy council, so rumours were begun to suggest that Elizabeth must have been replaced by a man in order to explain why she was so successful."

Piper curled her lip in contempt.

"There have been other rumours about historical doubles, though," said Callum. "The one about Elizabeth was online and there was a list of historical figures who have supposedly used doubles at some point: Stalin, Saddam Hussein, Hitler and

General Montgomery. And, if these letters are true, Elizabeth was replaced, too?"

"There are things I don't understand, though," said Alistair, turning to Perdita. "In the latter part of Elizabeth's reign, after the death of Robert Dudley, the queen's new favourite was Lettice's son, Robert Devereux, Earl of Essex. There were many lewd suggestions that she was his lover — one tale has him running into her rooms when she was still in her night-clothes…"

"If we take it that by then Lettice was playing the role of monarch, it wouldn't be unusual for the earl to run in to see his mother," said Perdita. "He'd probably been doing it all his life. Not only that, it explains why the queen would be so intimate and caring about Lettice's children when in the accepted version of events, Elizabeth is said to have banished the countess of Leicester. It was something I'd never understood. Hate the mother but adore the children. If you take the usual version, this follows with Mary, Queen of Scots, too. Behead the mother but anoint the son. Contrary doesn't even begin to cover it but if you filter in all that we've discovered, these strange decisions begin to make more sense."

"I hadn't thought of that," admitted Alistair. "Although, we do hit the snag that Robert Devereux was beheaded on 25 February 1601 at the Tower of London, along with his stepfather, Christopher Blount, who was executed on 18 March 1601. Essex had led a rebellion against the queen."

"Was he, though? Perhaps his execution was a fabrication created by The Scribe. I'm beginning to feel that these letters are the best source we have to work out what really happened and what The Scribe changed. If the facts aren't stated here, we need to view events with suspicion."

"My goodness, Perdita, that's a sweeping statement," said Deborah, shock registering on her face.

"It isn't something I say without careful consideration," replied Perdita, "but it's a thought that has been growing for a while. Not only that, we're the first people to touch or read these letters for years, possibly centuries, so we can confidently surmise they haven't been tampered with or changed. These tell the real version of events."

They stared at her and for a moment, Perdita felt uncomfortable, but then her academic experience and her conviction that her words were correct rose to her aid and she shrugged off any doubts.

"There is enough in MI1's version of history to fit into the gaps of our letters and the codex," she explained. "Take Penelope Rich as an example — she was Lettice's eldest daughter and, rather like her brother, Robert Devereux, she was a favourite at court, despite the fact Elizabeth supposedly hated her mother. However, as Elizabeth's reign began to fade, Penelope very much turned towards the rising sun that was James I. She and her brother had been writing to the Scottish king for some years, assuring him of their allegiance. In this correspondence, which is documented in her biography, she uses the codename Rialta, which she also uses in our letters.

"I would suggest that the letters written to James I, rather than an isolated series which were discovered by Burghley, were actually part of our letters written by the collective of women known as the Ladies of Melusine. For whatever reason, Penelope's letters escaped from Katherine Newton's extensive filing system and were revealed to historians. However, as they were out of context from the knowledge gathered in the entire collection, they merely suggested that Penelope was either working against the queen, which was unlikely, or was keeping an eye on her future prospects once there was a new monarch; an idea which can't be entirely dismissed."

"And what do the letters tell us about the queen dying?" asked Kit.

Perdita rifled through the pile of printouts and fished out the translations of the letters from the period around 24 March 1603, the day Queen Elizabeth I was officially recorded as dying.

"Elizabeth was said to have spent some weeks ailing, lying on silk cushions on the floor before finally succumbing to death," said Perdita. "However, Lettice Knollys, the dowager countess of Leicester, is recorded as dying at the age of 91, at her family home of Drayton Bassett in the village of Rotherfield Greys in Oxfordshire on Christmas Day 1634…"

"But history tell us that James I ascended the throne in March 1603," interrupted Alistair.

"The letters around the time Elizabeth was supposed to have died are a bit sketchy," said Kit, "but they suggest that Lettice, who was approaching 60, was showing signs of illness and fatigue. Although it isn't stated anywhere, I wonder if perhaps she decided it was time to step down to make way for the next generation."

"What I don't understand," said Deborah, "is why Lettice reigned for so long? Even if she did retire in 1603, that was 16 years after Elizabeth supposedly died, yet one of the letters stated that Elizabeth had left instructions for Lettice to remain as Queen for six months before stepping aside for Catherine's son, 'Apollo'. Why didn't she follow those instructions?"

"Do you think she enjoyed the power?" asked Piper.

Perdita shrugged.

"And, why name James I as her heir when she knew there was another Tudor prince, whom Elizabeth had requested be the next monarch?" asked Kit.

"There must have been a reason," said Deborah, "because, even if he had died, we know that 'Apollo' had a son who could have inherited instead. He's mentioned briefly in some of the later letters. His codename was Prometheus and Apollo's wife was referred to as 'Lady Fortune'. I suspect she was Mary Seymour, the daughter of Katheryn Parr and Sir Thomas Seymour."

"What?" Perdita's voice was surprised by this unexpected revelation. "When did you discover this?"

Deborah held up a letter. "Here," she said, walking over to Perdita to show her. "This was another one we had no real reference for, then I remembered that Katheryn Parr had been known for publishing two books: *Prayers or Meditations* and *Lamentations of a Sinner*. Lady Fortune refers to her mother's books and quotes a small section from *Lamentations of a Sinner*. I've only just finished the reference."

"But I thought Mary Seymour died as a baby," said Kit. "She vanishes from the records shortly after she was fostered by Katherine Willoughby, the duchess of Suffolk."

"I suspect she was written from the records," said Deborah.

"Deborah, this a brilliant piece of detective work," enthused Perdita. "It gives us evidence that Catherine's son, 'Apollo', whoever he was, grew up, married and had a son but for whatever reason, their line has been obliterated."

"And Lettice's supposed marriage to Christopher Blount in March 1589?" asked Alistair.

"A fabrication by The Scribe?" suggested Kit.

"It's possible," agreed Perdita. "Or maybe she occasionally went back to Kenilworth to be herself for a few days and really did marry him."

"And James I?" asked Piper. "Why name him as heir rather than 'Apollo's' son? Or even Arbella Stuart, who had a very strong claim to the English throne?"

Perdita gazed at the reams of paper strewn across the boardroom table, her eyes lifting to the white boards with their scribbled notes and thought, allowing her active mind to sift through this new version of events they had discovered. Walking over to the largest board, she wiped a section clean and began drawing an elaborate family tree, then she turned to the others who had gathered around her and began to explain, pointing to the names as she explored her theory.

"One of Mignonne's letters stated that Mary had asked Elizabeth to pass their secret through the women," said Perdita.

"Which would lead to Arbella, wouldn't it?" said Kit.

"Not if you take into consideration the fact that Mary, Queen of Scots was a legitimate Tudor," said Perdita. "For the moment, we must disregard the mysterious Apollo and focus on the information we have in the letters. If Elizabeth had been able to name an heir, it's possible Mary would have been next in line to the throne. She was Elizabeth's younger sister, a daughter of Henry VIII and therefore, the next monarch if they were sticking to Henry's laws of succession.

"However, Mary predeceased Elizabeth, so if Lettice had disregarded the unknown male line, for reasons we're yet to discover, the next legitimate Tudor heir would have been James I, the son of Mary, Queen of Scots. He also had a claim through his father, Henry Stuart, Lord Darnley, who was the eldest son of Lady Margaret Douglas, the niece of Henry VIII.

While Arbella's claim was strong, she was only connected to the succession through Lady Margaret Douglas and her second son, so whichever way you look at it, James was the next heir."

"But Mary's comment — 'through the women'?" persisted Callum.

"It is through the women," said Kit, pointing at the line to Mary. "It's through Mary, Queen of Scots."

Perdita turned to look at the tired faces all working through her comments and beginning to nod or make murmurs of agreement. The sky was dark now and the harsh overhead lights of the boardroom made everyone look pale and exhausted.

"Shall we call it a day?" she asked and there was a wave of relief.

"Although, before we finish," said Deborah, "one last thing — my team and I have worked out most of the codenames now. Lady Griffin is Kate Howard, Lady Effingham, who was the daughter of Henry Carey, Kathryn Carey's brother; Hebe is Katherine Newton and, we should have guessed, Lady Glass is Bess of Hardwick."

Perdita gave a tired laugh. "Of course," she said, "the rhyme about Hardwick Hall, 'more glass than wall'. She was famous for building an extravagant home with huge windows."

Deborah gathered her things and disappeared, while Alistair remained, perusing Perdita's diagram.

"Are you done?" Piper asked her sister but Perdita shook her head.

"I want to check a couple of quick things," she said.

Piper nodded. "We'll wait for you," she said but made no attempt to do any more work, instead curling up on the sofa and making herself comfortable.

Perdita bustled back to the table and, once again, consulted the printout of the letter sent to Bess of Hardwick from her granddaughter. Mignonne's voice resonated through the centuries, her words conveying the sadness and devastation at the brutality of the Scottish queen's end, the words as impactful in the twenty-first century as they would have been in the sixteenth. If this was then followed by the murder of Elizabeth I by Fortescue's men, it was no wonder the English were ready to fight Philip out of the water when he launched his Armada, she thought.

"What about all the stuff with the privy council — the death warrant, Elizabeth refusing to sign it and all the other convoluted plots?' asked Kit.

"All made up afterwards by The Scribe?" suggested Perdita.

"The detail of it, though," said Kit, still unable to let it go, "could anyone make it up?"

"Yes," said Perdita, her quiet voice a stark contrast to Kit's sceptical tones.

"Seriously?"

"I suspect the details are based on real events — other real events — ones that took place before or after and have been altered to make them fit with the story The Scribe had been told to tell."

"But why?"

"The Scribe must have been instructed to carry out these changes by someone in power who decided it was time to hide the real trail of events," said Alistair.

"The thing I don't understand is why, though?" Kit persisted. "Why would anyone go to these lengths? These stories are fascinating but why does it matter? The past doesn't change anything, it's still the past. Why kill people today over things that were changed hundreds of years ago?"

"You need another perspective, Kit," said Alistair.

"You're right, Dad, I do," he said. "Help me understand why Perdita and Piper's lives are in danger because of events that happened in the sixteenth century!"

"But Kit, you know!" exclaimed Alistair. "History was changed, an enormous event was hidden — a secret which could have cataclysmic consequences if it were revealed today. I think with these discoveries, we're getting closer. Mary Fitzroy began to uncover these truths — you and Perdita took it even further with your incredible discoveries about Catherine Howard and now, with us all working together, we've uncovered even more and in a shorter space of time.

"We know Catherine gave birth to two legitimate Tudor heirs, we know the little girl replaced the legitimate Stuart heir: each born to royal parents, each a princess. Mary's line is the one we know, it led to the Stuart dynasty, to the Hanoverians, to Saxe-Coburg and Gotha and, finally, to the Windsors. Yet now we know she wasn't a Stuart at all, she was a Tudor. Should this be exposed, such a revelation is enough to send enormous shockwaves through society and around the world. It would beg the question: what else has been changed? Can anyone trust history?

"If we added to that the possibility that Elizabeth I was murdered at the same time and replaced on the throne by her cousin Lettice Knollys, there would be bedlam. Historical records the world over would be called into question, our national identities would be in tatters and in a climate like that, it doesn't take much for civil unrest to take hold.

"There's something else you must also consider," continued Alistair, when no one spoke, "although we have the codename 'Apollo', we still don't know what happened to the male line. It's vanished without trace. For some time now, I've wondered whether discovering what happened to Catherine's son, Nicholas, is the key to solving this."

"Are you suggesting it doesn't matter about discovering the true identity of baby Elizabeth Tudor, Catherine's daughter?" asked Piper, ready to defend her sister.

"No, of course not!" Alistair replied. "It was essential, and the more we delve into it, the more the ramifications of this duplicity will become apparent. We need to finish this, to find the ring and the locket. To see if what the Watchers say is true. They believe that when all three pieces of jewellery are reunited they will provide irrefutable proof of real events. Is it any wonder MI1 is scared, Kit? They have no idea what it could reveal. With what we've discovered here and even without verifiable proof, we could use this information to start a revolution, to hold governments to ransom. This is another reason why I think Randolph Connors is so desperate to take control of Marquess House. I wonder if he believes the final proof is hidden there. Whether it is or not, whoever finds and controls it holds the power."

"But, Dad, why was history changed in the first place?"

"When things are happening, when you're in the middle of events, it's all that you can think about, all that matters. It is only with the passage of time and the wisdom of hindsight that you realise your actions may not have been rational. It's clear that whatever other events followed those we have discovered, someone in power wanted the details changed and it would seem their objective may have been to eradicate the evidence of the other male Tudor line."

"Alistair, are you suggesting that perhaps Lettice did as Elizabeth asked and the male heir became king, but something happened and his entire reign has been expunged from all historical record? Even from what we've discovered, that's quite a suggestion," said Perdita.

"Believe me, my dear, there is more to come, another secret, maybe multiple revelations. Remember Kit," he said turning to his youngest son, "you're on The White List, too, and, despite the fact the Home Secretary claims it doesn't exist, I am not completely convinced any of you are out of danger. I will do everything I can to keep you all safe."

There was silence. Perdita stared at Alistair, then her gaze went to Kit who was white-faced. Callum was standing behind him looking unnerved but when she locked eyes with her sister, Piper radiated defiance and Perdita felt a surge of adrenalin. Kit might be unsure but she knew her sister was still at her side, fighting.

"These letters are a huge and important historical discovery," Alastair continued, when none of them spoke. "Please give yourself plenty of time to consider your next move. Doing something impulsive now could have fatal consequences."

His words sent a shiver down Perdita's spine and she turned to face him, her expression quizzical. Did Alistair know she and Piper were planning to search out Hannah White themselves? Their conversation had taken place some days ago and had since been superseded by the discovery of this new version of events surrounding the death of Mary, Queen of Scots and the build up to the Armada. *You're imagining it*, she thought, mentally shaking herself. *How could he possibly know?*

"Of course, Alistair," she said. "I won't do anything hasty."

"Thank you," he replied. "You and Piper have only known me for a few months but I've known you all your lives and I will guard you with the same ferocity I would employ to protect my own children."

Swallowing an unexpected lump in her throat, Perdita nodded.

"I promise, Alistair," she said, mentally crossing her fingers behind her back.

Alistair gave her a searching look, then with a rueful smile, strode towards the door, leaving the four of them alone among the piles of research and empty coffee cups.

Kit threw himself into one of the chairs and dropped his head into his hands. Callum took the seat next to him, his face ashen with exhaustion but determined to stay.

"Do you think these letters are really viable?" Kit asked, his voice muffled.

Perdita and Piper exchanged a look. Perdita wandered over to examine the timeline Deborah had been compiling. Perusing the many names and the links between the families, she considered all they had discovered before she responded. Gazing at the names: Elizabeth I, Arbella Stuart, Lettice Knollys and Mary, Queen of Scots, she screwed up her face as she decided on her next course of action.

"Yes, I do," she said. "If Mary, Queen of Scots was murdered by representatives of the Spanish king, it would explain why the Babington Plot is so very odd. Would someone as astute as Mary really allow herself to be implicated in such an amateur attempt on Queen Elizabeth's life? I don't think so, not when you assess it dispassionately."

Kit stared at her. "And Elizabeth's murder?"

"Plausible, if she truly did break into Fotheringhay Castle to say goodbye to her sister."

"Would she have taken such a risk?" asked Callum.

"I would," said Perdita and Piper in unison.

Kit smiled. "And the missing son?" he asked.

After a moment, Perdita replied, her tone thoughtful, "The duke of Hereford."

Piper, Kit and Callum exchanged a confused look.

"Who?" asked Kit.

"In the letter," Perdita walked over to the table and the printout of Mignonne's final, terrible message concerning Mary Stuart. Pulling it towards her, she read: "The duke of Hereford and his men arrived not long after and they carried her body to her chamber. We have prepared her with the love and reverence she deserves. The duke was said to be much affected by the death of the Scottish queen and was brought in by his men. His injuries, sustained as he and Lady Venus left us two nights ago, have weakened him considerably. His leg and his arm are both most heinously damaged, however, he sat beside her with his head bowed, sobbing as though she had been his great love…"

"The duke of Hereford?" said Kit.

"In all my years of research," said Perdita, "I've never come across a duke of Hereford for this period."

"Yet, from what Mignonne's letter says, he's at the heart of the situation," mused Kit.

"He sobbed as though she was his great love…" echoed Piper. "Or he's grieving for a beloved twin sister."

"And remember the mermaid analogy for Mary?" said Perdita. "The mermaid and the hare? It's always been suggested the hare represented her third husband, the earl of Bothwell, because there was a hare on his coat of arms. What if it wasn't him? What if it was a play on Hereford — 'hare' is the first part of the name. The mermaid and the hare, the missing twins."

"My goodness, Perds, you're right," said Kit. "The truth hidden in plain sight all along."

Perdita's eyes flashed with determination. "It isn't conclusive but it's a possibility," she said, then her eyes returned to the letter. "Arbella Stuart also gets a name-check," she said, in a considered voice. "In her most respected biography, it does state that Mary, Queen of Scots left Arbella her Book of Hours. Arbella sent it to her husband, William Seymour, 2nd Duke of Somerset, as both a souvenir and a valuable piece of property when he fled to France. She was supposed to meet him there, but she was captured and forced back to England. It seems he sold the book during the French Revolution — it was repurchased by a man called Peter Dubrowsky on behalf of the tsar. It's still in the Hermitage museum in Russia."

Perdita walked over to the window and stared out into the black night. Stars were strewn across the heavens, basking in the silver light of the moon.

"Artemis, the goddess of the moon..." Her voice trailed away.

"What are you planning, Perds?"

Turning away from the window, she realised Kit was staring at her. His eyes narrowed.

"We need the second ring," she stated.

"Why?"

"When we have both, we might understand how they reveal the truth. They might even give us a clue to the whereabouts of the locket."

"The locket?" he said, giving a short, harsh laugh. "Could we focus on one thing at a time?"

"Pipes, would you be able to search the database again?" Perdita asked her sister.

"I have," replied Piper. "There were no hits and I wanted to try a few variations before I told you. I'm sorry, Perds, I didn't want you to be disappointed."

"Then the ring is our best option," said Perdita, a thrill of excitement and fear running through her. "Are you sure you know where Hannah White is staying?" she asked and Piper nodded. "Then we should do it."

"What, you mean go?" exclaimed Kit. "Without telling anyone?"

"Yes," said Perdita. "We appreciate all your dad does — in fact, we'll never be able to repay him — but we're the best shot we have at getting this ring."

"Dad will go mental."

"He will. Are you in?"

Perdita stared into Kit's eyes, wondering if he would advise caution. He glanced at Piper, who raised her eyebrows at him, then his grin unfurled across his face.

"Try and stop me," he said, a dark edge lacing his voice. "Cal, how about you?"

"Of course," he said. "I'll ask Elliot to fly us there."

Chapter Two

Perdita hoisted her bag on to her shoulder and scanned her bedroom one last time. She did not know when she would return to Castle Jerusalem but she was grateful for the shelter its thick walls had offered during their time of crisis. Giving silent thanks to the apartment that had been their sanctuary, she gave the room one last nod of farewell and knocked on Piper's door.

The previous night, they had made a decision, one she hoped they would not regret. After they had found Hannah, they intended to return to Marquess House and trust to the Milford Haven Treaty to keep them safe from MI1, while increased private security, would, they hoped, keep them safe from Randolph Connors.

"It feels like home," Perdita had said to Piper. "Even more so than the Chiswick house. It's not only that Pipes, but I feel the answers are there. Everyone here is brilliant but I think we'll discover more in The Dairy and the research centre. Is that selfish?"

"No, I feel the same way," Piper had admitted. "Do you think Alistair and Susan will be offended? They've done so much to keep us safe — I hope they don't see this as a slap in the face?"

Perdita had pulled a face and shrugged. "Who knows — hopefully they'll understand, but even if they do think we've insulted them, we can't let that stop us. They might offer legal brilliance and protection but this is our quest, not theirs, not really. We have to do what's right for us, or Mum and Granny will have died in vain."

Now, as her twin joined her, Perdita felt nervous about her decision and wondered if perhaps they should return to the castle after their trip to Hannah's cottage. *There's still time to change our minds*, she thought, as they crept down the stairs. *Elliot will have to return the plane at some point, so we can always come back.*

They made their way across the impressive entrance hall, heading towards the back of the castle and the exit into the courtyard. It was 4am and outside the sky was pitch black. Inside, the castle was lit by low night-lighting that cast eerie shadows on the walls. Perdita was relieved when they arrived at the side door and were able to escape from this strange and disturbing version of Castle Jerusalem. She glanced at her watch; they were a few minutes early and there was no sign of either Kit or Callum.

"Do you think they've changed their minds?" asked Piper, shoving her gloved hands into her coat pockets in an attempt to keep warm.

"No," replied Perdita. "They'll be here."

As the words left her mouth, the door opened and two figures emerged.

"Hey," said Kit, his breath forming a cloud. Perdita smiled. Callum glanced at his watch.

"Elliot said he'd send someone to meet us in the lay-by down the road," he whispered.

Piper picked up her bag and made to walk across the courtyard but Callum grabbed her arm.

"Follow me," whispered Kit. "The whole area is covered with CCTV cameras but Megs, Stu and I worked out a path that avoids most of them."

"We used it when we were teenagers," Callum added. "Then we could deny the lateness of our return home every Saturday night."

A shadow of a grin flashed across his face. Perdita imagined the two of them sneaking back, impressed with their subterfuge, although she suspected Alistair and Deborah had probably known all about it.

On silent feet, they followed Kit as he kept to the shadows. The courtyard doubled as a car park for the inhabitants of Castle Jerusalem and the tall gates opened on to the main road leading down the mountain. Kit keyed in the passcode and when the gates swung open on smooth, oiled hinges, they exited on to the empty road. It was a short walk to the lay-by where they waited, their breath rising around them in clouds of nervous anticipation.

Perdita slid her arm through Piper's, who in turn rested her head on Perdita's shoulder. Callum walked into the centre of the road, looking up and down, while Kit hovered beside the twins, nervously scuffing the piled-up snow. Perdita watched him, understanding this was more difficult for him than for herself and Piper. She knew he loved and respected his father; this early morning flit must seem like a huge betrayal.

It'll be worth it though, she told herself as her own feelings of misgiving rose again. *When we have the ring, it will all have been worth it.*

"Better to ask for forgiveness than permission," murmured Piper and Perdita grinned.

"Our teenage motto," she said but before Piper could reply the headlights of a large SUV blinded them.

"Callum?" the blonde woman behind the wheel hissed into the freezing air and he stepped forward. "Elliot sent me. He said you're scheduled to fly in an hour. Get in."

Callum took Piper's bag and headed for the boot, which had sprung open. As Perdita moved towards him, preparing to stow her own bag, Kit caught her arm.

"Are you sure about this?" he asked.

Perdita looked into his pale, tense face. "Yes," she said.

"But it feels as though we're betraying Dad," he said in a rush.

"I know and I'm sorry. You don't have to come, Kit, we'd understand."

"And what if something were to happen to you? I'd never be able to live with myself."

"You don't need to protect me."

"I know I don't," he retorted, "but what if you were killed? I couldn't bear the thought of never seeing you again and always wondering if I could have made a difference."

His blue eyes bored into hers and she hesitated, unsure how to respond.

"Get a move on you two," hissed Callum, dragging Perdita's bag from her shoulder and hefting it into the car. "You can have a lover's tiff once we're safely away from here and on the plane."

"What... We weren't..." began Kit but Perdita had already climbed into the waiting vehicle.

Callum threw Kit's bag into the boot and smirked. "Come on, lover boy," he said and guided him towards the open door.

In comparison with their dramatic arrival in Andorra, their departure was smooth and simple. The early morning start had made them all quiet and sluggish. No one spoke much and they all dozed fitfully as they flew into the breaking dawn. It was only as they were making their approach to Bodmin airfield in Cornwall that Sam served coffee.

"We've hired you a car," she said. "It had to be in Cal's name and we have Kit as a named driver under Dr C Mackensie. I'm sorry Perdita but we were worried that if we booked anything in your or Piper's name it might trigger alarms somewhere."

"Good thinking," agreed Perdita.

"What time do you think you'll need a return flight?"

Perdita and Piper exchanged an uncomfortable look; they had not yet discussed their plans with Kit and Callum.

"We're not sure," replied Kit, taking their silence for nervousness.

"Hannah White is staying in Polzeath, which is about half an hour's drive from the airfield but we don't know how long we'll be after that," explained Perdita.

"OK, well, keep us posted," came Elliot's voice over the intercom. "I'll need some warning if we plan to fly back this evening."

"No problem," Callum shouted through to his elder brother in the cockpit.

Less than an hour later, as the sun rose into a clear sky, Perdita gazed out of the window. In the front, Kit and Callum were discussing their route, while she gazed at the beautiful Cornish coastline. The bleakly rugged cliffs and crashing waves reminded her of Pembrokeshire and she was overwhelmed by an unexpected wave of homesickness.

"Do you think she'll talk to us?" asked Piper, her voice little more than a whisper, bringing Perdita back to the present.

"I think so, especially if we're honest about the reasons why we need the ring," replied Perdita. "Anyway, we have this to convince her." She reached into her coat and pulled out a small leather pouch.

"Our ring."

"Yes, our ring," Perdita confirmed. "What do you think we should offer her?"

"We don't want to go in too high," replied Piper. "Alistair told me that he'd offered £4,000 on his email but she hasn't responded. Although, I checked online and an ordinary Tudor ring could fetch as little as anything between £50 and £350. Those with provenance are more, but if we go in with an opening bid that's too high she'll be suspicious."

"I thought they'd be far more expensive."

"No, it's surprising how reasonable they are when you consider their age. If she doesn't think it has much monetary value — and I bet she's looked up Tudor ruby rings on the internet, people usually do when it's a family heirloom — it's probably the reason she wears it as a pendant."

"Should we tell her the truth then?" mused Perdita.

"A version of it, I think," replied Piper.

They pulled up outside the cottage where Hannah White was staying. Perdita slipped their ruby ring on to her finger, the jewel with the emerald clip, engraved with the Latin words *iuncta sanguine*, hiding a portrait of Anne Boleyn, that had belonged to two formidable women: Anne of Cleves and Elizabeth I before being passed to Arbella Stuart. The weak morning sun caught the fire in the stone and it glinted.

"Come on," she said, squeezing Piper's hand, "let's see if we can get the second ruby ring and take another step closer to proving the truth."

The cottage stood alone, looking out to sea. Perdita suspected it had once been a fisherman's storage hut but an enterprising developer had transformed it into a wooden-floored, white-washed weekend retreat with a veranda running along the front. Its position offered uninterrupted views of the roaring ocean with its magnificent sunrises and sunsets. A faux-antique knocker shaped liked a mermaid was positioned in the centre of the eau-de-nil painted door. Perdita grinned at Piper when she saw it.

"Let's hope it's a good omen."

The woman who opened the door was almost six foot, with long, straight brown hair, pulled on top of her head in a messy bun. She was wearing a large fisherman's style jumper over thick pyjama bottoms and on her feet were battered Ugg boots. Her hazel eyes were warm and welcoming.

"Are you here for the Reiki healing? Because if you are, I'm not ready," she laughed. "I forgot to set my alarm clock and I overslept. Come in, come in."

Perdita glanced at Piper and they both smiled back, delighted to have a reason to be invited inside, before following her into the cottage. They had decided it would be less threatening if Kit and Callum remained in the car at the end of the lane.

"Keep your phone on," Kit had insisted, "and if anything goes awry, ring us and we'll be with you in seconds."

The interior was bright and warm, a small log burning stove glowed in the fireplace.

"This is so kind of you," enthused Hannah, tipping a pile of clothes off the sofa and straightening the cushions so Perdita and Piper could sit down. "I'm still training and I really need the practice. Would you like tea? Real tea, none of the herbal nonsense."

"Thanks, that would be great," said Perdita, wanting to keep things friendly. She suspected Hannah would be less open when they revealed their true intentions.

"We both have it with milk and no sugar," she called as Hannah bounded off to the other end of the large room that served as both sitting room and kitchen, divided up with an old-fashioned wooden table in the centre. As the kettle boiled and she assembled mugs and biscuits, Hannah chatted. Perdita and Piper murmured the occasional response but the cheery string of conversation flowing from Hannah's lips did not need much encouragement.

"Here we are," she said, sweeping back to the living room and placing the tea tray on the long low table in front of Perdita and Piper. "This is for you," she handed a shocking pink mug to Piper, then she passed a vivid green one to Perdita, who took it with her right hand, ensuring the ruby ring was in view. For a second Hannah faltered and her stream of chatter halted. She folded herself into the armchair opposite the twins and picked up her own tea, sipping it.

"Your ring," she said, her voice tentative for the first time. "It's very unusual."

"It's a family heirloom," said Perdita, smiling, trying to exude calm and trustworthiness but she was aware that Hannah's cheerful, open demeanour was hardening.

Hannah narrowed her eyes. "Really?" she responded; her tone suspicious.

"It belonged to our grandmother and when she died earlier this year, she left it to us as part of her estate."

"You're sisters?"

"Yes, we're twins," said Piper, her voice mirroring Perdita's, low, warm, calm.

Hannah considered them. "I can see that," she said. "Your colouring is different but your faces are almost identical."

Perdita placed her mug back on the tray, taking a deep breath; she knew this was the moment.

"Hannah, we're not here for the Reiki," she said, trying to keep her tone even, non-threatening. "My name is Perdita Rivers and this is my sister, Piper. We've come to see you because we have something important we need to ask."

"You're not here for the Reiki?"

Perdita shook her head.

"You have a ring that matches this one," she said, deciding honesty and directness would be the most effective way to charm Hannah. Despite her carefully cultivated scatter-brained behaviour, Perdita was aware that Hannah was no fool and was even now considering either throwing them out or calling for help.

Hannah placed her mug on the table, too. "What do you want?" she said, her voice cold — all trace of the amenable young woman who had welcomed them had vanished. Although, thought Perdita, she has not denied my claim or even asked how I know.

"Has someone else approached you about the ring?" she asked. "Someone other than an antiques dealer named Alistair Mackensie?"

"So what if they have?" snapped Hannah. "You two are getting beyond weird!"

She pulled her phone from under a cushion and held it on her lap where the twins could see it. She flipped the timer on. "You have five minutes to explain yourselves and what you say dictates whether or not I call the police."

"Alistair Mackensie works for us," said Perdita. "He's not an antiques dealer, he's our solicitor and he approached you because he was concerned about your safety."

"My safety?"

"Yes," said Perdita. "I'm an archaeologist and Piper is an artist. Earlier this year, our estranged grandmother died and left us an enormous stately home. This ring was part of the legacy. It dates from Tudor times and is key to my research.

"Our ring has an emerald clip, which when pulled, opens a secret compartment under the ruby. It reveals a Latin

391

inscription: *iuncta sanguine* that means 'joined in blood'. Under a moveable golden plate at the bottom is a portrait of a woman whom we believe to be Anne Boleyn, as it is engraved with the initials AB. We think the ring you inherited from your grandmother Honor Westcote née Winchester is the matching pair, only your ring has a sapphire clip."

Hannah stared at Perdita, agog. "How do you know my grandmother's name?"

"While we were searching for the ring, we came across information about her," said Piper. "It was how we were able to locate you. I'm sorry, Hannah, this must be very difficult to comprehend."

Hannah stared at them. "I didn't know it opened," she said, looking at Perdita, who gave her what she hoped was an encouraging smile.

"Yes," said Perdita. "It was quite common during this period for people to use rings or other small items of jewellery to pass secret message."

"And you think mine was used this way?"

"We do. We believe that in the middle of your ring is a portrait of a woman whom we think is Catherine Howard, Henry VIII's fifth wife," continued Piper. "We also think there could be an inscription saying: *Semper Sorores* — Always Sisters."

"Hannah, these rings can help to prove a secret hidden so deeply in history that there is a government agency whose only function is to stop it being revealed," said Perdita. "They want the rings. They want them so badly they've already murdered our mother and our grandmother. We think reuniting the rings will help to save our lives, as well as yours."

"A government agency?" Hannah made a brave attempt at a contemptuous laugh. "Who are you people? You're insane!"

"It does sound that way, I know," admitted Perdita, "but we're telling you the truth."

There was a clang as Hannah's five-minute alarm sounded. She switched it off with trembling fingers and pointed to the ring on Perdita's finger.

"Open it," she demanded. "If you can show me all the things you've described, I won't call the police."

"Of course," said Perdita. She unwound the soft woollen scarf from around her neck. Piper moved the tea tray on to the floor and Perdita stretched the delicate fabric across the table. From her handbag she extracted her roll of jewellery making tools and a small torch before removing the ring from her finger and placing it in front of Hannah.

"Pick it up if you like, check it's real," she offered and with cautious fingers Hannah grasped the ring, placing it on her palm as she examined it. Returning it to the table, she made no comment, crossing her arms as she waited. Her face was a mixture of doubt and curiosity.

Smiling with as much warmth as she could muster, Perdita unrolled her tools, then with measured movements, ensuring Hannah could see her working, not wanting to be accused of sleight of hand, Perdita took a steel scribe and turned the ring over.

"The green stone is an emerald," Perdita explained, "and it is on the head of small clip. When it's pushed back," she made a firm movement and felt the click, "the ruby in its golden cage opens to reveal its secret."

Levering the ruby back on its hidden hinge, Perdita tilted the ring to enable Hannah to watch as she slid the cover away from the miniature.

"Here is the inscription," said Perdita, indicating with the point of the steel scribe, while Piper flooded the cavity with light from the torch, "and this is, we believe, a portrait of Anne Boleyn."

Hannah put out her hand and with a small tremor of reluctance, Perdita placed the ring on her palm. Lifting the ancient jewel up to eye level, Hannah peered inside and her eyes widened. For a few moments, she stared at the interior of the ring, then she returned it to Perdita, who placed it on her scarf, leaving it in view, trying to encourage Hannah to trust them.

Perdita gazed at Hannah. There was not much difference in their ages, perhaps five years, and this young woman held their future safety in her power. As the silence stretched, Perdita threw a quick glance at Piper who had dropped her gaze. Hope was draining from Perdita and she wondered if they had made a grave error coming here and trying to appeal to Hannah's better nature. Perhaps she should have left it to Alistair with his many years of persuading people to part with valuable historical artefacts through his work with Jerusalem. Kit might have been able to charm her and she kicked herself for not asking for his advice. He, too, was an expert at negotiating and convincing people they were correct in selling them their heirlooms.

I'm a fool, thought Perdita, *I've ruined our chances by not listening to Alistair. Before we arrived, Hannah had no idea the ring was anything other than an old piece of costume jewellery left to her by her grandmother, now I've told her it's a valuable piece of proof. I may as well have rung MI1 myself and handed it over to them.*

Perdita swallowed hard, trying to remain calm. For all she knew, Hannah could already have been approached by MI1 and was hesitating in order to keep them here until agents arrived. Or even Randolph Connors, a ruthless man who would stop at nothing to get what he felt was rightfully his.

Perdita shuddered at the thought and decided Hannah was not going to relent. It was time to leave.

As she stirred, reaching forward to reclaim their ring, preparing to go, Hannah placed her phone on the table and fished around the neck of her sweater while Perdita and Piper exchanged a hopeful glance. Hannah pulled a long golden chain from where it had been hidden. Lifting it over her head, she held it front of her.

Hanging from the golden chain like a pendant was the ruby ring.

Perdita and Piper both gasped.

The ancient jewel glinted in the morning light. It was oval shaped with a deep, dark hue and encased in a delicate golden filigree cage, identical to their own. The wide golden band was set with the same pattern of diamonds, five on either side, although whereas only a few of the delicate rose-cut stones remained in their ring, Hannah's had been restored as all ten diamonds were present.

"You claim your mother and your grandmother were murdered because of this jewel?" she asked.

"Yes," replied Piper. "After our mother died, our grandmother also removed herself from our lives in order to protect us from the people who murdered Mum."

Hannah shuddered, shaking her head in revulsion. "They wrote to me," she said, "the other people who wanted this ring. The letter claimed to be from collectors of antique jewellery but the company name, C. Fitzroy Antiques, and the name they used to sign the letter, P. F. Allan, were false because I did some research into them online. It was part of the reason I came here. It made me nervous that they knew where I lived." Chewing her thumbnail, Hannah looked from one twin to the other, then her gaze rested on Perdita. "You said you need this ring to keep you safe?"

Perdita nodded.

"I only wear it because it's antique and a bit quirky. I don't love it so much I'm willing to endanger my life for it," she said. "If this has all the things inside it that you claim, then I'll let you have it."

As Hannah placed the ring in her palm, Perdita felt a leap of excitement. There was no doubting this was the second jewel, the twin to their own. Underneath, in the same place was the clip. Her heart beat faster when she saw the shimmer of the sapphire. Once more positioning the steel scribe with great care, Perdita pushed on the clip, waiting for the click. Piper and Hannah watched, spellbound. She pushed again, using more pressure and this time it came: click and the hinge released.

Perdita held the ring out to Hannah.

"Open it," she said. "It's your ring, you should be the first to see what it has been hiding for centuries."

Hannah's eyes were wide but her hands were steady as she took the jewel and the steel scribe that Perdita proffered. She bit her lip in concentration as she slid open the golden cover at the base of the cavity.

"Gently," murmured Piper, leaning so far forward on her seat, Perdita thought she might topple on to the floor at any moment.

"Oh," whispered Hannah. "It's beautiful."

Handing the ring back to Perdita, Piper moved in closer and the twins gazed on the portrait. It depicted a young woman in a Tudor headdress with her red hair showing across the front. Her eyes were blue and she had a sweet, innocent expression. The most fascinating detail, however, was the image of the silver locket that she wore around her neck. Above her head, were the initials CH and at the base was engraved the phrase: *Semper Sorores.*

"The second ruby ring," breathed Perdita. "Oh Granny, I wish you were here to see this."

"Take it," said Hannah, her voice croaky but firm.

"Hannah, this has been in your family for years," said Piper. "You don't want to make a hasty decision now that you might regret later."

"Take it," she repeated. "Ever since I received the letter I've been uneasy and when your Alistair Mackensie contacted me, too, it freaked me out."

"We'll pay you," said Perdita.

"OK," said Hannah, chewing her lip. "How much?"

"Name your price," said Piper and Perdita winced. Hannah would sense their desperation in this comment and might change her mind. Instead, she narrowed her eyes and in a voice ringing with defiance said, "£5000 and it's yours."

Perdita exchanged a glance with Piper — they had been prepared to go far higher.

"Done," said Perdita, "but we will need you to sign a receipt to say it's legally ours."

"Anything, just get it away from me," said Hannah. "I'll find some paper and write you a letter saying I sold it to you willingly and you paid for it, all legal and above board."

Piper pulled out her tablet and logged into her bank account.

"Give me your bank details and I'll transfer the money now," she said.

The transaction was complete within ten minutes, although Hannah was in such a state she did not notice that Piper had added an extra zero to the end of her requested £5000. She had shown Perdita the amount before sending it and she had nodded. Both still felt they had secured the ring at a reasonable price.

Perdita scribbled her and Alistair's contact details on a piece of paper.

"If anyone else contacts you or you're worried about anything connected to the ring, call us immediately," she said. "We'll collect you from wherever you might be and take you to a place of safety."

"Who are you people?" she muttered, echoing her question from earlier.

"No one special," said Perdita.

Hannah gave her an appraising look and glanced at the phone numbers Perdita had written down. She keyed one in and Perdita's phone rang.

"Just checking," she said, then a stern expression flooded her face. "Now, please leave."

"Thank you, Hannah, and good luck with the Reiki," said Perdita.

"Goodbye," called Piper and they stepped out into the cold winter morning as Hannah slammed the door behind them.

Aware Hannah was watching from the window, Perdita linked arms with Piper and walked down the narrow lane.

"Don't react until we're out of sight," she whispered but their faces were wreathed in delighted grins. The moment they had rounded the corner and could no longer be seen from the cottage, Piper leapt into the air in excitement, then turned a cartwheel.

"We've done it, Perds," she exclaimed. "We've found the second ring!"

Kit and Callum were parked at the end of the lane, laughing at Piper's antic.

"It's good news then?" called Kit but as Perdita opened her mouth to answer, Kit's phone rang.

"Hey Dad," he began, pulling a face, then his comical expression fell, "they're here…" He beckoned Perdita and Piper over, putting Alastair on speaker phone.

"Do you have the ring?" Alistair's voice was urgent.

"Yes, we…"

"Hide them both somewhere about your person and don't give them up to anyone."

"What…?"

"There is no time to explain," he snapped. "You are in great danger. A SWAT team with orders to kill you on sight is an hour away from Hannah White's cottage…"

But before he could say any more, the line went dead.

"Drive," said Kit, throwing open the car doors for Perdita and Piper to scramble into the back, while he leapt into the front. Callum was already gunning the engine and they were barely inside when he slammed his foot on the accelerator and sent up a huge spray of mud as he roared the car out of the lane.

"Cal, stop!" screamed Piper.

A black van had skidded to halt, blocking their only exit. Callum stamped on the brakes, missing the other vehicle by millimetres. Ten men, clad from head to foot in black, their faces covered, guns aloft, leapt out of the van, shouting instructions to each other, filling the air with the sound of threats and violence as they surrounded the car.

Perdita, Piper, Kit and Callum exchanged panicked looks, then the four doors of the car were wrenched open simultaneously.

Perdita shouted, "No!"

She fought with all her might as two strong arms reached inside, intent on dragging her out. Piper was swearing and punching her assailant and in the front, Kit and Callum were doing the same, then a sweet smell filled the car and the man grappling with Perdita caught hold of her hair and tipped her head backwards. Screaming and shouting, struggling against his terrible grasp, Perdita felt a cloth being pushed over face. Writhing and twisting, she clawed at the man's hands but she knew it was too late. Even as she fought, her limbs were growing heavy and no longer responding as blackness descended and she knew no more.

Chapter Three

Perdita's head was pounding as she clawed her way back to consciousness. Despite her best efforts, her brain was sluggish, unresponsive, her limbs were heavy and her mouth was dry, with an unpleasant, sweet taste. Reaching out her hand, she felt soft blankets covering her and a smooth linen pillow beneath her cheek. Sitting up, she winced and paused while a wave of nausea passed. As her eyes swam into focus, she began to make sense of her surroundings. She was lying on a bed in a room that was small but luxurious. Someone had removed her muddy boots and they were placed side-by-side next to her rucksack, which was resting on the floor. Her jacket was on a coat hanger on the back of the door.

"What the...?" she muttered. A jug of water was on the table beside the bed. Dipping her finger in it and tasting a tiny drop, she could not detect any strange tang that might indicate it was drugged or poisoned. Although she was desperate for a drink, she would not risk it, instead she fished around in her jeans pocket and pulled out a handkerchief. Soaking it in the cold water, she held it to her forehead, trying to clear her head.

Taking deep breaths, she pieced together the events of the morning, forcing herself to remember each detail — their flight from Andorra to Bodmin, the drive to Hannah's cottage, finding the ring and persuading Hannah to sell it. The rings! Cold panic swept through her: did she still have the rings? Looking up, she ensured she was alone in the room before sliding her hand under her top to check they were safe. In their moment of panic, she had shoved the rings inside the only place she had hoped no one would search, in the lining of her bra. To her relief, they were still there, wedged into the padding which in turn stopped them digging into her skin. If they had remained where they were, despite the fact she must have been manhandled into this room, she decided it must be secure to leave them in their current hiding place.

Beginning to feel more alert, she swung her legs off the bed and reached for her boots, only to find herself lurch backwards. At first she assumed it was as a result of sitting up too quickly or possibly the after-effects of the chloroform, but as she struggled upright again, she realised the room was moving and a row of round windows opposite the bed revealed the reason why.

"No," she whispered, horrified, as realisation of her current whereabouts hit her. Lacing up her boots, she pushed herself into a standing position and crossed the room in three strides.

All she could see for miles around was water. Churning, grey waves and icy, torrential rain. Perdita felt cold terror envelope her and she began to tremble, whether with fear or anger she could not differentiate. She was on what appeared to be a powerful speed boat, considering the way it was slicing through the waves and throwing up spray, heading into the Bristol Channel, perhaps into the Celtic Sea, and it was nobody's fault but her own for impulsively rushing to Hannah's cottage. It would take very little effort to tip me overboard, she thought, and in this freezing water, I wouldn't last more than a few minutes. Her heart pounded: was she about to become the next woman in her family to be murdered like her mother and grandmother?

There is no way out, she thought. *If I was in a car, I could scream to other drivers, I might be able to fight my way out but here, there is no hope.*

Piper's face swam before hers, her laughter and cartwheels in the moments after they had bought the ring from Hannah, followed by Kit's smiling face and Callum's broad grin. Where were they? Were they somewhere on board?

Stop feeling sorry for yourself, she thought, *this was all your idea and you've led the others into danger, you need to pull yourself together and find them. Maybe together we can think of a way out of this dire situation.*

With this flimsiest of plans in her mind, she wrenched her jacket from the coat hanger, pulled it on, then grabbed her rucksack. It was only as she spun around and hurried to the door, she realised it was probably locked. Gripping the handle, she turned it and to her amazement, it clicked open. With great caution she edged the door open, a little at a time, peering out to see if there was a guard blocking her way. Through the gap, she could not see anyone and hope flared in her again. Finally, the door was wide enough for her to creep out into the sitting room, but any false hope she had created for herself was crushed as a voice said: "Good afternoon, Dr Rivers. I hope you had a pleasant sleep."

Perdita tried to step back into the small bedroom as the true danger of her situation took hold but a tall man was behind her, blocking any chance of escape. She was standing in the main seating area of the boat and, sitting opposite her, drinking tea, as though this were an afternoon pleasure trip, was Stephen Haberfield.

"Where are the others?" she hissed.

"They are safe," he said with an avuncular smile that made Perdita want to lash out and punch him, as anger replaced her fear. "I'm sorry our next meeting is under such difficult circumstances."

His remorse sounded genuine but Perdita was in such shock, she barely heard his words.

"Get away from me," she gasped.

Stephen Haberfield did not move.

"Gary, would you please fetch Dr Rivers a brandy — she's in shock," he said to the man behind her. "Ma'am, I see you are dressed for outside." He nodded to her coat and rucksack. "If it makes you feel better, we can go on deck and discuss events. Not everyone can stomach being down below on a boat, although I've never suffered myself, or we can remain here where there is heating and comfortable seats."

Perdita stared at him, confusion, fear and anger battling each other as she tried to make sense of what was happening.

"Where's Piper?" she managed at last, dropping her rucksack.

"In a launch that is a travelling a short distance behind us — would you like to see?"

He pointed to the window at the back of the boat and beckoned her forward. Keeping as much distance between them as she could, she peered through the salt-encrusted window. In the distance was a vast, sleek, black speed boat, slicing through the waves.

"Gary, get Mrs Davidson on the radio please, I can see Dr Rivers won't relax until she knows her sister is safe," instructed Haberfield.

"Yes, sir," said the tall man who had been hovering behind Perdita. He left the room.

"Please, Dr Rivers, there is no need for you to worry about your belongings — no one here will steal them."

Perdita glared at him. Was he laughing at her? She had never felt so angry.

"When you feel ready," Haberfield continued, "we shall step through this door and go up a short flight of steps on to the bridge where you'll be able to speak to your sister."

Perdita did not reply. She was so confused, she could not form words, but when Haberfield stood and did as he had described, leaving her alone in the beautifully appointed cabin, she decided to follow him, although she kept her bag and jacket with her like a safety blanket. He was speaking into a radio when she emerged. On seeing her, he smiled and handed her the mouthpiece.

"Your sister," he said and Perdita leapt towards the device with a sob.

"Piper!"

"Perdita!" came her sister's voice. "Oh thank God, we thought, we thought..."

"Are you alright?"

"Yes, Cal and I are here, but they've taken Kit. Where are you? They said you're in the boat in front of us."

"I am," she said. "But where's Kit?"

"I don't know..."

"Say goodbye now," said Haberfield and the line went dead as he took away the radio.

"No," screamed Perdita, clawing at him, but Gary Ashley stepped forward and caught her wrists.

"Please don't force us to use restraints, Dr Rivers," he said. "Something my colleagues have unfortunately had to apply to Dr Mackensie in order to subdue him."

"What?" she shrieked, her fear for Kit overwhelming her. Now she knew Piper was safe, he was the next most important person and the thought he was in danger filled her with such intense terror she felt faint.

Haberfield considered her for a moment as she struggled. Then he spoke, his voice soft but firm: "I understand that you have every reason to distrust me but, please believe me when I say, you have my word as an officer that neither you, your sister nor your companions will come to any harm," he assured her and something about the weariness of his tone calmed her. "Gary, release Dr Rivers and fetch the brandy please, as I requested and, before you ask, the drink my colleague Mr Ashley is about to give you is neither poisoned nor drugged. In fact…" He took the glass and gulped a sizeable mouthful from it, then after wiping the rim of the glass clean, handed it to Perdita. She hesitated only a moment before downing the remaining contents of the glass, then coughed, her eyes streaming, before handing it back to Gary Ashley, who smothered the ghost of a grin.

"The reason we have been forced to restrain Christopher Mackensie," he said and Perdita's befuddled brain took a moment to realise he meant Kit, "is because he was so determined to fight his way out of their boat in order to find you, we feared he would injure, not only himself, but other members of the crew. He has been sedated but the dosage given has been calculated to have worn off before we arrive at our final destination. I assure you; he will come to no harm. Now, shall we?"

Stephen Haberfield indicated the stairs to the cabin and, because it took her away from the churning grey waves and the possibility that this still might be a trap, Perdita nodded and followed.

406

The cabin was warm and comfortable with soft, butterscotch-coloured leather upholstery and polished wood. Perdita perched on the edge of a banquette. Haberfield stood opposite her and for a moment it struck her that he seemed to be waiting for something. After a slight hesitation, he sat down.

"Dr Rivers, now that you have spoken to Mrs Davidson, do you believe that your sister and your friends are safe?" he asked.

With great reluctance, she muttered, "Yes," then added, "Why couldn't we travel together?"

"It is unwise to have you both in the same transport," said Haberfield.

"Both? What are you talking about?"

"It's a precaution," he continued. "You will be reunited when we reach the end of our journey."

Perdita shuddered. Despite his reassurances, she did not trust this man.

"And where are you taking us?"

"To Mill Bay, near Milford Haven, where you will be collected and returned to Marquess House."

Although she heard the words and knew he had spoken them, her mind was having difficulty making sense of this bizarre situation.

"I don't believe you!" she snapped. "Last year, MI1 issued arrest warrants against myself, Piper and Kit Mackensie. You wanted to charge us with treason. Why would you deliver me safely to Marquess House?"

"Well," said Haberfield, "things have changed."

"What things? This is a trap, isn't it? When we get to Pembrokeshire, your boss, Inigo Westbury is going to be waiting..."

"Inigo Westbury is no longer a member of this unit," said Haberfield, his voice laced with contempt. "He was relieved of his position a short time ago and no longer has any ties with MI1 Elite. The man was always unstable and the power of being in command of such a prestigious department fed his arrogance to such a level he believed he was above the law. No one has that privilege. He has left the employ of Her Majesty's government. Unfortunately, he has joined forces with people whom we would rather not associate and has no doubt given them detailed and secret information. He is one of the most wanted men in Europe."

Perdita stared at Haberfield, her expression sceptical.

"His actions and those of his predecessor, his uncle, Jonty Westbury have caused your family a great deal of sorrow. It is therefore on behalf of Her Majesty that we apologise and ask your forgiveness for the deaths of your mother, Louisa Rivers, and your grandmother, Mary Fitzroy."

"You want me to forgive you for murdering my mother and grandmother and for trying to kill me and my sister?" Perdita's voice was rising again, laced with anger, fear and bewilderment.

"I'm giving you the official stance of MI1 Elite; however, I don't expect your forgiveness. Your family has been torn apart — how could you ever forgive the crimes perpetrated against you?" he replied. "In order to, perhaps, enable you to come to terms with these events, you need to understand the remorse felt by many in my department at their demises. Both were remarkable women."

"Don't you dare speak to me about them," shouted Perdita, her control slipping as a lifetime of sorrow, pain and loneliness churned inside her. "How dare you even say their names? Especially as neither of their murderers were ever brought to trial. You even allowed that man, Morton Keller, to accompany you to my grandmother's funeral to gloat…"

"He was not there to gloat," snapped Haberfield, his control slipping. "He was there as the request of a dying man to try and make amends. However, it was ill-judged and caused more damage than good."

It was a moment before Perdita registered the meaning of Haberfield's words.

"What do you mean? A dying man?"

"Morton Keller died two weeks after your grandmother's funeral. He had terminal cancer. It was his final wish to meet you and your sister and ask for your forgiveness."

"What?" Perdita could not comprehend what she was hearing.

"If you will let me, I would like to explain," said Haberfield. "You see, no one was supposed to die that day, certainly not your mother."

To Perdita's astonishment, Haberfield eyes filled with tears, which he blinked away.

"I knew your mother, not well, admittedly, but I was born and brought up in Dale until I was 11 years old. She was only a few years older than me and everyone knew she was the girl with the remarkable touch when it came to helping animals. I found an injured owl once and my parents drove me to Marquess House where Louisa offered to care for the bird," said Haberfield in a rush before Perdita could interrupt him. "The owl wasn't badly hurt, more stunned I think, but she nursed it back to health and when it was ready to be released, she insisted that her parents collect me, so we could release it together.

"It was a small thing but she was a remarkable person, and even as a young child I could see her goodness. I will admit to being a little in love with your mother. My father worked in the oil industry that was burgeoning in Milford Haven around then. He was good at his job and was offered work abroad. My mother was delighted and they moved to the US, where they lived for the rest of their lives. I was sent to boarding school and never lived in Dale again, although I bought a home there recently."

Perdita glared at Haberfield; her eyes wide with confusion as to why this man was telling her his life story. This man who was her sworn enemy.

"And what has that got to do with Morton Keller?" she asked.

"On that terrible day, he was only supposed to scare your grandmother by driving at her in an aggressive manner…"

"But you'd tampered with her brakes," interrupted Perdita. "If you hadn't meant to kill her, why did you disable the car?"

"You're correct, we did," he said, his voice bitter. "The plan, however, was to cause her to swerve in a place where she would land in a ditch, thus shocking her and showing her we had the power to reach her if she did not desist with her research; nothing more."

"You took out the seatbelt mechanism," hissed Perdita.

Haberfield looked wretched but he did not deny it.

"If your grandmother had swerved in the place we had selected, even that would have done her no damage. It was carefully planned, but something unexpected happened which, in the end, showed the stupidity and cruelty of our methods. As you know, your mother borrowed your grandmother's car. Keller and his men were caught unawares. According to their intel, your grandmother had not intended to leave the house so early. They didn't know it was Louisa behind the wheel and that when her car had refused to start, she had hopped into Mary's in order to collect some hay for the horses. Believing he had missed his chance to scare Mary and desperate to salvage the operation, Keller and his team leapt into their vehicles and were rushing to the agreed rendezvous site when your mother came flying around the corner in your grandmother's car. Keller was driving far too fast and swerved, as did Louisa. She skidded on mud and the car smashed through a wall and over a cliff. It was an accident."

Perdita stared at Haberfield in revulsion. "I don't believe you," she whispered.

"Of course you don't," said Haberfield, "I wouldn't have expected you to."

"And, accident or not, Keller killed my mother and went unpunished."

"No, he did not," Haberfield replied.

"He was questioned and released by the local police…"

"The local police," snorted Haberfield. "We were hardly going to let them deal with the case. Keller was court marshalled and spent the rest of his life in a private prison for the murder of your mother. When he was diagnosed with cancer and he heard about Mary's death and your subsequent inheritance, he became obsessed with the idea of telling you and your sister the truth and begging your forgiveness."

"Alistair told us the same thing, that he wanted forgiveness…" Perdita murmured.

"Mackensie said that, did he?" Haberfield seemed almost amused. "If only we could have persuaded him to join us — he is without doubt one of the cleverest and shrewdest men I have ever met."

411

"Does he know what you've just told me?" asked Perdita. "That Mum's death was a real accident?"

"No, no one knows. It had the highest level of security and I can only tell you now because I am head of the department and, therefore, have special clearance."

"You weren't head of MI1 when you attended my grandmother's funeral," she pointed out.

"No, but I volunteered for the job, partly because I had known Keller — he had been my first mentor in the service — but also because I have always been very involved in the Marquess House case and, I admit, I was intrigued to see you and your sister. You look very like your mother, you know, although you're taller."

Perdita ignored this comment. She felt uncomfortable with the knowledge that this man had known her mother in their youth.

"And the man who murdered my grandmother, my former 'fiancé'?"

"Are you referring to Warren Dexter?" asked Haberfield. Perdita gave a short, angry nod. "He didn't murder your grandmother."

"Liar," she spat. "He was in the area that night or how else would he have been able to get to me so quickly to break the news the following morning?"

"Because we were made aware of your grandmother's death almost immediately and Dexter was flown to Withybush airfield, where he was given an identical car to his usual vehicle, with the same number plates, in order to get to you. I swear on my son's life that Warren Dexter didn't murder Mary Fitzroy."

"Then who did?"

"We have a few ideas and, believe me, when the murderer is apprehended, they will be suitably punished. Your grandmother was not killed on the orders of MI1 Elite."

Perdita wondered if perhaps the brandy had been laced with a hallucinogenic drug because Haberfield's words, spoken with such conviction, were so far from the version of events she had been told, she was unsure what to believe.

"We suspect Inigo Westbury may be the key to discovering who murdered your grandmother," continued Haberfield when Perdita did not respond. "As you know, he is an old friend of Randolph Connors and we believe they are working together. It seems it was he who discovered you had left Andorra and were heading to Bodmin, probably through a contact somewhere in air traffic control. Westbury is very well connected. After listening to chatter collected by our agents at GCHQ, we also became aware that you and your sister were returning to the UK. It was then that our listeners picked up a plot to have you kidnapped and murdered…"

"What?"

"We think Connors is pulling the strings but Westbury is his go-to man for arranging disappearances and deaths that could be construed as accidental. One of Alistair Mackensie's informants within Connors's organisation contacted him as soon as he was made aware of the danger you were in. We also have a spy within Connor's ranks and when we were informed about your early-morning flit, Mackensie and I realised the only way to save your lives was to join forces — even if only temporarily. Despite what you may believe, Dr Rivers, I don't want you, your sister, Kit Mackensie or Callum Black dead."

"Randolph Connors sent a SWAT team after us?"

"Yes."

Everything Haberfield said was incredible, yet he claimed that he and Alistair had joined forces with MI1 Elite to save their lives. The Watchers had not murdered her mother and grandmother. Perdita's mind was whirling.

Another door opened and Gary Ashley entered carrying a tray of tea and coffee, along with the decanter of brandy.

"We will reach Mill Bay in approximately two hours," said Haberfield. "Until then, you are our guest, so please, relax and make yourself comfortable. The bedroom where you were placed when we first arrived is at your disposal as is this sitting room. Mr Ashley and I will be on the bridge should you need anything. I will ensure nobody disturbs you."

Perdita stared at him. It was madness, yet instinct told her that he would not harm her. She realised she had no option but to remain calm and try to understand this new and unexpected layer of information.

"It really is an honour to meet you properly at last, Ma'am," said Haberfield and to her amazement, he stood to attention and saluted her before leaving without another word.

Chapter Four

"PERDITA!" Piper was up to her knees in the waves, shrieking her sister's name but being held back from plunging into the choppy water any further by Callum who was fast losing his grip.

"PERDITA!" Kit's voice took up the shout as he threw himself into the freezing surf to meet the launch carrying her to the shore. Moments later, he was joined by Billy and Larry Eve as they endeavoured to manhandle the military dinghy on to the beach. Suddenly, Perdita felt Kit's arms around her as he lifted off the deck and carried her ashore.

"What are you doing?" she half-laughed, half-shouted as he collapsed on to the freezing sand with her still in his arms.

"I thought you were dead," he said, hugging her so tightly she was worried he would crack her ribs. "I didn't think I'd ever see you again…"

Before he could say any more, Piper had flung herself, sobbing, on to Perdita.

"Piper," Perdita cried, tears of relief streaming down her face as they squeezed each other with a ferocity fuelled by their shared experiences of too much loss and grief. "Oh, Piper, I'm so sorry, this was all my fault."

The short winter day was dipping into dusk and the rain lashed them with frost-twisted fingers. Callum hauled Kit to his feet and behind her Perdita heard a car door slam. More people were running towards them, including Dr Black who threw herself on her youngest son. Susan, usually so calm, had enveloped Kit in a bear hug and was sobbing into his shoulder.

Then, to Perdita's surprise, Sarah Eve appeared and grabbed the twins.

"Your mother might not be here," she said, tears sliding down her face, "but I'm your godmother so you'll have to make do with me."

Perdita felt Sarah's arms tighten around her and Piper. It was the closest thing they had experienced to a mother's love since they were seven years old and it was bittersweet.

Over Sarah's shoulder, Perdita saw Alistair walking towards Stephen Haberfield. Giving Sarah a watery smile, she ducked out of the hug, leaving her and Piper hanging on to each other and ran across to where the two men were standing near the dinghy that had delivered her to shore, talking, their expressions serious.

They were so deeply engrossed in conversation that it was a few moments before they realised she was within earshot.

"And you will ensure their protection if they return to Marquess House?" she heard Alistair say, his voice low and urgent.

"Consider it done," replied Haberfield. "It will be unobtrusive but until we have apprehended Connors and Westbury, we will take no further risks with their safety. As Section 10, sub-section 4b of The Milford Haven states, 'In times of national security, the heirs will be protected using all suitable methods available to Her Majesty's government…'" He saw her and broke off. "Still no sign of Westbury?"

"Alas, no," confirmed Haberfield, "however, we have despatched Warren Dexter and his team, and Dexter is ruthless…"

"Tell me about it," said Perdita, interrupting the two men.

"Ma'am," Haberfield greeted her with deference, while Alistair reached out to pull her close to him in a protective paternal manner, but she shook him off, turning to look Haberfield in the eye.

"I'd like to thank you for keeping my sister, Kit and Callum safe and also for saving us from what appears to have been a far worse threat," she said.

Now she was safely on land and surrounded by those she loved, her curiosity was beginning to reassert itself. Why had Haberfield agreed to help? Would it not have made his life easier if they had been murdered? And what had he meant by that last comment? Who were the 'heirs'?

With her brain restored after the food they had served her on the boat and a short restorative sleep, her questions were coming thick and fast but before she could ask any, Haberfield, who seemed to sense this torrent was about to overwhelm him, was already stepping away from her.

"It was an honour, Ma'am," he said.

"Tell me, why do you keep calling me 'Ma'am'?" she asked but Haberfield shook his head.

"Another time, Ma'am," he said. "I must return to my vessel."

Gary Ashley was standing in the prow of the small craft with three other MI1 officers behind him, all armed. The boat that had delivered the others was idling its engine a few metres away from shore. Haberfield vaulted over the side and on to the deck, where he positioned himself beside his second-in-command. On a nod from Haberfield, the officers in both vessels turned to face Perdita, stood to attention and saluted. Moments later, the men were aboard the powerful speed boats and, with a roar of engines, both craft vanished around the headland and into the gathering gloom.

"What was that about?" said Kit, who had disentangled himself from his mother and joined Perdita but, as they watched the disappearing boats, she could only shrug.

"I've no idea," she replied.

The wind was whipping up into a storm and there seemed no reason to stay on the cold beach any longer.

"Let's get you home," said Alistair, who had been joined by Alan Eve, his shotgun across his arm. "I won't be able to breathe freely until we're all back at Marquess House."

As the others trudged across the sand and shingle towards the waiting cars, Perdita stared towards the horizon, wondering.

On arrival at Marquess House, Perdita had gathered them all together to show them the matching rings and reveal the secrets within. Over the next week, the four of them spent hours reliving their stories, coming to terms with their near miss with Inigo Westbury, Randolph Connors and the violent SWAT team. However, when Perdita had felt able to reveal Haberfield's claim that MI1 had not intentionally killed Louisa and had not been responsible for Mary's murder, the two deaths that had ripped her and Piper's lives apart, there had been an outcry from everyone. Alistair was the most shocked by this unexpected version of events and had agreed he would look into things further.

"After all," he had said, "we know the Watchers are proficient at altering the past, perhaps this is another bluff."

A few weeks on and Perdita was beginning to feel things were returning to normal. She and Piper had explained to Alistair that they intended to stay at Marquess House and, having heard Haberfield's reassurance at extra security, they were happy to trust the Milford Haven Treaty to protect them.

Seeing their implacable expressions, he had resisted the urge to dissuade them.

A rearrangement of people had begun. Callum, Dr Black, Susan and Kit had returned briefly to Andorra, while Alistair had travelled to his London home. Piper had begun to plan her studio where the cabins let to artists stood and Perdita had immersed herself in examining the rings and looking for ways they might help to solve the final mysteries of Catherine's children. But now, everyone was returning and as spring made itself felt in the vast gardens, Marquess House was coming alive once more.

Sarah cooked a vast celebration dinner when the Mackensies returned, bringing Callum with them to upgrade the Marquess House computer systems. A laughter-filled evening that ended with everyone sprawled in the chairs in the Lady Isabel room seemed, to Perdita, to mark a new beginning.

Wandering over to Alistair, carrying two cups of coffee, Perdita placed them beside him, then reached over and kissed his cheek, making him smile.

"I'm sorry, Alistair," she said, sitting down.

"Whatever for, my dear?"

"You asked me not to do anything hasty and I ignored you."

"Perdita, I expected nothing less of you and Piper," he chuckled. "If I'm honest, I was delighted when it became apparent you had taken matters into your own hands. Your grandmother would have done the same thing. She was never one to wait for others to do her research for her."

"It did result in us obtaining the second ring," she said.

"Yes, we have the rings. How do you feel about reuniting them?"

Her eyes shone in the firelight. "On an academic level, honoured and excited. If the provenance we have for these rings is correct, then we have jewellery that once belonged to Anne of Cleves and Catherine Howard. As an historian who specialises in the symbolism of jewellery, this is overwhelming. The rings were made as a pair and prove the two queens were friends. It's the discovery of a career, of a lifetime."

"And on a personal level?"

Perdita sipped her coffee, considering her answer before she spoke. The events of the past few weeks had been extraordinary but then, so had everything since her grandmother had died and they had received their inheritance. What did the two rings mean to her?

"They unnerve me," she said, at last.

"Why?"

"The fact we have them in our possession proves that they exist, they are discussed in many of the documents we have discovered, so they prove our version of history has some weight. MI1 is still out there watching us, although they seem to be in a protective role at present, which I can't quite understand, and Randolph Connors wants us dead so his granddaughters can inherit Mary's — our — estate. The rings are a tangible part of that, so yes, having them in our possession unnerves me."

"Do you regret finding them?"

"No, but I'm frustrated that we still don't know how they prove the truth," she replied. "I've been examining them for weeks and apart from the fact they're fascinating, there doesn't seem to be any way to link them. There are no secret codes inscribed that only make sense if the rings are somehow slotted together or images that might have led us to another clue. I even climbed up to take a closer look at the frieze where the rings are depicted as joined together to see if I'd missed something but the carving shows them next to each other — they're not joined."

"What will you do?" asked Alistair.

"Keep looking," she replied. "Inspiration might strike when I'm least expecting it."

"And the Lady Pamela letters?"

"Jenny and Deborah are dividing up the compiling of the other letters between their teams. Izabel and Eveie will be overseeing the translation of the remainder. The final letter is dated 12 December 1662, so there are probably more revelations to come but it'll take us a bit longer to discover them."

"What do you intend to do next?" he asked.

"Find the locket," she replied without hesitation. "We must complete the puzzle, Alistair."

"How?"

"I don't know yet," she admitted. "We've been lucky so far because Mary had already facilitated most of the research for us — she'd discovered the Catherine Howard codex and completed the majority of the groundwork. All Kit and I did was fill in the gaps…"

"You did more than that," spluttered Alistair, but Perdita continued undeterred.

"And she gave us a huge start with the Lady Pamela letters and the first draft of her other unpublished manuscript. I know she'd only translated a few but she'd realised they were important. It was as though she kept pointing us in the right direction. Now that we've used all her research and followed all her clues we're on our own."

"Your discoveries have been incredible, Perdita, please don't underestimate what you've achieved. You've revealed the truth about Catherine Howard and you've unravelled the tangled web around Mary, Queen of Scots's execution. Write them up, my dear, there may come a day when you're able to publish your findings."

"When might that be?" she laughed. "You've been responsible for saving our lives — wouldn't publishing our findings put them at risk again?"

Alistair grinned. "Times change, Perdita," he said. "Times change."

"What are you plotting?" asked Kit, sliding into the seat beside Perdita.

"Nothing," she replied and smiled when he raised his eyebrows in disbelief.

Piper wandered over and threw a log into the roaring flames.

"Have you discovered anything more about how Mum and Granny died?" she asked.

Perdita froze. She had been resisting asking — there was something in her that did not want to believe Haberfield's story.

"I'm still waiting for official confirmation but, off the record, I spoke to the Home Secretary and he corroborated Haberfield's version of events," Alistair said.

Perdita and Piper stared at each other.

"Mum wasn't murdered, it was an accident, and their intention had never been to kill Granny either?" confirmed Perdita.

"Correct. They also believe that your grandmother was murdered by someone in the pay of Randolph Connors," he continued.

"Her nephew?" gasped Piper, outraged. "How could he?"

"Connors is an unpleasant man. At present, he has returned to his vast tea plantation in Darjeeling. He is no doubt plotting his next move but until we have new information on his plans, we must try not to let his brooding presence mar our lives. As for MI1, they are once again spying on academics and removing documents they believe to be suspicious from archives around the world — that is, of course, unless Jerusalem gets there first."

Perdita looked around the room. All eyes were on Alistair and glancing at him, she realised he thrived on the mysteries and adventures as much as she was beginning to. *I wonder if Granny was the same?* she pondered.

"Why did the Watchers help us, Dad?" asked Kit, breaking into her thoughts. "Wouldn't it have made their lives easier if Connors had murdered us? It would have saved them the trouble of putting us all on The White List."

"Since Inigo Westbury has been sacked, MI1 has returned to its former remit: to retain historical 'truth' by suppressing documents, by halting publication of material that is thought to be subversive or could invite too many academic questions. It does not search, it watches, it blocks and it sends the occasional threat. Stephen Haberfield is an honest man. If it wasn't for fact we held different beliefs as far as what we perceive to be is the correct way to deal with the past, we could have been friends," said Alistair. "However, I trust he will do a good job. He had no wish to see the four of you killed by a despot like Connors, hence the reason we joined forces. He has the power to scramble soldiers from anywhere in the country. He could save you when I couldn't. When I approached him, he agreed without hesitation."

"It still doesn't add up, Dad," said Kit.

"People often behave in ways we can't rationalise," said Alistair, draining his cup and standing. "Be thankful he did, Kit, or the outcome of your adventure could have been very different." He smiled at his youngest son and Kit nodded acknowledgment of his words. "Good night all," said Alistair. "I'll be upstairs if you need me to scramble a SWAT team."

They laughed, all calling goodnight as he left. The four of them — Perdita, Piper, Kit and Callum — settled around the fire.

"We have the rings," said Kit, grinning at Perdita.

"We need the locket," she replied.

"Do we have any leads?" asked Callum.

"Not yet," said Piper, "but we'll find them. Until then, I'm going to work on the mermaid cup — you never know, it might reveal a secret of its own."

"I'll have my head in a computer for the next few months doing the upgrade," said Callum. "I doubt I'll discover any secrets there. Lots of dust, but no secrets."

"What about you, Kit? What's your next move?"

"Business as usual for a while, until we decide on a plan to find the locket."

"And you, Perds?" asked Piper.

"I'm going back to the dig," she announced, enjoying the surprise on everyone's faces. "It's resuming in a few months and it'll give me a chance to discuss raising the wreck with Olaf."

"What?" exclaimed Kit.

"You never said," laughed Piper.

"Olaf emailed a few days ago, asking if I fancied getting involved again, so I said yes. After all, it's our land they're digging on," she said. "It'll only be for a month or so, but I've also suggested they use our resources while they're here. Until I've worked out our next move, it'll do me good to have something else to occupy my busy mind."

424

An hour later, they wandered up to bed. Piper and Callum climbed the ornately carved staircase and went in separate directions as the landing divided.

"Don't wait for me, Pipes," called Perdita and blew her sister a kiss. "There's something I've remembered; I want to check it while I think of it…"

"Of course," said Piper, giving her a knowing look. "Midnight is a good time to check things. See you in the morning," and with a smirk, she disappeared.

Perdita paused, looking at the intricately carved wooden relief on the wall. It was the mirror-image of the beautiful stained-glass window above the front doors. Across the top were the words of their family motto: *Fide sed cui vide.*

"Trust but be careful in whom," translated Perdita as she had on the first day she had entered Marquess House.

"Who knew it would be so prophetic," said Kit, who was watching her from the doorway of the Lady Isabel room.

"Not me, when I first saw it last summer," replied Perdita, waiting a few steps up as Kit crossed the vast entrance hall with its vivid carpet.

"A lot has changed since then," he said, stopping in front of her.

"Yes," she replied. "I'm no longer engaged to Warren; you're not going out with Lydia. We've uncovered two huge historical secrets and we know there's more to come. I suppose it was always going to make a difference coming to live in a place like this — a house full of history, packed with never-ending secrets. Especially when Granny had already paved the way."

Her eyes travelled around the enormous hall with its carvings, elegant stained-glass windows, priceless paintings and artefacts.

"It's been an unexpected time," he agreed. She smiled and turned to leave but he caught her arm. "And us? Are we good?" he asked, his voice unsure. "You know, after everything that's happened in the past few weeks?"

With Kit standing on the stair below her, their faces were level. Looking into his serious blue eyes, Perdita was overwhelmed with a sudden rush of emotion, fuelled by the thought that they might have lost each other.

"Yes, Kit," she said, running her finger down his cheek, "we're good."

And, very gently, she leaned forward and kissed him.

A NOTE TO THE READER

Dear Reader,

Thank you for taking the time to read *The Elizabeth Tudor Conspiracy*. I hope you enjoyed joining Perdita as she delved even further into the historical mysteries connected with Marquess House.

Although this is the second book in *The Marquess House Saga*, for me, this was the starting point of my story. Both Elizabeth I and Mary, Queen of Scots have fascinated me since I read the Jean Plaidy books *The Young Elizabeth* and *The Young Mary, Queen of Scots*, when I was a child. The idea of two women, cousins, both being queens seemed to capture my imagination and never let go.

As I stated in my note in *The Catherine Howard Conspiracy*, the final piece of my story came to me while I was researching my family tree: the uncovering of secrets, the *what-if?* but those strands were the last fragments of the puzzle which were all created to frame the first idea: What if Tudor history was even more complex than we had first imagined? Obviously, I could not mention this in *The Catherine Howard Conspiracy* because I did not want to spoil the surprise.

It was from my theory concerning Elizabeth and Mary that I worked backwards to see if I could make the idea viable historically. The dates led me to Catherine Howard and my research into her made me realise that with a bit of fiddling about with dates combined with the final layer of the family secrets, which would bring it all together, it could work. My heart really did begin to race. As for the secrets yet to be revealed in book three, which all fell rather easily into place historically, too, it was quite eerie!

Once again, this is a work of fiction, and the conspiracy theory I have built around Elizabeth I is entirely my own creation. However, I have researched this period extensively and as far as it has been possible, I have tried to use verifiable historical fact for the rest of the story. The more seemingly farfetched suggestions are usually factual and the most prominent are listed below with their references for further reading.

As in *The Catherine Howard Conspiracy*, I have tried to tell this story through the voices of women, which is why my interpretation of certain characters is rather different from the accepted norm.

The suggestion that Mary, Queen of Scots was first a sickly child named Elizabeth, before a few months later, she was being described as a child who was now thriving and named, Mary, was information I discovered at the very beginning of my research in Antonia Fraser's, *Mary Queen of Scots* (London, 1969). The original source material for this information is recorded in The Hamilton Papers that are available to view online at The Hamilton Papers: https://archive.org/details/cu31924091786040.

The information concerning the way the evidence about Darnley's murder is recorded that exonerates Mary of any involvement is listed in John Guy's, *My Heart is my Own, The Life of Mary Queen of Scots* (London, 2009).

The other historical reference that surprised me was the disappearance of Mary's death warrant as listed in John Guy's biography *Elizabeth, The Forgotten Years.* The document that Elizabeth supposedly signed and to which the Lord Chancellor, Sir Thomas Bromley added the Great Seal of England, has vanished and all that remains in the official records are hastily made draft copies that have not been signed by Elizabeth and have no official seal attached. It is the seal that would make them legal and binding.

Elizabeth going into official mourning for six months after the death of the duke of Anjou is in: John Guy, *Elizabeth, The Forgotten Years*. The poem that is accredited to her and purports to be about Anjou is entitled: *On Monsieur's Departure* and can be read here: https://en.wikipedia.org/wiki/On_Monsieur%27s_Departure.

The locket ring containing images of Anne Boleyn is pictured in Plate Section One, Tracey Borman's, *Elizabeth's Women: The Hidden Story of the Virgin Queen* (Vintage, 2009).

The anomalies concerning Robert Dudley, Earl of Leicester and his wife Lettice Knollys have come from Simon Adams, (Editor), *Household Accounts and Disbursement of Books of Robert Dudley, Earl of Leicester, 1558-1561, 1584-1586* (London, 1995). Although there is now a biography of Lettice Knollys, it was unavailable while I was researching this novel and all the information I have gleaned about Lettice has come from the household accounts and from other people's biographies.

Penelope Devereux's list of codenames can be found in the Cecil Papers, Volume 3, at: www.british-history.ac.uk. There are also more details in Sally Varlow's, *The Lady Penelope* (London, 2007) (Listed as 'Rialta affair' in the index).

Arbella Stuart did inherit Mary, Queen of Scots's Book of Hours: Sarah Gristwood, *Arbella, England's Lost Queen* (London, 2003), and it is now in a collection in Russia.

The Babington Plot is a complicated, cynical and convoluted piece of entrapment. I have tried to glean details from multiple sources, including all the texts already mentioned and also: Mary S Lovell, *Bess of Hardwick, First Lady of Chatsworth* (London, 2005); Stephen Alford, *The Watchers, A Secret History of the Reign of Elizabeth I* (London, 2012); Robert Hutchinson,

The Spanish Armada (London, 2013) in order make it as detailed as possible. I have followed the facts in Kit's explanation to Perdita in order to show the true strangeness of this piece of subterfuge and the manipulative lengths the men around Elizabeth would stoop to in order to achieve their own agendas.

This also includes the information about the sighting of Spanish ships off the Welsh coast. Although I have fabricated an invasion and Spanish Inquisition involvement, it is factually correct that Sir William Cecil, Lord Burghley did inform Elizabeth there were sightings of ships off the Pembrokeshire coastline, when it was a complete lie. He did it in order to scare the queen into thinking Philip II was about to invade in order to rescue Mary. Coupled with the 'discovery' by her privy council members of the second plot by Michael Moody to assassinate her, which had, in fact, been thwarted two years earlier, Elizabeth reluctantly felt she had no choice but to sign the execution warrant to protect herself and her realm from a potential Catholic invasion. More details are in John Guy, *Elizabeth, The Forgotten Years*.

Katherine Newton née Paston is a real historical figure and her relationship to Catherine Howard is accurate. More details about Katherine can be found at www.tudorwomen.com.

The names of the servants are real and are mostly taken from *Household Accounts and Disbursement of Books of Robert Dudley, Earl of Leicester, 1558-1561, 1584-1586* (London, 1995).

And, the place where Perdita hides the rings is viable. In the name of research, I tried it with two quite spiky rings and they did not move all day.

Thank you to the staff at the Pembrokeshire Archives for all their help with my research into what was happening in Pembroke Castle during the Tudor period. The results were converted into Kit's research and the pamphlets he names are real. Any mistakes are mine.

Thanks to James Meek at Dyfed Archaeology, who spent a long time discussing the finds at the dig at Pembroke Castle which Perdita and Kit mention. Any mistakes are mine.

If you have enjoyed the novel and would like to leave a review on **Amazon** or **Goodreads**, I would be so grateful as reviews are very important to authors. I love hearing from readers, so if you would like to contact me, you can through **Twitter**. You can also follow my blog on my website.

And one last thing before I leave: the title. Think about it carefully, it may not refer to the person you first think!

Thanks again for reading *The Elizabeth Tudor Conspiracy.*

Alexandra Walsh

www.alexandrawalsh.com

Sapere Books is an exciting new publisher of brilliant fiction and popular history.

To find out more about our latest releases and our monthly bargain books visit our website:
saperebooks.com

.

Made in United States
Orlando, FL
28 November 2022

25181296R00264